Between the Signal and the Sound

Book One in The Weight of Light Series

Jae Silver

This is a work of fiction. Names, characters, places, and incidents are either the product of the author's imagination or are used fictitiously. Any resemblance to actual persons, living or dead, events, or locales is entirely coincidental.

For inquiries or permissions, please visit: www.theweightoflight.net

Published by Refracted Press

An imprint of Aeon Media LLC

Paperback Edition

ISBN: 979-8-9934306-2-1

Cover design by Jae Silver

For the ones still learning the weight of light.

Content Note

This story contains references to medical trauma, chronic illness, emotional dysregulation, grief, and themes of spiritual awakening and existential crisis. While these topics are handled with care, they may be triggering for some readers. Please proceed with awareness and take care of your emotional well-being.

For more detailed information, visit:

www.theweightoflight.net

Contents

Prologue VIII

Chapter 1 1

Chapter 2 6

Chapter 3 10

Chapter 4 35

Chapter 5 50

Chapter 6 55

Chapter 7 69

Chapter 8 75

Chapter 9 83

Chapter 10 91

Chapter 11 99

Chapter 12 105

Chapter 13 115

Chapter 14 122

Chapter 15 126

Chapter 16 131

Chapter 17 136

Chapter 18 148

Chapter 19	155
Chapter 20	161
Chapter 21	169
Chapter 22	177
Chapter 23	189
Chapter 24	194
Chapter 25	201
Chapter 26	207
Chapter 27	218
Chapter 28	222
Chapter 29	233
Chapter 30	243
Chapter 31	248
Chapter 32	253
Chapter 33	266
Chapter 34	272
Chapter 35	280
Chapter 36	285
Chapter 37	298
Chapter 38	304
Chapter 39	312
Chapter 40	325
Chapter 41	334
Chapter 42	339
Chapter 43	343
Chapter 44	348

Chapter 45 355

Chapter 46 381

Chapter 47 387

Chapter 48 405

Chapter 49 413

Chapter 50 426

Chapter 51 435

Chapter 52 440

Chapter 53 447

Chapter 54 450

Chapter 55 471

1. Review Invitation 484

Prologue

The Quiet Part

I found the box again today. The one with the lyric sheets, old set lists, a few photos that still make us laugh, and a couple of flash drives containing files that could shatter my mood.

I wonder if they still work?

Do I even want to know?

I'd been searching for something else entirely, digging through the back of my bedroom closet. Trying to locate the sweater I'd promised to lend to a friend. But it's weird how synchronicities work, because I was just talking to him the other night, and now here it is.

Aside from my key, the contents of the box are really the only tangible items I have left from back then. After so many years, so many moves, spring cleaning projects, and emotionally driven purges, it's amazing that this box has survived.

Of course, surviving is subjective.

I've learned that lesson well.

I've learned a lot of lessons over the years.

Some, I've had to learn more than once.

It took me years to understand what really happened back then. The strange coincidences. The energy I couldn't explain. The way time seemed to bend when he looked at me. I didn't believe in anything beyond what I could prove. Not until everything broke.

But when you're young, you don't think about things like that... until they actually do *break.*

My real learning started in 2000. We had flip phones, burned CDs, and the World Wide Web. Life was good.

I was ambitious and fiercely analytical. Qualities I was proud of—for despite fueling my anxiety, they also fueled my success. I had plans. I'd been strategic. My ducks were in a row. My story was written. So I thought.

But now... I'm staring into this damn box. And I'm realizing... I've never really talked about *It.* I've never really told our story. Not from the beginning. Not the way it lives inside of me.

Maybe it's time.

I used to think this story was just about love. About how he walked into my life and flipped every switch. But this isn't just his story.

It's mine.

It's the kind of story that begins with someone else's heartbeat—and somehow, ends with your own.

Chapter 1

"So you're coming along to the rest of these shows, right?" Tony asked—for the second time that evening.

I hesitated. Watching the guys perform was always a thrill, but after a while, even the subtle setlist changes couldn't keep it from feeling... routine.

No wonder Jon complained.

Night after night, it had to be grueling—especially for someone who wasn't exactly *Mr. Spotlight.*

"How many more shows are we talking about?" I asked.

"Tomorrow, then a week's break. After that, seven more, then they're done till June," Tony said, leaning in with that familiar New Yorker intensity. "C'mon, Via. I'll introduce you to all the big shots who'll actually pay for your work. These guys are dying to outshine each other with the slickest websites. You'll make good money."

He wasn't wrong. I'd seen the internet boom coming a mile away and dove headfirst into web development—one of the few careers where creativity and logic could hold hands without strangling each other. Finishing my accelerated associate's degree had been hell, but worth it. Now I could take my time with my bachelor's while making money doing what I loved.

Jon's music connections had already brought in some cool gigs. And now Tony dangled even more opportunities in front of me like bait.

I laughed. "Are you seriously bribing me to hang out with my own boyfriend?"

Tony threw up his hands—a classic Italian gesture, as if his New York accent didn't already give him away. "What can I say, Via? The guy's crazy about ya. And when you're not around, he's a pain in the ass. Moody as hell. And when Jon's miserable, everyone's miserable. Save us all, will ya?"

We both laughed. It was flattering, sure. But I knew Jon loved me. And to be fair, calling him miserable was a stretch. Moody? Sometimes. But that had more to do with the fact that he wasn't a natural performer. Music was in his blood. But being on stage every night? That was a fight he had to win over and over again.

***

Jon was, in every sense, a prodigy. He'd been blessed with perfect pitch, a mind wired for composition, and fingers that made a guitar sing before he could even spell the word. By eight, he had mastered multiple instruments and was better than every local musician—including the ones who'd been teaching him. By 16, he'd been offered a full ride to the top music conservatory in the country.

The whole *"band"* thing? That was an accident. A really successful one, thanks to Tony.

Jon, Mike, Cary, and Shawn had stumbled into a wildfire of success they weren't fully prepared for. Jon and Mike had been inseparable for years. Mike, the older of the two, ran his own tattoo shop and played drums like he was born behind a kit. Odd time signatures, wild techniques—he and Jon fit together like puzzle pieces and always had.

Cary had wandered into the music store where Jon worked, asking about lessons. They'd been 15 at the time. One session together, and that was it—they clicked. Cary always said that even back then, Jon wasn't just a good teacher, he was exceptional. Patient, sharp, instinctive. Teaching music came naturally to him, like a second language. Cary switched to bass not long after, and somehow, Jon helped him unlock it. Like it had always been waiting there, just under the surface.

Occasionally, Jon, Cary, and Mike would jam out together, just for fun. I still remember the time they played at Nelson's house party that first summer break at college. Nelson practically lost his mind over how good they were, swearing they had to enter the city's battle of the bands. He was their biggest fan, even before they *were* a band.

Two months before the competition, Nelson's roommate found him dead from an accidental overdose. He just... went to bed and never woke up.

The guys were devastated. Nelson had been clean for nearly two years. Jon once told me Nelson's home life was a mess, and he'd started numbing the pain young. Thirteen. Drugs, alcohol—the whole bit. But then, he'd turned things around. Or so we thought. One slip. One night. And he was gone.

In his honor, the guys decided to enter the competition. Nelson had wanted it for them more than anyone. They even named themselves *Final Relapse*—a bittersweet nod to him.

There was just one problem—they didn't have a vocalist.

But Mike knew just the guy. A client he had met at a tattoo convention. Shawn. Shawn was a rhythm guitarist who worked as an audio engineer. He wasn't super outgoing, but he knew a lot about recording, and he wasn't afraid to unleash some wicked-sounding vocals. It worked.

It worked so well that Final Relapse made it into the top five. One final round. One song. One crowd vote. The prize? Recording gear and a deal with a small but respected NYC label.

Then, fate stepped in. Or, rather, Tony did. A short, fast-talking Italian guy who stormed up to the band after their set and dropped a bombshell.

"Drop out," he said, like it was the most obvious thing in the world.

The guys stared at him. So did the rest of us.

"Why the hell would we do that?" I remember thinking, probably out loud.

"Because," Tony said, all confidence and hand gestures. "You're gonna win. Hands down. But that deal? It's garbage. I can get you something better. One of the big dogs."

Shawn, the most experienced, pulled the others into a huddle. Saying that, yeah, talent scouts hit up these competitions all the time.

Jon didn't care about labels. Or winning. Or fame. Not then. He just wanted to play. At least... at first. They had nothing to lose.

Four months later, they had a pro studio demo and a contract that felt too good to be true. Nelson would've been proud. Not surprised, though.

Tony pushed them hard. He always said success took grit. His first radical move? Mid-rehearsal, he made Jon and Shawn swap places.

Yet again, Tony's natural instincts were correct. "I just want to hear Jon run through the vocals."

The guys had all exchanged glances, unsure of what to make of it.

"Just humor me!" Tony had insisted.

And the minute they did—*we all knew.*

Jon didn't have the angry, growly voice that Shawn did. Instead, he delivered an edgy, melodic rendition that was sharp and haunting. The song morphed into something unrecognizable. And it was *perfect.*

"Shit, dude!" Shawn grinned after a stunned silence. "Why didn't you say you could sing like that?"

Even I hadn't known he could sing like that. We'd been together for a year, and I had *no idea.*

Jon? He was the hardest to convince. Tony pushed. The band encouraged. Friends rallied.

Jon resisted.

But, eventually, he gave in. He was incredible. Undeniably.

Tony coached him at first—eye contact, crowd engagement, all that. But Jon didn't play the charming frontman. On stage, he retreated inward, pulling dark, brooding vocals from somewhere deep and unreachable. It became his signature. Authentic. Magnetic.

Tony gave up trying to change him. Jon didn't need to be anything else.

Maybe that's why people couldn't look away. Maybe it was the rawness. Maybe it was that he demanded the audience meet him where *he* was—distant but captivating.

Probably all of the above.

But it drained him. Every time. Jon was the textbook introvert.

So... was Tony right to call him moody?

Yes. And no.

Chapter 2

That last seven-day stint had proven to be more grueling than most. Mainly because Jon had gotten sick early on. By the second day, he was pale, damp with cold sweat, and unsteady on his feet. The rest of us dosed up on vitamin C and tried to keep our distance.

"I don't want whatever the fuck you've got!" Cary had said. We all laughed, but I still felt bad for Jon. Performing was hard enough without feeling like hell on top of it.

By night four, he looked *bad.* He'd leave the stage looking like a ghost, shoulders slumped, breath coming too fast. After the set, we'd head straight to the hotel, where he'd shower, down some NyQuil, and crash straight through checkout the next day. Then, on to the next show. Rinse. Repeat.

I thought maybe he needed an antibiotic, but he brushed it off. *No big deal,* he said. *Probably something viral.*

On night six, he actually needed to sit down after coming offstage. I'd handed him a water bottle, and his hands shook so badly that I had to take the lid off for him.

"You good?" Mike asked, watching him closely.

Jon nodded, jaw tight. "Yeah," he muttered. "I'm just tired. One more night—I can make it."

Tony pulled me aside on the last night. "Via, make him go see a doctor when you get home, will ya? I don't like how winded he's been getting. He could have walking pneumonia or something."

I agreed. I meant it, too.

***

We rolled into Jon's driveway around 12:30 Sunday afternoon. Technically, he still lived at home, but it never really felt that way. Sharron, his mother, traveled for work, sometimes gone for ten or fifteen days at a time. His dad, Jeff, was a detective, always working long hours, sometimes traveling, too.

Jon had planned to get a studio apartment in the city when he first started grad school, but his parents and I had convinced him to commute from home and bank his money instead.

Plus, there was Maize—Jon's border collie, smarter than most people and bursting with energy. She was used to a sprawling backyard and would've lost her mind in an apartment. That pretty much sealed the deal.

Now the house was empty as we threw our bags inside and greeted a wildly excited Maize. She didn't like when Jon was gone too long—despite the neighbors taking excellent care of her.

Jon didn't even make it to the couch. He dropped straight onto the floor, letting Maize climb over him, lick his face, and roll against his chest. He just laughed, rubbing her fur, until she finally stilled—settling directly on top of him, like a weighted blanket.

I smiled, then shifted. "So... about that doctor's appointment," I said, raising an eyebrow.

Jon sighed, rolling his eyes. "It's Sunday, Vee. I'll call tomorrow. But I feel better already. I think I was just run-down." He tilted his head toward me, voice dropping, coaxing. "Can't we just hang out in bed today? The three of us?"

I laughed. *The three of us.* Me, him, and Maize. It sounded pretty good.

Also, the way he said my name. *Vee.*

I had plenty of names, starting with Livia Sullivan. My family called me *Liv.* My friends called me *Via*. But Jon had taken it upon himself to call me *Vee.* Short, sweet. And when he said it, I liked it.

Maybe he *was* just run-down. And if he were contagious, I would've been sick by now. *Right?*

***

Despite not feeling tired myself, I ended up crashing with Jon and Maize—and we didn't wake until dinner.

Way to waste an afternoon, Via. I scolded myself. Except... it hadn't felt like a waste. It was nice. Relaxing. And even if I hadn't *needed* it, I knew Jon did.

And he really did seem better.

We even ordered pizza for dinner, splitting it with Kyle, the neighbor kid, who had been almost as excited to see Jon as Maize had. At seven, Kyle had boundless energy, and Jon had long since taken on the role of his honorary older brother. Watching them together was always kind of cute. When Jon was home, Kyle stuck to him like glue.

I called it *pestering.*

Jon called it *visiting.*

Jon had even let Kyle talk him into coaching his soccer team. *Coaching.* Him. Of all people. Fortunately, he shared the duties with a dad from the team—because between work, school, and touring, Jon *did* occasionally miss a game.

And when he did, he always felt guilty.

Like he did now. Hence, the extended backyard playdate, practicing soccer drills.

When Kyle finally headed home for a bath and Jon strolled in from the backyard, I tried to glare at him. "I thought you were sick?" I mock-scolded.

He grinned, stepping in close and wrapping his arms around me.

"I feel better now. I swear."

I rolled my eyes, but he just kept smiling, cocky and smug.

"Do you love me?"

"Obviously."

Chapter 3

Rewind a few years. It wasn't love at first sight. It was curiosity. Followed by fascination. And then, maybe, just a little bit of obsession.

But before that—I'd been thinking about dating Drew. He'd dropped enough hints to suggest he was interested. But we hadn't actually done anything about it yet. Which is why I wasn't sure how to answer when Nikki brought him up.

I hadn't known Nikki that long then, but we'd bonded instantly when we met at one of Nelson's epic parties. One of those rare, best-friend-level connections that just clicks. Following that night, we actively pursued plans together, and I quickly became part of her local friend group—which, incidentally, is how I met Drew and Jon.

"So, you and Drew hooking up?" She asked, a sly smile creeping across her face.

"No. Why?" I tried not to sound defensive.

"You gonna?" She prodded.

"Maybe. He's cute. Why?"

She shrugged, feigning innocence. "No reason! It's just that..." she trailed off, looking like she wasn't sure whether to say more.

Oh God. She knows something.

Was Drew a player? Did he have a bad rep?

I sighed. "What's wrong with Drew?"

"Nothing!" she blurted. Too quickly. "He seems cool." Then—that look again. "But I think Jon is into you, too."

I blinked.

Who?

"...Jon Stetson?" I said incredulously.

She rolled her eyes. "Yeah—as in my almost-neighbor. How many Jons do we both hang out with?"

Just the one...

But that couldn't be right.

I snorted. "Doubtful. I've never gotten that impression."

"He literally asked me yesterday if you and Drew were a thing." She made air quotes and smirked.

"So? Maybe he was just curious."

"He's not just curious. And besides, if it were that, he could ask Drew himself."

I considered this.

Still.

Jon was friendly and polite—but never in a way that suggested I'd even have a chance. In fact, he was one of those guys who was so attractive that I had subconsciously dismissed him from consideration.

Nikki was watching me, waiting for a reaction, and I was trying not to give her the satisfaction.

"Unlikely."

She let out an impatient sigh. "Trust me. I've known Jon since I was eight, and he was ten. Hell, I even had a little crush on him back in the day. But I gave up on that."

"Why?"

"Because. He wasn't interested." Then she snickered. "For a while, I even thought he might be gay because I never saw him with a girlfriend."

I laughed. "Figures. The hot ones usually are."

"He's not," she said. "And I've seen the way he looks at you."

The fuck?

I shifted uncomfortably, too embarrassed to even entertain the idea.

"Honestly, Via, you should pull your head out of your ass sometime—the view is much better out here," Nikki said dryly.

We both laughed.

"Seriously," she added. "Now that he thinks Drew might beat him to the punch, I bet he makes a move on you."

I rolled my eyes.

Yeah, right.

***

Nikki and I stood in her driveway, a trash bag between us, all four doors of her car hanging open. She had offered to drive for the night while we ran around with some friends. Then—mid-offer—admitted she needed to clean the trash out of her car first.

Had I known how bad the situation was, I would've politely declined. I held the bag open while she chucked handfuls of granola bar wrappers, straw papers, and crumpled fast-food bags into it. I was debating whether I should start charging for manual labor when I noticed her eyes move past me.

"Well, speak of the damn devil," she muttered, failing to hide whatever *else* was in her expression.

I turned to see Jon heading our way, hands in his pockets, moving with that unhurried ease of his.

Nikki immediately turned her back and resumed flinging garbage.

"Hey," he said casually.

"Heyyy!" Nikki called over her shoulder.

"What are you guys up to?" he asked me.

"Cleaning out the Jetta," I said with an exaggerated eye roll.

As if to illustrate my point, Nikki tossed another handful into the bag—except this time, a half-eaten burger tumbled loose, landing unceremoniously on the pavement.

Jon's gaze flicked to it. Then to me.

I allowed myself a moment to appreciate how unusually pretty his eyes were—amber, ridiculously expressive. Right now, they sparkled with humor, matching the grin spreading across his face.

"Seriously?" he said, amused, as Nikki scooped up the burger and tossed it in the trash.

"Hey!" she snapped. "I'm always on the go! I eat in the car a lot."

Jon arched an eyebrow. "You don't pass any trash cans during your travels?"

I *barely* stifled a laugh.

Nikki ignored him.

Jon looked like he was about to *really* lean in and antagonize her, then changed his mind, shifting his focus to me.

"So, Via." His voice was easy, casual. "There's a new pub starting up on Prince Street. Grand opening Tuesday night. Cary's hosting on behalf of the radio station, and he asked me to stop by. Wanna come with?"

A rush of heat hit my face. I *refused* to look at Nikki.

"I know it's weird timing—midweek. No pressure if you're busy."

Cary worked for a local radio station with solid reach, and his on-air persona was exactly like him in real life—comedic, slightly ridiculous, and somehow always entertaining. If he was running the event, I knew it would be fun.

"I'll go."

Jon smiled. "Cool. I can pick you up?"

"Maybe Via doesn't want you to know where she lives," Nikki interjected, tone dripping with mischief. Clearly still paying him back for the garbage comment.

Jon stayed perfectly calm, meeting her gaze. "Maybe..." he said evenly. "Or maybe she doesn't mind and will text me her address."

"Maybe she's afraid you're some creepy weirdo."

Jon shrugged, unfazed. "Maybe..." he echoed. "But she's known me for a while. She knows where I live. She's been in my house."

Their odd little standoff continued, as if I weren't standing right there. I found their banter thoroughly amusing. Deciding to play along, I pulled out my phone. As Nikki kept giving Jon shit, I texted him my address. A moment later, from somewhere in his pocket, his phone made a ka-dunk sound.

"Ooah," he said, eyes still locked on Nikki. "I wonder if that was her."

Nikki cracked first, breaking into laughter. I followed.

"I guess you got lucky," she shot at him.

"Score one for the good guys," Jon quipped. But instead of checking his phone, he just looked at me, completely confident.

"Pick you up around five?"

"Sure."

Jon gave us both a half wave before heading back down the driveway. Then—just before crossing the street—he turned back.

"Oh, and Via?"

Our eyes met.

"I promise you won't have to wade through any trash when you get in my vehicle."

He grinned, dimples on full display, before continuing on his way.

"Eat a dick!" Nikki called after him.

Jon threw his head back, laughing.

Before I could even wipe the stupid smile off my face, Nikki spun toward me.

"I *fucking told you.*" She beamed.

***

Murphy's was nice—a cozy spot downtown with a horseshoe bar, plenty of seating, and a small stage for comics and open-mic nights.

The grand opening had drawn a solid crowd, but we'd lucked out, snagging a corner table early—big enough for our friend group. Nikki, of course, spent most of the night shamelessly flirting with Mike.

The only real one-on-one time Jon and I got was in his vehicle. Which, as promised, was spotless. Talking to him was easy, though. We'd already known each other for—what, six months? We skipped right over the awkward getting-to-know-you phase, diving straight into deeper things. Our families. His sister Jill. My roommates, Kenny, Krissy, and Justin. Goals for the future.

Still, it was a 40-minute drive back to my apartment.

"I should've driven myself," I said apologetically. "Now you have to take me all the way north, then turn around and go *all* the way back."

Jon just shrugged. "I don't mind. *I* invited you. Would've been rude not to pick you up." He glanced at me. "Besides, it was so loud at Murphy's. At least we get to talk on the way."

He hadn't made a single pass at me all night—which I appreciated. And even when we pulled up to my apartment building, he didn't make a move.

Nice. And different.

I had my hand on the door handle when he stopped me.

"Hang on. I have something for you."

I turned back as he reached into the center console, fishing out—

A keychain?

It was thin and rectangular, silver with an anodized purple sheen.

"Wow," I said, surprised. "That's really pretty."

Jon shook his head. "Not pretty. Functional."

He flipped open the top—

Wait. Is that a USB?

I blinked.

"It's a flash drive," he said. "I remember that weekend you had to leave early because you forgot some files for school."

Holy shit.

He remembered that?

That was at least a month ago. I'd been crashing at Nikki's, only to realize I'd left the files I needed back at my apartment—and had to drive all the way home. I was furious.

I hadn't even realized Jon had been paying attention.

Huh.

I turned the keychain over in my fingers, still a little thrown. "This is really cool," I said honestly.

Jon just smiled. "You're welcome."

Then—without hesitation—he simply said, "Have a good day tomorrow."

That was it. No *pause* to see if I'd invite him in. No expectation.

Just *that.*

I smiled, shutting the door behind me, then gave him a small wave as I headed inside.

Huh.

***

I untwisted my damp hair from the towel and threw on an old T-shirt for bed when my eyes landed on the keychain I'd left on my desk.

That's seriously a cool idea. And it might actually work.

I picked it up, turning it over in my hands.

I wonder how much space is on this?

For a second, I considered plugging it into my laptop. Then I hesitated.

What if it's compromised? What if it puts a virus on my computer?

...But why the hell would he do that?

Jon was a musician, not some cybercriminal. What possible motive could he have for sabotaging my laptop?

Still.

I stared at the drive, full-on overthinking it.

For fuck's sake, Via. Just plug it in.

I finally gave in, holding my breath as I inserted the end of the flash drive into my computer.

Waiting for...

What, Via? A full system meltdown? FBI agents busting down your door?

The drive popped up in the file explorer. 64MB. *Not bad.* More than enough to store files for a few website projects. I double-clicked to open it.

There was nothing on it. Except for a single text file. I frowned, hovering over it.

What if it's some kind of auto-executable malware?

Oh my God. He's a musician. Not a hacker. YOU are the one being the weirdo right now.

I double-clicked.

The file opened.

Thanks for hanging out with me tonight, Livia. Maybe we can do it again sometime. Are you free for dinner tomorrow?

-Jonathan

I exhaled a laugh.

Huh.

He'd used both of our full names. Interesting.

And he'd clearly had this ready before we even went to Murphy's. What if the night had gone horribly? Would he have just not given me the keychain? I sat back in my chair, twirling the USB between my fingers.

I had dinner plans for my roommate Kenny's birthday. But *damn it,* Jon had me intrigued. I glanced at the clock. 11:43. He'd be home by now. *I wonder if he's still awake?* My heart did this weird little thing—a flutter, a shift—right before I took a deep breath and texted.

Via: *I have dinner plans for tomorrow. But I'd love to hang out again. Maybe after? Like around 7 PM?*

I held my breath.

A minute later, my phone chimed.

Jon: *Perfect. I know just the thing. Pick you up at 7.*

Oh God. This was happening.

And I couldn't stop smiling.

***

Jon sent me a text saying that he was parked out front.

"Bye, birthday boy." I threw my arms around Kenny before heading for the door.

"Bye, luv! Behave yourself! Don't do anything I wouldn't do!" he called, then cackled.

"Bring him up here so we can interrogate him!" Krissy chimed in.

"*Hard pass!* Byeee!" I shot back, slipping out the door before anyone else could pile on.

Jon smiled as I slid into the passenger seat, the door sealing shut with a quiet *thunk*.

"Hey," he said.

"Hey."

I felt... not nervous. Excited, maybe?

"Where are we going?" I asked as we merged onto the main road.

Instead of taking the highway toward town, he took the ramp heading north.

"It's a surprise. That okay?"

"Uh... sure!"

Silence settled between us for a beat, comfortable and unhurried. Then, a thought popped into my head.

"What made you so sure I'd even open that text file?"

He smirked. "Because you're curious. I can tell. You *had* to check."

I stared out the passenger window, then muttered, "I thought maybe you were going to crash my computer or something."

Jon let out a genuine, full laugh.

"I *wish* I had that skill set," he said. "But if you're that paranoid, it makes me wonder exactly what kind of websites you're developing. And for whom."

I laughed, shaking my head. It was *so* easy with him. Conversation flowed effortlessly, and before I knew it, thirty minutes had passed. And we were *still* heading away from civilization.

Up into the mountains.

Well. If he planned to butcher me, this would sure be the way to go.

I scolded myself for always being so cynical.

Jon was a nice guy. He'd grown up next to one of my best friends. Nikki had known him forever. She said he was a nice guy.

But he kept me guessing.

And I found that both intriguing and unnerving.

He must have sensed my hesitation, because he laughed.

"Relax," he said, nodding toward the backseat.

I squinted into the dim light. Something metallic sat there, tangled and folded up. It was dark now, making it hard to tell exactly what I was looking at. Then, he pulled off into a large gravel turnout and cut the ignition.

"We're here."

My stomach flipped.

Fuck, Via. This is how every bad movie starts.

Jon didn't hesitate. He stepped out and popped the back door open. The dome light flickered on—illuminating the shiny object in the backseat.

A telescope.

"There's an astronomy club that meets up here once a month," Jon explained, carefully unpacking the equipment. "But it should be pretty quiet on a Wednesday."

I hesitated, glancing around. Dense trees lined both sides of the deserted road.

"Here?" I asked skeptically.

Jon handed me an enormous flashlight—the kind that comes with a tripod.

"You'll see."

Then, without waiting for a response, he started walking toward the trees.

Fight or flight, Via. Which are you?

I exhaled and followed, flicking on the flashlight to illuminate the path. We'd only gone about twenty paces when the trees suddenly thinned out. And I realized—

We weren't walking into a forest at all. It had just been so dark from the road, I couldn't tell. We were standing on a lookout. My breath caught.

The world opened up before me—a vast valley stretched out beneath a sky so sharp and clear it almost didn't look real.

"You can see the entire valley from here," I whispered.

Jon grinned. "Yep. And you get a good view of the stars from here, too. Full moon tonight. That's why it's so bright."

I turned in a slow circle, taking it all in.

"I had no idea this place was up here."

Jon's smile widened. "Surprise."

Yeah. No shit.

My skepticism flared back up.

"You bring all your dates up here to hook up?" I teased.

Jon, still wrestling with the telescope legs, didn't even glance up.

"Nope. Never been here before."

I smirked. "Oh yeah? Then how'd you know about it?"

"My sister's fiancé." He straightened up, dusting off his hands. "He's really into astronomy. Told me about it a while ago, I just never had a good reason to come. Borrowed this from him."

I observed him. He seemed sincere.

And also—completely lost as he squinted at the telescope knobs.

I folded my arms. "Do you even know how to use that thing?"

Jon finally looked at me, breaking into a shit-eating grin.

"No clue."

I gawked at him.

"I mean, Ben gave me a crash course," he admitted. "But..." He gestured vaguely at the telescope. "It seems complicated. You're smart. I thought we could figure it out together."

I stared at him.

Then, we both burst out laughing.

After twenty minutes of fumbling with various knobs and settings, we managed to pull a few stars into an impressively close view. Ultimately, though? It was more peaceful, just sitting on the rocks, looking out over the valley. We talked. We laughed.

I had no idea what time it was. I hadn't been paying attention. Because, for once, I didn't want to. I totally hadn't seen this coming. Not any of it.

***

"This is nice," Jon said after a lull in our conversation. "I enjoy spending time with you."

A small rush of warmth curled through me. Not quite nerves. Not quite excitement. Something quieter.

Me too.

Feeling a little emboldened by the dark, with the vastness of everything stretching out ahead, I pushed.

"Well," I said, tilting my head, "why'd you take so long to ask, then?"

He let out a short laugh—nervous.

"I wasn't sure what you'd say." He glanced over at me. "You've never really paid me much attention."

What?

Was this guy *for real?*

"Seriously?" I scoffed. "I've had to put conscious effort into *not staring at you*. At your eyes."

Shit. Instant regret.

Had I just inflated his ego?

I braced for some cocky retort, but instead—Jon looked away, shyly.

And somehow... that made him even more adorable.

"Well," he said after a beat, voice a little softer. "Why didn't *you* make a move, then?"

I sighed. "I don't know. You're the guy," I added quickly. "Guess I was waiting on you."

Jon smirked. "You don't strike me as the type to care about the traditional status quo."

I shrugged, then flashed him a grin. "Maybe I'm *very* traditional. How would you know?"

His smirk widened. “Guess I screwed this up then, huh? This is about as untraditional as it gets for a date.”

I was starting to enjoy flirting with him.

“Oh, so *this* is a date?“ I teased. “And you didn’t even bring me roses? Bastard.”

“You’re right.” He said it so seriously, for a split second I thought he actually felt bad. “I didn’t.” He nodded, solemnly. “Sorry.”

A pause.

Then we both cracked up laughing.

The conversation drifted naturally after that. Jon was so easy to be around. I loved that he could make me laugh.

***

After a while, the chill in the air finally drove us to our feet.

Jon gathered the telescope, packing it into the backseat while I took one last look at the twinkling valley lights below us. And the bright, round moon.

This has been a beautiful night.

The gravel crunched under my feet as I made my way back to the truck. I opened the passenger door—

And froze.

Lying on my seat was a bouquet of flowers. Not roses. Lilies. They weren’t open yet, but I could tell—white, soft pink and deep reds. The buds were huge.

I stared. My eyes moved from the flowers to Jon.

He grinned. “Sorry. Not roses. I opted for lilies. They felt more fitting.”

I reached out, gently brushing a fingertip over one bud. “They’re going to be beautiful.”

He nodded toward them. “Each color has a different meaning. They’ll open in a day or two.” Then—his voice dropped just slightly, almost teasing, almost not—“So, hopefully, you won’t forget about me before the weekend.”

Forget about him?

I was going to have a damn hard time thinking about anything else.

Wait.

Was this a line? Something he used on every unsuspecting girl?

I narrowed my eyes. "How do you know so much about lilies?"

Jon let out a laugh, completely unbothered by my suspicion. "The lady at the flower shop taught me *way* more than I needed to know."

Then—he shrugged. "But I told her the chick I was into was *unique*, and I wanted something less cliché than roses."

I stared at him. Did he actually just *say* that?

"Did I screw up?" he asked, still smirking.

No.

I could barely contain the smile on my face.

"I love them."

***

Jon's devious plan had worked exactly as intended.

I had not forgotten about him.

In fact, I found it difficult to perform even basic tasks without thinking about him.

This isn't good, Via.

The lilies had already started to open when I left for class the next morning. By the time I got home from running errands, they were fully open. Giant. Gorgeous.

And Jon?

Hadn't texted me once.

Should I say something to him?

Thank him again for the flowers?

Or was it too soon? I didn't want to seem clingy.

Were we in one of those hold-out situations? Seeing who would break the silence first?

Or maybe he was just busy.

I didn't care much for typical cat-and-mouse games. And Jon didn't strike me as the type, either.

So why hadn't I heard from him?

He's the one who said he hoped I wouldn't forget about him before the weekend.

Maybe he's waiting for me to reach out?

Fuck it.

I was at least going to call his floriculturist bluff.

I grabbed my phone and quickly banged out a text, hitting send before I could second-guess myself.

Via: *Thanks again for the lilies. They're beautiful. One of the red ones opened first. What does that mean?*

There.

We'd see what special-meaning bullshit he tried to feed me now.

It wasn't even a full minute before my phone lit up.

Jon: *It means you should go on another date with me.*

I snorted.

Damn. He answered fast.

And...

I liked his answer.

Which also meant he wasn't put off that I'd texted him so soon.

God.

I was really starting to like Mr. Stetson.

I was still wrestling with my internal dialogue, debating how to respond, when—

Another text came through.

Shit.

I hadn't even replied yet.

Jon: *What are your plans for this weekend? Will you be coming over?*

I smiled.

It was ironic, really.

I typically spent at least one night a week at Nikki's.

And because of our mutual friend group, we *always* ended up at Jon's house eventually. It was the place everyone gathered. This had been routine for so long. And yet, somehow, it had never once crossed my mind that Jon Stetson would ask me on a date.

Via: *Yeah. I'll be there.*

Jon: *Cool. We'll figure it out then.*

A pause.

Then—

Jon: *See you soon, Livia.*

I stared at my screen.

Something about the way he used my full name made my chest tighten.

I hadn't even realized I was smiling.

***

When I pulled into Nikki's driveway, I could already see a few extra cars lined up along the street in front of Jon's.

"Bonfire in Jon's backyard tonight," Nikki announced as I stepped inside and slung my bag into the corner.

Then she smirked.

"Of course, I guess you know that. You're probably the one who started it."

I glared at her.

She just laughed. "Just kidding... *love yyyouuu.*"

I rolled my eyes.

Despite my best efforts to act normal, not make it weird, or pretend nothing was different—

It *for sure as hell* was. And after a while, I gave up the charade, because everyone else seemed to be aware of it. And Jon? Didn't seem to mind. He'd been doting on me all night. Bringing me drinks. Offering me food. Not in an over-the-top way. Just enough to be noticed. And by the time the night wound down, it was obvious.

Everyone had eventually filtered down to the basement to check out Jon and Mike's recent handiwork. The space had always been a sprawling, finished basement—livable, carpeted, but mostly vacant. Until recently.

Now, they were turning it into a recording studio. And they weren't half-assing it. They were spending money. Doing everything by the book. They'd installed acoustic paneling, two isolation booths, and had already started running wiring for all the mics, amps, and gear. Mike had moved in his full drum kit. Jon had bought a new computer to run his recording software. It was starting to look pretty damn impressive.

"You should hang out for a while after," Jon had said casually. "I can show you the specs of my workstation."

I smiled and nodded.

Yes, please.

He'd been discreet when he asked. But Nikki was like a damn bloodhound. Before she headed upstairs, she slinked over to me and whispered—

"I'll leave the back door unlocked. Come back whenever you want. *If* you want."

Then she smirked. "I know you wanna check out the size of Jon's hard drive."

I turned five shades of red. We both cracked up laughing.

And then—just like that—everyone left.

Except me. And Jon.

The funny thing? We *actually did* geek out over his new computer. And it was impressive. No pun. It was *seriously* cool. But eventually, the inevitable moment arrived. Where it felt more awkward to not kiss than to finally just kiss—

So we did.

And fuck, why did that take so long?

This wasn't my first rodeo—not in *any* capacity—but this guy was making me giddy as a horny teenager.

And then—

Right before I expected things to escalate—

He pulled back.

I blinked.

Jon leaned back in his chair, watching me carefully.

"Do you like me, Livia?"

The fuck?

I stared at him. "Uh... *yeah?*"

His gaze didn't waver.

"Enough to be my girlfriend?"

I froze.

Jon grinned.

Are you kidding me?

NO, Via—maybe this is just how an emotionally mature individual approaches things, and you're too dumb to recognize it.

I felt like I was in the Twilight Zone.

But somewhere, my inner brain saved me.

Fucking answer him, Via.

I swallowed, feeling my lips curve into a smile.

"That sounds amazing."

His grin broadened.

God.

He was going to kill me with those dimples, wasn't he?

"Good," Jon said. But then, his expression turned more serious.

"But I mean, like... exclusively. Us—as in, an actual couple. I hate the hook-up scene. Not that I'm going to pressure you into anything."

His voice was steady, deliberate.

"I'd actually prefer if we took time to really get to know each other first. But only if that's okay with you."

Then—slower, "I want to be respectful of what you want."

I sat there. Dumbfounded. Listening as the words spilled out of his mouth.

Was this guy for real?

I had never had someone be so blunt with me. I'd never even heard stories of such a thing happening out in the wild. I like to think I have a strong moral compass. But I'd be lying if I said I wouldn't have been ready and willing to consummate our relationship status right then and there. *Oh, I would have.*

But *this*?

I was not expecting this.

Never had anyone been so direct with me about exactly what they wanted. It was so...

Refreshing.

I pulled myself out of my thought spiral long enough to meet his gaze.

And return his candor.

"I would love that very much, Jon."

***

And no, it wasn't as bad as it sounds.

It's not like he was teasing me—we just... literally never did things that would have naturally led to that. Instead, he continued to surprise me with unexpected outings. Trips to museums. Little day trips to places I'd never been. Things that actually required conversation.

One night, he even took me back to the lookout—this time, when the astronomy club was meeting. And this time, we actually learned how to use Ben's telescope properly. He hadn't been kidding when he said he wanted to get to know me first. And honestly? I enjoyed it.

By the time a month had passed, I'd become convinced of one thing—

Jon Stetson was, quite literally, the nicest guy I had ever met. I didn't even realize guys like him existed. Had he not had one of my best friends to vouch for him, I'd have been looking for the catch. But Nikki had known him for most of her life. Her older sister had been friends with Jon's sister. And as it turns out—

They were just a really nice family.

Go figure.

What Nikki couldn't believe, though, was that after a full month, we still hadn't slept together. In fact, that very first night I'd gone back to her place after hanging out at Jon's, she had cornered me immediately. Demanding details.

"How was the sex?" she had asked, eyes gleaming.

When I told her what he'd said—about wanting to take things slow—

She had burst into giggles. Her eyes sparkled with amusement.

"No way." She'd kept saying. "No. Fucking. Way."

***

And from that point on? It became a weekly tradition. Nikki's Interrogation Hour. Every time I saw her:

"Did you two finally do it?"

"What the hell is he waiting for?"

"Is he in a cult?"

I had to admit...

It was starting to get to me.

Why *was* he holding out so long?

Was there a reason?

Was it me?

Did he secretly suck in bed?

I knew it wasn't a size issue. There were a few times we'd made out enough that I could feel him pushing up against me—and I was certain that we were working with a sizable package. And that just made me more curious. More eager.

Nikki and I debated these points frequently. And for once, she had no answers.

"I told you," she said, shaking her head. "I never saw him with a girlfriend."

I let that sink in.

Then—

Her eyes suddenly widened.

"Oh my GAWD."

She grabbed my arm.

"I wonder if he's a virgin."

Oh, fuck. That thought hadn't even occurred to me. Jon was two years older than me, even.

"No way," I scoffed. "Nobody that hot makes it all the way into their twenties without sex."

...Right?

Right??

I considered just point-blank asking him. But Jon had never once asked me about my past. And I really appreciated that. It always struck me as a sign of insecurity when guys fixated on that kind of thing. So, I wasn't about to become the thing I hated. Besides—I didn't want to ruin the enigma that was so beautifully just... Jon.

Nikki shrugged. "I don't know," she said. "He went to private school. And I know his sister is engaged—but Ben is the only guy she's ever been with."

I gaped. *"Seriously?"*

Nikki nodded. "That's what Tamara said."

I considered that.

"That's actually kinda sweet."

Nikki smirked. "*Welp.* I guess you'll find out."

Then, with pure evil in her eyes—

"Eventually. If you can hold out long enough."

She cackled.

***

By the sixth weekend, Nikki didn't even need to ask me. I tried to play it cool. I really did. But I couldn't hide the triumphant glee on my face.

Nikki's eyes locked onto me like a heat-seeking missile. She took one look at my face, and practically did her own little happy dance. And the craziest thing? After all the waiting and debating... I didn't even tell her all the details.

I had *thought* I'd had good sex before. But compared to Jon?

Nah.

Not even close.

With Jon... it felt too personal to share. Nobody had ever so effortlessly taken control. Or looked at me. Or communicated with me... the *whole time.*

Not like he had. He had made me feel safe enough to completely let my guard down. My body had won out—over my mind. And that had never happened before.

He had made that happen.

And that, alone, was saying something. Whether or not he realized it, Jon had set a new standard. And God help the next poor asshole who might have to follow that up. Secretly, I was already hoping I'd never need to go looking.

***

I'm not sure what had finally changed for him—or what made him decide it had been long enough. One thing had led to another, and we ended up on the bed.

At one point—I didn't even think about it—I just... gently put my hand on him.

For a split second, he tensed.

Just long enough to make me panic and wonder if I'd crossed a line.

But then, he kept kissing me, and any reservations that I'd had about the moment melted away.

He knew *exactly* what to do.

Where to touch.

How to caress, and kiss...

Why the *hell* had he been holding out for so long??

We went slowly.

He was tantalizingly deliberate.

Guys his age didn't fuck like this. *Did they?*

NO.

And also, *this wasn't "fucking."*

I don't even know why I was so surprised by him anymore.

He had asked me, "Is this okay?"

And *damn,* was it...

He made eye contact—more than I was used to.

It was both intimate and exciting in a way I wasn't prepared for.

I was starting to feel self-conscious because the type of smashing orgasm I was headed towards—*probably not sexy.*

Not a good look, Via. Especially not the first time you finally hook up with the guy.

Keep yourself in check.

And then—

He kissed the side of my neck, right below my earlobe, and murmured, "You're almost there."

The fuck?

Did he just—

Was he asking me?

Or TELLING me?

Either way, it didn't really matter, because he was right.

I was struggling to maintain control of my body, my mind, and my reaction to his intentional, methodical movements.

My thoughts were fighting against the intense physical pleasure.

"You're okay," he murmured.

His voice was low.

Soothing.

Was it possible to be both reassuring and sexy at the same time?

Apparently, it was.

And then—*"Let go."*

Oh hell.

His words...

You're okay.

I believed him.

God help me—*I believed him.*

I finally exploded—the sensation swallowing me whole—starting down deep and vibrating through my body in waves. I was helpless to control it. It rolled through me. Repeatedly.

Nobody had ever made me feel like that before.

Not ever.

He was so gentle.

So controlled.

It felt like he had handed himself over to me.

I was *tingling.*

When we'd finished, he brushed my nose with his and grinned.

And then—he kissed my forehead.

It was so sweet.

Slow—just like everything else had been.

And dammit, I was going to fall for this guy.

Is that why he'd waited?

I was reeling from the entire experience.

My first sexual encounter with him had evolved in such a beautiful, natural way that it felt like there was nobody else in the world I was meant to be with.

And that was dangerous.

I knew it.

I already had feelings for him.

That scared me more than anything.

Fuck.

Chapter 4

Over two years later... He was still every bit as charming. Every bit as irresistible as he had been in those first weeks together. I never forgot it. *I felt safe with him.* Always.

"You're still going to the doctor tomorrow," I said with resolve. "I promised Tony."

Jon grumbled. "Fine."

Then, flashing me that grin—

"But right now... let's eat more pizza and watch a movie."

I laughed.

And this.

This is why I would never be free.

He had me.

Hook. Line. Dimples.

***

June and July flew by. It hadn't been a lazy summer—far from it. Between school, work, and everything else, we'd all stayed busy. Productive. A little scattered.

FR had officially wrapped their second full-length album. Thirteen meticulously recorded tracks. Professionally produced. Mixed. Mastered.

And Jon? Was pissed.

"They polished the life out of it," he'd said bitterly.

But sales numbers told a different story. Fans loved it.

And it wasn't hard to see why.

By then, FR had carved out their own sound—a blend of sharp-edged contrast and nuance. Complex riffs layered over hard, addictive rhythms. Murky, angst-driven distortion punctuated with bursts of clarity—an echo of Jon's deeper compositional instincts.

His academic background in classical composition gave the album unexpected weight. Subtle orchestrations. Atmospherics. Fully scored backtracks recorded by some of the top musicians at his conservatory. You could feel it, even if you didn't know what you were hearing.

Shawn's engineering skills gave the recordings precision. Even when rough cuts started in Jon's basement studio, they always ended up crisp, deliberate—refined into a distinct breed of dark rock.

Only... more cinematic.

Like a film score that had slipped into a nightmare and grown teeth.

And Jon's voice? Haunting. Powerful. Controlled. But always threaded with something raw beneath the surface.

Live, they were minimalist. No gimmicks. No costumes. No attitude. And somehow, that only amplified their presence.

They just *were.*

The music was bold enough to carry itself. Which was good. Because that's what fit them best.

***

I had helped design the new merch, including T-shirts, for their upcoming promotional tour.

The label's marketing strategy had been intentional—

Nine dates. One month.

A "teaser," Tony had called it. Enough to create buzz before the band dropped an additional EP in December. And after the new year FR would be co-headlining a full-length tour with FaultCode.

FaultCode had been around longer—more seasoned, more established. But their fan bases overlapped and their sounds worked well together. The guys had met up once over the summer, and personality-wise, they had clicked well enough to survive a few months on the road together. At least, that was the hope.

***

August arrived. The first weekend of the mini-tour had three back-to-back shows. Thursday: Virginia. Friday: DC. Saturday: Maryland.

They were well-received. Everything had gone according to plan.

Except, Saturday night, something felt off. Jon had seemed quiet after the show. Withdrawn. He hadn't wanted to engage with anybody. Hadn't even wanted to go out with the group for a late dinner. Jon never ate before shows—he didn't like to perform on a full stomach. That was normal. But *after* a show, we usually found some hidden gem restaurant—a local favorite, off the beaten path—good food, quiet vibe, a chance to wind down.

But Jon?

"Not hungry."

So, we skipped dinner entirely.

***

The following weekend's Friday night show in Philadelphia was a repeat of the previous Saturday. The show itself was flawless. But afterward, Jon shut down again. Said he had a headache. We grabbed takeout, and aside from Cary—who had vanished off with some "new friends" for the night—we all retreated to the hotel.

And then came Saturday. New York City. The show was already fucked before it even started. A phone call from Matt had sent Jon into a rage spiral.

Matt Conner handled contracts. Not just for Final Relapse—but for Jon personally. Because of Jon's exceptional talent, companies were constantly approaching him with sponsorships, endorsements, and strategic partnerships. Some deals were lucrative as hell. And Matt knew how to find them. Networking. Schmoozing. Knowing the right people. When it came to business, Matt was a damn good agent.

But he and Jon?

Clashed. Constantly.

Jon resented many of the deals Matt brought to the table.

Like the one that set him off on Saturday evening.

***

Jon was normally mild-mannered. Even-tempered. But after that phone call with Matt, I swear I could see actual steam rising off of him. Jaw clenched tight. Shoulders coiled like a spring.

Apparently, Jon had been very clear about not renewing a contract with a company that made effects pedals he deemed "shitty quality."

And Matt?

Made the deal anyway.

Now, Jon was fuming.

We were already at the venue—soundcheck was done. At least he had some time to cool off before showtime.

And he knew he needed to.

I watched as he downed an entire bottle of water in one go—

Then, crushed it into a tight, twisted knot of plastic with one hand.

His fingers were white-knuckled.

His whole body was tense.

He caught me watching him.

Paused.

Then, exhaling deeply, he walked over and planted a soft kiss on my forehead.

"I love you."

Quiet.

As if to reassure me that his irritation wasn't about me. I smiled and plucked the mangled plastic bottle from his hand.

"Let me find a trash can for this." I said, lightly teasing. But even as I tried to defuse the tension, I was pretty sure his hands were shaking.

"Thanks, babe." His voice was a little rougher than usual.

"I'm gonna take a walk... I need to blow off some steam."

Yes. Yes, you do.

I nodded. "Go ahead."

***

Backstage, I joined the others in the lounge. Nikki and I were sharing a loveseat, determined to demolish a family-sized bag of M&M's when Tony strolled in. After a few minutes of small talk, he glanced around.

"Where's Jon?"

All eyes snapped to me.

I popped an M&M into my mouth.

"Went for a walk."

Tony raised an eyebrow, waiting for me to elaborate. When I didn't, he looked at Mike.

Mike smirked. "He's pissed."

Tony threw up his hands. "Somebody wanna tell me what the hell is going on?"

Mike didn't even hesitate. "Matt."

That was all it took.

Tony sighed heavily, rubbing a hand down his face.

"Aw, Christ." He shook his head. "Those fucking two..."

Glancing at his watch, he muttered, "Well... we've got time. He better get the fuck over it."

***

But after the show—

Something was off again. Jon packed away his guitars, muttered something to Mike, and headed out the back exit to the lot. I followed a few minutes later, stepping into the cool night air.

Jon had already stowed one of his bags in the rack inside the trailer. Now, he was sitting on the edge of it—his elbows on his knees, staring out across the lot. I walked over. From the height of the trailer, he was still a little taller than me, even sitting down. But when I reached him, he said nothing. Instead, he just leaned forward and wrapped his arms around me.

I hugged him back—

And immediately noticed how sweaty he was.

It had been hot as hell on stage. Even backstage, the air had been stifling, which was probably why the rest of the group had started filtering outside.

Still—

Something about the way he felt against me—the way his breath hit my shoulder—

It didn't feel like normal post-show exhaustion.

"Hey, Via!"

I glanced over as Tony motioned me toward the stairs. Reluctantly, I pulled from Jon's arms and crossed the lot back to the others.

Tony didn't waste time.

"What the hell's going on with him?" He nodded toward Jon, still sitting on the trailer.

I hesitated. Shrugged.

"He sick?"

Another shrug. "I honestly don't know, Tony."

Tony's face darkened.

"Same shit as last time?"

There was apprehension in his voice now.

I considered.

Jon had been sick for practically the entire last stretch of shows. Tony had been convinced it was walking pneumonia—but when Jon went to the doctor the next week?

Clear bill of health.

My lack of an answer seemed to make Tony uneasy. He sighed, shaking his head. "I'll be back."

And without another word—

He turned and disappeared back into the venue.

***

"Here ya go!" Nikki skipped down the back steps, swinging my backpack toward me. Shit. I'd forgotten about it when I followed Jon outside.

"Thanks," I mumbled, slinging it over one shoulder.

I crossed the lot, tossed my backpack into the front seat of Jon's truck, then headed back to the trailer. Jon was inside, back turned, wrapping cables and stacking them into a road case. I walked up the ramp. "Hey, babe."

He glanced over.

Flashed me a reassuring smile.

"Hey, sexy."

I studied him for a beat.

"Why don't you let Andy do that?"

Andy was their road tech—he normally handled equipment load-in and out.

Jon shrugged. "No harm in helping."

And before I could push further—

A man's voice interrupted.

"Hey there."

Jon and I turned simultaneously. Tony was standing just outside the trailer—with two EMTs. A man and a woman. And before I could react—

The male EMT was already stepping up the ramp.

Oh. Shit.

My eyes snapped to Tony.

He motioned with his hands, a clear *What else was I supposed to do?*

"Jon?" The EMT extended a hand. "Nice to meet you. I'm Mark."

Jon shook his hand—but his eyes were locked on his uniform.

Taking him in.

Assessing.

"Feeling okay tonight?" Mark asked.

Oh, fuck.

This wasn't going to go well.

Jon's gaze moved to Tony.

His entire expression darkened.

"What the hell, Tony?" His voice was low. Tense. Pissed.

Tony sighed, throwing his hands up defensively.

"Just let 'em check you out real quick, will ya? You've got me a little freaked out, man!"

Jon's eyes moved back to Mark.

I could see it—

His jaw tightening.

Mark took a cautious step forward.

"Can I just take your pulse?"

He lifted his hands slowly.

Like he was approaching a feral dog.

Honestly?

Probably not far from the truth, judging by the look on Jon's face.

But he didn't resist.

Mark wrapped his fingers around Jon's wrist.

Held it.

Waited.

Then—

Made a monumental fuck-up.

"Your heart rate's elevated. Have you taken anything tonight that might cause that?"

FFFUUUUUCKKKK.

Jon yanked his hand away.

Took a step back.

Eyes blazing.

"What, I'm a musician, so I obviously have a substance abuse problem. *Right?*"

Cold.

Accusatory.

And I couldn't blame him.

It was such a bullshit assumption.

Not only was it unfair—

It couldn't be further from the truth.

Nobody in FR used drugs.

Nobody.

They had literally named their band after a friend who had died that way.

Hell, I did more drugs than Jon—

And all I ever did was smoke some occasional weed.

"Not at all." Mark said quickly. Backpedaling.

Buddy, you're not getting out of this riptide alive.

"That's not what I meant."

Mark lifted his hands, trying to calm the situation.

"I'm just trying to understand why your heart rate is so high."

But it was too late.

Jon was already storming down the ramp.

Already moving back through the lot toward the venue.

And as he passed Tony—

He threw him a seething glare.

I exhaled sharply.

Stepped forward.

"Really, Tony?"

The disappointment in my voice was undeniable.

Before Tony could reply, the EMT calling himself Mark, came down the ramp.

"Didn't mean to offend anyone," he muttered. "He *is* tachycardic, though."

"How bad?" the female EMT asked.

Mark hesitated.

"Probably 150ish."

That hit harder than I expected.

The woman turned to me. "What other symptoms has he been experiencing?"

I glanced at Tony.

He nodded for me to speak up.

"Cold sweats. Shaking. Shortness of breath. Lightheadedness?"

I didn't mean for my voice to sound uncertain.

But hearing it all listed out like that made my stomach twist.

The woman nodded. "Has he been under a lot of stress lately?"

Tony and I exchanged glances.

"...he was stressed today." I admitted.

Another nod.

"Could be that. Those are all symptoms of a stress response. Could he be having performance anxiety?"

Oh my God.

My eyes snapped to Tony.

Jon definitely had performance anxiety.

Is that what this was?

"That could be it."

For a second, I felt relief.

But then, that same relief twisted into something else.

Because if that was it—

What the hell did that mean?

Tony blew out a shaky breath.

Rubbed the back of his neck.

Muttered, "Fuck."

Shook his head. "*Fuck.* Yeah. That could be it."

"Maybe talk to him about it?" The woman suggested.

"He could try breathing exercises or meditation. Those things might help."

I didn't know if I'd ever convince Jon of that.

But I thanked her anyway.

Then turned, and headed back toward the venue.

***

I found Jon standing with a small group of six or seven people.

Talking. Laughing. Smiling.

Like everything was normal.

Thank God.

As I approached, Jon threw an arm around me, pulling me in close.

Like nothing had ever happened, including the altercation in the trailer.

Minutes ago, he'd been pale, sweaty, shaking.

Now?

He seemed fine.

I decided to go along with it.

Everything seemed to have smoothed over.

But about five minutes later...

"Hey."

Tony's voice cut through the conversation.

Jon turned his head slightly, arm still around me.

Tony met his eyes. "Can I have a word?"

I felt Jon's whole body tense.

His posture stiffened.

But after a beat, he stepped away from the group.

Tony's eyes flicked to me.

"Via. You too."

Shit.

I followed as Tony led us around the corner into a secluded area.

Jon's shoulders were tight. Guarded. Hands in his pockets.

"Listen, man." Tony exhaled. "I'm sorry for what happened back there. I—that's not how I meant for that to go."

Jon stood silently. Watching.

Waiting.

"We're just worried about ya. That's all." Tony added.

"So what—is this some kind of intervention?"

His voice was cold.

Tony shook his head. "I just—man, I know you're not yourself lately. I can tell you're not feeling good."

Jon didn't reply.

But he also didn't deny it.

I slid an arm around Jon's waist.

A silent *I'm with you.*

Tony's tone softened. "You're stressing pretty hard lately, huh?"

He motioned toward the stage. "I get it. This shit's hard. For anybody. But you're juggling a hell of a lot. Work, school, studio—and then going out there every night?"

And he was right.

Jon was still finishing his graduate degree in music, focused on composition and advanced studio training. He still taught, too—though these days, he mostly coached aspiring professionals and gifted students.

On top of that, he was writing and recording full-time with FR, juggling side projects, scoring gigs... And, for some reason, still coaching that neighborhood soccer team—because Kyle asked, and Jon couldn't say no.

"You're burning the candle at both ends, man."

Tony let the words settle.

Jon was listening. But I could still feel the tension in his body.

Tony tilted his head slightly.

"But you're *so* damn good. You know that, right?"

Jon nodded.

"Do you *like* it, though?" Tony prodded. "Do you still wanna do this?"

Jon exhaled.

Looked away.

"Yeah."

Tony's voice dropped even lower.

"Really?"

"It's okay if you don't, Jon. But you gotta tell me."

Jon's jaw flexed.

"No."

A pause.

Then—

"I do."

Tony studied him.

Then, quietly—

"Jon."

Jon lifted his head.

Their eyes met.

"Do you still wanna do this?"

The words came out slow. Even. Deliberate.

Something you never got from Tony.

Jon didn't flinch.

"Yes."

Tony exhaled.

Nodded.

"Okay."

And maybe it was just me—

But I could swear I saw relief flood Tony's face.

He clapped a hand on Jon's shoulder. "Then let me help you. I get that you're stressed. But I know a guy. A doctor. In the city. He works with performers. All types. He can prescribe you something to take the edge off."

The fuck?

Jon froze.

His jaw locked.

"No, fuck that." His voice was immediate. Sharp.

"I don't need some sedative that's gonna turn me into a walking zombie every day."

"No, no! Of course you don't," Tony nodded quickly. "That's not what I'm talking about. Not at all."

He hesitated.

Then—

"He can prescribe you a beta-blocker."

Jon stilled.

Listening.

Tony pressed forward. "They use it off-label for this. It helps with performance anxiety."

"You take it before a show. That's it. It won't fuck with your head. Won't mess with your creativity. Performers use it all the time."

Jon considered.

Tony softened. "Let me make you an appointment."

Jon was silent.

Thinking.

"We'll go see him this week. Okay?"

Another beat.

Then—

Jon nodded.

Tony grinned.

Clapped Jon's back. "Yeah?"

Jon exhaled.

"Yeah."

"There's my guy!" Tony pulled him into a quick hug. "We're gonna take care of this. I got you."

I felt a wave of relief.

And yet—

Something in my gut still twisted.

I wasn't sure why.

But I didn't like it.

Chapter 5

I walked up to Jon's front door, feeling uneasy.

He had gone with Tony earlier that day to see Tony's doctor connection.

At least the guy was a real doctor.

I had checked.

But now, as I sat on Jon's couch, reading over the label on the prescription bottle—

I felt my stomach twist again.

Propranolol.

A beta-blocker.

I flipped to the side effects.

Extreme tiredness. Fatigue. Dizziness. Slow heartbeat.

The list went on.

I frowned. "How in the hell is this supposed to make things better?"

Jon shrugged. "I don't know, Vee. I just took one a bit ago. So, we'll see."

What the hell??

My head snapped up.

"You took one?!"

The words came out louder than I intended.

But I couldn't stop the spike of panic.

Jon's tone was calm. Soft. "The doctor told me to try it ahead of time. So I know what to expect."

I stared at him.

"And???"

He shrugged. Nonchalant.

"I don't know. I don't really feel anything."

I don't like this.

But then again—

I didn't like the way Jon had been after shows lately, either.

I tried to have a normal night with him, but I couldn't help but watch him closely.

After another hour, I pressed again.

"How do you feel?"

Jon exhaled. "Honestly, it's not what I was expecting."

He tilted his head, thinking.

"I'm a little tired, maybe? But if I get up and move around, I don't even notice it. I think it'll be fine, Vee."

***

Turns out he was right. I had to hand it to Tony. He'd really come through on this one.

The rest of their shows went smoothly.

Jon would take the pill.

Finish the show.

Carry on with the evening.

No more shakiness.

No more cold sweats.

Just... Jon.

Normal.

Just like it used to be.

Crazy how something so small could make that big of a difference.

No wonder performers took them all the time.

August rolled to a close. FR's season was over. No more shows until the new year.

I was looking forward to a quiet fall. A relaxing holiday season.

Things were looking great.

The Hamptons trip was our last celebration for the new album.

And our reluctant goodbye to summer.

Four days.

No commitments. No deadlines.

Just us.

And even though it was only a long weekend, it felt like so much longer.

For all the right reasons.

Especially since Nikki and Mike had finally become an item. Their romance wasn't like mine and Jon's. It wasn't that electric, all-consuming passion, but that was okay. Because for them?

It worked.

It was easy. Convenient.

Mike was Jon's best friend, and Nikki was one of mine. Considering we spent half our time together anyway...

It only made sense that they'd end up together.

And better yet—

They were happy.

***

One night, Jon and I went out to the pool after everyone else had gone to bed.

It had started with a midnight swim.

It ended with us tangled on a lounge chair.

We had always been careful.

Responsible.

Condoms. Always.

I was on the pill, too—just to be safe.

But we had planned to go swimming that night.

And we didn't have a condom.

After a brief but serious discussion—

My birth control.

Our monogamy.

The fact that neither of us had ever done this before.

We gave in to the moment.

I knew it would feel good for him.

I was not expecting how stimulated *I* would be by all of it.

I could feel his warmth hit places that made me see stars.

Afterward, we just lay there.

Grinning at each other like two simpletons.

Jon sighed, smiling lazily.

"Please tell me we're never going to let latex come between us again."

His voice was low. Devilish.

I laughed. "I just hope my birth control works." I said it, not because I was trying to ruin the moment, but because, *damn.*

Jon hummed.

Turned his head to look at me.

"Would it be so bad if it didn't?"

The fuck?

I went completely still.

And he wasn't even looking at me anymore.

Like he had just casually dropped a nuclear bomb into the conversation.

"What?"

Jon shrugged. "I dunno."

Then, with a lazy grin—

"A mini-Via running around with long, dark hair and eyes so green we'd instantly forgive her sassy attitude. That sounds kinda nice."

I stared at him.

Longer than necessary.

"...that sounds like a nightmare."

Jon laughed.

"Give me time. I'll convince you."

I turned away.

Intentionally letting the quiet settle in.

I wasn't going to think about what he had just said.

I wasn't going to analyze it.

It was just something stupid he had said.

Caught in the grip of endorphins and exhaustion.

That's all it was.

Because NO.

***

Fortunately, my contraceptives had done their job.

And were continuing to do their job.

Thank. Fucking. Jeezus.

No need to further that conversation.

Chapter 6

The weekend after Thanksgiving, we took a trip to upstate New York.

Jon and Cary had plans to snowboard most of the weekend.

The rest of us?

Not so much.

I was going to attempt it again.

Beginner slopes. Low expectations.

Because after years of trying, one thing had become painfully obvious:

I sucked.

So did Nikki.

So did Mike.

We had all long since accepted this.

Which meant we'd probably end up in the lodge, drinking and watching the people with actual skill through the window.

But this trip had become an annual tradition.

And I was looking forward to it.

Jon was in the garage, packing up his snowboard gear.

I was upstairs, doing one last check to make sure I hadn't forgotten anything.

Scouring Jon's bathroom sink one last time, my eyes fell on his deodorant.

Yikes. Can't forget that.

Chuckling to myself, I grabbed it—

Walked over to his open suitcase.

Unzipped the top pocket to toss it in—

And stopped short.

A prescription pill bottle.

Jon's Propranolol.

The hell?

I reached down.

Picked it up.

Turned it over in my palm.

These were for shows.

Why the hell was he bringing them?

I glanced at the label, just to be sure.

Then, slowly, I shook the bottle.

A prescription that should have been nearly full.

Instead?

Maybe ten pills left.

What the actual hell?

My mind raced to connect the dots.

I didn't have to spend long thinking about it, because a few minutes later, Jon walked into the room.

I was still sitting on the bed.

Silently fuming. Looking at a bottle that should have had a lot more in it than it did.

Jon stopped mid-stride. Looking from my face to the bottle in my hands, and back to me.

I held it up.

Shook it once.

My voice came out sharp.

"Why the hell are you sneaking your medication along on this trip?"

"I'm not sneaking them, Vee." His voice was calm. Even. "They're right there. In my suitcase."

Oh, we're playing *this* game?

"Why?"

Jon shrugged.

And for the first time—

He looked like he didn't know what to say.

"In case I need them?"

"What the hell would you need them for? These are for shows!"

Before he could even respond to that—

A bigger, *more important* question slipped out.

"And why are there so many missing?"

I held the bottle up again.

"There should be, like, most of the bottle left."

I shook it again.

Jon blinked.

I waited.

Forced myself to stay quiet.

I needed his explanation.

After a beat—

"...I take them sometimes."

My eyes narrowed.

"For what?"

Jon exhaled.

Ran a hand through his hair.

"I don't know."

He lifted his shoulders in another shrug.

"They just... help."

"Help *what?*"

Jon sighed.

"They just help me relax sometimes, okay?"

My mind raced.

Could you abuse beta-blockers?

I didn't think so...

But I also wasn't sure.

Jon wasn't a pill-popper.

Was he?

Did he have a full-blown anxiety disorder?

And if so—

How the hell had I not known?

Jon sat down beside me.

"Please stop."

His voice was soft. Steady.

"Whatever you're thinking... it's wrong."

I lifted my chin.

"How do you know what I'm thinking?"

Jon huffed a quiet laugh.

"Because I'm looking at your face."

I paused.

The comment caught me off-guard.

For a second, I thought we both might laugh.

Jon didn't.

He was watching me. Waiting.

I let out a slow breath.

Reset, Via.

We don't want to fight.

Not right before our trip.

I tried again.

Softer.

"Are you okay?"

Jon nodded. Emphatically.

"Yes. I promise."

Then—

He kissed me.

Softly.

I wanted to believe him.

I didn't want to be mad.

Jon pulled back.

Smirked.

"Maybe you should try one."

My eyes snapped to his.

"Excuse me?"

He grinned.

But... he was serious.

"You're the one with anxiety issues. I'll share."

I hesitated.

Because...

He wasn't wrong.

Stress got to me.

A lot.

Jon handled way more than I did.

Maybe I was being too hard on him.

I let out a slow breath.

Choose your battles, Via.

This one slides.

It was time to go have fun.

And that's exactly what we did.

***

The fall months had been quiet. Relaxed.

Which meant I finally had time to pick up some new hobbies.

One of them?

Bass guitar.

I mean, I literally had the best teacher in the world at my fingertips.

And Jon had been more than happy to indulge me.

Which meant I pretty much knew what I was getting for Christmas.

Naturally, on Christmas Eve, surrounded by Jon's parents, his sister, his brother-in-law, and Mike and Nikki... I wasn't terribly surprised when Jon handed me a large, guitar-sized box wrapped in red and silver paper.

Except—

As usual—

Jon had made sure to knock me completely off my feet.

He had guaranteed I would be surprised.

Starting with the fact that he'd hidden my actual guitar in the closet.

Instead—

He had wrapped six more boxes.

Each one in a different paper.

Each one nested inside the next.

Every time I unwrapped a box,

There was another, smaller box inside.

What the hell, Jon?

I glanced at him.

He looked innocent.

But his eyes sparkled with mischief.

Would he punk me this way?

Absolutely.

But would his family sit back and watch?

If that's the case, I'm going to be pissed at everybody.

It'll be a Grinch Christmas.

Finally—

I worked my way down to a box small enough to fit in the palm of my hand.

I unwrapped it.

Flipped open the velvet container.

Inside—

A ring.

My breath caught.

What the actual fuck?

I blinked.

Looked at it.

Looked at him.

Jon was already on one knee.

"Marry me, Vee."

Did he just—

Did he actually just fucking say?

My brain glitched.

I couldn't process what I was seeing.

What I was hearing.

My eyes locked onto his.

Those beautiful. Golden. Eyes.

The ones that never stopped surprising me.

I heard Nikki squeal beside me—

Her hands clapped over her mouth.

I barely registered it.

I barely registered anything.

Oh God.

Everyone is watching.

I could feel my face burning.

My brain shutting down.

Was I going to melt?

Dissolve right here on the couch?

Via. You need to react.

OUTWARDLY.

And then—

Oh no. Oh, fuck.

Was I breathing??

I threw my arms around him. Held on tight.

I wasn't going to cry.

Except, suddenly—

While hugging him—

The reality slammed into me like a freight train.

I pulled back.

Jon tilted his head.

Looking hesitant. Hopeful.

His eyes sparkled.

He half-laughed.

But his voice was soft. Almost nervous.

"So... is that a yes?"

I nodded.

Laughed sheepishly.

I was on fire.

I didn't know what to do.

I had apparently forgotten I had a voice.

Jon smiled. Hugged me again.

His arms were grounding.

Keeping me from floating away.

I finally whispered, "I love you."

The room erupted in cheers.

People clapping.

Nikki was still practically jumping up and down.

As it turned out—

Everyone had been in on it.

Everyone except Nikki.

Jon had purposely left her out.

He knew she would accidentally ruin the surprise.

And, honestly?

She probably would have.

She pretended to be pissed.

We all laughed.

And just like that—

I was engaged.

To Jonathan Stetson.

***

Jon and I had stepped out onto the back patio.

The air was bitter.

Sharp enough to sting my skin.

But I didn't notice.

I needed a moment to decompress.

Away from the eyes.

Away from the noise.

Jon stood beside me.

Quiet. Watching.

My brain was still catching up.

I had just agreed to marry him.

And for some reason—

I just wanted to keep hugging him.

Like, as long as I held onto him, I wouldn't completely spiral.

Jon finally broke the silence.

His voice was soft. Gentle.

"Are you okay?"

I let out a breathless laugh.

I couldn't wipe the stupid smile off my face.

I nodded.

"Yeah. I'm sorry... I'm just... overwhelmed."

Jon's golden eyes softened.

"We don't have to rush into anything."

His demeanor was calm and reassuring.

"We both have a year of school left. I just... wanted you to know where my heart is. And I'm hoping you feel the same."

I shook my head instantly.

"Oh my God, Jon. I do! And yes. I want this, too."

He smiled.

I stepped forward.

And we embraced again.

This time, I let myself sink into it.

My forehead against his chest.

I don't know how long we stayed like that.

But eventually—

The cold sank its claws in.

And I finally felt it.

***

The next conversations were inevitable.

Naturally—

Nikki was already planning the wedding.

Even though we explained that we were waiting until after graduation.

- My bachelor's.
- His master's.
- Our new life together.

None of it mattered.

Nikki was unstoppable.

And Jill?

Not much better.

At the rate the two of them were going—

I wouldn't have to do a damn thing.

Jill & Ben's wedding had been extravagant.

Beautiful. Traditional.

It had been the first time I met Jon's extended family.

Most of them lived on the West Coast.

Everything was perfect.

But it was also the exact opposite of what I wanted.

Jon knew that.

At one point—

Jill and Nikki were mid-scheme.

Talking about venues, dresses, and color palettes.

My head was already spinning.

Then, suddenly—

Jon's voice cut in.

Casual. Easy.

"I was thinking about black and red. For the colors."

Wait.

I looked at him.

He was already looking at me.

A grin tugged at his lips.

And then—

A wink.

My stomach flipped.

He'd already thought about this?

Of course, *he had.*

And hell yes.

A dark, gothy vibe?

Classy. Unique.

Everything that we were.

Jill and Nikki exchanged a glance.

Then sighed.

Jill shook her head.

"Of course you would."

Nikki grinned.

"Honestly? That's kinda badass."

Yeah.

Yeah, it was.

***

I walked around on cloud nine the rest of the night.

I called my friends.

I called my family.

I told the story multiple times to multiple people.

And every time—

It felt amazing.

And surreal.

But the true weight of it—

The deeper meaning—

Didn't hit me until the following day.

Christmas Day.

And yes—

I had chosen to spend it with Jon.

Rather than travel home.

We would see my family between Christmas and New Year's.

But on Christmas?

I just wanted to be with him.

And it ended up being the perfect decision.

Ben and Jill had a very special gift for each of us.

They had waited intentionally.

Not wanting to overshadow Jon's proposal.

They wanted that moment to be ours.

So, they waited until Christmas afternoon.

Jill handed us each a wrapped box.

"Open them together." She grinned.

I tore the paper off mine—

Pulled out a folded T-shirt.

Flipped it open.

Across the front, in bold white lettering—

"World's Greatest Aunt."

My eyes snapped to Jon.

He was holding his own shirt.

"World's Greatest Uncle."

Next to us—

Sharron and Jeff unfolded their shirts.

The grandparent equivalents.

Jill was beaming.

Ben looked proud.

Jon—

I swear to God—

I saw his eyes well up.

Sharron outright sobbed.

Dramatic as usual.

But they were happy tears.

I truly saw how much she was invested in her family.

Then, she said it.

Just an innocuous comment.

A passing thought.

"You four kids have made me the happiest woman on the planet this Christmas."

You. Four. Kids.

Jill. Jon. Ben.

And...

Me.

Me.

I looked down at my shirt.

Read the words again.

"World's Greatest Aunt."

And it hit me.

I was part of this family.

They had already embraced me.

They had already chosen me.

And Jon—

He had invited me in.

I had accepted.

I had just officially gained a new family.

And I loved them.

And holy fucking shit.

I was going to be Livia Stetson.

Chapter 7

The morning air was brisk. Downright cold. But the sun was bright, making my pupils constrict almost painfully as I stepped out and walked the short half-block to the boutique coffee shop on the corner. I reminded myself not to complain. Atlanta in February was still mild compared to home.

Still, it was too damn early to be out. I would have preferred to stay snuggled up inside for a bit longer. The hotel had coffee, sure, but they didn't have my preferred sweeteners. And unlike Jon, I did not like my coffee black. Not all of us were complete psychopaths.

So, here I was, standing in line like a half-asleep zombie, letting the delicious aromas of espresso and caramelized sugar settle around me. The chatter of baristas, the hiss of steamed milk, the quiet hum of early risers—it all blurred together as I waited for my much-needed caffeine fix.

"Oh, heyyy darling!" purred a smooth male voice. "You're engaged to Stets, right? He's an absolute life saver!"

The voice was close. I turned to look at the man who had spoken. He was well-dressed—too well-dressed for 9 AM. Black jeans, a crisp button-up, and an absolutely gorgeous red and black damask jacket. His eyeliner was flawless, better than mine ever was, even on a good night out.

He looked familiar. One of the guys from a band opening for FR and FaultCode. Shane? I think that was his name? It was only day four of the tour, and I'd met a lot of new people. And I was already shitty at remembering names on a good day.

I blinked again, still trying to jump-start my brain. *"Stets."* Right. That's what some of them had started calling Jon, and the nickname had stuck.

I glanced down, suddenly hyperaware of the weight on my hand. I still wasn't used to it. The ring was stunning—a brilliant center diamond, flanked by glittering rubies, set in platinum. I didn't want to know how much Jon had spent on it, but Nikki guessed it was worth more than her car. And she was probably right.

I smiled, despite myself. "Yes! We just got engaged over Christmas. Still getting used to it."

Shane beamed. "Well, that's wonderful! Congratulations!"

Without hesitation, he took my hand, bending down to examine the ring like it was a rare artifact. "This is gorgeous, girlfriend! He did well."

I laughed. Shane was flamboyant, but in the most endearing way.

He gave me a playful wink, then circled back to his original comment. "He saved us all from a meltdown last night."

"Oh, yeah?" I raised an eyebrow.

Shane threw up his hands dramatically, and proceeded to tell me about how Jon had helped his band save a problematic song by rewriting a chord progression. Apparently, they were thrilled with his advice.

I grinned. I had no doubts. Jon had an incredible ear.

The barista placed my coffee on the counter, but before I could grab it, something about Shane's jacket caught my eye. The style, the colors... it reminded me of the wedding theme Jon had mentioned.

"I love your jacket," I said. "It's beautiful."

Shane's eyes lit up. "Thanks! You know Jess made it?"

Jess was married to Clay, FaultCode's frontman.

"FaultCode's Jess?"

"Yep! She's a wizard with a sewing machine. In fact—"

He took a step back, looking me up and down.

...the hell?

I stood there awkwardly as he appraised me, eyes sharp with sudden inspiration.

"You should come with me."

Uh. What?

"She's looking for a model for some of her pieces, and you have the body for it."

Oh hell no.

"Oh—I couldn't," I blurted out. "But I can't believe she made that!"

"Nonsense, girlfriend! At least come see the vest she's making me next."

I hesitated, but his enthusiasm was infectious. And now, I was curious.

Plus... I had a wedding to think about.

***

"Thanks so much for doing this!" Jess said, giving a hard yank that cinched me into the corset.

I winced. *Jesus Christ.* The woman had strength.

I still felt awkward, but I liked Jess. We'd hit it off after Shane's introduction earlier that afternoon, and she'd promised me that Clay was gone—leaving her with privacy to work.

"It's so much easier with an actual model," she continued. "Mannequins? I pull those suckers right over."

I believed it.

She was working on the intricate back stitching—an elaborate black and emerald green piece, gothic in style, detailed in leather and lace. I put my long hair into a loose bun to keep it out of the way.

"Just don't stab me with that needle," I teased.

We both laughed, but I was dead serious.

Jess was insanely talented. Most of her commissions were for artists and performers, but she also built up inventory for summer festivals—corsets, vests, unique statement pieces. Everything she made was elegant.

When I mentioned our wedding colors, her eyes lit up.

By the time we finished brainstorming, I was already excited, even though we had an entire year to plan.

"Nooo, that's a good thing!" Jess said as she tightened another lace.

I stood on a small wooden box, giving her easy access to my lower back while she worked from her chair.

"We'll need that time to pull everything together. But oooh, baby, once it all comes together—you guys are gonna have one hell of a dark and elegant look!"

She paused, then added thoughtfully, "You're beautiful. The possibilities for your dress—I can't wait to dive in."

I blushed.

"Your man's not too shabby, either," she added with a teasing grin. "And whatever we design for you? We'll make sure he matches."

That stupid, smitten smile took over my face again.

I hated I couldn't control it better.

I had once been so proud of the cool, collected cynic I'd built myself into.

Jon had ruined me.

Turned me into a sap. Just like that.

A while later, my phone pinged. I stepped down from the box, grabbed it, and reclaimed my place as I typed back.

Jon: *Where are you?*

I grinned. He probably thought I'd been with Nikki all afternoon.

"Is it cool if Jon comes up?" I asked Jess.

"Of course!"

Via: *Room 503.*

A long pause.

Then—

Jon: *Whose room is that?*

A devious smile crept across my face.

Via: *Clay and Jess's.*

I barely resisted the urge to laugh maniacally.

That was definitely going to rock his boat a little.

I waited an agonizingly long few minutes.

Then—

Jon: *Oh. Cool. Can I come up?*

Via: *Sure.*

Sure enough, five minutes later, a light knock at the door.

Jess hopped up to let him in.

Jon stepped inside—then stopped cold.

"Whoa," he breathed. His eyes moved slowly over me, taking in the corset, the low-rise pants, the way the lace and leather cinched at my waist.

The shock on his face was *priceless.*

But the look that followed?

That *hungry,* carnal expression?

Even better.

His voice dropped. "What's going on here?"

Before either of us could answer—

"God, you look beautiful."

My face heated instantly. Jess giggled.

"I needed a model," she said playfully. "Via's being a good sport."

Jon barely looked at her. His gaze hadn't left me.

"...and a great model," he murmured.

The corset had my boobs squished up just right, and I wasn't *not* enjoying the way his eyes took notice.

I loved when he looked at me like that.

Then, as if pulling himself back from an evil thought, he asked, "You make corsets?"

Jess chuckled. "And other stuff—like wedding dresses."

She paused deliberately.

Jon's eyes snapped to mine.

He didn't hesitate.

"Hell yeah."

I grinned. My face was definitely hot now.

"This one makes your eyes look so green," he said, voice low.

"I can make them in any color," Jess said casually. "This one's going into inventory for the fairs this summer."

Jon's brow lifted. "So it's not sold yet?"

"Nope."

"Then, yes. It is."

I let out an embarrassed laugh. *"Jon."*

He held my gaze. Unapologetic.

"And we want a red and black one, too," he added.

"I'll pay you upfront."

Chapter 8

It was nice being back in New York.

Someplace that felt more like home.

Even if there was snow on the ground.

Co-headlining meant FR and FaultCode alternated who closed. On nights FR played last, it was great—when they were done; we were done.

This, however, wasn't one of those nights.

While FaultCode was finishing their set, FR was tied up in conversation—tour manager, band managers, and one of the promoters.

I was flipping through some promotional shots Nikki had captured when Jon caught my attention and motioned me over, grinning.

He was leaning against a railing, a sheet of paper in his hand.

I made my way down the ramp and stopped behind him. "What's that?"

"The dates and locations for the second leg of the tour."

Ooh. We'd been waiting for this. My excitement about going to the West Coast was undeniable.

From my vantage point on the ramp, I was a good foot taller than him. Smirking, I leaned over, wrapping my arms around his shoulders from behind so I could read along with him.

Shit!

Four stops in California. Portland. Seattle. Two in Texas. One in Phoenix—

But then...

My focus shifted. Away from the list. Away from the excitement.

To my arm.

Draped over his chest.

And that in this position, I could feel his heart.

It was pounding. *Too hard.*

Was that normal?

It seemed awfully fast, considering he was just standing there.

Didn't it?

But... he seemed okay.

He wasn't acting weird.

He was saying something about visiting his cousin in San Francisco, but I wasn't really listening anymore.

"Did you take your pill tonight?" The words slipped out before I fully thought them through.

"What?" He blinked, surprised. For a split second, he looked genuinely lost.

Then—"Oh. Yeah, babe. I took it."

His tone was innocent. Truthful.

And just like that, he was already moving on. Back to Ryan, his cousin in San Francisco.

I hesitated. I wanted to say something else. I just wasn't sure what.

Before I could figure it out—

"Hey, man. Which two modules did you want to swap on your board?"

Andy, one of the audio techs, had approached from the right.

Jon turned instantly, already shifting gears. "Be right back, babe."

And just like that—

He was gone.

Well, fuck.

I stood there, my arms now empty, my thoughts scrambling.

He seemed okay.

And honestly, why did it always feel like he was being pulled in ten directions at once?

It's no wonder the guy was stressed.

Maybe he'd forgotten to take his pill?

Or maybe...

Maybe it was just in my head.

I checked my phone.

His "be right back" took forty-five minutes.

When I went looking, he and Andy were in the back of the trailer, soldering something.

Wonderful.

At least he was obviously feeling fine.

It must have been all in my head.

***

There wasn't a show scheduled for Sunday night, which meant we could head home in the morning. A pleasant break before the next leg in New England.

I was going to miss out on most of the following week's show schedule because of work and school obligations. Jon hated it when I couldn't be there, but I wasn't worried this time. He had developed a fast connection with FaultCode's lead guitarist, Jason. The two of them were on some entirely different wavelength—the kind of creative synergy that just happened when the right musicians met.

Jason wrote all of FaultCode's material and had considered himself a phenom—until he met Jon.

It was a bromance of creative geniuses.

They'd started co-writing during the days, and I couldn't have been happier about it.

Because the performance side of this? That was a struggle. But writing? Composing? Recording?

Jon lived for that.

So, the fact that he had an outlet to keep him distracted during the days? Fuck yeah.

And I knew Mike would have his back—always. They'd been best friends since they were kids, and honestly, I think Mike saw Jon more as a brother than a friend.

I'd meet back up with them in Connecticut on Friday.

Then, on Saturday, they were back in New York. They had a show in the city, and then Jon had an extra acoustic show right after.

A different venue. A different setup.

The additional set was special—a rare arrangement that had come from Matt.

And one that Jon didn't immediately hate.

After the usual show, there'd be a VIP event—an after-hours special. The venue was swanky, out on Long Island.

A one-off acoustic collaboration with Jon and Allen Houston—a seasoned vet in the scene, but one who'd been branching out beyond mainstream music.

Jon and Allen had hit it off a couple of years ago.

And now?

Matt had landed them a gig.

Two grand each for a 45-minute set.

Jon was thrilled.

Ironically, less for the money—more for the challenge.

The chance to do something acoustic. To push himself. To let his creative prowess shine.

So, as we packed up and left the hotel Sunday morning for home, I felt confident.

And happy.

***

We were right behind Mike and Cary pulling out of the parking garage Sunday morning.

Only, instead of following them toward the interstate, Jon turned left.

"Where are we going?" I asked immediately.

Jon shot me a quick smile. "Pit stop. We're meeting up with Tony and his wife."

I blinked. "Tony and Bev?"

I loved Bev. I'd only met her a handful of times, but she exuded a warm, nurturing energy that reminded me of my grandmother—though Bev wasn't quite that old.

Jon nodded.

"But where are we going?" I pressed.

He laughed, but something in his tone felt… hesitant. Nervous, even. "Just checking something out."

"What?"

A long beat.

Then— "A house."

What the actual hell, Jon?

I stared at him. "What?"

He exhaled a quiet laugh. "Okay, Via. Before you lose your mind—we're just looking. I just want to see what Tony's been telling me about. We'll look, and then we'll discuss it. *Together.* Okay?"

I gaped. "Discuss *what?* Jon, what the hell are you talking about?"

He kept his eyes on the road. "Bev's sister owns a duplex in Brooklyn. She lives in one half, but the other side is vacant. She's retiring and plans to move upstate. She's looking for a buyer."

I just… stared.

"We can't afford a house in Brooklyn."

Jon's grip on the wheel didn't change. "We can, if what Tony's telling me is true. But I don't want to get into it too much—not until we see it first."

My heart was pounding. Excitement. Hopefulness. Abject terror.

A house?

I was still at a complete loss for words when Jon reached over and rested a hand on my leg.

I thought I caught a glint in his eye.

***

The duplex was adorable—red brick, neat, tidy, and at the end of the block.

Not flashy. Not extravagant. But solid.

The yard was bare but well-kept. I could already picture flower beds and some low shrubs to frame the walkway.

Inside, the same.

Tony and Bev welcomed us into the left side. Her sister, Diana, still occupied the right—though she spent little time there anymore.

The house was clean, spacious, and well-maintained.

The front door opened into a cozy living room, leading into a dining area, then a kitchen at the back. Through the sliding glass doors, I spotted a fully fenced-in backyard—small, but private, with a little patio and a two-car parking lot behind it.

"Needs fresh paint and some air," Tony remarked, crossing his arms. "But wait 'til you see the basement."

I followed him down, my heart lodged in my throat.

It was finished.

And subdivided.

A full second living space—kitchenette, bath, and an open floor plan that could be a studio apartment.

I turned in a slow circle.

Upstairs was even better.

A primary bedroom, two additional bedrooms, and two bathrooms.

In Brooklyn.

Right where we wanted to be.

No fucking way.

"What's the catch?" I finally blurted.

Bev smiled. "There isn't one, really."

I raised an eyebrow.

"Diana's moving into a retirement community next fall," Bev explained. "But she's not ready to let go of the house completely. She still has friends here, comes back for holidays and weekends. She doesn't want it sitting vacant, but she also doesn't want to sell off just this half. So..."

She hesitated, then continued.

"...she's looking for buyers who will take the entire property when she's ready—but in the meantime, she'd still occupy her half."

I tried to process.

"And... what does that mean for us?"

Tony, ever blunt, cut in.

"Here's the deal. You kids lease this half. But in the agreement, it's written that you get dibs on the whole thing when she's ready to sell. Whatever you've paid so far goes directly toward that full price—even if the house appreciates in value."

Oh.

That actually... made sense.

"So, if the property value increases, we're locked into the lower price?" I clarified.

Bev nodded. "Exactly. She doesn't want to split the deed. It keeps the whole thing intact and lets her keep an affordable option until she's ready to move full time, which is still a couple years off."

Jon's voice was softer now. His expression was so hopeful. "And with the money I've already saved, by the time Diana is ready to sell the whole thing, we would actually be able to buy all of it."

I didn't have words.

Jon stepped closer, wrapping his arms around me. "We can talk about it. We have plenty of time to talk about it."

Tony shrugged, grinning. "Diana's not going anywhere just yet. But I thought of you two. You've got your eye on this area. You're good kids. You'd be good neighbors. And—" he smirked, "you got your yard for the dog."

He waved a hand. "Take your time. I just wanted you to see the place wasn't a dump."

It was far from a dump.

It was really nice.

Chapter 9

Sunday and Monday went quick.

And when Tuesday came, and it was time to say goodbye to Jon for a few days... I swear, I could see it in his eyes.

A hesitation.

A reluctance.

But it was only until Friday.

I tried to think back...

God. How long had it been since we'd gone that long without seeing each other?

The fact that I couldn't remember said it all.

But this was just a small trade-off considering everything we were experiencing.

We were both fast-tracking goals I'd barely dared to dream of not long ago.

This was going to be good.

***

Nikki had stayed back with me, so the two of us made the trip to Hartford together—leaving super early Friday morning.

We made good time and were at the hotel by 11 AM.

While I found a parking space, Nikki called Mike.

He told her the show the night before had been great—but long.

The band had decided earlier in the week to drive from Boston to Hartford right after the set, so they could catch up on sleep once they got settled.

To Mike's knowledge, Jon was still asleep.

"He seemed tired," Mike added.

Shit. Okay. Well, I'm sure he is.

After grabbing my key card from the front desk, I decided to surprise him.

I pushed open the door.

The room was dim; the curtains drawn shut, leaving everything draped in dark shadows.

I could hear the shower running; the bathroom door was closed.

I dropped my bag, about to call out and announce my arrival, when—

I saw it.

Sitting right on top of his pile of things.

The black and green corset.

My stomach flipped.

Jess must have finished it!

Then, a thought.

Could I get into it myself?

I picked it up, running my fingers over the intricate stitching. Jess cleverly hid a side zipper within the seam, allowing me to slip it on without help once it was laced.

I hurried, not knowing how long he'd been in the shower already, and quickly changed into my new outfit.

I pushed open the bathroom door just as the water shut off. He flung open the curtain and froze.

He looked briefly startled, but then his expression instantly changed.

"Holy shit." He said, his eyes dropping to look me over.

"It fits pretty good, huh?" I said excitedly.

He stepped out of the shower, dropping his towel without even drying off, and pulled me into him. His hot, wet body pressing against mine sent tendrils of excitement through my core.

And apparently, his mood had flicked on like a light switch. I couldn't help but fight a grin, even with his open-mouth kiss threatening to smother it.

We never even made it out of the bathroom, and between his fervor and the steam from his shower, I needed one of my own, once we were through.

He took off my corset, turned the water back on, and pulled me in with him.

For a while, we just stood and let the water run down over us. He'd embraced me tightly and was covering my neck and shoulders with kisses.

"God, I missed you." He said.

I smiled. Deeply.

I had missed him, too.

***

It ended up being a really long shower.

Round 2.

Afterward, Jon dragged me into bed with him, not even letting me get fully dressed.

"Take a nap with me?" he murmured.

A nap? He'd literally just woken up.

I raised an eyebrow.

"We have lost time to make up for," he added, voice lazy, thick with satisfaction. "I just want to hold you for a while."

Well fuck.

How was I supposed to say no to a gorgeous, half-naked man pulling me into bed for a cuddle?

He spooned me, his arm draped over my waist, his face buried in my neck.

I let my eyes drift closed, a lazy smile on my lips.

Before long, I could feel his breath slow.

Then—

Soft snoring.

He was out.

I sighed, content—but also a little surprised.

He really must be worn out.

I knew they'd had a long night.

Thank God there were only two nights of shows left.

Then, they'd have a few weeks break before heading to the West Coast.

That would give him plenty of time to recharge.

***

The city was prettier than I expected.

And the venue? Not what I expected at all.

It was huge, but the interior felt more like a lodge—all rich wood and warm ambiance, nothing like the cold, industrial spaces I was used to. The sprawling second balcony wrapped around the entire venue, and the upstairs bar was even bigger than the one on the main floor.

It almost felt like the venue expanded at the top.

I liked it.

Nikki and I decided to watch from the second floor.

Shane's band was on fire. I couldn't stop grinning, watching him work the crowd.

He was a natural—a born performer who played off his sense of humor, making the audience laugh between songs.

His boyfriend, Kit, was also the keyboard player—adding an edgy, industrial vibe to their sound. Sometimes, during long instrumental breaks, Shane would walk over and plant a dramatic kiss on Kit's cheek.

The crowd ate it up.

Shane loved the limelight.

It was a perfect contrast to FR and even FaultCode, who had a darker, heavier energy.

Because where Shane thrived on fun, Jon thrived on captivation—on being a presence that demanded attention.

***

FR was up next, and as always...

They didn't disappoint.

Most of the set list was from the new album, with a few older favorites thrown in. The crowd was locked in, completely with them.

I was locked in, too.

And then—

Something shifted.

They were on the second-to-last song when Jon did something weird.

He stepped back from the mic before the last verse.

I frowned.

But he kept playing, so the crowd didn't notice.

Only...

He didn't sing.

The instrumental kept going. The verse passed.

He didn't come back in.

When the bridge hit, he veered toward Cary and said something.

Cary nodded. The music didn't falter.

But Jon never returned to the mic.

What the hell was he doing?

I turned to Nikki. She raised a brow but shrugged it off.

I didn't.

On stage, Cary crossed over to Mike and leaned in. His back was to the crowd, so I couldn't see his face. But then—

He turned to Shawn on the far side of the stage.

And made a quick, sharp motion across his throat.

Cut.

My stomach dropped.

That wasn't right.

When the song ended, Jon stepped up to the mic.

"Thank you."

And then—

They walked off.

No final song.

No encore.

Oh, fuck.

***

Nikki and I hightailed it backstage.

And that's where I found him.

Leaning against the wall. Pale. Hands braced on his knees.

A few of the guys hovered nearby, hesitant, but in true Jon fashion, he waved them off.

Only Mike stayed close.

I pushed forward, my pulse thudding.

"What's wrong?"

Jon barely looked at me. "Just need some air."

His voice was thin.

And then—

As we walked toward the exit—

He went down.

Mid-stride.

One second, walking.

The next—

His knees buckled.

Mike lunged, catching him under the arms before he hit the ground.

If Mike hadn't been there, Jon would have gone down hard.

I sucked in a breath, heart slamming.

He was only out for a second.

By the time Mike had him seated against the wall, his eyes were already fluttering open.

And—of course—he tried to stand.

Jesus, Jon.

He took a shaky step.

Almost went down again before Mike slipped an arm around him and practically dragged him out the back exit.

Down the steps.

Into the frosty night air.

Jon collapsed onto the bottom step, head dropping between his knees, his skin damp with sweat despite the freezing chill.

I fought the panic clawing up my throat.

We'd never seen him like this before.

Not this bad.

Not even close.

***

Tony had already gone to get the car.

Within minutes, we had Jon inside and were speeding toward the nearest ER.

Mike stayed behind to stall the others.

Jon's request.

He didn't want to cause a scene.

Didn't want anyone to freak out.

So we just...

Disappeared with him.

Chapter 10

They rushed him straight through triage because his heart rhythm was off.

Even so, Jon was seeming more like himself now. Talking. Downplaying.

But the haste with which the nurses moved—the way they got him on a heart monitor immediately, the way the doctor was already ordering tests before asking questions—all of it sent a sharp spike of anxiety through my chest.

They started an IV, pushing fluids. Drew blood.

What the fuck was going on with him?

The doctor ordered an EKG, and while they were hooking him up, a nurse pulled me aside.

"We need some information."

I rattled off his full name, birthdate, address, the usual.

Then—another nurse. More questions.

"Has he ever fainted before?" "Does he have any known heart conditions?" "How long has he been taking his beta-blocker?" "What dosage? How often?"

I answered everything, but my jaw clenched tighter with each question.

I could feel Tony standing nearby.

And when the nurse finally disappeared, I spun toward him.

"What the fuck, Tony?" I hissed. "I'm gone four days, and this is what happens? Has he been like this all week?"

The words ignited something in me—a fresh wave of anger, frustration, and fear.

Tony's expression was a mix of remorse and concern. "Come on, Via. You know I wouldn't overlook something like this. For Christ's sake—if he's been feeling this bad, then he's done a damn good job of hiding it."

Deep down, I believed him.

Or... maybe not entirely.

But I trusted Mike. And Mike had said things had been fine.

He'd noticed Jon seemed tired.

Yeah. That was obvious.

But this?

This was more than that.

***

When Tony and I joined Jon back in the room, an RN was still hovering.

"His EKG showed a few minor abnormalities, but nothing too alarming," she said. "We're waiting on blood work now. In the meantime, we're going to monitor his heart. He's having some runs of NSVT—non-sustained ventricular tachycardia."

NSVT.

She said it so casually. Like it wasn't terrifying.

"It's self-terminating, which is good," she added. "That means his heart is correcting the rhythm on its own."

She turned to Jon.

"We've got fluids running—you're dehydrated. Have you eaten anything today?"

Shit.

I knew he hadn't.

He never ate before shows.

Jon hesitated. Then—when he saw me watching him—he shook his head.

The nurse smiled gently. “Okay. Well, you probably have low blood sugar contributing to this. I’ll go see what we can get you for a snack.”

And just like that—she was gone.

Tony and I both turned to Jon.

He looked... embarrassed.

Which made this whole thing feel even more insane.

I was staring at him, somewhere between terrified and furious.

Was he seriously just not taking care of himself to the point where his body was physically protesting?

Tony exhaled. “This is some pretty serious shit, yeah?”

Jon tipped his head back against the pillow, eyes closed, like he was waiting for the lecture to hit.

But Tony didn’t lecture.

Instead—an earnest question.

“What the hell’s going on, man?”

Jon looked away. His expression was hard to read.

Was he annoyed? Or, did he genuinely not know?

The silence stretched.

Then—Tony again.

“You only took one of those things tonight, right?”

Jon’s eyes snapped to Tony.

The instant fire in his expression was all the answer we needed.

“Okay, okay,” Tony held up a hand. “I’m just grasping at straws here.”

Jon sighed, voice low. Flat.

“I don’t know what to tell you.”

And something about the way he said it...

I believed him.

I felt the tears welling.

When he looked at me, his expression softened.

“I’m worried about you,” I whispered, my lip quivering. “I don’t think you should do this anymore.”

In my peripherals, I saw Tony turn to look at me. Jon's gaze flickered to Tony, then back to me.

He reached for my hand.

"I'm okay, Vee."

No, you're not.

"I just need to eat. I forgot to eat today."

You forgot to fucking eat?

Do you even hear yourself right now?

"You think that's it?" Tony asked cautiously.

Jon nodded.

***

An hour later, they ran another EKG.

Thirty minutes after that—the doctor came in.

He pulled up a stool.

"Are you feeling any better?"

Jon nodded. "Yeah. I am."

The doctor nodded back.

"Good. Your EKG looks normal now. Your heart had a few extra beats earlier, but that's not uncommon—especially with stress, dehydration, and performance anxiety. They're called PVCs—premature ventricular contractions. If too many happen in a row, that's when you get into trouble. But you've stabilized."

Performance anxiety.

The way he said it made it sound so small.

Jon latched onto it immediately. "So I'm good to go?"

Goddammit, Jon.

The doctor hesitated.

"There's one thing I want to address first." He glanced down at the chart. "You're on propranolol?"

Jon tensed slightly. "Yeah."

The doctor tapped his fingers against the file. "How long have you been taking it?"

Jon hesitated. "Few months."

The doctor tilted his head. "Any issues with it before now?"

Jon shook his head. "No."

Tony, ever pragmatic, cut in. "Is this because of the beta-blocker?"

The doctor sighed slightly, as if choosing his words carefully.

"It's possible it played a role." He paused. "Beta-blockers slow your heart rate, which is why they help with stage nerves. But they can also lower blood pressure. If you were dehydrated and had low blood sugar on top of that, it could've created a perfect storm."

"Is he gonna need to stop taking those?" Tony asked.

Jon's eyes were on the doctor. I could tell he was afraid of the answer.

The doctor shrugged. "I wouldn't say stop taking them entirely unless this happens again. But I'd suggest being careful with timing. Don't take it so soon before a show. Make sure you're hydrating and eating properly. And don't overexert yourself."

I saw Jon breathe a sigh of relief.

Tony did too.

"So, I'm good to go, then?" Jon asked. Again.

"If you're feeling better, then I'd say we can probably let you go. But you should get some rest."

Tony nodded. "Alright, well, we'll get you back to the hotel. Rest up. No rush."

Jon grinned. "Yeah. Okay."

But it wasn't that simple.

Because even as Tony said, "No rush," he was already checking the time.

They had to be in New York tomorrow night.

Jon had another show in less than 24 hours.

Except *No*—he had *two shows.* FR's normal show, and then the VIP event Matt had orchestrated.

Holy Fuck.

Tony was already thinking ahead. "We'll extend your room for another night so you can sleep in as long as you want tomorrow. Check out when you're ready. The rest of the guys can head out early, and you and Via can meet us in New York later."

Jon nodded. "That sounds good."

I wasn't so sure.

***

Tony dropped us right at the hotel.

Mercifully, he'd already coordinated everything else.

Both Jon and I had left our stuff behind at the venue in the rush to get him to the ER. Nikki and Mike had taken care of it for us.

Everything still felt chaotic.

I knew that, as far as crazy band adventures went, FR was mild.

But for the first time, I was starting to understand why you heard so many stories of artists drinking too much. Or worse—numbing themselves just to keep up with the demands of this life.

It wasn't for everybody.

And it definitely wasn't for Jon.

Was he going to realize that?

***

I woke up at our normal time that morning, moving quietly as I got ready.

Jon was still out cold, so I left him sleeping and went down to the lobby to reconnect with everyone else before they left.

Cary, Mike, Nikki, Shawn, and Tony were all waiting. Andy and Steve had already left with the trailer and gear.

Normally, Tony didn't hover this much. He'd pop in at random, especially when the shows were semi-close together, but the fact that he was still here, even now?

It meant that he was watching.

Even if he wasn't saying it outright, he was paying attention.

Good.

After a quick recap of the night before—and after I assured everyone that Jon was okay and resting—Tony moved on to business.

He handed me a folded piece of paper.

"This is the next hotel."

I unfolded it. An address on Long Island.

"Got you guys a nice spot—right down the road from Jon's gig."

My stomach twisted.

His gig.

Jesus.

Tony continued. "Via, when Jon's ready, just take your time. You guys can meet us there. You'll ride back to the city with Mike for the first show. Cary will take care of the soundcheck. All Jon has to do is walk on when it's time."

I looked between Cary and Mike.

They both nodded solemnly.

A rush of relief flooded in.

At least they were thinking ahead.

"You guys go last tonight," Tony reminded us. "So as soon as you wrap, Mike—you can get Jon back over to Hempstead. It'll be tight with traffic, but I think you'll be fine. If you're a few minutes late, fuck 'em. They'll wait."

Mike grinned slightly and nodded again.

But my pulse had picked up.

Tight with traffic.

A venue in the city.

Then, a second acoustic set on Long Island—on a hard deadline.

Jesus fucking Christ.

Tony took a deep breath, exhaled loudly.

"Okay. Everybody good?"

We all nodded.

Then—Tony turned to me.

His dark eyes were serious.

"Make sure he eats." His voice was low. Firm. "I don't give a fuck if he's hungry or not. He's got two back-to-backs tonight, and I don't want a repeat of yesterday."

I nodded. Swallowed hard.

Because, for the first time...

I wasn't sure any of us had control over that anymore.

My stomach was in knots, but at least now everybody was paying attention.

Tight hugs all around. Then, as the others headed out, I turned back toward the hotel room.

Jon was still asleep upstairs.

And when he woke up?

He'd have less than twelve hours before stepping onstage.

Twice.

Chapter 11

Jon woke up around 11:30.

While he jumped in the shower, I went down to the cafe and grabbed his cup of black sludge—or, as he called it, coffee.

By the time I got back, he was shaving, his hair still damp, a towel wrapped loosely around his waist.

I held out his coffee.

He reached for it—

And I pulled it back, raising an eyebrow as I waved a croissant in front of him.

Jon smirked, his face half-covered in shaving cream.

"I'll eat it as soon as I'm done here."

And he did.

We took our time checking out, not hitting the road until 1:30.

As we walked toward the car, Jon glanced at me. "Mind if I drive?"

I hesitated.

For a couple of reasons.

But honestly? He seemed fine.

The spark was back in his eyes.

Normal Jon.

He even said we'd stop for an early dinner once we got into the area.

Okay... cool.

Then—the second he slid into the driver's seat—

He ripped the steering wheel cover off and shoved it into the center console with a mischievous grin.

I laughed, shaking my head.

Yep. That was the other reason.

I had no idea why he hated that damn thing so much. But he did.

Normal Jon.

Good.

***

The rest of the day went as planned.

✔ We got dinner.

✔ We got to the hotel.

✔ We met up with Mike and Nikki.

✔ We made it to the venue.

✔ Everything was fine.

Then—

During the transition backstage, Clay spotted Jon.

His face lit up.

He beelined toward him, clapping a hand on Jon's shoulder.

"How's it going today, Stets?"

Jon nodded, smiling. "I'm good!"

Clay was full of animation. "You handled yourself like a true pro last night, man! That was a smooth exit. Well done. We got it turned around quick—I don't think anyone even noticed!"

Well done?

I knew what he meant.

The whole *"show must go on"* mindset.

But that was too damn close to becoming a complete fucking disaster.

Jon said something, grinning.

Clay laughed.

Then, as he walked away, he called back:

"Good luck tonight, man! With both of them! You're gonna kill it!"

You're gonna kill it.

The words lingered.

I swallowed hard.

I had originally been excited for the acoustic set.

Now?

I just wanted it to be over.

***

FR's set was stellar, as always.

But Jon and Allen's set was beautiful. Haunting.

And when the fuck had he even been working on THIS masterpiece of a performance?

They played songs I'd never even heard before, meshing as if they'd been playing together forever.

The audience was fully engaged. The whole vibe differed completely from earlier in the night.

Small tables lit with tea-light candles. Fancy black tablecloths. A bar serving drinks on sleek, black napkins embossed with the venue's silver logo.

I had to hand it to Matt. He was a crafty asshole.

***

Jon seemed okay afterward.

Unlike the night before.

He smiled. Talked. Shook a lot of hands.

Cary and Shawn had caught most of the set, lingering nearby.

But once things wound down, Jon just wanted to go back to the hotel.

I hugged him before we left.

His body was tense.

Like something wound too tightly inside him.

But his demeanor? Still Jon.

So, I told myself it was fine.

Still... even Cary came back to the hotel with us.

Cary.

Who normally would've found an afterparty somewhere.

Cary seemed cautious.

Cary stayed close.

***

Back in the room, I had a chance to truly embrace Jon. He'd flopped down on the bed, playfully pulling me with him.

But the moment I leaned against him, I felt it.

A freight train.

Pounding. Relentless.

Through his chest. His shoulders. Everywhere.

I jerked back.

My breath caught in my throat.

I stared at him.

He looked... *fine.*

Like he hadn't even noticed.

I sat up fast.

"What's wrong?" I demanded.

Jon blinked at me. Innocent.

Don't you fucking do this.

"Jon, your heart is racing."

Now, finally, a flicker of concern crossed his face.

But—

Not for himself.

For me.

Oh, fuck this.

"You don't feel that??"

Jon sat up on his elbows, brows furrowed. "Via..." His voice was too calm.

He's not lying.

He's not covering it up.

He genuinely doesn't feel it.

This... this is just normal for him.

He sat up fully now, reaching for my hands—trying to pull me into a hug.

"Vee," he said, his voice steady.

How.

How was his voice so steady?

"Vee, just give me a little bit." His expression was so damn soft. "I just need to rest. It's been a long day."

It *had* been a long day. It had been a long week. I guess I could be overreacting?

A playful knock at the door interrupted us, and when Jon got up to open it, an animated Cary stepped inside, toting a pack of beer, all smiles. He immediately snapped caps and passed around bottles before clinking the necks and conducting an impromptu toast to Jon's stellar acoustic performance.

"Damn man, that was some crazy alter ego shit you pulled! You could definitely go mainstream with that style and leave the rest of us assholes in the dust."

Jon smirked. "Fuck off," he said, laughing lightly before downing half a beer.

"Seriously, though!" Cary pushed. "You guys wrote some great material. People were really into it! You could write music that makes the girlies all emotional, if you wanted."

Jon just laughed.

Cary held up his beer, pointing dramatically. "I'm tellin' ya! You could make people cry!"

Even I laughed at that. It wasn't just the comical way Cary had said it, it was the fact that it was true. If Jon wanted, he could spin off in an entirely new direction and be equally successful, if not more so.

Cary turned towards me. "Via, back me up, here!"

I shrugged apologetically at Jon and nodded in agreement.

Jon rolled his eyes, downed the rest of his beer and then grinned widely.

"Fuck it!" he exclaimed, rubbing his hands together. "Let's go find the bar!"

I stared at him for just a moment, but he seemed much more relaxed now. At ease, with genuine smiles. Probably relieved to have this first half of their tour over with. And he deserved to celebrate. It had ended on a spectacular note. I was relieved that he felt up to it.

The first normal thing in a while.

Chapter 12

The next week flew by faster than I expected, and I had to admit—I was getting more and more excited about the West Coast trip.

Each band would have a sleek tour bus, making travel easier while keeping everyone together and on schedule. We'd still be staying in hotels at each stop, but the buses made the most sense logistically. FR already felt like its own little family unit, and I loved knowing that the planning was all handled, thanks to Matt. Large venues were scheduled for the weekends, with smaller, more eclectic theaters and performing arts centers filling the gaps midweek.

Adding to my elation was the fact that I'd just landed a web development job with a client that was a potential windfall—we'd been going back and forth for weeks. The job was big enough to carry me through the summer.

I'd arrived at my interview fully prepared, but the job was already mine.

I'd sensed it the moment I took my seat at the conference table. The interview was just a formality—putting a face to the name.

They hadn't even asked me anything challenging. My portfolio had spoken for itself.

I could work from my laptop while we were on the road. I'd be spending my spring break exploring new cities.

This trip would be epic.

***

Jon picked me up around nine, as promised. He needed to pick up a new audio processor and had asked me to come with—just for company. Our destination was around a half-hour east, and we grabbed coffee on the way. The independent music shop was a favorite of Jon's—he ordered custom parts and audio gear from Vince, the owner. Vince was a good guy. Knew his shit, had solid contacts, and networked with a lot of folks in Jon's circle. They had a friendly business relationship built on mutual respect.

We had just taken the exit when Jon's phone rang.

"It's my dad," he said, bringing the phone to his ear.

I was wiping smudges off my sunglasses, half-distracted—until I heard the shift in Jon's voice.

"What?" he said sharply.

My head snapped up.

A long pause. His grip on the wheel tightened.

"When?"

Another silence. Then, without warning, he flicked on his blinker and jerked the truck into a hard right turn, cutting straight into a grocery store parking lot. My stomach lurched as he whipped around the divider and shot back toward the traffic light—now in the left-turn lane, facing the way we had just come.

What the hell?

"Yeah," he said, voice clipped. "Okay. Yeah, I'm on my way now."

By the time he hung up, we were already flying back in the opposite direction.

Something was wrong.

"What happened?" I asked, trying to keep my voice steady, but my pulse was already pounding.

Jon's jaw flexed. His grip on the steering wheel was tight enough that the muscles in his forearms stood out. "They flew Jill out of Memorial to Creston Regional. Something's wrong with her and the baby."

Fuck.

Creston was a major medical center—a few cities over, known for its trauma unit and specialized care. They wouldn't have transferred her unless it was serious.

"Oh my God, Jon," I whispered.

He exhaled sharply through his nose. "She's not due for a few more weeks." His voice was tight.

I reached over, resting my hand on his leg.

"Do they know what's wrong?" I asked.

He shook his head. "I don't know. But the fact that they're not handling it at Memorial..." He trailed off, his meaning clear.

It wasn't good.

"We're just going to meet them there. That cool?" His voice was tight, as if he weren't really asking.

I stared at him. "Of course. I'm here for you. For everybody." My fingers squeezed his leg. "I'm just glad we were already together. And at least we're closer now than we would've been leaving from home."

He nodded, his eyes locked on the road.

And just like that, everything had changed.

***

Jeff met us at the ER entrance. As he led us past a woman behind a glass window who buzzed us through to another hallway, he explained that Jill had a placental abruption—the placenta detached from her uterus. They'd taken her into surgery and would deliver the baby by C-section.

Shit. This isn't sounding good.

The walls were too white, the air too sterile, when we entered a separate waiting area.

Ben and Sharron were already there, speaking with a lanky doctor in scrubs.

Sharron's eyes were red, puffy, her hands clasped tightly in front of her like she was praying. Ben looked like he'd seen a ghost.

The three of them turned at once, watching as we approached.

But the doctor's eyes went straight to Jon.

What the fuck?

He said something to Sharron, and she nodded quickly, pressing her lips together like she was trying to swallow a sob.

And then, we were standing in a tight circle, all eyes locked on the doctor as he dropped the next bombshell.

"Jill's lost a significant amount of blood. We've already used what we had on hand, and we've put in an emergency request to the blood bank—but because of her antigen profile, our emergency supply is limited," he explained.

Before the thought even had time to register in my mind, Jon was already there.

"What about me?" His voice was sure, unwavering as he looked between the doctor and his family. "Could I be a match?"

Oh, fuck.

Sharron let out a strangled sob, turning away briefly.

The doctor nodded. "Yes. There's a likelihood that you're a match. We'd like to test you for compatibility for a directed donation. It won't go to her immediately," he added, sensing our reactions. "But if her bleeding continues, it may be the safest and fastest source we have. I know this is a lot to process. But having a unit available from a compatible family member could be critical. If you're willing."

Jon didn't even hesitate. "What do I have to do? Let's go."

Ben exhaled a shaky breath, dragging a hand down his face.

The tall doctor gave a small nod, and paused, his eyes flicking to Ben and Sharron. "We'll monitor you closely, of course. It's a relatively simple procedure." His gaze flicked to the rest of us, as if trying to reassure us.

Jon's body was coiled tight, ready to snap. "We're wasting time standing here." His voice was sharp, final. "Let's do this."

Ben pulled Jon into a hug, his breath catching. "Thank you." His voice was raw, cracking at the edges.

Jon turned, wrapping his arms around me quickly.

"It'll be okay," he murmured.

And just like that, he was gone.

***

I was surprised to see Jon reappear barely ten minutes later.

"They have to do an antigen crossmatch check," he explained, running a hand through his hair. "They're rushing it through, but it could still take another 15 to 20 minutes."

He started pacing, agitated. "It shouldn't take so long."

I caught him in a hug. "Try to relax. They have to be sure. If you're not compatible, it could be dangerous for her."

The next ten minutes stretched into eternity, filled only with the sound of restless movement and anxious silence.

Then, a woman in scrubs appeared.

"Jonathan?"

We all stood.

"We're approved to collect two units. Are you ready?" she said, holding the door open.

A collective sigh of relief swept through us. Partial relief.

Then, perhaps sensing my hesitation, she added, "You can come along if you'd like."

Blood had always made me woozy, ever since I was a kid. It didn't even have to be a lot—just the sight of it, that deep, too-red color, was enough to make my vision blur and my stomach twist.

Jon knew this.

He turned to me, grinning, despite the situation. "You shouldn't come, babe. You'll pass out."

"I'll go." Ben didn't wait for an invitation.

I glanced at him and felt a flicker of relief. He needed this. Needed to feel like he was doing *something*. If he could take Jill's place in that hospital bed, he already would have.

Once they'd gone, Jeff chuckled. "That's right." He smirked. "Remember when Kyle lost his front tooth in our backyard? Thought you were gonna hit the ground."

I let out a weak laugh. God, I did. Kyle had been messing around with Maize, and when his tooth popped out, I had to sit down before I keeled over.

The memory—stupid as it was—helped. It cut through the weight in the room, softening the buzzing in my ears.

I exhaled. "Yeah. That was bad."

Sharron smiled faintly, and for the first time since we'd arrived, some of the tension cracked.

***

How long had it been?

When the door opened, I half-stood, expecting to see Jon, or the technician.

But instead, Ben was escorted in by someone who disappeared without a word.

Something was wrong.

Ben's face was ashen. His eyes—wild.

"Oh my God," he mumbled, voice so shaky it barely sounded like him.

The three of us spoke at once. Some variation of *What happened? What's wrong?*

But Ben didn't respond.

Didn't even seem to hear us.

"Oh my fucking *GOD.*" This time, it was a whisper—sharp, broken. He was taking too many breaths, hyperventilating.

A cold, sick feeling crawled up my spine.

Had something happened to Jill?

The baby?

Jeff shot up from his chair, kneeling in front of Ben, gripping his shoulders.

"Ben," he said, voice firm, grounding. "Slow down."

Ben sucked in a huge, gasping breath. Made a sound—almost a whimper. Then his breathing sped up again.

"Ben. What is going on?"

Jeff's voice was low and steady. The only thing keeping the room from tipping into chaos.

Sharron and I could only stare, horrified.

Ben's mouth opened, but for a second—nothing came out.

"Ben," he repeated, calm but firm. "Tell me what happened."

Ben struggled to form words. His lips moved, but nothing came. He squeezed his eyes shut like he was trying to force it out.

Then, suddenly, he snapped.

"I think he died. *JESUS CHRIST!*"

Silence.

I could feel my pulse in my throat, pounding.

The three of us just stared at him.

Trying to process what he had just said.

Jeff's voice sliced through the silence.

"Who?"

Ben's head shot up. His eyes were frantic.

"Jon!"

No.

No, no, no, no, NO.

This was bullshit.

The words barely registered.

No. He's confused.

He's making no sense.

A blotchy red rash had crept up his neck.

Sharron let out a choked sound, her hands flying to her mouth.

Ben was rambling now. Unraveling.

"He was fine at first—pale, but that's normal, right? For giving blood? I asked him if he was good, and he said yeah. He said he was good!"

"What happened?" Jeff asked again.

Ben's breathing hitched.

"He was shaking. Toward the end. Just a little at first. I asked him again—if he was okay, and he said he just felt a little weird, that was all."

Ben swallowed hard.

"The nurse was right there. She told him just to sit still. But then... then—he tried to say something, but ..."

I was staring at Ben. He never acted like this. Ben was an accountant. Calm and boring.

Why is he being so fucking dramatic?

Jeff's voice was maddeningly controlled.

"Ben. What happened?"

Ben's breath shuddered. His whole body trembled.

"Like... all of a sudden—out of nowhere—his heart rate just shot through the roof!"

His voice broke on the last word.

"He tensed up. Just stopped moving. Like he was trying to ride it out."

"I said his name."

"He looked at me."

"And then—he just..."

"He—he jerked, kinda? Just once—and then he went totally limp."

Ben shook his head. Like he was questioning his own memory.

His eyes flicked to Jeff. For the first time, really looking at him.

"They pulled me away from him."

His voice was thin now.

Breaking.

He started to cry.

"It all happened so fast—I don't understand it."

Then—

"I'm gonna be sick."

Ben lurched out of the chair and bolted toward the hallway, disappearing into the restroom.

Sharron suddenly shot up, moving like she'd just realized the room was on fire.

She grabbed the door handle—the one leading to the back. Yanked it.

Locked.

She tried again, harder this time, rattling it.

"We're not getting in that way," Jeff said.

His voice was even, but this time—I heard it. The waver.

"I'm going to the desk," he said.

And then, he was gone.

Leaving me and Sharron alone.

We stared at each other.

This isn't real.

It couldn't be real.

Ben was wrong.

He was already overwhelmed—he had just misinterpreted what he saw.

That's all.

***

Jeff returned a few minutes later.

His posture was stiff. His eyes—dark.

But his voice remained steady. Low. Controlled.

Ben still wasn't back.

Sharron and I stared at Jeff, waiting for answers.

Answers he didn't have.

"They can't confirm anything," he said quietly. "Only that there's an active code on this floor."

A silence stretched between us.

An active code.

On this floor.

My chest tightened.

Sharron started sobbing.

Jeff sat beside her, placing a steadying hand on her back.

Another few minutes dragged by.

Then, finally—

Ben reappeared.

His shirt and hair were damp. Like he'd tried to shove his head under a sink.

But now—he wasn't wild.

Not panicked.

Just… subdued.

Like something had been drained out of him.

And I wasn't sure if that was better.

Or worse.

Chapter 13

The minutes crawled.

Ten went by.

Twenty.

Thirty-five.

Are you fucking kidding me?

Jeff had gone back to the window once. Still nothing.

Not a word.

All of us were thinking the same thing.

We should have heard something.

Even if—

Even if he was dead.

If he were dead, they'd have told us.

Right?

Forty-five minutes.

When the door finally opened, I thought I might pass out just from the sheer weight of the apprehension.

A doctor introduced himself, but I didn't even register his name.

Sharron started sobbing before he even spoke.

And for once, I understood.

I rarely exploded outwardly.

I unraveled in my head.

And I had been. Spinning. Drowning.

But Jon was alive.

The doctor had said it.

He's alive.

But he'd experienced a sudden cardiac arrest.

Then came the questions about Propranolol. It was obvious that they didn't think Jon's problem was performance anxiety. He drilled me about Jon's symptoms. His recent trip to the emergency room. If there was any family history of heart problems.

Oh my God.

They think there's something wrong with his heart.

My ears were ringing… I felt detached from my own body.

The doctor grilled us for a solid five minutes, asking question after question. Some of them, Jeff answered. Most of them were directed at me. I knew Jon better than anybody at this point. I'd been with him at his shows, and now that I was being asked to recall every detail of every symptom he'd been experiencing over the last year, a bigger, more terrifying picture was beginning to form.

Details that had seemed innocuous and unrelated now felt like a series of warnings. Ones that had been consistently brushed off and trivialized.

The doctor held eye contact with each of us.

Spoke slowly. Intentionally.

Even though his words were anything but reassuring.

"Fortunately, he was here when this happened."

That wasn't comforting.

That was terrifying.

"Right now, our focus is on stabilizing him, then determining the cause of his arrest. We have some strong suspicions, but we'll need further testing to confirm."

A million questions flooded my brain.

Sharron beat me to the first one.

Except—it wasn't a question.

"We want to see him," she said through a shaky, tear-clogged voice.

The doctor shook his head, firm but not unkind.

"Not yet."

Sharron's face crumpled.

"Jonathan isn't stable," he explained. "He's in the immediate post-cardiac arrest phase."

Sharron tried again, but he gently cut in.

"I know this is difficult. And I'm sorry that I can't answer all your questions right now. But I promise—we'll talk again once there's more to share."

Silence.

None of us spoke.

What was there to say?

He stood.

"We'll keep you updated."

Then—with a small, polite nod—he disappeared.

***

We'd barely had time to process what had been said before the tall, thin doctor returned—this time for Ben.

Abby was here.

She was pre-term but stable.

Jill?

Out of surgery. Alive. But serious.

She was on a different floor. Different doctors.

And this family was being ripped apart at the seams.

My anxiety was suffocating.

They whisked Ben away and Jeff went with him. Ben needed someone. He was barely holding it together. I could see it all over his face.

Who could blame him?

And Jeff and Sharron—both of their kids in critical condition at the same time?

Unreal.

How the hell does something like this happen?

What kind of screwed-up universe does this to a family?

I watched them embrace, my heart aching. Then, Jeff left.

And it was just me and Sharron.

Waiting.

***

It took so long for anyone to tell us more about Jon that I started to wonder if I'd imagined the whole thing. Like, maybe he'd never collapsed at all. Like maybe none of this was real.

The lights in the waiting room were too bright—clinical and constant. The kind that made your skin look sickly. The walls were too white, despite the oversized photographs meant to distract us: water, trees, cliché horizons, and hopeful sunrises, framed like they were doing us some kind of favor.

It felt like bullshit.

The artificial flowers didn't help. Neither did the fake, potted tree in the corner. Still, I found myself counting the leaves—tracing the fake rings up the plastic trunk just to keep from losing it.

Jeff returned after what felt like hours—though he said it had been forty minutes. Ben was upstairs with Jill. Jeff offered to trade places with Sharron so she could go see her.

She shook her head. She wouldn't move. Not until we heard something about Jon.

***

Another agonizing hour passed.

The sterile lights buzzed overhead, a fluorescent hum that pressed into my skull.

The fake potted tree in the corner hadn't moved, hadn't changed—like everything was paused except time.

My body felt stiff from sitting, my mind brittle from waiting.

Then—

A different doctor stepped in. Silver streaked through his dark hair; his strikingly pale blue eyes scanned the room as he introduced himself.

Dr. Robert Brookens.

A cardiologist.

The room went still. No one breathed.

He took a chair across from us. His posture was calm and steady. But I could already tell—this wasn't over.

He cleared his throat. And then, in a measured, methodical tone, he began.

"When Jonathan went into cardiac arrest, he became asystolic."

Oh fuck.

"Asystole isn't a shockable rhythm, but there's still a protocol we follow—compressions, medications we administer to encourage circulation to return. He responded, eventually. But then he entered a rhythm called pulseless electrical activity, or PEA."

He paused, watching our faces. "That means he had no effective heartbeat for a total of eleven minutes."

Eleven minutes.

My ears were ringing.

"That's a long time to be without circulation," Brookens continued, his eyes moving slowly between us. "But he received continuous, high-quality CPR. Right now, he isn't showing signs of major neurological impairment."

Neurological impairment.

He's talking about brain damage.

Oh my God.

Brookens kept going.

I kept listening.

Processing? Not so much.

Ischemia, inflammatory markers, strain on the brain, heart, kidneys...

"We're transferring him to the cardiac intensive care unit. He'll be under the care of a full team—cardiology, neurology, post-arrest specialists. The next twenty-four to seventy-two hours will be critical."

And that was just to mitigate the fallout.

The real problem was still underneath it all.

The cause. "Jonathan has no structural heart disease. His imaging looks normal. That, combined with his age, the setting of his arrest, and the arrhythmia pattern we saw—all point us toward something called a cardiac channelopathy."

"What's that?" Jeff asked.

Brookens nodded. "It's a disorder of the heart's electrical system. In Jonathan's case, we're concerned about a rare one called CPVT—Catecholaminergic Polymorphic Ventricular Tachycardia. But I want to be clear—we don't diagnose this in a single moment. It's based on the pattern, on history, and on tests we'll arrange once he's more stable."

My stomach flipped. So all this time... On stage. Backstage. The dizzy spells. The fainting. Was he having arrhythmias? He could've died.

He did die.

That realization hit like a wave, sharp and breathless.

Brookens kept his tone steady. "It's often genetic. And it can be very difficult to diagnose. Early symptoms can be misattributed to far more common things—anxiety, vasovagal syncope, dehydration."

I felt sick. How could they have missed this? *How did WE miss this?*

"I don't understand why the other doctors didn't see it. They ran tests in the ER. He was just there! They saw PVCs, and they let him go anyway."

Brookens met my gaze, calm and earnest. "Occasional PVCs aren't usually dangerous. CPVT can hide in plain sight until something triggers it—and the beta-blocker he was already taking may have masked some clues."

He paused, giving us space to absorb it.

"Right now, we'll focus on stabilizing him. Then we'll put a plan in place for confirming the diagnosis and preventing this from happening again."

We nodded. There wasn't anything else to do.

***

The good news?

Jon was breathing on his own.

My brain snapped back.

Latched onto that piece of information like a lifeline.

Then—

"I know you want to see him," Brookens said. "I think that would be okay. I'll send someone to take you to him."

Thank God.

I nearly sagged with relief.

Brookens stood.

Then he hesitated—just for a beat.

"He's doing well, considering," he said carefully. "He's conscious."

My breath caught.

"But..."

Of course there was a but.

"I think it's important to manage expectations. His condition could change. Cardiac arrest affects every system in the body. We're monitoring him closely—for complications, for setbacks, for anything unexpected. I just want you to be prepared. The next few days could go in any direction."

My pulse thundered.

Just let me see him.

Chapter 14

I had never been in a hospital room like that before. It was huge.

The Cardiac Intensive Care Unit sat at the far end of the floor, bustling with RNs and highly trained staff. In a way, it was comforting to see how much attention Jon was receiving. In another way, it was terrifying that he needed it.

He was awake. Surrounded by an unsettling amount of equipment.

I knew I should be grateful. He could be in a coma. He could *still* end up in a coma, from what the doctor had told us.

They say your life flashes before your eyes when you die. I wasn't the one who'd died. But looking at him—pale, fragile, tethered to so many machines—sent a flood of memories crashing through me. A montage. Late-night talks. The beach house. His proposal. The way he'd look at me, like I was the only thing that mattered.

And then, the other memories. The warning signs. The post-show fatigue. The tension. The breathlessness. Had he been dancing on the edge of this the whole time? How many moments had we mistaken for stress or nerves... when they were actually red flags?

His voice broke through. "Come here."

I looked up. He was watching me. Smiling—though it was faint, and his eyes looked tired.

"Ignore all this," he said, gesturing vaguely toward the wires, the monitors, the IVs.

That was going to be hard to do.

Even as he reached out, my eyes scanned everything.

Electrodes scattered across his chest.

Needles, catheters, tubes—one in his wrist, one mid-arm, one near his collarbone.

Holy shit.

Why are there so many?

His skin looked colorless beneath the adhesive.

I stepped closer, leaning down to wrap my arms around him gently. He pressed his forehead to mine. Brushed his nose against mine—something he'd always done.

Something I'd always loved.

"Well, that didn't quite go as planned," he muttered with a cynical grin.

His voice was raspy from the breathing tube that had recently been down his throat.

"I'd say not," I whispered, forcing a smile.

I was scared out of my mind. But Brookens had been right. Considering what happened... Jon was still Jon.

Sort of.

And they were checking that. Constantly.

Nearly every time a nurse came in, she'd ask: "What's your name?" "Where are you?" "What day is it?" Each time, Jon answered. Sometimes quickly. Sometimes with a second of delay, like he was confused.

But he always got there. Still, it felt bizarre. Like we were living in a parallel version of reality where time had warped, and nothing could be taken for granted.

***

But there was one thing he didn't seem to remember.

We figured it out when Ben came in.

Ben, who immediately burst into tears when he saw Jon awake.

Thanked him over and over, voice breaking on every word. But Jon just... stared.

Blank. Spaced out.

"Do you remember what happened?" Ben asked, incredulously. "We were mid-conversation, and your heart just... stopped."

Jon's brows furrowed.

I watched as he tried to reel in the missing pieces.

"I... don't know. How's the baby?"

He asked like he'd remembered that part by association. He'd already asked for reassurance several times that Abby and Jill were okay. It was really kind of sweet how concerned he was about them. But also worrisome that he seemed to be missing a pivotal chunk of his own timeline.

"She's doing great." Ben said again. "And Jill's resting. They say she'll be okay. Thanks to you."

"Don't tell her." Jon suggested.

We'd all exchanged glances.

Ben frowned as if he didn't follow.

Jon gestured vaguely.

"Don't tell her about this. What happened to me."

"Jonathan!" Sharron scolded. "We can't keep something like that from her!"

"You can. For a while. She has enough to focus on."

I glanced at Sharron.

And in that moment, we had a silent, unspoken agreement.

We knew he was right.

"It's not a bad idea," Jeff agreed.

Ben looked between us, dazed. Then he nodded, slowly. Swiped at his eyes. His neck was still blotchy.

I felt for him.

Because as scared as I was—Ben was having the worst day of his life.

His wife almost died. His baby came early. And his brother-in-law coded in front of him.

That probably won some kind of award for the shittiest, most stressful day imaginable.

Chapter 15

I had called Mike, earlier, when we were waiting for Dr. Brookens to come back.

He had closed the tattoo shop early and made the drive east to the hospital, and I couldn't have been more relieved to see him.

I met him in the lobby, and without a word, he pulled me into a tight hug.

"Fuck, Via. I'm so sorry. I just... I can't believe this. It doesn't feel real."

I swallowed hard. "I know."

I think I was still in shock. Still grappling with the reality.

Because it *didn't* feel real.

Not even though I'd been staring at it all afternoon.

Not long before, Jon had dozed off.

And then, he'd spiked a fever.

Carolynn, one of the RNs, was especially nice.

The kind of nurse who made you feel human, even when you were barely holding it together.

She had told me it was common in the aftermath of a cardiac arrest.

As was his fluctuating blood pressure.

She'd explained it while showing me how to interpret his readings on the monitors. She didn't seem to mind teaching me, and I felt a desperate need to understand what I was seeing—to process everything that was happening.

There was so much to learn.

So much that could go wrong.

His body was in chaos.

Trying to regulate itself.

Trying to recover from so much time without circulation.

This hadn't just been a scare.

It had been a full-scale physiological catastrophe.

***

6:00 PM

Mike and I stepped outside for fresh air while he called Nikki—giving her an update and asking her to loop in Cary, Shawn, and Tony.

We were gone thirty minutes.

No more.

But when we returned to Jon's room—

Something was off.

There were more people around him than before.

I took one look at the cluster of nurses and staff adjusting machines, adjusting meds, and my stomach knotted.

Something had changed.

"What happened?"

Carolynn answered quickly, carefully.

"His rhythm got a little funky. We're making some adjustments."

Jon was awake again.

And cooperating.

But something about him seemed... off.

He still played it cool, reassuring us that he was okay.

But I could see it.

The subtle cracks in his exterior.

Or maybe it was just his washed-out complexion.

The faint, pink circles under his eyes.

***

7:00 PM

There was zero doubt now.

His condition was changing.

Devolving.

His responses were slower.

It was taking him longer to answer basic questions.

His eyes looked glassy.

Ben had come back, Jeff and Sharron had gone up to see Jill.

I didn't know what was worse—

The look of devastation on Ben's face when he realized Jon was getting worse, not better—

Or that Jon had stopped pretending he was okay.

Ben tried to smile through his obvious panic.

"Jill's asking about you." His voice wavered. His eyes immediately filled. "I told her they were just keeping you for observation after the donation. That's why you haven't been up to see her yet."

Jon gave the faintest smile.

"That's good," he murmured. Quiet. Small.

Ben nodded, but he looked nervous. "It'll be good once I can tell her you're on the other side of this."

He placed a reassuring hand on Jon's arm.

"You're going to be okay."

Jon didn't answer.

Just... diverted his eyes.

Oh fuck.

He doesn't even believe he's going to be okay.

***

By 9 PM, Dr. Brookens had already been in twice more.

Carolynn had spent more time at Jon's bedside than away.

And I was getting the distinct impression that Brookens wasn't normally around this late.

Yet—

Here he was.

And that knowledge didn't give me a warm, fuzzy feeling.

Jon drifted in and out of what I guessed was... sleep?

Every now and then he'd stir awake—sometimes barely.

Sometimes, with a start.

They said his heart wasn't pumping well.

That his whole system was inflamed.

A lot of explanations. A lot of fancy words for a simple, brutal truth:

He was getting worse.

And even though we were in the best hospital around—

It didn't seem to fucking matter.

***

They had a name for it. Post-Cardiac Arrest Syndrome.

PCAS.

I hated hearing those letters.

I hated that fucking term.

It made it sound official. Understandable.

But in reality, it was nothing but a slow-motion nightmare.

Why can't they just make it stop?

Each time he woke up—

He seemed a little less *him.*

Like he was slowly moving away from us.

Being pulled in a direction that made me feel helpless and sick to my stomach.

We all saw it.

No one said it out loud.

But even Mike—the one who was usually cool and collected—at one point just got up and left.

Right after Jon had drifted off mid-sentence, even as the nurses were still talking to him.

That's when I noticed how tense Mike looked.

Like he was going to put his fist through a wall just from the sheer, fucking frustration of it all.

He had reached his limit, and needed to walk away.

I understood.

But that wasn't me.

No way was I moving one step away from this guy.

The guy who had swept me off my feet years ago—

Who had never stopped making me smile.

The guy I had fallen hard for.

The guy with the dimples I was going to see again.

I wasn't leaving him.

And I had to believe—

He wasn't leaving me.

Chapter 16

Then, just after 10 PM—

Something happened.

Jon's heart slammed into an arrhythmia so severe that the entire room exploded into motion.

The monitors screamed.

Nurses rushed in.

Doctors followed.

They worked fast—adjusting drips, pushing meds, forcing his body to comply.

He was awake again.

Barely.

He lay there, breathing shallowly.

His heart was racing erratically, his body drenched in sweat.

I had tried—God, I had tried—to count the intervals between these episodes earlier in the night.

A futile attempt to impose order on the chaos.

But now they were coming faster.

Like time itself was closing in.

I hated seeing him like this: reduced to someone who could barely protest, who had to put his trust entirely in other people.

His skin was cold and clammy, a stark contrast to the warmth I wanted to offer.

Dr. Brookens was there.

Carolynn, too.

She exuded a calm confidence that I clung to.

They pushed another round of medication into his IV.

I counted the seconds.

One. Two. Three.

I knew it worked fast.

But standing there, each passing moment felt interminable.

Like waiting for an explosion you knew was coming, but couldn't predict.

At twenty seconds, Jon's body tensed.

His muscles contracted.

His head fell back.

His hand clenched into a fist.

My eyes darted to Carolynn, looking for reassurance.

She gave a small nod.

"It's okay, you're just starting to feel the medicine," she said gently.

But was it?

Is he okay?

He looked uncomfortable.

More than before.

His breath hitched.

And for the first time—

There was something else.

Panic.

It was fleeting, but unmistakable.

Then—

The monitor beeped.

The pause.

Expected.

This was how it worked.

A short reset. Then a slower, more stable rhythm.

Only—

The pause stretched.

Too long.

Way too long.

The jagged lines on the monitor didn't smooth out.

They fractured.

Twisting into something worse.

Even I—a complete layperson—knew this was wrong.

Jon's awareness slipped.

I could see it happening.

Like watching a tide pull away.

His gaze drifted past me—

Looking at something else.

Something I couldn't see.

What are you looking at?

His body slackened.

The tension didn't melt away in relief.

It was something scarier.

He was too still.

Too quiet.

Everything felt like slow motion.

But Carolynn moved fast.

She placed an oxygen mask over his face.

"Jon, look at me."

Her voice was sharp, steady.

Her actions were precise but gentle—almost maternal.

She tilted his head toward her, eyes locked on his.

"Deep breaths."

Jon's chest barely moved.

He coughed once.

Weak.

Then—

Nothing.

The monitor's tone shifted.

Flashing red numbers.

Oh my God.

This wasn't normal.

This wasn't even close to normal.

He's dying.

My mind reeled, screaming at me to do something.

He's dying right in front of me.

Carolynn's voice stayed steady—but her face betrayed her concern.

"Come on, sweetheart, stay with us."

She shook his shoulder.

Nothing.

I saw the exact moment the doctor realized where this was going.

"Fuck," he muttered, turning. "Get the cart."

As if on cue, the alarms erupted in unison.

No. No, no, no.

Jon's bed was flattened in seconds.

Their movements were practiced. Precise.

More people flooded the room.

I stood there, frozen.

The air was thick with beeping, clipped orders, and controlled urgency.

It wasn't like TV.

No shouting. No chaos. No dramatic music.

Just calculated precision.

They must have done this a thousand times.

But for me, this was the most traumatic moment of my life.

I felt myself backing away.

Like if I could just step far enough back, I wouldn't have to absorb what was happening.

My shoulder hit something solid.

Someone.

"Whoa—it's me."

Jeff.

His hand on my arm.

He must have just walked in.

"Come on."

His arm wrapped around me.

Steering me toward the door.

We'd just reached the hallway when Sharron nearly collided into us.

"What's going on?" she demanded.

Her wide eyes darted between Jeff and me, then beyond us, toward Jon's room.

"We can't be in there right now." Jeff said firmly.

His tone had changed.

Like he'd flipped into detective mode.

"What's happening?" Her voice was higher now.

Panicked.

She tried to shove past Jeff, but he caught her by the arms.

"Sharron. Listen to me. We need to let them do their jobs."

A nurse swiftly guided us away to a waiting area.

I sat down.

My stomach churned.

My thoughts spiraled.

I just watched my fiancé go into cardiac arrest.

Again.

Do I even still have a fiancé?

Chapter 17

I felt nauseous.

Completely at a loss for words.

Sharron, on the other hand, was the opposite.

She was masking her anguish with something sharper.

Frustration.

Her voice was clipped, demanding.

"What's happening?"

She turned to the RN, eyes desperate.

"Why can't you stabilize him?"

The RN—sympathetic, composed—kept her tone measured.

"I know this has been a difficult night. I can only imagine how upsetting this is for you."

Her words were gentle. But careful.

"Jonathan's case is uniquely challenging. Dr. Brookens will want to speak with you about that soon," the nurse went on.

My stomach twisted.

A pause.

Then, her voice softened.

"But right now, the team's only priority is restoring circulation and establishing a pulse. That's *all* that matters. Someone will update you as soon as we have news, okay?"

Sharron wiped at her face, silent but nodding.

The nurse offered a sympathetic smile before disappearing back through the door.

***

The wait felt endless.

Mike had apparently been on his way to Jon's room when someone intercepted him, redirecting him to the waiting area.

He hadn't seen what happened.

But the moment he walked in—

He could tell.

Sharron wiping away tears.

Jeff's stiff posture.

Me—silent, staring, unable to process.

He took the chair beside me.

After a while the door opened.

A small-statured older woman stepped in.

She didn't waste time.

She cut straight to the only thing we cared about.

"We have him."

The tension in the room cracked, but the rest of the conversation felt like déjà vu. A repeat from earlier.

Sharron had asked if he was awake, and if we could see him, both of which the answer was no.

"I wouldn't expect him to regain consciousness anytime soon. But I'll let the doctor discuss those details with you when he comes out."

Then, she took a deep breath.

And smiled.

A little too wide.

A little too forced.

Like she was trying to make us accept what good news she had.

"Jonathan is still with us."

Her voice bright.

Her head bobbing as if that should be enough.

But it wasn't.

Not really.

Then, she excused herself.

Leaving us alone.

To sit in silence.

To drown in a million unanswered questions.

***

After what felt like a lifetime, Dr. Brookens finally walked through the door.

Jeff stood immediately.

Brookens raised a hand.

A simple gesture. Sit.

Then, without hesitation, he grabbed a chair, spun it around, and dropped into it.

He positioned himself right in front of us, like he was taking a seat at an invisible conference table.

Heavy movements. Deliberate.

"So."

His voice was businesslike.

"Let's talk about where we are."

He started with the good news.

Jon was holding sinus rhythm, thanks to a drug called amiodarone. He'd spent time explaining the drug. What it was, how it worked... and the risks. He talked about the loading doses and the long half-life. He also stressed the fact that, so far, Jon was tolerating it well.

Then—the other shoe.

"However, the drug often causes low blood pressure and bradycardia—slow heart rate—which in Jon's case have been severe. Because of this, he may require pacing for the next several hours. Possibly longer."

Jeff straightened in his chair.

His voice was firm. Uncharacteristically so.

"Wait. Stop."

He leaned forward.

"How can that possibly be worth the risk?"

For the first time, I saw Jeff as truly assertive.

His usually quiet demeanor was gone.

Replaced with something raw. Protective.

"He's been through enough," Jeff pressed.

"Is this really the best option?"

Brookens held Jeff's gaze. His voice was unwavering.

"Mr. Stetson, this is the only option we have left." His words were quiet. Heavy. Final. "Right now, the benefits outweigh the risks. Jonathan's cardiac output is critically compromised. Sustained ventricular arrhythmias make it impossible for his heart to pump blood effectively. They also place a tremendous strain on his cardiovascular system. Stabilizing his heart is critical."

A pause. Then—softer, but unflinching:

"I agree—he's been through enough. But if we don't act, I fear he won't survive another cardiac event. Of any kind."

Jeff exhaled sharply.

Like someone had just punched him in the ribs.

Then, he sank back into his chair.

His whole body seemed to deflate.

The rest of us sat in stunned silence.

Brookens seemed to sense our despair. He shifted slightly, then added, "If Jonathan can make it through the next twenty-four hours, his chances of recovery increase significantly."

His voice was even. Practical.

"For now, I suggest we stay the course and try to remain positive. Everyone here is fully committed to achieving the best outcome."

"Can we see him?"

My voice broke slightly.

Beside me, Sharron leaned forward, eager for an answer.

Brookens hesitated.

For the first time.

He glanced down briefly—like he was choosing his words carefully.

Then—a nod.

"Yes. But only if you feel prepared."

His eyes locked onto mine.

His words felt like ice.

I nodded, though my chest tightened.

I was grateful for his explanations.

But knowing—no amount of preparation could possibly ready me for what was behind that door.

***

Once Brookens left the waiting area, the four of us sat in silence.

Each of us, in our own way, trying to come to terms with what we'd just heard.

Part of me wanted to see Jon.

Part of me was terrified to.

Earlier that day, when they'd finally let us in to visit, Jon had been conscious.

Not 100% himself, but at least aware.

Now?

I wasn't sure who I was about to walk in and see.

I remembered what Brookens had said.

His warning had been clear.

Due to the nature of Jon's cardiac arrest—and the systemic physiological repercussions—things could get worse before they got better.

He had literally told us Jon's condition could backslide.

But I had been completely unprepared for just how extreme that would be.

I was grateful to have Mike with me.

It was late, and the ICU was limited to immediate family.

But Jeff had made sure the staff understood:

Mike *was* family.

Nobody questioned it after that.

I turned to him. "Will you come with me?"

He nodded immediately.

"Yeah, of course."

He stood, offering me his hand.

Jeff exhaled.

"You kids go ahead. We'll be right there."

His tone was level, but something about it made me feel like he wanted a moment alone with Sharron.

Mike and I didn't ask.

We just walked.

With each step down the hall, apprehension coiled in my chest.

I wasn't ready.

***

Jon's room was massive.

And it had to be.

Not just because of the sheer amount of equipment.

But because when things went sideways—like before—

There had to be enough space for a whole team to work.

When it was empty, though?

It felt intimidating.

Like too much space.

Like a void.

The room had a set of sliding glass doors on each side.

One led to the main hallway—the one visitors used.

The other opened directly into the central hub.

I glanced through the glass.

A large octagon-shaped nurses' station sat in the middle, occupied with staff moving in and out, always watching.

The second set of doors was still open.

That gave me some comfort.

They were right there.

They were watching.

I hesitated the second I stepped inside.

I wanted to touch him.

To hold him.

But he looked so fucking sick that I froze.

Jon was unconscious.

Breathing, but with help—a full oxygen mask fogging slightly with each weak breath.

My eyes fell on the defibrillator pads.

I knew what they were.

The doctor had explained them.

But knowing didn't make seeing them any easier.

One was attached to the center of his chest.

Its edges curved slightly over his ribs.

The other—

Pressed against his back, just beneath his shoulder blade.

Like two halves of an invisible clamp, holding him in place.

Wires snaked from the pads to a device on a rolling cart beside his bed.

The same cart.

The same damn cart Brookens had calmly asked for right before shit hit the fan.

Another screen.

Another set of numbers.

Too much equipment.

Too many blinking lights.

The whole thing looked more like a sci-fi control center than a hospital room.

A nurse entered.

Warm smile, but there was something behind it.

Something reassuring, but practiced.

"You can touch him," she said gently.

I hesitated.

She must have noticed.

"I'll be right here," she reassured me.

***

I had resumed my place at Jon's bedside, gripping his right hand tightly.

His skin was cool against mine.

Unsettlingly cool.

But I refused to let go.

Across the room, Mike sat in a chair near the far wall.

His head bowed, hands clasped tensely between his knees.

Silent.

Staring at the floor.

It wasn't long before Dr. Brookens reappeared.

He was just outside the open door, speaking in low tones with a few staff members.

The RN who had promised to stay with us had joined them.

I tried to catch snippets of their conversation.

Tried to piece together anything useful.

But I couldn't make out a single word.

My stomach knotted.

Reflexively.

Then, they entered.

Brookens gave Mike and me a quick nod of acknowledgment.

Then—straight to business.

"We're going to increase the pacing threshold to keep his cardiac output stable."

His voice was calm. Even. Unshaken.

"With his blood pressure this low, we need to ensure his heart is beating fast enough to maintain perfusion."

I couldn't stop myself from overanalyzing.

As though I could logic my way out of this.

As though understanding what was happening would somehow change what was happening.

Brookens cleared his throat.

A subtle shift.

A change in tone.

"Now would be a good time to grab a coffee or take a walk."

His voice was neutral, but there was an expectation behind it.

I could take a hint.

My hand was still on his.

Still holding on.

I didn't want to let go.

Even if he was unconscious.

Even if he wouldn't know.

It felt cruel to leave him alone in this.

Slowly. Reluctantly.

I released his hand.

The absence of contact was immediate.

But the doctor wanted us out of the room.

Did he anticipate something?

Was he expecting an adverse reaction?

My brain spun with possibilities.

His earlier words echoed.

Jon might not survive another cardiac event.

Mike and I stood almost in unison.

A brief, wordless glance exchanged.

Then, we turned toward the door.

***

A walk did sound good.

A stress walk.

My body felt coiled, vibrating with anxious energy.

But my mind felt slow. Heavy.

Bogged down.

Like trying to wade through thick, unwieldy thoughts.

It was a strange, maddening contrast.

Hyperaware. Yet detached.

As though I were caught in some surreal, slow-motion nightmare.

***

Mike and I stepped outside. The crisp air hit me immediately, but somehow it still felt warmer than the cold, sterile hospital room.

I considered grabbing a coffee but decided against it. I already felt wired. Shaky. Instead, I opted for a bottle of water, the dryness in my mouth a constant reminder of my anxiety.

Mike lit a cigarette and handed me one, his silent way of offering comfort. I accepted it, hoping it might calm my nerves. It didn't, but I smoked it anyway while he made a round of calls, providing updates. I was grateful he'd taken on the burden of communication. Nikki had sent me a few texts earlier, but I couldn't bring myself to respond. Talking felt impossible.

Still, I wished she were here.

I paced further down the sidewalk, acutely aware of the humming fluorescent lights lining the walkway. Eventually, I made my way back to the entrance. Mike was sitting on a bench, his phone calls finished. "Nikki's riding up with Cary in the morning," he said. "She's bringing you some clean clothes."

I nodded, grateful. "I think I left a sweatshirt at her place," I murmured, wishing I had it with me now.

***

When we re-entered Jon's room, Sharron sat by his bedside, her hand resting gently on his arm.

She looked up at us, and smiled faintly.

But her red-rimmed eyes betrayed her.

She'd been crying.

"Jeff and I are taking turns," she explained softly, answering our unspoken question.

"He's upstairs with Jill right now."

"How's she doing?" I asked.

Sharron sighed.

Her voice was heavy with exhaustion.

"She's okay. Better than we are."

She rubbed Jon's arm gently, like she was speaking for both of them.

Mike and I settled into the couch-like bench against the far wall.

I watched Jon closely.

Tried to pretend he was just sleeping.

Not locked in a battle for his life.

The monitors glowed in the dim room, their steady patterns oddly comforting.

A slow, rhythmic reminder that he was still here.

Still fighting.

But I couldn't relax.

I was terrified that if I closed my eyes—

I'd wake to the sound of alarms.

As long as his heart kept beating...

We'd be okay.

Please, Jon.

Please be okay.

Chapter 18

I had dozed off lightly, curled up on the bench beside Mike.

Sharron had moved to a larger chair, arms folded.

She must have fallen asleep too.

I sensed Jeff's presence before I saw him.

The quiet shuffle of footsteps.

A brief hesitation.

Then—the gentle weight of a jacket draped over me.

The gesture was so tender that it nearly brought tears to my eyes.

It was easy to see why Jon had turned out the way he did.

With Jeff as a role model, how could he not?

Jeff moved toward the bed, pausing briefly.

Then, he leaned down, pressing a soft kiss to Jon's head.

His voice was barely above a whisper.

"Hey, Jonathan."

A breath.

"Dad's here."

He sank into the chair beside Jon.

Took his hand in both of his own.

Held it firmly.

"Hang in there, kiddo."

His voice was thick. Raw.

The kind of wavering tone that only came from holding back too much emotion at once.

But the way Jeff spoke to him—

It made me want to cry.

For both of them.

Jeff swallowed.

"I know this is hard."

A pause.

"And I'm so, so sorry."

Another pause.

Then—his voice dropped.

"But..."

He trailed off.

I saw him wipe his eyes.

Saw his shoulders rise and fall, as if trying to reset himself.

As if trying to find the words that didn't exist.

He exhaled.

And tried again.

"We just need you to hang in there."

A beat.

"I'm so proud of you."

He placed a hand on Jon's head.

Gently stroking his hair, like you would a child's.

"You're doing great."

A whisper.

A prayer.

A plea.

***

Jeff stayed there, holding Jon's hand.

Talking to him.

Softly.

Casually.

About Jill. About the baby.

About the kind of things that had nothing to do with hospital rooms and defibrillators.

It was comforting in a strange way.

Like he was trying to inject normalcy into a situation that had been anything but normal.

His calm, steady voice felt like a lifeline in the chaos.

At one point, a nurse entered.

She moved to check Jon's IV stack, adjusting a few settings.

Jeff started to stand, ready to move.

But she waved him off.

"No, you're fine," she said with a smile. "In fact, you should keep talking to him. He's responding to you."

Jeff blinked. "What?"

Sharron stirred, sitting upright. Her voice was tight with hope and exhaustion.

"He's responding?"

The nurse nodded enthusiastically.

She gestured toward the monitors. "His blood pressure fluctuates slightly when you talk to him. It's subtle, but I've been watching it from the station."

A pause.

"He's reacting. He might even be trying to wake up."

I sat up fully, my exhaustion evaporating.

For the first time in what felt like forever—

A flicker of hope sparked in the room.

***

At about 7:30 that morning, Jon finally stirred.

It wasn't much—just the smallest movement.

But it was enough.

Jeff sat bolt upright.

His hand darted out, gripping Jon's.

"Hey, buddy."

Urgent, but soft.

"Hey, Jonathan... come on, kiddo."

He turned, his face alight with cautious hope.

"Go get someone—I think he's waking up."

Sharron scrambled for the door.

But before she even reached it, an RN entered.

Followed closely by Carolynn.

Relief washed over me the second I saw her.

Mike and I instinctively stayed back, giving them space.

Jeff stepped away from the bed, joining us near the wall.

Carolynn's tone was cheerful, soothing.

"Hi, sweetheart."

Jon's hand fumbled weakly toward his oxygen mask.

"No, baby."

Carolynn caught his hand, guiding it gently back down.

"I need you to leave that on for me, okay?"

She pressed her stethoscope to his chest.

Her calm, practiced hands a stark contrast to the frantic urgency of the night before.

But watching her, I couldn't help the flashbacks.

The alarms.

The urgent voices.

The helplessness.

My stomach clenched.

I forced myself to stay present.

Carolynn's voice brought me back.

"Good job, sweetie."

Steady. Encouraging.

"Just relax and take some deep breaths. I know you probably don't feel too good, so we're going to take this slow, okay?"

Jon's shoulders eased.

A second nurse adjusted the bed, bringing him into a less reclined position.

His eyes moved around the room.

Still clouded with confusion.

But unmistakably alive.

A younger doctor entered then—not Brookens.

I could only hope Brookens was finally getting some rest.

The new doctor's voice was bright, reassuring.

They spoke to Jon gently, encouraging his responses.

Watching for any flicker of recognition.

Their words were measured. Calm.

A delicate balance between optimism and caution.

***

By the time the flurry of activity subsided, I finally stepped closer.

Jon seemed barely awake, but the moment I reached his side—

He smiled faintly.

And reached for my hand.

The warmth of his touch startled me.

I hadn't realized how cold his skin had been before.

"Hey," I whispered.

My voice trembled.

It was all I could manage.

A lump formed in my throat, and it took everything in me not to cry right then and there.

The others took their turns, greeting him softly.

Jon barely had the energy to respond, but his eyes tracked each person as they spoke.

It wasn't long—maybe ten minutes—

Before his eyes fluttered closed again, his exhaustion pulling him back under.

A pang of disappointment hit me.

But Carolynn was quick to reassure us.

"He's doing great—this is a big deal!"

Her enthusiasm was genuine.

"He'll be in and out like this for a while, and that's okay. The important thing is—he's been awake. He's breathing without a ventilator. And he understands what we're saying to him."

Her words brought some comfort.

But my eyes stayed locked on Jon.

I kept replaying the sight of his smile, like holding onto that moment would somehow anchor him here with us.

The doctor returned as Carolynn finished speaking.

His expression matched hers—hopeful, but measured.

"These are all great signs," he said. "The fact that he woke up, even briefly, is encouraging. It suggests no significant neurological impairment."

A flicker of hope.

But then—he tempered it.

"That said, he is still very weak. And this will be an uphill battle."

Uphill battle.

The words stuck with me.

They felt accurate.

Ominously so.

But for the first time since this nightmare began—

The tiniest ember of hope had taken root.

He had woken up.

He had smiled.

He had reached for me.

And that was enough to keep me going.

Chapter 19

Another hour passed without any movement from Jon. He looked every bit as sick as he had the night before—hovering on the brink. We all knew it. Still, I clung to the memory of that brief moment when he'd been awake. It was real. It mattered.

Ben came down from Jill's floor to check on Jon, and he looked like he hadn't slept in days. Exhaustion hung on him like a second skin. My heart ached for him. Becoming a first-time father, earlier than expected, would have been overwhelming on its own. Add this, and it seemed unbearable.

The five of us gathered in the hallway, an impromptu powwow forming. Jeff explained that they'd booked two rooms at the hotel across the street and suggested we start taking turns to catch up on sleep. He suggested Ben and I go first.

I was ready to protest fiercely, but Mike interrupted, reminding me that Cary and Nikki would be arriving soon and that we could meet them at the hotel. A hot shower and a change of clothes did sound tempting, though I hated the thought of leaving Jon.

***

Mike stayed in the lobby waiting for Cary while I headed up to the room. As soon as I closed the door behind me, I flopped onto the bed. Stretching out on my back felt heavenly. A few minutes passed...

Don't fall asleep, Via.

My inner voice scolded me sharply. It had only been a few minutes, right?

How can you even think about sleeping right now?

I sat up, trying to shake off the guilt. A soft knock came at the door. "Hey, it's me," said a familiar voice.

I opened the door to find Nikki standing there, beaming, with a backpack slung over one shoulder and a bag of McDonald's hash browns in her hand. Relief washed over me, stronger than I'd expected. I stepped aside to let her in, and she tossed the bags onto the small table before turning to hug me tightly.

For some reason, my eyes filled with tears, one hot drop trickling down my cheek. I hadn't really cried yet. I'd been holding it together so well. Why now?

Nikki held me for a long moment, then pulled back to look at my face. "How are you holding up?" she asked, her voice soft but probing.

I shrugged, wiping at my eyes with an embarrassed laugh.

Why the fuck are you crying, Via? Stop it.

"Where's Cary?" I asked quickly, trying to redirect.

"He's across the street with Mike, visiting Jon."

"Well, he's in for a treat," I muttered, sarcasm lacing my tone.

"I thought you might be hungry." Nikki shoved a hash brown in my direction, the salty aroma hitting me like a lifeline. McDonald's hash browns had always been our go-to after a night of drinking. The familiar gesture brought a faint smile to my face.

I didn't realize how starved I was until I took a bite. My stomach had been in knots for so long that I'd forgotten the difference between hunger and anxiety.

As I ate, Nikki dumped the contents of her backpack onto the bed: my sweatshirt, a pair of black fleece pants, a T-shirt, socks, and even underwear. We wore the same size, and I was touched to see she'd packed an entire outfit from her own closet.

"I even washed the underwear first," she teased, making me nearly choke on my hash brown with laughter. It was the first time I'd smiled in what felt like forever.

"That's not all," she added, pulling shampoo and conditioner from the front pouch. "Those little hotel bottles never cut it."

"Thank you," I said, my voice thick with gratitude. She waved me off, insisting she'd wait in the room while I showered. It was good to have a friend like Nikki.

***

Feeling refreshed in cozy, clean clothes, I walked with Nikki back toward the hospital. The campus was sprawling, giving us extra time to talk. As we approached the entrance, I spotted Mike and Cary standing outside.

The moment I saw Cary, my stomach twisted. His neck and face were blotchy, and his eyes glistened. He'd been crying.

Did something happen?

My adrenaline spiked.

Cary never gets emotional. He's the jokester, the forever comedian. If he's crying, it's bad.

I looked to Mike for reassurance. "Is everything okay? Is he awake?" The questions tumbled out of me in rapid fire.

Mike shook his head calmly. "He's still the same. We were just visiting, that's all."

Cary stepped toward me, his expression apologetic, and pulled me into a tight hug. "Hi, Via," he whispered. His voice, thick with emotion, broke my heart. When he pulled back, I could see fresh tears in his eyes.

"I didn't mean to scare you," he said, wiping at his face. "It's just... a lot."

"Yeah," I replied flatly. What else was there to say?

"You never cry," Nikki said, her tone equal parts concerned and teasing.

"Well..." Cary trailed off, shrugging helplessly. "I just wasn't expecting... he looks so bad."

Nikki slipped her hand into mine. "Jon's tough. He'll pull through."

Thank God for good friends.

The four of us sat outside for a while, each of us wrestling with the realization that for the past year, Jon had been trying to tough out something far more serious than any of us could have imagined.

Cary called Shawn, putting him on speaker so he could talk with the group. It was hard to keep things positive, but Cary tried his best. "Jon's totally going to kick my ass when he gets out," he added, half serious, half amused.

"Yeah man." Shawn spoke in a cautionary tone. "For all the shit you've given him about being contagious and making us all sick."

Nikki and Mike both laughed as Cary's eyes widened.

It was true. There'd been a time we all thought Jon was fighting something viral. But even after it became obvious he wasn't, Cary had clung to that excuse—and seized every opportunity to playfully harass him about it.

He'd even bought Vitamin C lozenges and sprinkled them in everyone's bags. His way of lightening the mood. But now? Bitterly ironic.

"Ffffuck," Cary muttered, hands laced behind his head. "Yeah. He's for sure gonna beat my ass."

We all lost it laughing.

I tried my best to make conversation. The warmth of the sun was refreshing, but all I could think about was Jon. I felt like I'd been away from him forever, though it had only been a couple of hours.

Finally, I stood, restless. "I'm going to go check on him," I announced.

Nikki stood immediately. "We're going to visit Jon now, okay?" she told the guys. "You two go find something to do."

***

As Nikki and I neared his room, we saw Jeff standing just outside the doorway, talking to a nurse. My anxiety spiked, until Jeff caught my eye and smiled. Relief swept through me when he winked and motioned toward the room.

"You'd better get in there," he said warmly.

Inside, Jon was sitting upright, propped by pillows. He was no longer wearing the oxygen mask, and he looked awake—alert, even—talking quietly with Sharron and Carolynn. When his eyes met mine, he grinned faintly and said, "Hey."

A single word, mirroring my own greeting earlier.

So he does remember.

I went to take his hand, but he surprised me by opening his arms for a hug. I leaned in carefully. "I don't want to hurt you," I said nervously.

"You're not going to hurt me," he replied with a faint smile. "It's her I need to worry about," he added, nodding toward Carolynn.

She laughed. "Lord, I try not to, honey. But you're pretty bruised up right now."

When she pulled his gown down slightly to check his chest, the deep purple bruises spreading across his ribs and sternum made my stomach turn. CPR compressions.

A wound from the thing that saved him.

"Oh my God," I whispered.

"I guess this ruins our plans for the west coast. We'd better tell Tony I found a more expensive place to spend the time," Jon added with a faint smirk.

We all chuckled, a welcome reprieve from the tension. Even Sharron managed a smile.

"Actually, Tony's on his way here," I said, watching Jon's expression shift to surprise.

"What? Seriously?" he asked, his voice rasping slightly.

"Yeah..." I hesitated, gauging his reaction. "He'll be here soon."

"Why?" Jon asked, incredulous.

Nikki stepped in before I could answer. "Because Mike and Cary have been giving him updates on you, and there was no stopping him. He's worried about you. We all are. And, well, you know Tony—he doesn't take no for an answer."

Jon didn't respond right away, his eyes shifting toward the bed rail as if he were trying to process her words. Or maybe he was just too tired to respond. The exhaustion was etched across his face, the pink circles under his eyes even darker than yesterday. He looked utterly drained.

"Well..." Carolynn began, her tone light but firm. "We don't mind if you have a visitor or two later, if you're up for it." She directed her next words toward Jon. "But right now, neurology is coming to give you a checkup, and we need you awake for that."

She glanced around the room meaningfully, clearly signaling it was time for us to leave. "And later today, when Dr. Brookens is back, he'll bring the electrophysiologist to talk about what's going on with your heart." Her tone shifted, growing slightly more serious. "In the meantime, Jon, it's really important that you rest."

The unspoken weight of her words settled over us. Rest wasn't just a suggestion; it was critical.

Chapter 20

By the afternoon, Jon had been examined by both the neurologist and the electrophysiologist. None of us had been allowed to stay in the room, but the neurology report came back surprisingly good. Just like the day before, the conclusion was that Jon had miraculously avoided neurological damage from the cardiac arrests. Each hour that passed without further incident increased the chances he would avoid those complications altogether. So, there was that.

The results from his cardiac evaluation were, at first, kept quieter. Dr. Brookens didn't return immediately after the exam; instead, he disappeared with the other specialist. Over an hour passed before he re-entered Jon's room, and by then, Jon was sleeping. Brookens led us to a conference room. There, we were introduced to Jon's electrophysiologist, Dr. Kahn.

Dr. Brookens opened the discussion, taking the lead as he usually did. He began by explaining Jon's current condition in great detail, starting with what he called "severe left-ventricular dysfunction." His heart wasn't pumping enough blood with each beat—a low ejection fraction caused by the aftermath of his cardiac arrests. The medication stabilizing his rhythm was making it worse, dropping his blood pressure even further. Brookens made it clear that, as risky as it was, the medication was still necessary—for now.

That's when Dr. Kahn pulled up a 3D model of a heart and walked us through how electrical signals are supposed to travel—and how Jon's weren't. He explained their strong suspicion: a rare condition called CPVT—Catecholaminergic Polymorphic Ventricular Tachycardia. He described it as electrical chaos, how adrenaline could send Jon's heart into a deadly spiral.

"This is our leading theory based on the pattern of arrhythmias we've seen and Jon's history," Dr. Kahn said. "But I want to be clear—we'll need to confirm it with further testing once Jon's stronger. Right now, our priority is keeping him safe."

I tried to keep up, but the sheer volume of detail made my brain buzz.

Then Dr. Kahn spoke about Jon's rhythms.

"Since yesterday, Jon has had several brief but dangerous arrhythmias—episodes where his heart shifted into polymorphic ventricular tachycardia. Each could've triggered another arrest, but the medications and immediate care prevented that."

His message was clear: Jon was high-risk. The conversation shifted.

They introduced the ICD.

An implantable cardioverter defibrillator.

They passed around a sample device—small, metallic, no bigger than a pocket watch. It was strange holding something so unassuming, knowing what it was for.

They explained how it worked, how it would monitor Jon's heart every second of the day. If his rhythm slipped into something dangerous, it would deliver therapy—a correction, or a shock—to bring him back.

It was high-tech. Life-saving. Invasive.

Holding it in my hand felt surreal. It wasn't just a device—it was Jon's second chance.

How long had he needed this, and we just didn't know?

The thought gave me chills.

Dr. Brookens, ever cautious, wanted to give Jon a little more time to stabilize first. They laid out their opinions, each backed by risk assessments and protocols, but it boiled down to this: wait, and risk another arrest. Or move quickly, and risk pushing his fragile body too far.

We asked questions—so many questions—and they answered every one. Toward the end, Jeff voiced the one I hadn't even thought to ask.

"Does Jon know? Have you had a chance to tell him?"

Brookens nodded. "He does. He was awake earlier, and I took the opportunity to explain what we're recommending. He seemed to understand."

His voice softened. "This procedure is always a significant adjustment for patients, and we don't take that lightly. In addition to the physical risks, there's a psychological element. Jonathan seems to grasp the severity of his condition—probably better than any of us. He's been living with a symptomatic heart rhythm disorder for some time now, whether he knew its name or not."

Brookens paused, letting his words land. And he was right.

But as I replayed what he'd said, something hit me. Between Jon's meeting with the doctors and this conference, we'd been with him. He'd already known about the ICD by then.

Yet... he hadn't said a word about it.

That's odd, right?

Then again, maybe not. He'd seemed so sleepy. So quiet. Maybe he was too sick to care. Or maybe... maybe he didn't want to talk about it.

The realization made my chest ache.

"What can we do?" I asked. "How can we help him deal with this?"

Brookens gave me a small, approving nod, like I'd asked the one thing he wished more people would.

We spent the next ten minutes talking about psychological recovery—what Jon might face emotionally, how we could support him, and how the timing of the procedure would depend just as much on his mental readiness as his physical strength.

My mind reeled. There was so much to think about. So much to worry about. *I can't believe this is happening.*

***

Before we'd left the conference room, his doctor had diplomatically suggested that Jon had had enough company for the day. I knew it was fair. Honestly, I was pretty sure they were already bending the rules for him—likely for reasons that went unspoken but were universally understood.

When we returned and realized Jon was awake, I asked if he wanted to say a quick goodbye before everyone else left. He did, of course. He hadn't been awake during Cary's earlier visit, and I knew he'd appreciate the chance to see him. I was glad to witness their brief interaction, especially after the way Cary had surprised me earlier with his softer, more emotional side.

Jon extended his arm for a good-natured handshake, and Cary eagerly accepted, holding on a few seconds longer than necessary. His smile was genuine, but I noticed his eyes glistening again. With an awkward swipe of his sleeve, he brushed the tears away.

"Shit," Cary muttered, visibly embarrassed.

Jon grinned, breaking the tension with his usual easy humor. "Damn, bro, you look like you lost your best friend or something."

The room broke into laughter, including Cary, who shook his head. "Fuck," he said, smiling despite himself. "I'm usually the funny one."

Jon's grin widened. "I kinda like the sappy side of you."

Tony chimed in, his voice full of warmth. "Yeah, well, you're bringin' out the sap in all of us. I think you've sufficiently scared the hell out of everyone, okay? You're makin' people cry."

Jon smiled faintly.

"How are you feeling?" Cary asked, his voice quieter now.

Jon shrugged. "Okay," he said simply.

Cary sighed, visibly relieved. "Well... you look like shit," he added, grinning.

Jon laughed, the sound weak but genuine. "There it is," he said with a smirk. Then, "At least I'm not contagious."

His remark immediately elicited laughs from us and Cary nodded guiltily. "Yeah. I know. I'm never going to live this down."

The goodbyes were brief but heartfelt. Nikki hugged me tightly, promising to come back the next day. Cary gave Jon one more shoulder squeeze before stepping out, still visibly emotional. Tony offered a handshake in parting, his usual bravado tinged with something softer.

As they walked away, I felt torn. Part of me didn't want them to leave. Their presence, their humor, and their support had been a lifeline, helping to lighten the unbearable weight of the day. But another part of me—perhaps the larger part—just wanted to rest. To be with Jon. Alone. To finally sit quietly by his side and let the gravity of everything settle.

***

I walked with the group to the elevators, where Tony gave me a big hug. "Christ, Via. I'm sorry." He mumbled as he stepped back. He looked between me, Mike and Cary, a genuine sadness in his dark eyes. "I had no fucking idea it was this bad. Honest to God. If I had… I'd have never pushed him so hard. You know I would have pulled the plug on all of this a long time ago."

"None of us knew, Tony." I offered quietly. "How could we have?"

"I'm gonna make some calls when I get home. Pull you guys outta this tour, and everything else. Okay?" His eyes went from Mike to Cary. "We'll make a plan. But PR can wait, for a bit. Don't answer any calls that aren't from me. And I don't want anybody talking to Jon about *any* of it. Okay? We're not going to stress him with this bullshit. He's got one job right now, and that's to get better. Got it?"

We all nodded.

Tony looked back at me. "I'll be in touch. If you need anything—anything at all—don't hesitate to ask."

I smiled. It was a small comfort.

Jon certainly had everyone's attention now.

But it all felt way too late.

***

With everyone gone and the room quiet, things felt strange again—different. Jeff had lingered, and I didn't mind. I loved Jeff. In many ways, I felt closer to him than I ever had with my own father. He took a seat in one of the chairs, his gaze fixed on Jon, observing him thoughtfully. Jon looked exhausted.

"How are you doin', buddy?" Jeff asked softly, reaching out to squeeze Jon's arm.

"I'm okay," Jon repeated, his voice thin and flat. Nothing more, nothing less. He was ready to sleep, that much was clear. Neither Jeff nor I said anything else, letting the quiet fill the space. It didn't take long before Jon drifted off—and, not long after, so did I.

I startled awake some time later, disoriented. Jon's room had no windows to the outside, and for a moment, I struggled to piece together where I was. I grabbed my phone. It was almost 6 pm.

Holy shit. How long was I asleep?

Jon was still asleep. Sharron was now sitting in the chair Jeff had been in.

"Has he been awake at all?" I asked, rubbing my eyes.

"Just once, but only for a few minutes," Sharron replied, her voice tinged with weariness. "The doctor came in, too."

How the hell did I sleep through that?

"Is everything okay?"

Sharron sighed heavily, her expression melancholy. "Honestly… he's not doing so well."

My stomach dropped. "What?" I sat up, fully alert now, my eyes darting instinctively to the monitors, searching for reassurance.

"His blood pressure is down—again. And…" She trailed off, glancing at Jon with a mother's worry. "I don't know. He wasn't very talkative the last time he woke up. I think he's just… in low spirits."

I considered this. Sharron had a flair for the dramatic—this was her youngest child, after all—but I believed her. Who could blame him? His entire life had been turned upside down. Of course he was in low spirits.

"Ben said he'd bring the baby down later if Jon's up for it," she added.

The thought brightened me immediately.

That might actually help.

"That's a great idea!" I said. "I know he'd love to meet her. I would, too."

***

When Jon woke next, Sharron's concern was validated. He seemed... off. Polite, even pleasant, but subdued. Quiet. I couldn't tell how much to attribute to his physical state versus his mental one. When the ICD subject came up briefly, his reaction was indifferent—apathetic, even. But when I mentioned meeting Abigail, his face lit up ever so slightly. That was encouraging.

Not long after, Ben arrived with a nurse from the maternity ward. Abby was swaddled tightly in a blanket. She was so tiny—but healthy. Strong enough for this "field trip" from the nursery, thanks to some logistical wizardry (and undoubtedly a bit of rule-bending) from the staff.

Jon's entire demeanor changed the moment Ben placed Abby in his arms. His face softened, and for the first time in days, I saw a genuine smile.

Oh god. This is easily the most beautiful moment I've ever witnessed.

The room was filled with bittersweet irony—Jon and Abby, together in the hospital, each for their own battle. Both had fought so hard to be there, alive, in that moment.

Abby snuggled into Jon's chest and, to everyone's amazement, fell asleep almost instantly.

"I guess I'm boring," Jon mused, his grin widening.

"No, she really likes you!" Ben exclaimed. "She hasn't been this good for me yet."

"She's been our little fussy pants today!" added the nurse with a laugh. "This is the most content she's been since I got here this morning."

Jon held her close, cradling her affectionately for fifteen minutes before the nurse suggested they head back. It had less to do with Abby, I suspected, and more to do with Jon, who was beginning to look exhausted again.

Chapter 21

They'd barely left the room when Jon drifted back to sleep. Jeff and Sharron decided to return to the hotel to shower, eat, and maybe get some rest. I promised to call if anything—anything at all—changed.

The quiet settled in once more, but this time it felt heavy, oppressive. Jon's stats were low—lower than earlier—and the nurses were checking on him frequently. Their subdued, purposeful movements only heightened my unease. My stomach churned with that all-too-familiar gnawing anxiety.

Were we headed for another long night? Could any of us, especially Jon, endure another night like the last?

The whole thing was starting to feel like some cruel, rigged game. If one misfortune didn't claim him, another was always lurking. *One step forward, two steps back.* How long could this go on? Jon was tough, but even resilience had limits. This was taking its toll—on his body, on his spirit, on all of us.

I was spiraling when I heard a familiar voice drifting down the hall—Carolynn's warm, southern drawl. I felt relieved that she was back for another shift. A moment later, she strolled into the room, her voice lowering as she noticed Jon was asleep.

"There's my favorite guy," she said warmly, directing the greeting at me. "I hear Trina got a picture of him with that adorable baby. That'll be a treasure to hang onto."

Trina—that was the nurse who'd come with Ben and the baby. I nodded, remembering how she'd quietly snapped the photo while Jon was holding Abby. Carolynn was right; the picture would be a treasure. Maybe not in a traditional sense, but in an emotional one. I just hoped—desperately—that it wouldn't be the only picture the family had of Abby with her Uncle Jon.

My thoughts must have shown on my face because Carolynn gave me a concerned look. "You okay, hun?"

I wasn't okay. None of this was okay. I was terrified.

"Do you think tonight is going to be as bad as last night?" At this point, it was a valid question.

Carolyn drew in a long dramatic breath, and sat down on the chair closest to mine. "Oh, gosh, I sure hope not." She said sincerely, looking thoughtful.

Not the answer I wanted, but at least it was honest.

"How long does this normally go on?" I asked bluntly. "It seems like he's getting worse again."

Carolynn hesitated, nodding slowly. "Well... I can tell you this—he's doing a lot better than most, under similar circumstances."

That wasn't exactly an answer, but I accepted it as the most honest she could be.

"I know we're on shaky ground right now, but we mustn't lose sight of the small wins. Did you notice what happened to his blood pressure while he was holding the baby?" Carolynn asked.

I hadn't. Disappointment swelled in me—I'd been too caught up in the moment to notice something that was clearly significant.

"No... what happened?" I asked eagerly.

Carolynn's smile deepened. "Well, it came up. Quite a bit. That's a normal, healthy reaction. It's encouraging that his system was able to respond, even if he's too weak to maintain it for long."

I let her words sink in. It was reassuring to know the team was always paying such close attention to him. Maybe that was even part of why they'd agreed to the visit—so they could observe his response. It made sense. Jon had been so excited to become an uncle, more than I'd fully understood.

Jon loved kids, and kids loved him. He had the patience of a saint, while I... well, sometimes kids got on my nerves. But not Jon.

This brought another thought to mind—a brief conversation Jon and I had shared the day before. After his first cardiac arrest, but before everything had gone to hell. He had seemed confused at times, and his throat had been sore from the intubation, so he hadn't said much. But at one point, he told me it was Carolynn's voice that had brought him back from the brink. Something she'd said had motivated him to fight.

He'd admitted feeling so tired, so impossibly heavy, but Carolynn just kept talking. Rubbing his arm, his shoulder, his head. Telling him to wake up—almost to the point of being annoying, he'd said. All he'd wanted was to sleep. But then she'd told him he needed to wake up because it wasn't fair to Abby. It was her birthday, a day meant to celebrate new life, not to mourn a death. If he died, the day would always be shadowed. That wouldn't be fair to Abby. So, he needed to wake up.

And he did.

I remembered this now, feeling compelled to share it with Carolynn.

"Thank you, by the way, for being so good to him."

Carolynn's face softened, a deep smile spreading across her features. "Aw, honey, I'm just doing my job."

"Well, he told me what you said to him yesterday and how much it helped."

Carolynn tilted her head, her expression curious. She didn't seem to follow.

"When you told him it wouldn't be fair to Abby if he died on her birthday?"

Recognition flickered across her face, followed by something else—surprise. Her smile widened, and she tipped her head back, laughing, her shoulders shaking.

"Yessss. Lord Jesus, yes. I did say that to him." She wiped at her eyes, which glistened with tears. "But when I did, he was in the middle of a code. He was in complete asystole. So, I started talking to him. And that's what I said."

Her words left me stunned. "Sooo... he wasn't asleep when you said that to him? He was in cardiac arrest?"

The phrase sounded alien on my tongue, like it didn't belong.

"Honey, he was clinically dead. No heartbeat—not even a trace of activity—for a very long time."

"So, he couldn't have been consciously aware of anything. He shouldn't have heard you." I spoke slowly, my thoughts coming out one by one.

"But he did, didn't he?" Carolynn's eyes sparkled. "Thank you for telling me. That's the kind of thing that makes it all so worth it."

I stared at her, still trying to catch up. My mind raced back to another conversation from the day before. Jeff had asked Jon if he remembered anything about what had happened. Jon had hesitated, thinking deeply, like someone sifting through an abstract dream.

"Not really..." he'd said at last. "I remember Carolynn telling me I needed to wake up."

I thought about how his gaze had drifted, how he'd shrugged faintly, a wry smile tugging at his lips. "I don't know. It all seems kinda fuzzy. I think I had a dream, though. I saw the baby."

Jeff's eyes had widened. "You did?"

"Yeah. It was strange," Jon had said hazily. "Everything was blue."

I'd asked him what he meant, and he'd shaken his head. "I don't know... just everything was lit up. Bright blue."

At the time, I'd dismissed it as a semi-conscious hallucination. But now, I wasn't so sure.

I leaned toward Carolynn, sitting up straighter. "He also said he had a dream about the baby. He saw her, and everything was blue. Bright blue light."

Carolynn's eyes widened. "You know—" she began. "He asked me about the baby, too. He kept asking if she was okay. If something was wrong with her liver."

I nodded, suddenly recalling Jon asking us the same thing. "Jeff told him she was fine."

Carolynn leaned forward, placing a hand on my knee. "Hun, do you know they put newborns under blue light? It's called phototherapy. It helps their liver break down bilirubin."

"Blue light?" I echoed, my voice hollow.

Carolynn nodded. "Yes, and considering she came early, she would've been under the bili lights."

There was no way Jon could have known that. None.

How in the hell did he know?

My mind wrestled with the impossibility of it all. Had he experienced something beyond the physical? Some kind of supernatural moment while—God, I hated the word—while he was dead?

Did he have some sort of out-of-body experience?

My eyes met Carolynn's. Hers were bright with emotion, her smile unwavering.

"How is that possible?" I asked.

Carolynn chuckled softly. "Well, honey. Anything is possible. That's why I spoke to him in the first place. Sometimes, I think they can hear us. Even when we think they're gone... they're not far."

***

I wasn't sure how long I'd been sitting there—half awake, half lost in thought. My head rested against the chair, legs stretched out, everything about me slack except my mind. That was still spinning. Maybe I'd dozed off. Hard to tell.

But then, out of nowhere, a sharp, rhythmic beeping jolted me upright. The sound wasn't as shrill as last night's alarm, but it was enough to spike my adrenaline.

I whipped my head toward the monitors. This time, the alert wasn't from his heart monitor. It was the arterial line monitor, where his blood pressure values blinked ominously in red.

Below them, a flashing box read: **MAP BELOW LIMIT**.

Oh God.

What does that even mean?

The air thickened with urgency as the room came alive.

The young doctor from earlier swept in with a small team, their movements deliberate and quick. No chaos, but enough controlled commotion to make my pulse race.

One nurse adjusted an IV, another placed a mask over Jon's face, which only deepened my panic.

Is he struggling to breathe?

My head buzzed, ears ringing as if my own body was on the verge of short-circuiting.

My legs prickled with an unsettling, tingly feeling.

I stared at Jon. He looked too still.

The steady hum of their voices around me only made it worse.

"Sit down, hun." Carolynn's voice broke through the static, her hand gentle on my shoulder. "You don't look so good."

Her words felt misplaced—*I* didn't look good?

What about Jon?

"Why does he need oxygen?" I blurted, my voice high and wobbly. "Can he—can he not breathe?"

Carolynn crouched in front of me, her voice soft. "He's breathing. We're giving him oxygen to take some strain off his heart. That's all."

That's *all*?

My brain latched onto the words, trying to make them mean something reassuring.

They didn't.

I nodded mechanically, not fully understanding.

My gaze darted between Jon and the monitors. The flashing numbers burned into my mind.

The alarm had stopped, but its echo lingered.

She stood, giving my shoulder a reassuring squeeze. "It's under control, okay?"

I nodded again, not trusting my voice.

The crisis seemed to subside, but the tension in the room didn't. Staff came and went in a steady stream, a silent testament to how fragile things were.

As soon as I felt steady enough to stand, I slipped out to call Jeff. He needed to know.

Then I called Mike. He picked up on the first ring.

"Via?" His voice was sharp with concern.

"Mike..." My throat tightened, and my voice cracked.

"What's wrong?" He sounded panicked now.

The words tumbled out before I could second-guess them. "He's not doing well."

"I'm on my way," he promised. I could hear the fear he was trying to mask. "I'll be there soon."

***

When I returned, I was relieved to find Carolynn still at Jon's bedside, calm and steady as ever. "He's hanging in there," she said with a smile that didn't quite reach her eyes.

I sank back into my chair, feeling the cold sweat on my palms. The air was thick with unspoken fears.

Tonight would be another long night.

A short time later, a woman I didn't recognize poked her head into the room. She gave Carolynn a quick nod. "Oh, good. Carolynn. Just checking—I saw this room flagged for code watch and wanted to see who was on tonight."

Code watch?

Fuck.

"I'm here all night," Carolynn replied smoothly. She shot me a quick glance, then turned back to the woman, clearly trying to shift the topic. "Jen, this is Via."

Jen waved at me, friendly enough, then turned toward Jon. "And this must be Jonathan," she said, her eyes widening slightly. "He's the patient the Telemetry girls were talking about earlier."

Carolynn grinned. "Oh, yeah. You should share that story with Via. I'm sure she'd get a kick out of it."

I wasn't sure I was going to get a kick out of anything, but a potential distraction sounded nice.

Jen hesitated for a moment before leaning in, her voice taking on an almost conspiratorial tone. "Okay, so, my friend CeCe is an RN on another unit, way down the hall. This morning, one of her elderly patients asked if the 'nice gentleman from down the hall' had died last night."

Seriously lady?

I blinked, unsure where this was going.

"CeCe told her no one had passed, but the woman insisted—adamant, even—that she'd spoken to him. She described him as 'just a baby, way too young to be in the ICU with heart problems.' And apparently, they had a lovely chat. Said he was polite, charming, and had remarkable eyes. 'Tiger eyes.'" Jen made air quotes around the words, clearly enjoying the story.

I froze, chills rippling through me.

Jon's eyes were exactly that—golden amber, striking, unforgettable.

Carolynn winked at me. "Sounds like our guy, doesn't it?"

"Yeah," I mumbled, unsure what else to say.

How was I supposed to process that?

"She said he visited her during the night. CeCe tried to tell her it wasn't possible, but the woman wouldn't let it go. Swore he'd been there," Jen added with a grin.

My gaze flicked to Jon, still lying there, oblivious.

How could that woman have known what he looked like?

When Jen finally left, I turned to Carolynn, my voice low. "That's true? What the woman said?"

Carolynn nodded, her expression thoughtful. "It is."

She didn't elaborate, and for some reason, that made it even stranger. Her words hung in the air, heavy with implications I wasn't ready to confront.

Chapter 22

Seated to the left of his bed, I appreciated a rare moment alone with Jon.

I rested my head in the crook of my arm, propped on the bed's railing. My other hand wrapped around his, careful not to disturb the catheter taped to the inside of his wrist or the IV further up his arm.

I stared down at my engagement ring, absently tracing the veins on the back of his hand with my thumb—something I'd always found strangely attractive. It wasn't just the shape of his hand but what it represented: strength, warmth, and commitment.

And soon, it would wear a wedding band.

That thought clenched my heart. I wanted that moment for us more than anything. Damn this fucking situation that was trying to steal it away.

Please, Jon. Please get through this.

Let me see that ring on your finger.

Let me have that moment.

My eyes drifted closed, clutching that thought like a lifeline.

Then, I felt it—a faint squeeze of my hand.

"Vee?" His voice came so softly, barely more than a whisper, yet it struck me like a bolt of lightning.

That one, single syllable. A breath of air for my drowning soul. Only he called me that.

I instantly straightened, turning to meet his gaze. He'd pulled the oxygen mask off just enough to speak.

"You're still here? You should get some rest."

"I *was* resting." My eyes, almost involuntarily, slid to the monitors, quickly scanning. Heartrate. Blood pressure. Stable—for now. I took a breath, willing away my anxiety, and looked back at him, his warm eyes.

Tiger eyes.

"You should be wearing this," I murmured, reaching for the mask. But before I could put it back on him, his fingers gently intercepted mine, pulling my hand to his lips. He kissed my knuckles, soft and deliberate.

"How are you doing? Are you okay?"

How can he possibly be so sweet, even while struggling like this?

I nodded, a watery smile breaking through as my eyes burned with tears I didn't want to shed. Not now.

For a split second, unease slithered through me like a cold draft. "I should get the nurse," I said, starting to rise.

"No—wait." His voice was a tether, warm and grounding. His eyes met mine, full of quiet strength. "Just us. Just for a minute."

He reached up and brushed a strand of hair behind my ear. Such a small, familiar gesture, but it melted the tension gripping my chest in a way only he could.

I laid my head back down, resting on my arm, this time I turned to watch his face. He looked pale, and the purplish circles under his eyes were sharper than ever, accentuating his exhaustion.

But his smile—it was soft, steady, encouraging.

It wasn't much. Just a moment. But it was exactly what I needed.

***

The ICU couch wasn't exactly comfortable, but it didn't matter—I wouldn't have slept any better anywhere else. I'd woken up stiff and unrested for the second morning in a row, tangled in the hospital-issued blanket, feeling more like a fixture in the room than a visitor.

Jon had woken up multiple times throughout the night, each time only briefly. Whether it was from discomfort or the sheer absurdity of his current situation, I wasn't sure. But exhaustion always won.

That morning, he seemed a little better—awake for nearly an hour straight, giving us all a sliver of hope.

Then, with Mike, Jeff, and Sharron at my side, we found ourselves in a hauntingly familiar situation: seated across from Dr. Brookens, discussing Jon's fragile state.

Only this time, the topic of conversation was heart failure.

As always, Brookens explained the complexities of Jon's condition with meticulous care, his words measured but not sugar-coated. He detailed the factors contributing to Jon's alarmingly low ejection fraction and walked us through the cocktail of medications they were using to prop up his blood pressure. It was a delicate balancing act: supporting his circulation without putting undue strain on his heart. He mentioned the latest test results, which were concerning. While it wasn't unexpected after what Jon had endured, it left him teetering on the edge of further complications.

A silver lining, if you could call it that, was that the new medication had been effective in keeping Jon's arrhythmias at bay. Of course, the same drug was also contributing to his dangerously low blood pressure, but compared to the alternative—another cardiac arrest—it was an acceptable trade-off.

Don't lose sight of the small wins, Carolynn had said earlier.

She was right. That was a win. Yet it was hard to celebrate small victories when every moment felt like walking a tightrope over a bottomless pit. One step forward, two steps back.

I'd settle for two steps forward, one step back.

Still, I clung to the thought that Jon could get there. He had to. We'd made it to day two, and that in itself was significant. I kept replaying Brookens' words from the first night: the next 72 hours would be critical. We were halfway through the window he'd so ominously defined. And Jon was still here.

***

All afternoon and evening, it was more of the same. No steps forward, but no steps back either. And that, I kept telling myself, was good enough.

Jon had finally dozed off again when I decided to take a stress walk—maybe even call Krissy, if I could manage the energy to hold a conversation. But as I headed down the hallway toward the elevators, I saw them.

Shit.

Their neighbor, Cindy. She had Kyle with her. She was talking to Sharron.

They were sitting in the small waiting area by the elevators, Cindy and Sharron deep in conversation. Both of them crying.

Damn it.

Cindy had asked earlier if she could bring Kyle to see Jon. Under any other circumstances, the answer would've been a resounding *hell no*. Jon wasn't well enough, and Kyle wasn't old enough to understand.

Except... he understood more than he should have.

Kyle was smart—too smart for his own good. He'd overheard his parents talking two nights before, their words never meant for little ears. Jon might not make it. That's what he'd heard. And since then, he'd been inconsolable.

Refusing to go to school. Not sleeping. Begging to see Jon.

The doctor had hesitated, but ultimately, he left the decision up to Kyle's parents. *If he's old enough to ask, maybe he's old enough for answers.*

Now, here they were. And I still wasn't sure it was a good idea.

I sighed, my initial irritation softening as I took in the sight of Kyle. He looked lost. His hands were fidgeting, his big brown eyes darting anxiously between his mother and Sharron.

They weren't helping. They were making it worse.

He was taking his cues from the adults, and they were failing him spectacularly.

He caught sight of me then, his face flickering with something between recognition and relief. I forced a smile, waving as I approached.

Kyle sat up a little straighter, his voice barely above a whisper. "I wanted to see Jon. Is he okay?"

Something in me cracked.

This poor kid.

"He's sleeping right now," I said, forcing a bigger smile than I actually felt. Then, making a split-second decision, I looked at Cindy and Sharron—still lost in their own emotional spiral—before turning back to Kyle.

"Wanna come with me to his room?"

His eyes lit up immediately, his head bobbing in an eager nod as he scrambled to his feet.

God, I hoped I wasn't making a mistake.

Cindy wiped at her tear-streaked face and managed a grateful nod. "Thank you, Via."

I held my hand out to Kyle, and he took it without hesitation. "C'mon," I said, trying to sound cheerful, even though I felt anything but.

***

We had barely stepped two feet into Jon's room when Kyle froze.

I felt it before I saw it—his small hand tightening around mine like a vice, his feet suddenly glued to the floor.

His wide eyes scanned the room. The monitors, the machines, the wires, the IV stacks—all of it. And Jon... asleep, pale, fragile in a way Kyle had never seen him before.

This was not the same Jon who had coached his soccer team. Who had given him guitar lessons in the basement. Who had played video games with him on lazy Saturday mornings.

This Jon looked...

Bad.

Shit. He's going to cry.

My throat tightened as I tried to fix it. "It's okay," I said softly, reassuringly. "He's just sleeping."

Kyle didn't move.

"Well! You must be Kyle!"

A voice cut through the tension behind us, making us both jump.

I turned to see Dr. Brookens stepping through the doorway, his expression warm, his tone deliberately light.

He maneuvered around us, stopping just long enough to offer his hand to Kyle, bending slightly to meet his eye level. "I'm Dr. Brookens. I'm Jon's doctor."

Kyle barely whispered his response. "I'm Kyle." His voice was small, his hands still fidgeting.

The poor kid was scared to death.

His mother should be doing this, instead of bawling in the hallway—not me.

Brookens glanced at me and winked. A silent *I've got this.*

Then he turned back to Kyle, his smile kind. "It's really brave of you to come visit. Jon's lucky to have a friend like you."

Kyle twitched in my grasp, his face almost relaxing. Almost.

Then, his voice wobbled. "Well..." He swallowed hard. "I heard my mom tell my dad that Jon might die."

Oh fuck.

My stomach plummeted. I knew that was what he'd overheard, but hearing it in his own little voice? Out loud?

Brookens hesitated. Just for a second. And then, he nodded, like the weight of that truth hit him too.

But only for a beat.

Then he sighed, crouching slightly. "Well... your mom is just worried." He paused, lowering his voice like he was about to share something top secret. "But I know a secret that she might not know."

Kyle's big brown eyes flickered with curiosity. "What?"

Brookens smiled, gesturing to Jon. "Your friend here? He's one tough cookie."

And just like that—Kyle smiled.

Brookens grinned. "I'm serious! You know what I like best about Jon?"

Kyle's voice was still quiet. "What?"

"He doesn't give up." Brookens winked. "And neither do I."

Kyle's shoulders finally relaxed. I stared, genuinely impressed.

Brookens leaned in conspiratorially. "Do you wanna see something really cool?"

Kyle nodded.

And just like that, Brookens flipped the entire visit.

Within minutes, Kyle was grinning, perched on a chair beside Jon's bed, stethoscope in his ears. Brookens showed him the heart monitor, explained the numbers, made the machines less scary.

Kyle followed along, mesmerized.

When Jon stirred, Brookens glanced at me. A silent cue.

Jon was usually pretty groggy and disoriented when he first woke up.

Even though he was doing much better now than before, I still didn't think he would appreciate waking up to unexpected company.

Or a kid in his face.

Time to wrap this up.

I smiled at Kyle. "Hey, wanna go find Ben? Maybe he can introduce you to the new baby."

Kyle lit up. "Really?"

Brookens nodded. "And maybe, after Jon wakes up, you can come back to say hi."

Kyle slipped his hand into mine again, and I threw a grateful glance toward Brookens.

That could have been a disaster.

Instead, it was perfect.

***

"Do you think they're going to always dress her in pink?" Kyle asked, frowning at the memory of Abby swaddled in a light pink blanket. His disapproval was barely concealed.

I laughed. "Not if her Uncle Jon has any say in it."

We were waiting in line for Kyle's milkshake—my effort to kill a bit more time before heading back to Jon's room.

"Good!" Kyle huffed. "Jon won't let her look like a dork."

That made me laugh harder.

"Hey! Alyssa's one of the best players on your soccer team, and she wears pink cleats," I pointed out.

Kyle rolled his eyes. "Yeah, but she'd be way cooler if she didn't wear pink."

"You're a lost cause." I scruffed his hair, shaking my head.

Once he was slurping on his chocolate shake, I checked the time again. It had been twenty minutes—long enough that Jon should be more alert. A little more prepared for an energetic visitor.

As we approached Jon's room, one of the nurses gave me a wink. "He's all set for a visit."

Whew. Good.

Inside, Jon was sitting upright, propped on pillows, smiling as he chatted with Sharron and Cindy. He looked better, but still pale. Still exhausted.

"Hey, buddy," he smiled at Kyle.

Kyle shot across the room like a rocket, scrambling onto the bed without hesitation. He flung his arms around Jon in an enthusiastic hug.

Jon winced—*fuck, that had to hurt*—but he returned the hug anyway.

"Oh my God, Kyle!" Cindy gasped. "Get down! You're going to hurt him!"

Kyle instantly drew back, startled, but Jon tightened his hold on him, keeping him close.

"I'm okay," he reassured Cindy, shifting Kyle so he could sit beside him comfortably. That was a lie. But Jon would never let Kyle know that.

We chatted for a while, Jon doing his best to act normal, like nothing was wrong. Like he wasn't in a hospital bed, barely on the other side of a near-death experience.

After a short time, Dr. Brookens happened to pass by in the hallway. He paused when he spotted Kyle, then stepped into the room with a smile.

"Well, well! Look who's back!" He greeted Kyle warmly.

Kyle beamed. "Hi, Dr. Brookens!"

Jon looked confused, glancing between them. "Wait—you two know each other?"

"We met earlier." Brookens winked at Kyle. "Kyle helped me give you a checkup while you were sleeping."

Jon arched a brow at Kyle. "You did?"

"Yep!" Kyle nodded matter-of-factly. "I listened to your heart! It sounds AWESOME!"

His animated excitement was so pure that it made everyone chuckle.

Jon smirked. "Well, I'm glad somebody around here thinks so."

His sarcasm went right over Kyle's head, but the adults in the room lost it. Even Brookens had to stifle a laugh.

Once the laughter settled, Brookens patted Kyle on the shoulder. "Glad you got your visit in, buddy." Then he glanced at Cindy and Sharron. "We should probably let Jon get some rest soon, okay?"

Cindy nodded, already gathering her things.

Brookens gave a small wave and disappeared down the hall.

"Come on, Kyle. You heard the doctor. It's time to go." She said.

Kyle sighed. "But we just got here! He hasn't even been awake that long!"

Cindy shot Kyle a warning look, but Jon laughed. "You're taking good care of Maize for me, right?"

The diversion worked. Kyle immediately brightened. "Yep! And she's sleeping in my bed at night!"

Jon smiled. "That makes me feel better. Thank you, buddy."

Kyle nodded proudly, but before he could hop off the bed, Jon gently caught his arm.

"Can you do something else for me, too?"

Kyle stilled, giving Jon his full attention. Cindy, Sharron, and I did the same.

"Go to school tomorrow?"

Cindy sighed softly, nodding gratefully.

Kyle groaned. "How did you know I didn't go to school today?"

Jon grinned. "Because you just told me."

Sharron and I burst out laughing. Cindy did not look amused.

"Really, Kyle," she said firmly. "Now you've seen Jon—you know he's okay. You can go to school."

Kyle still looked skeptical.

"You gotta go to school, bud." Jon's voice softened into something almost paternal. "And soccer practice, too."

Kyle sighed dramatically. "When are you having your heart operation?" His eyes flickered with concern. "Are you gonna miss our game on Saturday?"

Jon visibly stiffened, caught off guard by the question.

Oh shit.

His eyes flicked to Cindy—who immediately looked guilty.

"Oh man, buddy." Jon exhaled, clearly searching for the correct response. "Yeah, I won't be at your game on Saturday. I'm sorry. I'll still be here."

The weight of those words hit the room like a ton of bricks.

And damn Cindy and Steve for putting Jon in this position.

Kyle's shoulders slumped. He looked crushed.

Jon didn't let go of his arm. "Hey," he said gently, waiting for Kyle to look at him again. "This just means you guys have to play extra hard for me, okay? If you keep up your winning streak, you'll make it to the playoffs. And by then... hopefully, I'll be well enough to come see you play."

Sharron turned away, wiping her eyes.

I felt my own throat tighten.

Jon pulled Kyle in for another tight hug.

I knew how much it physically hurt him—but he did it anyway.

"It's gonna be okay, buddy," Jon whispered. "You do your part, and I'll do mine. Alright?"

Kyle nodded, finally climbing down from the bed.

Jon held up his fist. "Deal?"

Kyle smiled and bumped it.

***

Sharron walked Cindy and Kyle out, and I moved over to sit beside Jon.

"Are you okay? How's your bruising?"

He winced, shifting in bed. "It's fine." Lie. He smiled anyway.

I shook my head. "You're amazing with him."

Jon sighed, rubbing a hand over his face. "So how much does he know?"

Enough to be afraid of you dying.

I hesitated. "I think he overheard way too much of a conversation that wasn't meant for him."

Jon exhaled sharply. "Fuck."

I nodded. "But you handled it perfectly."

Jon gave me a small, tired smile.

Then—he chuckled. "So do you think the little shit has really been playing hooky?"

I blinked at him. "What do you mean?"

Jon raised a brow. "I mean, was he actually skipping school?"

Wait... what?

"I know he didn't go yesterday or today," I said. "He's been too upset. Cindy didn't tell you?"

Jon frowned. "No. She didn't mention it."

My stomach flipped.

"Then how did you know?"

Jon shrugged, looking unbothered. "I don't know. I just had a hunch."

For a moment, I felt that same eerie feeling from before.

Like when Carolynn and I talked about the blue light.

Like when he remembered things he shouldn't have been able to remember.

But his exhaustion was catching up to him—his body finally giving out after spending so much energy pretending he was okay.

No more questions.

Not now.

He needed to rest.

Chapter 23

I stepped out of the elevator and turned right. By now, I could walk this path in my sleep—and probably had. But that morning, following a shower and a power nap at the hotel, I felt more rested than I had in days.

Still, as I approached the ICU, the familiar knot of nervousness settled in. It's amazing how quickly uncertainty can become the only certainty. The last 72 hours had taught me one thing: certainty was an illusion. Progress could vanish in an instant.

He'd been awake more often the day before, held longer conversations. But I'd already learned that these things couldn't be trusted. These things can turn on a dime...

Where will we be, today? A step forward, or a step back?

Entering Jon's room, I was greeted by something I hadn't seen in what felt like forever: a genuine grin, complete with dimples. It caught me off guard, a welcome change. And there was something else different—something tangible.

The arterial line was gone, replaced by a simple blood pressure cuff wrapped around his arm. No more invasive monitoring.

"They took away your ART line?" I asked excitedly.

Jon nodded, his grin widening. "I'm officially stable."

Stable. The word immersed me like a ray of sunshine.

"They're going to be moving me out of here soon." He added with a casual tone that didn't match the significance of the milestone.

"What??" I said with astonishment. I leaned toward him, hugging him close. Careful not to squeeze too tight. If I could have pulled his whole being into

mine, I would have. "Jon, that's incredible." I whispered into his neck, before backing away to look him in the eyes.

He shrugged. "Baby steps." His voice was nonchalant, but his eyes held a spark that I'd been missing for days.

"It's not a baby step. It's a big deal!" I said, and it was.

He's stable. Without an ART line.

That meant they were satisfied there was no risk of his blood pressure tanking. No more abrupt, scary fluctuations in his vitals. This was in fact, a very big step.

"So, where are they moving you to?" I asked with a mixture of curiosity and excitement.

Before he could answer, Elizabeth bounced in. "Liz" was the youngest of the RNs that had been caring for him. I guessed she was probably not more than a few years older than Jon. Since day 1, she'd been very friendly with all of us. She found him attractive, I suspected, although she'd never been anything but professional. And how could I blame her? She'd have to be blind not to notice.

She'd also instantly recognized him, from FR. She'd chatted a few times with Mike and I, about the band and their music. She was a fan. Had even been to one of their shows.

"Hey, good morning!" She said to me cheerfully. She looked at Jon, beaming. "Did you see? He's been upgraded from analog to digital!" She pointed toward the cuff around his arm.

I nodded, laughing.

"How'd ya like my audio pun?" she teased.

Jon gave her a blasé smile. "Nice. I see what you did there."

"So what happens next?" I inquired, just as Jeff and Sharron rounded the corner.

The next few minutes were a repeat celebration, as they absorbed the implications of Jon's freshly upgraded status. During that time, Carolynn had joined us. The room was now abuzz.

I waited impatiently for the excitement to die down, and then asked the question again. "So, you're moving him?"

Carolynn nodded in confirmation. "Jon's stable enough to move to telemetry later today. He'll still be monitored closely there, but it's a step down from ICU."

I could feel the collective relief in the room.

"But –" she added. "Before that happens, we'll have another meeting with the electrophysiologist."

My stomach dropped like lead.

***

It was eerily surreal. Only a few days ago, everything was normal.

Now, I was sitting in a hospital room with Jon's cardiologist Dr. Brookens, *and* his electrophysiologist, Dr. Kahn.

We were bracing for an update on his procedure, but Dr. Brookens spent the first few moments praising the fact that Jon was stable, allowing us another opportunity to feel some relief before breaking news that was harder to hear.

With a kind but somber expression, he explained that Jon's heart was still struggling. His ejection fraction was still lower than they would have liked, and he hadn't regained enough strength yet. He needed more time to recover.

My stomach dropped, even though I'd suspected it. Hearing it made it real.

Jon nodded slightly, but his expression was unreadable. *Is he resigned, detached, or simply too exhausted to show how he feels? I can't tell.*

Dr. Kahn launched into a longer explanation about how the heart needs time to heal after an arrest, explained the risks of proceeding too soon, and discussed how waiting would help ensure the best possible outcome for ICD implantation. He provided a lot of detail to support a simple fact: Jon wasn't ready, and we had no choice but to wait.

They gave us time to absorb the information and ask questions. Jon was agreeable, yet stoic.

The rest of us seemed to be grappling with a mix of emotions—relief and fear tangled together, like finding a moment of calm in a storm that wasn't yet over.

When the doctors finished, silence settled over the room like a heavy blanket. Finally, Jeff spoke. "We'll take this one step at a time. Right, Jon?"

Jon gave a faint smile. "Baby steps," he echoed. It was something, at least—a small flicker of the person he used to be.

***

My footsteps echoed softly as I walked through the upstairs hallway that afternoon. The house felt cavernous and unnaturally still, like it was holding its breath, waiting for life to return. Not even Maize was there to greet me when I stepped inside. She was with the neighbors, probably wearing Kyle out with endless games of fetch. But the silence pressed in, heavy and smothering, wrapping around me like a weighted blanket.

While they were settling Jon into his new room, it seemed like a good time for me to head home and grab some essentials for him. A few comfortable changes of clothes, clean but presentable enough for the hospital. Notes and textbooks he'd specifically requested.

Mike had driven me back in Jon's truck. It had been sitting idle in the hospital parking lot for four days, much like its owner—stuck in limbo. When Mike offered to drive it home, Jon had agreed with a curt nod, though the unspoken implications hung in the air between them: Jon's world had narrowed to the confines of the hospital, his independence traded for quiet reliance.

We climbed into the Tacoma, closing the doors against the brisk air. For a moment, silence lingered.

"Fuck," Mike muttered finally, his voice heavy. "That sucked."

I nodded, but the words felt too big to respond to. The ride home passed mostly in silence, each of us lost in our own thoughts.

Now, as I packed Jon's things into his weathered backpack, my mind refused to settle. The far corner of his room drew my attention—a shrine to his music, with guitars hanging neatly on the wall and a few favorites resting on stands, quiet and waiting. It was hard to look at them, knowing how much of himself he had poured into his music.

How long will it be before he plays again?

Will he play again?

Music wasn't just a hobby for Jon; it was his identity. How would he cope without it?

My gaze shifted to a stack of music manuscript notebooks on the desk. The thought came suddenly: *Should I bring them?* Even now, Jon could score music in his head, translating notes and chords into something tangible without touching an instrument. It was a rare gift—one that had earned him his scholarship. Music was how he expressed himself, his subdued personality finding its voice through melody and rhythm.

Maybe having a creative outlet would help occupy his mind while his body recovered.

Or maybe seeing the notebooks would only frustrate him.

The uncertainty lingered, but I decided it was worth the gamble.

After a quick shower, I rummaged through a pile of my own belongings that had collected in a corner of his room. I managed to piece together a clean outfit, but remembering how cold the hospital could be, I opened his closet again and grabbed an oversized black hoodie. Pulling it on, I felt a small pang of comfort in the familiar fabric.

Chapter 24

The new room was smaller—maybe a touch cozier, though it still felt sterile, crowded with equipment and those persistent blinking lights. It was only down the hall from where he'd been before, the ICU still close enough to remind me how far he had to go.

"Thanks, Vee," Jon said as he pulled his books out of the backpack. My heart hitched as I watched him sift through the stack, eventually landing on the manuscript paper.

"That's just in case... you know, if you get bored and inspiration strikes," I blurted, my words tumbling over each other as I tried to gauge his reaction.

He paused, staring at the notebook for a moment. The silence stretched, and my stomach tightened.

Oh God... what's going through his head?

Then, to my relief, he looked up and smiled—a genuine smile that softened his features. "Thank you," he said again, quieter this time.

Before I could respond, his gaze dropped. "Is that my sweatshirt?"

"Yeah. I was cold. Hope you don't mind."

He grinned, his voice lighter. "Nah. Looks better on you anyway."

***

It was nice sitting with him. Despite everything, a tentative sense of safety was beginning to creep in. Or maybe I was simply adjusting to this new baseline of constant low-level anxiety. Either way, I couldn't help but notice the changes. He was awake longer now, holding conversations that lasted more than a few exchanges. I clung to these small improvements.

The small wins.

The first nurse I met in the new unit was Julia, a warm, older woman with silver hair who introduced herself with a friendly smile. She chatted pleasantly as she worked through her routine checks.

"How are you feeling, sweetheart?" she asked, "Can I get you anything?"

"A shot of bourbon would be nice," Jon replied, his expression deadpan.

Julia burst out laughing, clearly charmed, but I watched him closely, unsure if he'd meant it as sarcasm or something else entirely.

When she finally left the room, I caught him rolling his eyes.

"What's wrong?" I asked.

"She's as bad as Carolynn," he muttered.

What the hell is wrong with Carolynn?

I wondered what had triggered this reaction, his irritation catching me off guard. "What do you mean?"

"With all the pet names," he said, still avoiding my gaze.

"You mean because she called you 'sweetheart?'" I asked, struggling to keep my amusement in check.

A beat passed before he turned to look at me, his expression serious. *"Yes,"* he said emphatically.

He's seriously bothered by that? Of all fucking things?

I took his hand, hoping to ease his sudden shift in mood. "Jon, Carolynn is amazing. She genuinely likes you. They all do. And I'm pretty sure they've been bending a lot of rules for you."

A few more seconds ticked by before he sighed. "I know. I'm sorry. I guess I'm just tired."

Not long after, he drifted off. I stayed by his side, watching the steady rise and fall of his chest.

His frustration felt justified, even if it was misdirected.

This is probably a good sign. He's feeling well enough to complain.

It was a far cry from the listless demeanor he'd had in the ICU, when he'd been too frail to care about anything.

Maybe this was actually another win.

***

The next morning, Jon was cleared to shower and change into some of the clothes I'd brought—a pair of soft running pants and a plain gray T-shirt. It was another milestone, one that felt monumental in the grand scheme of his recovery. I passed the time chatting with Ben and Jill in her room, trying not to let my nerves show.

Her and Abagail were both doing well. Thank God. In fact, they'd probably be cleared to go home soon.

I was happy to hear it—despite the irony of being stuck there with Jon. I could tell that Jill and Ben were feeling the same. Every time I'd been up to visit, Jill would inevitably cry. And sometimes Ben too—feeling a sense of personal responsibility for Jon's circumstances. Even though I'd explained to them multiple times that no one was at fault. And I meant it.

In fact, if anything, this whole cascade of events had been a blessing in disguise. Because prior to that, none of us realized he was at risk for sudden cardiac arrest. And if that had happened outside of the hospital—as it easily could have—he wouldn't have stood a chance.

So. If It had to happen, I was grateful that It happened in the hospital, just the way it had.

These were the facts that I reminded myself of daily. And now, waiting while Jon took another hard-earned step toward normalcy, I reiterated it yet again to Jill and Ben.

But when I returned to the room a short time later, the sight of Jon stopped me in my tracks. He was sitting on the edge of the bed, pale and visibly out of breath, the effort of being on his feet for even a short time leaving him drained. The nurses were already by his side, urging him to lie down.

"Your heart rate's too high, sweetheart," Julia said gently. "You've got to take it slow, at least for now."

I did my best to keep the worry off my face when Jon glanced over at me from the bed. "Look at me," he said with a wry smile, gesturing to his outfit. "All dressed up, and no place to go."

The other nurse chuckled but gave him a playful scolding. "Now, Jonathan, we told you this would take time. You can't do everything at once. Rest for a bit, and then you can try again later."

Jon was clearly not thrilled with the advice, but too tired to argue.

As we waited for his vitals to settle, the other nurse lifted his shirt to show me the wireless monitor, a sleek device that would let him move around freely. It was progress, albeit slow.

"Pretty fancy, huh?" she said cheerfully.

I nodded, forcing a small smile. But my attention drifted to the deep bruises on his sternum, now a dark, angry purple.

"Sexy, huh?" Jon teased, catching my gaze. He threw in a wink for good measure.

"Always," I shot back without hesitation, my response more earnest than his sarcasm.

His grin flickered, but the moment lingered with unspoken weight. It hurt to know he saw all of this—the monitors, the bruises, the limitations—as evidence of weakness. To me, it was just the opposite. Every day, my admiration for his strength grew, both for his body's fight to recover and for his quiet endurance through it all.

By the time Cary and Mike came to visit that afternoon, Jon was up again, wearing his zip-up hoodie. From a distance, he looked almost normal. For a little while, we could all pretend that was true.

We needed that.

He did too.

***

The next day unfolded in a pattern that was becoming familiar. With Jon finding ways to occupy himself between visits and much-needed rest, I felt comfortable stepping away for a while. I used the time to catch up on sleep, run errands with Nikki, and recharge. That evening, we met Mike and Cary for dinner at the diner we'd all frequented several times since It had happened.

Cary updated us on his and Tony's conversations with the label. It seemed FR would be released from any further obligations. The second half of the tour they'd been scheduled to complete in the coming weeks would have marked the natural end of their contract anyway, and now that Jon's participation was impossible, no further action was needed.

"Everyone's been incredibly supportive," Cary said, sitting across from me. "Tony and I have been flooded with calls and emails all week—people checking on Jon, asking if there's anything we need. Honestly, the response has been better than I'd hoped. The PR statement is ready to go out, too."

"Will Jon have a chance to look at it first?" I asked. Knowing how private he was, I couldn't help but worry about how he'd handle this situation.

Tony had spoken to him about it a few days earlier, gently but firmly. "Jon," he'd said, "we need to control the narrative. FR is dropping out of the tour. People are going to want an explanation, and if we don't give them one, they'll make something up. We don't want that."

To my surprise, Jon had agreed. He'd even seemed relieved that Tony was taking charge of the situation, "staying ahead of it," as he'd put it.

"Of course," Cary said, nodding. "Tony's coming down tomorrow to go over everything with him."

I studied Cary's face for a moment. This wasn't just hard on Jon—it was hard on all of them. FR had been on a fast track to success, and now, just like that, it was over.

"Are you okay? With everything?" I asked softly.

Cary met my gaze with quiet sincerity. "Livia," he said, using my full name for emphasis. "The only thing that matters to any of us is Jon's wellbeing. We're here for him, in whatever way he needs."

His words were slow and deliberate, conveying the depth of their true friendship.

***

After dinner, Mike and I headed back to the hospital while Nikki and Cary went home. Four visitors at once would have been too much for Jon, and keeping the excitement to a minimum was a priority.

As we approached his room, we saw Matt already inside. "Shit," Mike muttered, echoing my thoughts exactly.

Matt's presence was never welcome. His professional relationship with Jon had always been strained, despite Matt's attempts to play the role of buddy. As Jon's agent, Matt constantly pushed for more public appearances and new vendor partnerships—things Jon actively avoided. Their clashes had become infamous.

"Hey, guys!" Matt greeted us with an overly cheerful smile, oblivious to the tension he was causing. He motioned toward Jon, grinning. "I was just telling him how he always manages to step in shit and still come out smelling like a rose!"

What the fuck?

I blinked, stunned by the audacity of his comment.

"What?" Mike snapped, his tone sharp.

"He looks great!" Matt said, entirely missing the point.

Neither of us responded, and the room fell into an awkward silence as Matt continued to drone on about "exciting new opportunities." It was completely inappropriate, and I could see the stress visibly building in Jon. The monitor confirmed it—his heart rate had been steadily climbing since we'd walked in.

We need to get Matt out of here.

I shot Mike a look, subtly tilting my head toward the door. He caught on immediately and stood. "Matt, we were just coming to say goodnight to Jon. He needs to rest."

Matt hesitated for a moment, still grinning broadly. "Okay, okay, I can take a hint," he said with a laugh. But instead of leaving, he rambled on for another minute, oblivious to the tension in the room. Finally, he walked out, his voice carrying down the hallway.

Jon let out a long, audible sigh, absently running a hand over his head.

"You good?" Mike asked, his voice low.

"Yeah," Jon replied quietly, though his irritation was clear. "I just can't... with him." He trailed off, rubbing his temple.

"He's an asshole," I said bluntly.

The room fell silent for a moment. Then Jon glanced toward the corner of the room, his agitation flaring again. "And *that,*" he said, pointing to an excessively oversized vase of flowers, "is fucking ridiculous."

We couldn't help but laugh. It was classic Matt—always trying to impress, but his efforts rang hollow.

What the hell is Jon going to do with flowers?

Judging by the way he glared at the arrangement, I guessed he'd like to shove them somewhere Matt wouldn't appreciate.

Chapter 25

The following afternoon, Sharron and I grabbed lunch together in the hospital café after visiting Jill and the baby. I'd held her for the first time—so tiny in my arms that I was almost afraid I'd break her.

"You'll catch on when it's your turn," Sharron said with a knowing smile. She and Jill exchanged a glance, one I deliberately chose to ignore.

When we returned upstairs, Dr. Brookens was finishing up with Jon.

He greeted us. "Is it just the two of you today, or... is Jeff around? Anybody else?"

Unease prickled at the back of my neck. Why was he asking?

"Jeff's here somewhere," Sharron said cautiously.

Brookens nodded. "Okay. Why don't you see if you can track him down? Let's all meet back here in, say, 15 minutes."

My stomach clenched. His tone felt cryptic, unsettling. What was wrong? Why did we suddenly need a family meeting? My mind raced, anxiety bubbling up to a level I hadn't felt since the ICU.

Sharron's face reflected my own apprehension. "I'll call Jeff," she said shakily, glancing at me before hurrying out of the room.

Left alone with Jon, the air felt thick, heavy with unspoken worries. I couldn't muster the energy for small talk.

"I wonder what that's about," I said aloud, my voice barely above a whisper.

Jon shrugged, forcing a faint smile. "Guess we'll find out." But the look in his eyes betrayed him—resignation, mingled with weariness.

I reached over and took his hand, squeezing gently, unsure what else to do.

A few minutes later, Sharron reappeared with Jeff in tow. Their matching expressions were grim.

"What's going on?" Jeff asked Jon softly. "You feeling okay?"

Jon shrugged again, then nodded. His demeanor said he was bracing himself, preparing for another blow.

The room grew quieter still, the ticking of the wall clock filling the silence.

Finally, Brookens returned, Julia following a step behind. She nodded at us but said nothing, leaning against a cabinet like an observer waiting for a cue.

Brookens shook Jeff's hand briskly before rolling over a stool and sitting beside Jon. His light blue eyes maintained their usual intensity, his expression unreadable. My stomach twisted into tighter knots, and I fought the urge to throw up.

Brookens straightened, taking a breath as he clasped his hands over his knee. He locked eyes with Jon, holding his gaze deliberately. "Jonathan, how do you feel about going home?"

Wait- What?

His words landed like a bomb. The silence that followed rippled outward, the weight of his question filling every corner of the room.

Jon looked as though he was trying to decide whether the question was rhetorical or a cruel joke. After what felt like forever, he smirked faintly but stayed silent. I could clearly see hesitation in his eyes. He didn't know how to respond.

Brookens offered a small, reassuring smile. "It's not a trick question. I think you're ready to have this conversation. With the medications you're on, your rhythm is stable. Your ejection fraction is still low, but that's expected this soon after your arrest. I'm hopeful it will improve over time."

He glanced at all of us. "Discharge doesn't mean you're out of the woods. It means you're stable enough to continue recovery at home under strict limitations. We'll arrange close follow-up—repeat imaging, rhythm monitoring. If there's any concern, we act fast."

He launched into an analogy about strained muscles: "If you strain your leg, you stay off it. But your heart doesn't get that luxury. It has to keep working while it heals—that's why this recovery is slow."

Then he locked eyes with Jon, his expression firm. "You've been up and about a little. How do you feel after moving around?"

Jon hesitated. "I feel alright, I guess."

The doctor looked skeptical, like he didn't quite believe that. "Do you feel your heart racing? Any shortness of breath?"

After a pause, Jon nodded reluctantly. "Sometimes."

Brookens nodded back. "That's your body telling you when to stop. That's what you'll need to listen for, every day. If you overdo it, we risk setbacks—or worse."

"Yes, sir," Jon replied quietly.

"Good," Brookens said approvingly, his gaze shifting to me. "Something tells me you'll make sure he follows the rules." He winked, eliciting a chuckle from Jeff.

"We'll go over all the details and provide you with a list of instructions before discharge," Brookens continued, his tone professional but reassuring.

Julia nodded along in agreement.

"For now, do you have any immediate concerns about leaving the hospital?"

"No," Jon said quickly, his voice firm.

Of course he'd say that.

Meanwhile, a dozen concerns churned in my stomach, tangling with a cautious sense of excitement I hadn't dared to entertain until now.

Brookens turned his question to the rest of us. "What about you? Any concerns?"

Jeff, Sharron, and I exchanged hesitant glances, each waiting for someone else to speak first. I gave in.

"What about his ICD?"

Brookens nodded, as if expecting the question. He reiterated the concerns expressed by Dr. Kahn.

"How long?" Jeff asked. "Before he's ready for that?"

Brookens lifted his hands, palms up, a gesture of tempered honesty. "There's no way to know for sure. Some people never recover fully after cardiac arrest. Others improve significantly. Based on the progress Jon's made over the last few days, I'd say he's one of the lucky ones. And I'm hopeful we'll continue to see improvement."

The room fell silent. There was so much to process.

"The decision on your device depends on how much your heart recovers. Right now, we're giving your body time. If your ejection fraction improves, we can opt for a simpler device. If it doesn't, or if you have further dangerous arrhythmias, we may need a more complex system or additional heart failure treatments." Brookens leaned back slightly, addressing the room as a whole. "This recovery period isn't just about making sure you're strong enough for the procedure—it's about determining what type of device will best suit your long-term needs."

His explanation hung in the air like a heavy cloud, but Jon seemed unbothered.

Brookens raised an eyebrow, breaking the tension. "Now, what additional questions does that bring up?"

Before any of us could respond, Jon spoke up, his voice steady. "So when can I go home?"

***

"He didn't look too bad!" Krissy said with her usual upbeat positivity as the hospital faded into the rearview mirror. "I mean, all things considered. Has he lost weight?"

"Yeah... he's lost some weight," I replied wistfully. Weight he didn't need to lose. Jon wasn't a big guy to begin with, so the five or so pounds he'd dropped over the last few days felt noticeable. Especially when I hugged him.

"Well, still. It wasn't as bad as I expected. I was bracing myself for him to look awful. If that's even possible."

We both giggled, the tension easing a bit. I wasn't sure it *was* possible, actually.

"It was pretty awful, for a while," I admitted. "It was really bad... right after..." I trailed off, unable to finish the thought.

Krissy didn't push. Instead, she changed the subject, pulling into the Starbucks drive-thru. "Let's stop for lattes."

She had offered to pick me up from the hospital and drive me back to our shared apartment, despite the hour-long trip. I hadn't been home since It happened. I needed things—clothes, personal items, and my car.

After the unexpected conversation with Dr. Brookens, it was decided Jon shouldn't be left alone for a while, at least until he got settled into a routine. Jeff's long, irregular hours, and Sharron's frequent work travel made that challenging. Sharron had even offered to cancel her upcoming trip to Chicago, but Jon had adamantly—and predictably—insisted she go. I'd had to turn my back during their conversation to hide my smirk. He wouldn't be able to stand her hovering, and she wouldn't have been able to stop herself.

Luckily, I still had my spring break coming up. If there could be such a thing as "perfect timing" for all this, Jon had found it. I'd pack enough to stay at his place for the next couple weeks. Ironically, the same couple weeks we'd been planning to tour the west coast. It's funny how quickly plans can turn on a dime.

***

The savory smell of spices greeted us as we walked into the apartment.

"Hi, luv!" Kenny called from the kitchen. "I hope you're hungry!"

I followed the delicious scent and found him and Justin bustling around, cooking what appeared to be an elaborate Mexican dinner. They each greeted me with a warm hug. I was touched. It was rare for all four of us to be home at the same time, but Krissy must have told them she was picking me up, and they'd made a point to be here.

"How's Jon?" Justin asked, his expression sincere.

I shrugged. "He's been through it. But... he's doing well, considering. They might be sending him home as soon as tomorrow."

"He's one tough SOB," Kenny said with a nod.

We chatted over dinner. Hearing about Kenny's work drama and Justin's ongoing "women troubles" was a welcome distraction. When I reminded Justin that the plural "women" was likely the root of his conflicts, the whole table erupted into laughter.

After dinner, I packed several bags—probably more than I needed. Scanning my bedroom for anything I might have forgotten, I considered lying down in my own bed for a bit. But I dismissed the idea. A mix of anxiety and excitement kept me restless, and being this far from the hospital—away from Jon—made it impossible to fully relax.

Before leaving, I hugged each of my roommates, promising to keep them updated. With my bags in tow and keys in hand, I headed back, eager to be closer to him again.

Chapter 26

I'd barely settled into my usual spot by Jon's bed when an unexpected surprise appeared in the doorway. Ben stood there, toting Abby in a baby carrier, followed by a nurse pushing Jill along in a wheelchair. They were all bundled up, clearly ready to go home. Jill, who hadn't been able to visit Jon until then, had understandably insisted they stop by his room before leaving.

The moment she saw him, her face crumpled, and tears spilled down her cheeks. "Oh my God," she sobbed as Jon bent to hug her. She clung to him tightly, her arms wrapped around his neck. "I love you. I'm so sorry."

Jon let her hold on a moment longer, his hand rubbing her back in gentle circles. Their dynamic had always struck me as unique. Jill was nearly five years older, but Jon somehow slipped into the role of the protective older brother. I'd always found it kind of sweet, a subtle reversal of their expected roles.

Finally, Jon pulled back and straightened. "You have nothing to be sorry for," he said firmly. "This has nothing to do with you."

"Yeah... right," Jill sniffled, wiping her eyes.

Meanwhile, Abby had been fussing in the carrier through their exchange. Ben and I exchanged a glance, and I offered him a sympathetic smile, trying to mask my annoyance at the noise.

"She's mad because we stuck her in that carrier," Ben said with a grin.

As if to confirm his suspicion, Abby's soft fussing erupted into a full-blown wail.

"Can I hold her?" Jon asked suddenly, his tone calm and steady.

Jill's tear-streaked face lit up. "Of course!"

Ben set the carrier down and unbuckled the wiggling bundle of noise. Abby flailed as he lifted her out and handed her to Jon.

"Hey," Jon said softly, cradling her close to his chest with a natural ease. "What's all the fuss about?"

To everyone's amazement, Abby stopped crying mid-wail. The silence was so sudden it felt like someone had hit a mute button.

Jill's eyes widened. "Oh my God, you're a natural!" she exclaimed.

"I told you she likes you," Ben said, shaking his head. "I can't get her to calm down like that."

Jon smiled down at Abby, completely unfazed by their comments. He swayed gently, holding her as though it was second nature.

We chatted about Ben's parents, who were on their way from Lexington, Massachusetts, to visit. As we talked, Jon continued to hold Abby, who had mercifully fallen asleep in his arms. He seemed utterly at ease, as if holding her grounded him somehow.

After a few minutes, Jon carefully placed Abby back into the carrier, his movements slow and deliberate to avoid waking her.

"I don't know how you did that," Ben remarked again, shaking his head in disbelief.

I didn't know how he did that either. A strange feeling tugged at the edges of my awareness, like a faint whisper I couldn't quite catch. There was something about the way Abby quieted in his arms that felt... unexplainable. But before I could linger on the thought, Jill's voice drew me back.

"I hate leaving you here," she said, her breath hitching as she turned back to Jon.

"It's okay," Jon replied soothingly, his voice steady. "I'll be right behind you. I promise."

***

I woke up the next morning feeling stiff. I'd slept in the recliner in the corner of Jon's room, but "recliner" was a generous term. My back ached in protest.

"I'm going to stretch my legs and grab some coffee," I said, my voice still raspy from sleep. Jon was just beginning to stir. "Do you want anything? A decaf?"

Jon liked coffee as much as I did, but we'd been told he should avoid caffeine when possible.

"Sure," he said with a groggy smile. "Black."

I wrinkled my nose. Jon was the only person I knew who preferred his coffee black. "I know," I said with a mock sigh before heading out.

In the café, it felt strangely quiet—almost lonely—without the chance of bumping into Ben or Jeff. It amazed me how quickly the past week's chaos had settled into a kind of routine. As surreal as it had been, it had become familiar.

It's okay.

We made it through this.

That's all that matters.

Only days ago, I would have traded anything to be standing here, buying coffee on the day Jon was finally going home. But the reality felt heavier than I expected.

When I returned to the room, coffee in hand, Julia was helping Jon disconnect from the heart monitor. The device lay to the side as she peeled the electrodes from his chest and ribs. This was the final step. The last tether to the machines that had stood as silent sentinels, guarding him through the week.

The sight felt oddly final.

A wave of emotions swept over me, catching me off guard. I should have felt nothing but relief—elation, even. And part of me did. But another part felt like we were stepping off a ledge without a safety net. The machines and monitors I'd come to trust were being left behind. He was free now, but that freedom felt precarious.

As Jon showered and got dressed, I sipped my coffee, lost in thought. The muted hum of the hospital around me, the quiet shuffle of nurses in the hallway—it all felt surreal. My phone buzzed with a text from Sharron. She and Jeff were packing up, checking out of the hotel, and heading to the hospital for Jon's sendoff.

I stared at the message for a moment, the weight of the day settling over me.

He was going home. *We* were going home.

And the life waiting on the other side of this felt like an uncharted expanse.

***

I watched Jon with a newfound sense of appreciation as he packed his belongings into the backpack I'd brought a few days earlier. His movements were deliberate but unhurried, his focus shifting suddenly to the oversized vase of flowers.

"What the hell am I going to do with those?" he muttered, irritation flashing across his face at the memory of Matt's visit.

I glanced at the flowers, considering. "They're still really pretty," I offered. "Maybe you can give the vase to one of the nurses? They could take it to someone else."

Jon's eyes lit up, and he nodded. "Yeah! That's a great idea—I know exactly what to do with them!"

Before I could ask what he meant, he grabbed the vase and headed for the door. Curious, I followed a few steps behind, assuming he'd take them to the nurse's station. But instead, we passed the station entirely, walking down the hall, past five or six rooms, before Jon turned the corner.

"Where are we going?" I asked, quickening my pace to keep up.

"Right here," he said simply, stopping in front of a room and stepping inside.

"Jon!" I whispered sharply, glancing around to see if anyone noticed. "What are you doing?! You can't just—"

I was cut off by an elderly voice, warm and delighted. "Awwwww, lookie here, Bob! He came!"

I stepped into the room behind Jon and found an elderly woman lying in the bed, her face lighting up like the sun. Beside her sat an older man in a chair, his wrinkled hands folded neatly on his lap. The woman was beaming.

"There's my angel!" she cooed. "Look, Bob, I told you!"

I blinked, trying to process what was happening. Jon had walked into a complete stranger's room, yet they weren't questioning it. If anything, she seemed to know exactly who he was.

"Bless your heart, dear," the woman said, her voice trembling with joy. "Look at those beautiful flowers! Set them right over there, please."

Jon obliged, carefully placing the vase on the table beside her bed. The elderly man extended his hand, and Jon shook it.

"Can I have a hug?" the woman asked softly.

Jon bent down and hugged her gently. As he pulled back, she turned to the man. "Just look at those eyes!" she exclaimed, her tone full of wonder. "See? I told you."

Oh. My. God.

Tiger eyes.

The phrase struck me like a lightning bolt.

It was so specific, yet it had been there all along, waiting for me to connect the dots. Why had it taken me so long?

The exchange was brief, sweet, and unsettling in a way I couldn't quite articulate. Jon said goodbye, and we headed back down the hall.

"That was nice of you," I said cautiously as we walked toward his room. I wanted to ask more, but Julia spotted us from down the hall, her pace quickening as she approached.

"Where did you go?" she scolded, her tone brisk. "I've been looking for you!"

"Sorry," Jon muttered. "I was dropping off some flowers."

"Oh." Her expression softened, her sternness melting into a smile. "Well, you can't just take off like that. You're waiting to see the doctor. You *do* want to go home, don't you?"

"Yeah," Jon said with a grin.

"Well then, stay put!" She pointed at him like a teacher scolding a student, though her playful smile betrayed her true feelings.

"Yes, ma'am," Jon said, still grinning.

As we reached his room, Julia stopped abruptly, turning back to face us. "Did you give them to Mary?"

"Yes," Jon replied simply.

Mary. Had anyone mentioned her name before?

Her smile widened, and she nodded approvingly. "Good! I'm sure you made her day."

She turned to leave but hesitated again, pivoting back to us. "Wait a second. How did you know where her room was?"

The question hit me like a jolt. My gaze darted to Jon, then to Julia. I'd followed him absently down the hall, assuming he'd been told where to go. But now...

"How *did* you know where her room was?" I asked, my voice edged with disbelief.

Jon shrugged casually, as though the answer didn't matter. "I dunno. I guess someone told me."

"No, sir, we did not," Julia countered firmly. "We don't share patient information."

My stomach churned. I stared at Julia, then back at Jon, who seemed entirely unbothered by the exchange.

"I must've overheard someone," he said, his tone dismissive. He turned away, clearly done with the conversation.

Julia frowned but let it drop. "Alright. Just stay here now. Dr. Brookens should be by soon for your discharge."

With that, she finally left, leaving me alone with my spiraling thoughts. The question echoed in my mind: *How did he know?*

***

The doctor appeared a while later, his demeanor softer and slightly more casual than usual. He reiterated the most important rules, though the RNs had already gone over everything thoroughly. They'd reviewed Jon's medications one by one, listing potential side effects and specific dos and don'ts.

We were given an electronic blood pressure cuff and shown how to use it. For the first few weeks, they explained, it would be crucial to monitor Jon's vitals, especially with the medications he was taking.

Now, as Dr. Brookens ran through the restrictions *yet again*, I could see Jon's patience thinning. Sensing his growing frustration, I quietly excused myself and stepped into the hallway.

Julia was down the hall, writing on a whiteboard. A sudden compulsion overcame me, and I found myself walking toward her without fully knowing what I intended to say. She glanced up as I approached, her face brightening.

"Today's the big day," she said with an encouraging smile. "Are you ready?"

I nodded. "Um... yeah." I hesitated, choosing my words. "So, that woman down the hall..."

"Mary?" she asked, her tone still cheerful.

"Yeah."

Before I could elaborate, Julia raised her hand, motioning to another nurse. "Hey, CeCe!"

The name rang a bell instantly. *CeCe.* The name from that story I'd heard in the ICU. My mind scrambled to piece together the fragments. The nurse in the ICU had been telling me about her friend—CeCe from Telemetry—but back then, it hadn't seemed important. I'd been focused on Jon's precariously low blood pressure, and my brain had automatically sorted everything else into irrelevance. Now, though, the memory resurfaced, clearer with each passing second.

CeCe approached with an effervescent smile, her pixie cut and bright pink glasses radiating energy. "Hello!" she chirped.

"This is Via, Jonathan's girlfriend," Julia said by way of introduction.

"Oh, hi!" CeCe said again, her enthusiasm undimmed. "Your boyfriend has been the talk of the town around here! I hear he's in a band?"

Was in a band, I thought, but I didn't say it aloud.

"Via was asking about your patient, Mary," Julia said.

CeCe's smile broadened as recognition dawned. "Oh yes, Mary..." she laughed. "Boy, she swore up and down she saw him that first night he was in ICU. She even described him perfectly."

"I heard," I said flatly. My voice lacked the energy to mask my unease. "That was the night he coded." I stopped there, unsure how to continue.

CeCe and Julia exchanged a glance, one that seemed too perceptive. "Oh..." CeCe said, her voice softening. Her smile lingered, but now it felt tempered by sympathy. "I think I know what you're going to say. If you want my advice, don't spend too much time thinking about it."

Thinking about what? How do you know what I'm thinking?

"If you spend enough time working in these critical care units, you see some weird things," CeCe continued, her voice matter-of-fact but unsettling. "It's just part of it."

Part of what?

Julia nodded in agreement. "She's right. If you ask any of the seasoned nurses around here, most of them have heard a story or two. This one was especially compelling, though," she added with a small smile.

I stood there, staring at them, unsure how to respond. Words failed me.

CeCe reached out, giving my upper arm a light squeeze. "We don't know what happens to them when they leave us for a while," she said gently. "We just appreciate the signs when they appear."

***

Dr. Brookens was standing in the doorway when I returned, clearly on his way out. He shook each of our hands, then turned back to Jon. His steady blue eyes held a quiet sincerity as he extended his hand.

"Jonathan," he said. "Until we meet again."

"Thank you," Jon replied, gripping his hand firmly.

Brookens nodded once, holding the handshake for an extra beat. "Go easy," he said, his voice low but deliberate.

Jon nodded in return.

As Brookens disappeared down the hall, Jon grabbed his backpack. "Ready?" he asked.

The question felt so understated, almost casual—like we were heading to the grocery store. It didn't come close to capturing the gravity of the moment.

Just as he turned toward the doorway, Julia rounded the corner, pushing a wheelchair toward him. "Perfect timing!" she said with a grin. "Have a seat."

Jon looked at her like she'd lost her mind. His expression alone conveyed everything he was too polite to say.

Here we go, I thought, biting back a laugh.

"It's a long way," Julia said, completely unfazed.

"Come on, buddy," Jeff interjected, his voice calm and encouraging. "She's right. I've been walking this route multiple times a day—it's far."

That was true. The hospital was sprawling, and Jon would be exhausted by the time we reached the lobby. But I also knew this was a losing battle. I didn't even bother to add my two cents.

"I have legs. I can walk," Jon replied with finality. Then, perhaps not wanting to leave on a sour note, he squeezed Julia's shoulder fondly and added, "Thank you, Julia. For everything."

With that, he started down the hallway.

Julia rolled her eyes but couldn't hide her smile. She wasn't surprised.

As we passed by the ICU, the familiar knot of unease twisted in my stomach—a strange mix of dread and nostalgia. I glanced toward Jon's old room, surprised to find it empty. The glass doors stood wide open, offering a clear view of the central hub beyond.

There, a familiar figure stood with her back turned. She glanced over her shoulder, then did a double take, her face lighting up with a beaming smile.

"Praise the Lord Almighty!" Carolynn's voice rang out, her southern drawl unmistakable. "Get over here and let me see you!"

She motioned for Jon to come through.

Jon took my hand, and we stepped into the room. Carolynn met us halfway, enveloping him in a bear hug.

"Oh, honey," she fussed, her voice thick with warmth. "You look wonderful! Just look at you!"

While she fussed over Jon, I let my gaze wander around the room. It felt liminal, as though the space still held the echoes of those harrowing days. The memories felt both close and distant, like I was peering into a different timeline. A strange sense of déjà vu prickled at the edges of my awareness.

Carolynn's embrace pulled me back. "I'm so happy for you, honey," she said, her eyes misting. She looked again at Jon, her tone turning gently serious. "You take good care of this one, now. Okay?"

I smiled. "I will."

***

The four of us reached the front lobby and stopped, giving Jon a moment to sit down on a bench. I sank down beside him.

"I'll grab the car and pull up out front, okay?"

"Okay," he said softly.

He didn't argue—a sure sign that he was spent.

Five minutes down the road, Jon was sound asleep in the passenger seat. It struck me as odd, being the one driving. Jon had always been the driver.

But things were different now.

A kind of different that would take some serious getting used to—for all of us.

Still, as I glanced over at him, I felt the weight of gratitude settle over me. Jon was alive.

He was asleep in the passenger seat of my car.

And we were going home.

Chapter 27

"Are you sure you don't need me to stay?" Sharron asked, her gaze flickering back to Jon, who lay sprawled on the couch, oblivious to the conversation. He'd been out for about an hour after a shave and shower—two basic tasks that now drained him completely.

"I think we've got it," I said with a polite smile. It was only his second day home, and already he'd grumbled about Sharron's hovering.

She sighed, shifting her purse on her shoulder. "I suppose it's for the best. He probably wants me out of his hair. And Ben's mom is still visiting through the rest of this week, so they don't really need help with the baby, either."

I nodded sympathetically, catching the wistfulness in her tone. Jeff, waiting at the door to drive her to the airport, grinned slyly when our eyes met, as if sharing a secret joke about Sharron's reluctance to leave.

"We'll be fine," I assured her, wrapping her in a quick hug before stepping back.

I stood at the window, watching the car disappear down the street before collapsing onto the loveseat. "Just us, girl," I said to Maize, who paused mid-chew on her toy to glance up at me. She cocked her head slightly, her quiet acknowledgment oddly comforting.

Jon spent more time asleep than awake, which, under the circumstances, might have been a blessing. His medication made him nauseous, and his coordination was off—two things that rendered his guitar-playing impossible for now. He never said a word about it, though the absence of music in the house felt almost deafening. I told myself it was fine—it was temporary—but even I didn't believe me.

I looked down the street to see if Nikki's car was in her driveway. Maybe she'd want to come over and watch a movie.

***

As it turned out, I watched a lot of TV. That first evening with the house empty, Nikki and I binged The Sopranos, half-watching and half-chatting. I missed a lot of the details. But the company? Worth it.

At one point, Nikki glanced at Jon, her brow furrowed. "I don't think he's moved the whole time I've been here," she said, keeping her voice low.

For a moment, we both just sat there, watching him.

"Mike mentioned they talked earlier today," Nikki said, breaking the silence. "Jon's the one who brought up moving the gear from the storage unit into the basement."

Ah. So that's why he got so quiet. The phone call.

After he'd hung up with Mike, Jon had seemed… off. Distant. Brooding, even.

It made sense, though. Between them, the band had amassed an impressive collection of gear—some of it still sitting in the trailer they used for shows. With their schedule cleared, Jon wouldn't want the expensive equipment collecting dust in a storage unit a few miles away. But I knew him. The thought of moving it back into the basement probably hit him like a gut punch. It was like signing a lease on a future he didn't want to imagine yet.

"Do you think he's really okay with that?" Nikki asked, her voice careful.

I shrugged. "I doubt it. But what's the alternative? They can't just leave it sitting there."

We sat in silence again, each caught in our own thoughts.

"What about Mike? Is he okay with that?" I asked. Jon wasn't the only one whose world had flipped upside down.

Nikki shifted, thoughtful. "I think he's just... worried about Jon. He hasn't had the chance to think about anything else yet."

That seemed to be the common theme for everyone. Unprocessed emotions, and overwhelming concern.

***

The next day was quiet. Just me and Maize while Jon slept off another rough morning. His routine had become heartbreakingly predictable: wake up, vomit, take the pills that made him sick, then fall back asleep. Rinse and repeat.

I hated watching him like this. It made me feel helpless. Like I should be doing more, even though I knew there wasn't anything to fix.

He didn't talk about it much, which somehow made it worse. "Fine" was all I ever got when I asked how he was feeling. That was it. One word. If I pressed, he'd just shut down. Most of the time, he seemed... somewhere else. Lost in a world I couldn't see, and he couldn't explain.

The only time he seemed to spark was during a visit from Mike, who found himself on the receiving end of Jon's mounting frustrations. He'd come over to move the gear down to the basement. As Mike unloaded his 4Runner, Jon grabbed an amp and made his way to the basement stairs.

"Whoa, I've got it," Mike said, stepping forward to take the load.

Jon recoiled sharply. "*I've* got it!" he snapped, his voice brittle. "I'm not a fucking invalid!"

The outburst stunned us both. It wasn't like Jon to lash out, especially at Mike.

"It's cool." Mike had said to me later in the driveway. "I shouldn't have stepped in like that."

"He shouldn't have been lifting that heavy equipment." I muttered.

Mike shrugged it off. "I get it though. He's frustrated. Let's just forget it."

Afterward, the house returned to its quiet rhythm. Jon didn't mention the confrontation with Mike, and in fact had seemed to compose himself rather quickly, even offering an apology before Mike left.

That night, dinner was a protein shake—about the only thing he could keep down. I couldn't help but wonder how much more weight he'd lose if this kept up.

He threw a ball for Maize in the back yard a few times. Even she seemed to know he wasn't himself. She'd return the ball gently, her usual enthusiasm curbed, almost like she was trying not to wear him out. When he got tired, she didn't beg for more. She just sat there, wagging her tail softly, watching him.

It's like she could sense things were off. *He* was off.

We watched TV until Jon fell asleep. I picked up a book, the pages blurring as I tried not to think too hard about how fragile everything felt—but of course, I did.

Chapter 28

I placed my hand gently on Jon's shoulder, trying to nudge him awake. He'd already slept through his alarm—a first. I hated waking him, but it was time for his medication.

He didn't stir.

I gave him a small shake, ignoring the pang of worry clawing at the edges of my thoughts. "Hey," I whispered, leaning in to kiss his temple.

Finally, he moved, stretching slowly before opening his eyes.

Thank God.

He gave me a lazy smile. "Hey."

The exchange tugged at a strange sense of déjà vu, like we'd been here before—only in a different way.

"It's time for your pills," I said softly. "Do you want me to bring them up?"

He glanced at the clock, his brows lifting slightly. "Wow," he mumbled. "No, that's okay. I need to get up. Maize is going to want out."

"I already let her out," I said, smiling a little, proud of myself. Maize had followed me downstairs earlier, as if adjusting to some new routine. She'd stopped just at the edge of the patio, done her business, and trotted back inside without even waiting for her usual treat. She'd bounded right back upstairs and into the bed like she hadn't even left.

Jon looked over at Maize, who was sprawled diagonally across the bed, watching him like she was trying to read his thoughts.

"Traitor," he said with a lopsided smile.

Maize lifted her head, snorted, and licked her lips before resting her paw on Jon's arm.

I laughed. "I think she's hungry, though."

***

I was pouring my second cup of coffee when Jon wandered into the kitchen, his steps unhurried. I busied myself with the cream and sugar as he got a glass of water and took his meds, barely glancing at them as he swallowed.

"Do you want some toast?" I asked, trying to sound casual.

Silence.

Before I could turn around, I felt his arms wrap around me from behind, pulling me into a backwards hug. He kissed the back of my neck. "Do you want me to want some toast?" he asked, his voice warm.

I smiled, recognizing his roundabout way of saying no—but also offering to humor me. He needed to eat, and I decided to take what I could get.

Still, I wished his appetite would come back on its own.

As I popped bread into the toaster, Jon prepared Maize's breakfast. The clatter of dry kibble hitting her metal bowl echoed through the quiet kitchen. Then came the wet food on top, just how she liked it.

The can opener slipped from his hand, clanging onto the counter before hitting the floor. I pretended not to notice. So did Maize. She sat still, watching him with quiet patience.

As Jon bent to place her breakfast down, his foot knocked into her water bowl, sending a wave of it spilling across the floor. The sudden wetness made him stumble, sidestepping quickly. His elbow caught the empty dog food can, sending it tumbling off the counter.

Under any other circumstance, it might have been funny. I might have laughed at the scene—Jon fumbling through the morning while Maize sat serenely, waiting for her meal.

But today? Today, something about the way he sidestepped—like he was off-balance, dizzy maybe—made the humor vanish.

I tried to force a smirk, a feeble attempt to lighten the moment. "You okay?" I asked.

"Yeah," he grumbled, giving a small laugh as he reached for the paper towels.

I didn't believe him.

***

I puttered around the kitchen, washing the small stack of dishes from breakfast—including Maize's bowl. The rhythmic clinking of plates against the sink felt oddly grounding. I wiped down the counters, letting a quiet sense of accomplishment settle over me. This wasn't quite my house, but it was starting to feel close.

Eventually, I wandered into the living room and flopped down beside Jon on the couch. He was watching the news, though his face was unreadable—somewhere between disinterest and detachment.

After a pause, I asked the question.

"Did you check your blood pressure?"

I already knew the answer. He wouldn't have, not without prompting. But still, I pretended to give him the benefit of the doubt.

Jon sighed, his head tipping back slightly before he extended his arm toward me. No words. Just a resigned gesture that said everything.

The blood pressure cuff whirred softly as it inflated. I glanced at Jon out of the corner of my eye. He stared at the wall, his arm limp in the cuff, barely acknowledging the tightening pressure around his bicep.

A sharp hiss broke the quiet as the cuff deflated. The screen blinked to life, and the numbers appeared: 100 over 68. Lower than last night.

I stared at the tiny digits, willing them to change, even though I knew they wouldn't.

"Am I gonna live, doc?" Jon's voice was flat, his sarcasm cutting through the silence.

I ignored the jab, choosing practicality over a reaction. "We're just doing what they told us to do," I said evenly. "And actually, it's kinda low."

Jon glanced at the screen, his expression vacant. "It's normal," he muttered.

Barely normal.

I held my tongue. The numbers hovered at the bottom of the range they'd given us, but arguing wasn't going to help. Instead, I set the cuff aside and jotted the reading in the small journal I was keeping.

As I wrote, I couldn't shake the sense of awkwardness that always seemed to hang between us during these checks. Maybe he felt like I was invading his space. Whatever it was, I knew he hated it. That much was clear.

But if he wasn't going to look after himself, I would. End of story.

I decided to move on, changing the subject the way I'd learned to when things felt too heavy.

"What do you want to do today?" I asked brightly, forcing some cheer into my voice. "I was thinking we could do a little online shopping. Maybe pick out some cool outfits for Abby? Kyle's worried your sister is going to dress her in all pink."

Jon's shoulders eased, his demeanor softening as he let out a small laugh. "Sure," he said. "We can't have that."

***

After a late morning nap, I suggested we go outside for a bit. Jon had seemed lethargic—more than usual. His face was pale, and the pinkish-purple circles under his eyes hadn't faded. The sun was warm. Maybe some fresh air would help.

He agreed easily enough and even seemed to perk up at the idea. He grabbed one of Maize's favorite toys—a rope attached to a slobbery tennis ball—and she sprang to life, prancing excitedly as she followed us to the back door.

Jon drew his arm back and threw the toy hard, sending it sailing across the yard. Maize barreled after it, her enthusiastic "boof-boof" noises making us both laugh. She grabbed the toy and raced around the yard with the zoomies, her energy infectious.

Eventually, she brought it back, and Jon threw it again. This went on for a while, until he sat down on the edge of the patio.

It caught my attention. The chairs and table were just a few steps away, but he chose to sit on the concrete instead.

I walked over and sat down beside him, trying not to be obvious as I studied him. He looked really washed-out, and yes, he was sweating. *It's not that hot outside.*

I played mental tug-of-war with myself before deciding to speak up. "Maybe we should head inside?" I suggested gently.

To my surprise, he smiled faintly. "Yeah, I might go in for a minute," he said, nodding toward Maize, who was still bounding around the far end of the yard. "But you stay out here—she's not done playing yet."

The door clicked shut behind him, and I felt uneasy. I made myself wait a few minutes. Slowly. Agonizingly.

When Maize finally realized he was gone, she trotted back to the door, waiting to be let in.

As I passed the downstairs bathroom, I heard the water running. The sound made my stomach tighten. Feeling suddenly nervous, I sat on the couch and fidgeted with the remote, pretending to browse the guide but not registering anything.

Finally, Jon walked through the dining room into the living area, collapsing onto the couch beside me. He looked worse than before.

"Feeling okay?" I asked hesitantly.

"Yeah," he said, forcing a cheerful tone that didn't quite match his expression.

I wasn't sure if he believed that—or just needed me to.

I sat there, debating whether to push. Instead, I reached for his hand. His skin was cool and clammy, a sensation that sent a jolt of memory through me. It felt like before.

I pretended to watch TV until he fell asleep. Then I turned my attention to him, studying the rise and fall of his chest. Was it shallower than usual? Faster? Probably.

Eventually, I forced myself to get up and find something to do. Watching him rest was making my anxiety worse.

I started at the back of the house, tidying up just to keep my hands busy. I was vacuuming the rug in the front foyer when it happened.

The cord caught around the coat stand, sending it crashing onto the hardwood floor. The noise was deafening, even over the vacuum.

"Shit, sorry!" I called, flipping the vacuum off and poking my head into the living room.

It was quiet. Too quiet.

My smile faded as I realized Jon hadn't moved. Not a twitch. Not a muscle.

He's too still.

My heart pounded as I dropped the vacuum cord and walked over to the couch. "Jon?" My voice sounded hollow.

I placed my hand on his knee. Nothing.

I sat down beside him, gripping his shoulder. "Hey." My tone sharpened. Still nothing.

"Jon!" I said forcefully, panic edging into my voice. He was never this hard to wake up.

I braced myself, gripping both his shoulders and ready to shake him hard, prepared to deal with the consequences if he woke up mad.

Finally, he stirred.

He woke slowly, blinking as if through a thick fog. I watched, my heart racing, as he sat up and ran a hand over the back of his head, glancing at me like he was wondering why I was staring.

"Are you okay?" I asked.

His reply was delayed. "Ah... yeah," he said, his tone groggy. "I'm thirsty."

As he moved to get up, he stumbled slightly, taking another one of those odd sidesteps.

I caught his elbow. "Why don't you let me get it for you?" My voice wavered, betraying my unease.

He gently pushed my hand away. "I'm okay," he said softly, trying to reassure me.

I followed him into the kitchen, unable to quell the gnawing pit in my stomach. He managed to pour a glass of water without spilling, drinking it all at once before setting the glass down with a faint smile.

"See? I'm okay," he said, holding out his hands as if to prove it.

But I really didn't think he was.

I could feel it in my gut, gnawing with relentless certainty: something was wrong.

***

I stared out the kitchen window, tapping my fingers nervously against the countertop. The sun reflected harshly off the grill lid, still untouched this year. A robin hopped through the yard, plucking something from the grass. Probably a worm. Everything outside looked bright. Normal.

Inside, it felt anything but.

I turned toward the living room. *I'll offer to make him something to eat.* My own stomach churned—I couldn't have swallowed a bite if I tried—but food might help him. I thought I'd seen his hand tremble earlier when he reached for his glass. A boost in blood sugar could be good.

A boost in blood pressure would be better.

"How 'bout I make us a snack?" I called as I entered the living room through the dining area. My steps slowed. Jon was already asleep, his head tipped back against the couch cushions, his usual spot.

Already? It's been, what, three minutes?

I sat beside him. This was going to be a long afternoon.

I gave up trying to find distractions. My thoughts ran on a single track, and there was no stopping the train.

I curled my legs beneath me, adjusting the pillows so I could sit sideways, my head resting on the back of the couch. *I'll just watch him. That's all I can do.*

Somehow, my own eyelids grew heavy. Anxiety always had a funny way of making me sleepy, like my brain decided to shut down instead of spiraling further. I drifted in and out of a light doze. Not dreaming, but feeling dreamlike. Time didn't pass the same way in this new world.

***

A slight bounce of the cushions and a soft jingle pulled me from the edges of slumber. Without moving, I opened my eyes to see Maize had joined us on the couch, curling up beside Jon. She looked at me, her tongue lolling as she panted gently, her eyes steady in the quiet room.

My gaze shifted back to Jon, then to the clock on the wall. 3:30. We'd been resting for nearly an hour.

Slowly, I sat up and turned to look at him again. His skin felt cool beneath the back of my fingers as I brushed his cheek. I squeezed his shoulder gently, but like before, he didn't stir.

I reached for his hand, my arm resting over Maize's warm body. His palm was clammy, a stark contrast to her steady heat. For some reason, having her there was comforting.

I sat for a moment longer, my mind debating my next move. Finally, I readjusted my grip, sliding my fingers around his wrist to find the faint pulse just below his thumb.

I sat motionless, focusing intently on the rhythmic throb. The secondhand on the wall clock ticked steadily in my peripheral vision. Its movements felt faster than his pulse.

That couldn't be right. He should at least be keeping up with the clock.

Straightening, I patted Maize gently on her flank. She hopped down reluctantly, looking back at us once before settling on the floor.

I scooted closer to Jon, moving to the edge of the couch.

"Jonathan."

I slid my hand beneath the back of his head, tilting it forward slightly, as though helping him sit up. "Jonathan, wake up."

He opened his eyes, and for a split second, relief washed over me. Confusion flickered across his face before recognition set in, and he moved, sitting up slightly. I didn't look away, giving him a moment to orient himself.

Finally, his eyes met mine.

"Hi," I said, the word heavy with restraint I wasn't sure I truly felt.

"You're starting to scare me a little," I admitted, my voice betraying a tight edge of control.

That was a lie. He was scaring me a lot.

***

He sat quietly for a moment, staring into the middle distance like he wasn't fully present.

Where are you right now?

"How are we doing?" I asked, intentionally choosing an open-ended question. Something that would require more than a nod or a shrug.

After a beat, he nodded.

That's not an answer.

His detachment scared me almost as much as the way he looked—too pale, too still.

"Okay," I said, keeping my tone as calm as I could manage. My mind raced for the next step. "Do you want a drink? I can bring you some more water."

"No," he said softly, his voice distant. "I don't need anything right now. Thanks, Vee."

He seemed so out of it. I thought about trying to get him to stand, to shake off whatever fog he was sinking into. But remembering how unsteady he'd been earlier, I decided against it.

"Do you think you can stay awake for a little while?" I asked, trying to sound steady. My voice didn't feel like my own.

He nodded—just barely—and then closed his eyes anyway.

I don't even know if you heard me.

As he seemed to drift off, I made a decision.

"Jon? I'm going to check your blood pressure, okay?"

"Mm-hmm," he mumbled, not bothering to open his eyes.

I took a couple of deep breaths, willing my hands to steady. Kneeling beside him, I gently unzipped his hoodie, sliding his arm free from the sleeve.

The cuff whirred softly as it inflated, the sound mechanical but somehow suffocating in the silence of the room. The seconds dragged like hours as I waited for it to finish, each beep making my chest tighten further.

When the numbers finally appeared, it felt like lightning struck me.

88 over 60. HR 56.

This isn't right. This can't be right.

Adrenaline surged through me, making my vision blur for a moment. My mind raced, trying to process, to decide.

What do I do now?

A desperate thought flashed through my mind. Tamara. Nikki's sister. She was an RN at the memorial hospital not far from here. On top of that, her husband, TJ, was an emergency physician.

I thought I still had her number saved in my phone. Didn't I?

Tamara was Jill's age, and they were good friends. She'd already heard about what happened to Jon. She'd know what to do now.

My hands shook as I scrolled through my contacts, searching.

Please pick up. Please pick up.

Chapter 29

I opened the front door as Tamara's SUV pulled into the driveway. She stepped out quickly, her expression warm but serious.

"Hi, Via," she said, offering a sympathetic smile as she hurried up the walk.

"Thanks," I said, my voice tight with nerves. "Sorry to bother you on your day off. I'm just not sure what to do."

"It's okay," she replied, following me inside. "Is he still awake?"

"Off and on."

More off than on.

Tamara perched on the arm of the couch and leaned toward Jon. "Hey, Jon," she said brightly, her tone cutting through the quiet. "Can you wake up for me?"

He stirred, but barely.

She pulled a purple stethoscope from around her neck and pressed it to his chest.

Maize, who had been sitting nearby, stood abruptly, her body tense. Her tail went still, and a low growl rumbled from deep in her throat—a sound I almost never heard from her.

"Shhh, it's okay, girl," I said softly, running my hand down her back. "She's a friend."

Tamara stayed calm, her movements steady, but her eyes flashed with something that made my stomach twist.

"Where are his medications?" she asked, her tone too pleasant, like she was trying to keep things light.

"In the kitchen," I answered.

She set the stethoscope aside and looked at me. "Do me a favor—grab them. All of them. We'll want to bring them along."

The words took a second to land.

"Are we going to the hospital?" I asked. My voice sounded distant, like someone else was speaking.

"Yep!" she replied curtly, already moving to the blood pressure cuff.

In the kitchen, I rifled through the cabinet, my hands shaking as I fumbled with a box of freezer bags. I shoved all of Jon's pill bottles into one and rushed back to the living room.

The blood pressure cuff had just beeped. Tamara glanced at the numbers but didn't say a word.

I don't think I want to know.

She looked at the bag of medications and nodded approvingly, loosening the cuff and setting it aside.

"Okay," she said briskly, sliding an arm under Jon's back and propping him up. "Let's see if he can walk."

Walk? He can't even stay awake.

"Jon," she said again, cheerful but firm. "I need you to wake up."

To my surprise, he did. His eyes opened, and he blinked a few times, disoriented but awake.

"We're gonna take a walk," Tamara continued, not wasting a second. "Are you ready?"

Jon mumbled something that might have been an answer. Tamara glanced at me.

"You get his other side," she instructed. "We're going to walk him to the car and get him into the backseat."

I nodded, my anxiety growing, but Tamara's confidence steadied me enough to act.

Jon stumbled once but managed to make it to the car, where he slumped into the backseat. For a moment, he seemed oddly alert, his eyes meeting mine.

"I'll be right back," I promised.

He nodded faintly.

I ran back inside, grabbing my bag, my phone, and my keys from the hook on the wall. I darted to the living room to grab the bag of medications and gave Maize a quick pat on the head.

"Be good, girl," I murmured, my hands trembling as I locked the front door.

As I reached the vehicle, Tamara motioned for me to get in the backseat with Jon. She was holding her phone to her ear with her free hand.

I climbed in and shut the door hard, turning toward Jon. He was already asleep.

Tamara's voice broke through my swirling thoughts. "Okay," she said into the phone. "Be there soon."

She hung up and met my eyes in the rearview mirror. "TJ's waiting on us," she said reassuringly.

Not much could comfort me at this point, but knowing that brought a small, fleeting sense of relief.

***

The hospital wasn't far—as the crow flies. We made good time for the first couple of miles. But as we got closer to town, traffic thickened, grinding to a predictable halt at a stoplight.

The seconds ticked by, maddeningly slow.

Why is this light taking so long to change?

Every second felt like a mountain Jon had to climb. My mind screamed at the delay, but my body stayed frozen, glued to the seat.

Another block and a half passed before we stopped again.

"Via." Tamara's voice cut through the silence, calm and measured, as if we were having a casual conversation. "There's a pink duffle bag behind the back seat. Do you see it?"

I twisted around, peering into the back. "I see it."

"I need you to get it and bring it up here, please."

I pushed onto my knees, stretching over the seat until my fingers grazed the bag. Grunting, I dragged it up and over, finally dropping it onto the seat beside me.

"Open the big pocket," she instructed. "The one with the zipper, not the snaps."

I unzipped the main compartment, my hands moving without thought.

"There's a blood pressure cuff in there somewhere," she said, her tone still steady. "Under my scrubs. You might have to dig around, but it's in there."

I pulled out a shirt, a pair of pants, some books—finally, the cuff. I yanked it free.

"It's similar to yours," she explained, her eyes on the road as she veered onto a side street to avoid the next light. "It goes around his arm the same way, except the power button is on the side."

Nodding, I wrapped the cuff around Jon's arm, fastening the Velcro. My fingers fumbled as I located the button, finally switching it on. It felt like I was running on autopilot, every movement mechanical.

The machine beeped—a different sequence from the one I was used to. Then a solid tone.

"What's his pulse per minute?" Tamara asked, her voice calm and direct. "Bottom left of the screen."

I stared at the display, blinking.

That can't be right.

"Thirty-eight?" I heard myself say. The word felt foreign, hollow.

Silence.

"Tamara?" My voice cracked.

"It's okay," she said, her tone still steady. "We're almost there."

I glanced out the window. The hospital was just a block away now. I could see the top of the building peeking above the trees and rooftops.

Tamara picked up her phone. "Hey," she said to whoever answered. Her tone stayed even, but her words felt clipped. "We'll be there in a couple minutes." A pause. "Okay." Another pause.

I watched the mirror as her eyes darted to Jon, then back to the road.

"No."

The single word hung in the air, heavier than anything else she'd said.

I wondered what the question had been.

"Okay. Bye."

Tamara's eyes met mine briefly in the rearview mirror. "We're almost there," she repeated.

***

Tamara veered into the lot from a narrow alley entrance, pulling up to the emergency wing where the ambulances unload. The car had barely come to a stop before three people emerged from a large set of sliding doors, a gurney rolling between them.

One of them was TJ.

Still on autopilot, I got out of the car and stepped aside, watching as the team moved with startling precision. In one fluid motion, they slid Jon from the back seat onto the gurney.

He seemed blissfully unaware of the commotion around him, as they whisked him inside.

TJ's expression was stoic, his focus razor-sharp.

This has to be weird for him, right?

He knew Jon. They'd sat across from each other at backyard barbecues and birthday parties. Would that familiarity help him? Or make it harder? Are doctors even supposed to treat friends?

A light tap on my elbow jolted me from my spiral.

"Come on," Tamara said, her tone brisk. She'd already closed the back door and opened the passenger door, motioning for me to get in.

I hesitated, my eyes darting to the sliding doors where Jon had disappeared.

"I need to move the car," she called as she hurried around to the driver's side. "We're in the ambulance lane."

I hesitated for a split second, and then decided to go with Tamara. This was her hospital, and Jon was now in her husband's care—Dr. White.

***

Tamara parked in a side lot, and I blindly followed her into the building. My ears were ringing. My hands and feet tingled.

And worse—I was going to be sick.

My eyes darted around until I spotted a door marked **Restroom**. Without a word to Tamara, I broke from her side and bolted inside, barely making it to the toilet before I vomited violently.

Once the heaves had subsided, I stood there, trying to catch my breath. The ringing in my ears grew louder, and my face felt prickly and numb. I turned to the sink and ran the cold water, splashing it over my face in handfuls, not caring as it soaked my shirt.

I closed my eyes—no. That made it worse. I snapped them open, gripping the edges of the sink as I tried to steady myself. *Deep breaths.*

"Jon—deep breaths," Carolynn's voice echoed in my mind, unbidden. The memory sent a cold shiver down my spine.

Was this going to be a repeat?

I wasn't sure I could handle it.

I wasn't sure Jon could handle it.

"I fear he won't survive another cardiac event. Of any kind." Dr. Brookens' voice haunted me, cutting through my panic like a blade.

The dizziness swelled. My mind raced, and I tried to shut it off, but the thoughts kept coming.

A light knock on the door broke through the spiral.

"Via?" Tamara's voice came from the other side. "Can I come in?"

I willed myself to pull it together.

Before she could knock again, I opened the door and stepped out.

***

Tamara led me down another section of the emergency department. "Here, let's find someplace to sit," she said, guiding me into a small vacant room and pulling the curtain closed behind us.

I dropped into one of the two chairs against the wall without hesitation.

"Will you be okay for a minute?" Tamara asked. "I'll be right back."

I nodded mutely, and she disappeared around the corner.

The emergency department buzzed with distant voices and the hum of activity. This space was quieter, tucked at the far end, away from the chaos. The closed curtain gave me a thin layer of separation from it all, but not enough to quiet my mind.

Where did they take him?

Before I could spiral again, Tamara reappeared, holding a bottle of water. She handed it to me, and I drank half of it in large gulps, my throat parched and raw.

That was stupid, Via. What if you throw up again?

Tamara sat down beside me and placed a steady hand on my knee. "I'm going to go see what I can find out, okay?" she said gently.

Tell your husband not to let my fiancé die.

I nodded, the words lodged somewhere deep in my chest.

***

Time crawled. It felt like a lifetime, but the clock said it had only been a little over 15 minutes. I was starting to think time, in hospitals, wasn't a fixed reality but some cruel construct that stretched and warped, dragging my mind along for the ride.

"Okay," Tamara said at last, slipping back through the curtain. "It's as I suspected."

As you suspected?

A jolt of anger crashed through me, sharp and sudden.

"If you suspected what was happening, then why didn't you say anything?" I snapped before I could stop myself.

Tamara didn't flinch. She calmly reclaimed her seat beside me. "Because," she said slowly, "I didn't know for sure. I'm not a doctor. And I didn't want to tell you something that wasn't right."

Fair enough.

She turned in her chair to face me directly, her expression solemn. "Jon has something called AV block. It's when the electrical signals in the heart are disrupted. And it's being caused by his medication."

But... he needs that.

She hesitated, clearly unsure how to phrase what she needed to say next.

"What?" I urged, my throat dry.

"Well..."

"How bad is it?" I hated having to drag the information out of her. Maybe it was because we were friends. Either way, I wished Dr. Brookens were here. He always explained things clearly, directly.

Tamara shifted uncomfortably. "His ventricular rate dropped into the twenties, and that's really dangerous."

Cardiac arrest dangerous?

"Did he code?" I asked flatly, the numbness creeping back into my face.

"No," she said quickly. "They're inserting a temporary pacemaker. A catheter with a wire will be threaded through a vein into his heart." She gestured to her own chest, just below her left collarbone. "It will keep his heart beating until they can determine how to manage the medication that caused this."

My mind reeled, spinning with questions that refused to line up.

I needed air.

The panic was overwhelming, pressing down on me like a weight.

"Via?" Tamara's voice felt distant, as though it were coming from underwater.

"I need to go outside," I whispered.

"Okay, okay," she said quickly, standing to guide me. "Come this way."

I followed her down the hallway, my footsteps feeling detached from my body.

When I saw the exit door up ahead, I quickened my pace, brushing past her.

The moment I burst into the daylight, I turned and vomited into the bushes, the water I drank splashing uselessly onto the ground.

***

I sank down into the grass, leaning my back against the cool bricks of the building. The air felt heavy, and thick with humidity.

Tamara emerged a moment later. I was grateful she hadn't seen me throw up, though I was certain she could tell. Her concern was obvious, but I didn't want company.

I felt like I was teetering on the edge of a mental cliff, and I needed to stand there alone.

"Will you come get me when the surgery's over? Or when you know something?" I asked, my voice hoarse—whether from puking, anxiety, or both, I couldn't say.

She hesitated for a moment, then nodded. "I will."

I watched as she disappeared back inside.

The back of the building was deserted, save for the solid hum of HVAC units that merged with the ringing in my ears. No one would come back here. There wouldn't be any foot traffic, no interruptions. And I needed the privacy—to fall apart completely.

It didn't make sense.

No—that wasn't right. It *did* make sense. It just wasn't fair.

The past week had been an unrelenting rollercoaster, its emotional havoc eclipsed only by the toll it had taken on Jon's body.

But we'd come so far. Somehow, Jon had managed to pull through, to come home. It wasn't the same as before—our new normal was fragile, tinged with fear—but I'd been willing. I'd latched onto the strand of hope it offered, desperate to believe we'd turned a corner.

And now this.

It felt like we were right back where we'd started.

Except we weren't.

Jon was weaker now.

Still recovering.

How much more can he take?

I dropped my head into my arms, and the gates opened.

I cried—hard. My entire body shook with silent sobs, the kind that hollow you out.

I didn't know how long I sat there, crumpled in the grass, or why the tears were finally coming now. I'd been so good at holding it together all week. But now that it had started, I couldn't stop.

At some point, I felt movement nearby.

I lifted my head, blinking through blurred vision, and saw Nikki.

She must have come around the side of the building; the door I'd exited hadn't opened. Tamara must have called her.

Nikki didn't say anything. She just sat down and wrapped her arms around me, pulling me into a quiet hug.

And I cried some more.

Chapter 30

A heavy click and the creak of the door opening snapped me out of my haze. I'd cried myself dry and sat slumped, exhausted and quiet, with Nikki still beside me.

My stomach clenched instinctively. Tamara stepped out. "Hey, Via," she said gently. "TJ would like to talk to you."

TJ.

Or Dr. White, in this case?

Somehow, both.

I stood reluctantly, Nikki rising with me, and followed Tamara inside.

She led us back to the same small room I'd been in before. TJ was waiting. The sight of him there felt surreal. I was used to him as Nikki's brother-in-law, cracking jokes around a pool—not this.

Not here.

At least there was no need for introductions. Thank God, he got right to the point.

"The procedure was a success, Via," TJ said, his expression serious but soft. "He's doing much better now, with the pacemaker."

I nodded, too drained to muster much else.

"He's been admitted, of course. They're getting him settled in a room now, and you'll be able to see him soon."

That sparked a faint flicker of relief, though I kept my guard up.

"What about his medication?" I asked cautiously.

"We had a consultation with his cardiologist," TJ replied. "We're going to pull back on the dosage."

"Dr. Brookens said to do that?" The words came out before I could stop them. They might have sounded sharp, but TJ didn't seem fazed.

"Yes," he said simply. "Did they explain to you how amiodarone works?"

I nodded, then cursed myself.

Use your words, Via.

"It has a long half-life," he continued, "meaning it's metabolized very slowly. Sometimes it takes a while before it reaches its full effect."

I knew this already—Dr. Brookens had explained it before—but I didn't mind hearing it again. Nikki stood beside me, hanging on every word.

"The drug works by slowing the electrical signals in the heart," TJ said. "That's why it's so effective at controlling arrhythmias. But in combination with the beta-blocker, it slowed those signals down *too much.* That's what happened here. And this reaction has likely been building for several days."

"So, it would have just kept getting worse?" Nikki asked quietly.

TJ nodded. "You did the right thing, Via. Your actions saved his life."

I doubted that. All afternoon, I'd been replaying everything I could have done sooner, better. He'd almost died.

On my watch.

I pressed on. "What happens with the dosage now? How do we know we'll get it right?"

TJ hesitated, just for a moment. "We'll monitor him closely to make sure his heart rhythm stays steady without risking another block. In the meantime, the pacemaker will ensure his heart rate doesn't drop too low."

"How long will he need it?"

"We'll see," TJ said. "Right now, he's reliant on the pacing. Over time, we'll monitor how much his heart starts pacing on its own. Once he doesn't need the pacemaker anymore, we'll take it out."

I exhaled slowly, trying to let the relief sink in.

TJ smiled faintly. "Tell you what—let me go see if they're ready for you. He's already asking to see you."

A wave of optimism rushed in. "He is?"

"He is," TJ confirmed with a nod.

***

Nikki, Tamara, and I were still in the ER room when the curtain rustled slightly. Ben peeked in, hesitating for a moment before stepping inside. As soon as he saw us, he strode over and pulled me into a warm, lingering hug.

"Tamara called me," he said softly.

Shit.

The realization hit me like a brick—I'd completely neglected to call anyone else during my meltdown. Over Ben's shoulder, I mouthed a silent *Thank you* to Tamara. She winked in response.

Ben pulled back, quickly wiping his eyes. I figured my face was a blotchy mess, my eyes puffy from crying, but I was surprised to see that his were red, too.

"Uhh," he muttered, a hint of embarrassment in his tone. "I think I cried the whole way here."

"Join the club," I replied flatly.

"Well, we're all done crying now," Tamara said, her voice bright as she tried to lift the mood. "TJ was just telling us Jon's doing well."

"Really?" Ben asked, still dabbing at his eyes. "That's great. Oh—Jeff's on his way. Said he'd be here within the hour," he remarked, almost as an afterthought, glancing at me.

"Thanks for doing that," I said, meaning it.

"You've had your hands full today," Tamara added gently.

The nurse poked her head in, smiling cheerfully at Tamara. "Room 204. He's all set."

"You two go ahead first," Tamara said, gesturing to Ben and me. "We won't smother him all at once."

***

Elevators had become my personal mental reset containers. You step in, the doors close, and you pull your shit together. By the time they open, you're ready to face whatever's waiting.

Today was no exception.

Ben and I stepped into Jon's room. TJ was perched on a stool next to the bed, legs crossed casually, chatting with Jon like this was just another day.

Jon grinned the moment he saw me. It was the kind of grin I was starting to treasure—small, soft, but so completely him.

"Sorry about that," he said sheepishly, his dimples showing. "Are you okay?"

I raised an eyebrow. "I know you didn't just ask me if *I'm* okay," I teased, leaning in to hug him—not too tight, just enough to feel his warmth.

There was a clarity in his eyes, a spark that had almost disappeared earlier. I wasn't sure he realized how much his eyes revealed about how he was really feeling.

"You look better!" I said, relieved to see some semblance of his usual self, returning.

"I told ya," TJ chimed in. "He's alright. He's got this pacemaker to keep him in line now."

Jon's faint smile deepened. "I can't seem to get it right," he said. "I'm either too fast, or too slow. There's no pleasing these damn doctors."

TJ and Ben burst out laughing, and Jon's grin widened.

But I couldn't quite see the humor. There was something in Jon's tone—an undertone that made me wonder if he saw it, either.

***

I tossed an extra blanket onto the downstairs couch, along with my pillow. I'd showered in Jon's bathroom but couldn't bring myself to sleep in his bed without him.

After finishing my coffee, I carried the empty cup to the kitchen sink.

Jeff had brewed us a pot when we got home from Memorial—Jon's decaf, the same one Sharron had picked up a couple of days ago. "Figured neither of us needs the extra stimulation," he'd said with a grin.

He had Jon's dimples and dark hair, though his eyes were a deeper, chocolate brown.

I'd asked him what Sharron had said about everything.

He laughed. "I spent 30 minutes convincing her she didn't need to come home. She had to talk to Jon herself before agreeing."

"I'm surprised she agreed at all," I'd replied.

"I thought about not telling her," he'd remarked, a mischievous glint in his eye.

"Really?"

He snorted into his coffee cup. "No. Well... maybe." He wiggled his eyebrows.

I laughed despite myself.

"Seriously, though. You did good today, hun," he'd said, his voice warm.

I thought about that. He wasn't the first to say it, but the day had left me feeling anything but successful.

"I should have acted sooner," I admitted. "This could have been bad."

"You were here, and you were paying attention. Nobody could have seen this coming," he said gently. "I know my son. He wouldn't have admitted anything was wrong until he dropped over. And even then..." Jeff waved his hand, the gesture finishing the sentence for him.

I was still turning that over in my mind as I slipped onto the couch, pulling the blanket up around me.

It had been too close for comfort.

Maize jumped up beside me, circling once before curling up at my feet.

"I know, girl," I murmured, stroking her fur. "I miss him, too."

Chapter 31

"Wow, this came fast!" I exclaimed, carrying the package into the living room. "We only ordered this three days ago!"

Inside was one of the outfits we'd picked for Abby—a black and red sweatsuit and a black onesie featuring *The Clash* with the *London Calling* artwork. Jon's idea, of course.

He smiled approvingly as I held it up. "Nice," he said, then smirked. "Seems even more appropriate now that we know she's a brat."

I laughed. "That's not very nice."

He shrugged, still smirking. "Hey, Ben's the one who said it first."

That was true. During his last visit, Ben had gone on about how Abby always seemed grouchy and took forever to settle down at bedtime.

"Maybe she's just cranky like her uncle," I teased.

Jon smiled but didn't respond.

I folded the outfit and placed it neatly in a gift bag, tucking in tissue paper as Jon spoke. "What are your plans for this afternoon?"

It seemed like an innocuous question, but I knew better. I sighed. "I guess I'm going to read through the syllabuses for my classes."

"Good idea," he remarked, his tone almost parental.

I rolled my eyes.

Still not sold on the idea of attending classes at all.

***

I'd made up my mind earlier in the week to take the semester off. The thought first crossed my mind after It happened. I began toying with the idea after we'd all agreed I should spend my spring break at Jon's house. Convenient timing, sure, but we all knew he wasn't going to recover that quickly.

The day he landed back in the hospital with a pacemaker sealed the deal. And it wasn't just about being there for him—I was too preoccupied to focus on school. Anxiety doesn't make for good study habits. So, I resolved to hit pause. Just for one semester.

I'd also decided not to tell anyone. I didn't even tell my roommates. I figured I'd wait until it was too late to intervene, once classes started.

The problem is that through methods I still can't explain—*somehow*—he'd figured it out. His intuition had been eerily on point lately.

The first time he brought it up, I'd been hanging out with him in the hospital—killing time until he could ditch the pacemaker. He'd asked me about one of my web development classes.

Fortunately, there were enough distractions to dodge the question. Easy enough.

But then there was the ride home from Memorial.

Kicked back in the passenger seat, he brought it up again. "So, you never did tell me about your classes," he prodded.

My grip tightened on the wheel. Why was he pressing me about this? I shrugged. "I dunno. What is there to talk about?"

"Plenty!" He declared. "Which class are you looking forward to the most?"

I sighed. "I don't know. All of them?"

None of them.

He was staring at me with that same curious look.

"Viaaa," he said, in the same tone he used with Maize when she was up to no good.

I kept my eyes on the road, but I could feel his stare.

"Why are you grilling me about school?" I asked, exasperated.

"Because I have a feeling you're thinking of doing something dumb."

Shit. How does he know?

I sat in silence, scrambling for a response. No point in dodging—he wasn't letting this go.

"Livia," he said. "Tell me you're not thinking of doing something dumb."

I sighed. "I'm not thinking of doing something dumb! I've decided to do something logical."

"You'd better be ready to tell me you're finally getting rid of that steering wheel cover."

I burst out laughing. My fuzzy unicorn steering wheel cover drove Jon crazy. He was always trying to convince me to get rid of it. "The cover stays," I said, grinning.

A few beats passed before he asked, "Seriously. Is there something going on with school?"

Resigned, I told him about my plan.

His reaction was immediate. "Absolutely not!" he said, repeatedly.

"What would you even do all day?" he'd demanded. "Take naps? Watch TV? Watch me not play guitar?"

Even after we pulled into the driveway, we sat there debating for another ten minutes. Eventually, I promised to reconsider, though I was mostly just trying to end the conversation.

Still, Jon wasn't moving.

"Get out of my car!" I said, a mix of frustration and amusement.

"Not until you promise you're going to your classes next week."

"Uhhh, fine!" I moaned, pounding on my fuzzy unicorns.

***

Maize was mid-zoomie with her ball when the neighbor came sauntering over through the grass—Kyle's dad, Steve. Thank God Kyle was at school, or we'd never get rid of him.

"Hey, Jon!" Steve called, nodding at me as well. "Via."

"Hi, Steve," Jon replied, turning toward him.

Steve's eyes moved over Jon, taking in the weight loss, the worn look. He seemed to be working through his own silent checklist. "How are you feeling?"

"I'm good."

"I didn't expect to see you out here so soon again," Steve said, overly friendly.

So soon? Again?

Nice to know the neighbors were keeping tabs.

"It's a nice day," Jon said dryly, turning back to Maize, who was prancing impatiently at his side, ready for him to throw the ball. He sent it flying down the yard with a hard pitch.

"You sure you should be doing that?" Steve asked cautiously.

I saw Jon's shoulders tense, his jaw clench.

Shit.

"What? Play with my dog?" Jon's tone was cool, but the edge in his voice sliced through the air like a knife.

Steve shifted uncomfortably. I started to wonder if he'd been sent on a reconnaissance mission by Cindy—Sharron's friend.

"Well," Steve stammered, "we know how energetic Maize can be... border collies..." He chuckled nervously. "Boy, she sure had a blast over here with Kyle while you were—"

He cut himself off.

Smart man.

"Anyway," Steve finished awkwardly, "Cindy just wanted me to let you know we're here to help out if you need it."

There it is.

Jon turned fully to face Steve now, his eyes sharp. "What do you think is going to happen? If I play with my dog?" His voice was steady, controlled, but the resentment was unmistakable.

Steve shrugged, shaking his head as if to wave it off. "Nothing," he mumbled.

"Give Cindy my best," Jon said flatly, turning back to the yard and launching the ball with precision. The silent *fuck off* was loud and clear.

Steve took the hint and headed back home. "All right then, take it easy!" he called cheerfully, nodding at me again as he left.

I stood in silence as Jon threw the ball again, trying to think of something to ease the tension. "They're just trying to be helpful," I said quietly.

"Umhm," Jon mumbled, his tone dismissive. "They, and everyone else."

I assumed that was a dig at Cary, who had stopped by earlier that morning on his way to work—*just checking in,* like everyone else. Jon had been gracious enough at the time, but I could tell the constant inquiries were starting to wear on him.

The first few sprinkles of rain speckled the patio.

"Looks like playtime's getting cut short," I commented as Jon threw one last hard pitch into the yard.

He shrugged. "Seems like a good time to review a syllabus," he teased, giving me a sideways grin.

For once, I welcomed the shift in topic.

I rolled my eyes, grinning back, feigning more annoyance than I actually felt.

"I'll keep you company," he offered, his tone light again.

Chapter 32

We headed inside, Jon stopping to give Maize her treat. Determined to tackle the syllabus, I started upstairs, assuming Jon was right behind me.

I got to his room, still talking to him, only to realize he wasn't there.

I found him two-thirds of the way up the stairs, sitting on one of the steps with his arms folded on his knees, head down.

A jolt of panic arced through me. He was pale, white as a sheet, and in a cold sweat. My stomach twisted as I hurried back down to him.

"Oh my God," I breathed. "Are you okay?"

Not again.

He nodded faintly. "I just... need a minute."

I instinctively reached out, placing a hand on his shoulder. "What can I do?"

He shrugged me off quickly, almost defensively. The gesture startled me.

"Nothing, Via. I just need a minute, *okay?*" His tone was quiet, but irritation simmered beneath the surface. I'd never heard that edge directed at me before.

Something about the way he said it told me to back off. I forced myself to turn and head back upstairs, flopping down on the bed. Confused. Anxious.

A few minutes passed, my thoughts racing. Heart block. How it starts. What it looks like.

Is this what I just saw?

Finally, Jon appeared in the doorway. He still looked awful, his T-shirt soaked with sweat, a dark V-shaped patch down the front. He reminded me of someone fresh out of an intense workout.

I tried to reassure myself.

TJ said it could take weeks for his body to adjust. It's all normal for now.

But normal or not, he didn't look like he'd recovered fully. I watched as he went to his dresser, pulled out a clean T-shirt, and swapped it for the drenched one without a word.

I stayed quiet, uneasy. Memories of a few days ago—the couch, his shallow breaths, his cold skin—played in my mind, igniting fresh anxiety. I was trying to decide what to say or do when he caught me staring.

"What?" he snapped, his tone sharp.

"Um…" I hesitated. "Do you think maybe we should check your blood pressure?"

He scoffed. "No. I don't. I'm fine."

Oh, the fuck you didn't.

Anger surged, unbidden and hot. Was he seriously implying I was overreacting?

After everything?

"Are you serious? Dude, you are so FAR from fucking fine!"

Jon tilted his head back, sighing dramatically. "For Chrissake, Vee! Why bother? There's nothing we can do about it! It'll pass in a minute!"

"But they said we should check if you feel faint or woozy! Isn't that exactly what just happened?"

"Well, if you expect to check my blood pressure every *single time* that happens, I may as well be back in the hospital!"

The way he emphasized "single time" flipped a switch in me. His dismissive tone, the sharpness of his words—it all felt too much, and the molten anxiety I'd been suppressing finally erupted.

"You know what?" I exclaimed, my voice louder than I intended. "You probably should be in the hospital! Don't tell me you didn't almost pass out just now! But *nooo,* you're fine! Fine like you were a few days ago? Fine like *that*? When you almost fucking died on the couch?"

The words came out like daggers, slicing through the air. My own anger shocked me, but there was no stopping now.

"I think you should still be in the hospital. Yeah. I'd feel better if you were."

We stared at each other, the silence thick. His expression shifted from shock to something more muted—hurt. My words had landed like a slap, but I couldn't take them back.

"Wow... okay," he said numbly, shaking his head.

A moment later, he mumbled, "You're afraid to be alone with me."

Was I?

It was too late to take back what I'd said, and worse—I didn't want to. How could he still insist he was okay? Clearly, he wasn't.

My mind spiraled back to several days earlier. If I hadn't been concerned about his blood pressure, I wouldn't have called Tamara. She wouldn't have checked on him, and we wouldn't have realized how serious it was. He would have died in his sleep. That's it. That's how it could have happened.

So maybe I *was* afraid to be alone with him.

The anger inside me began dissolving into a familiar, gnawing anxiety. My stomach twisted uncomfortably.

Pull it together, Via.

I took a steadying breath and tried again, forcing my voice to stay calm. "Look, all I mean is that I can't help but wonder if they discharged you too soon." I hesitated. "It's not that I want you in the hospital, Jon. But when things like this happen, we *have* to track your heart rate and blood pressure."

He glared at me. "You are such a control freak."

"I'm not! We need to know these things! We have to know how you're doing!"

"You could just *ask me!*" His amber eyes glistened fiercely as he paced across the room and flopped into the oversized armchair in the corner. "You don't have to obsess over some stupid numbers."

No, I can't just ask you—because your answer will always be the same, no matter what.

"The numbers are important!" My voice rose in exasperation. "Why are you being so stubborn about this?"

He didn't answer immediately, sitting there instead in tranquil fury, his gaze fixed on the floor.

From down the hall came the sound of Maize playing loudly, her paws thumping against the hardwood as she entertained herself. The noise provided an odd contrast to the silence in the room, and finally, Jon spoke.

"You know," he began slowly, "when I was in the hospital, there were times—more than once—when you'd walk into the room, and the first thing you'd say was, 'How are you feeling?'"

"What, was I not supposed to ask?" I quipped, the sarcasm slipping out before I could stop it.

"Sure." His tone darkened. "But you weren't even looking at me when you asked. You'd walk in, and your eyes would go straight to those fucking monitors."

It hadn't registered yet what he was getting at, or why he seemed so angry.

"They were there for a reason," I argued. "It's pretty useful to look at them."

"Maybe so. But they weren't going to tell you how I was *feeling*, were they?"

Yes, actually.

I swallowed the retort. His point was starting to sink in, clawing into my gut with sharp precision.

"You use numbers as a coping mechanism," he said, lowering his voice. "You can't reduce someone's health—or who they are—to a few numbers on a screen, Vee. That's not fair. There's more to it than that. There's more to *me* than that."

I stared at him, dumbfounded. Was it true? Had I been guilty of reducing him to numbers? Of using data to make sense of something I couldn't control?

"I'm sorry," I said quietly, my words faltering. "I never meant to make you feel like..." I trailed off, unsure how to finish.

He shrugged, brushing off the memory like it didn't matter. But his eyes betrayed him—hot resentment replaced by a glimmer of sadness. He looked resigned.

"It wasn't just you," he muttered. "It's no big deal. I just... you're still doing it. Even now. Even at home. I'm a person, Vee. Not a statistics project, or a buggy line of code you can troubleshoot."

I was speechless. His words felt strange—unexpected—but they hit deep. Was there more to this than he was saying? I wanted to ask, but the timing felt wrong.

"I didn't realize it bothered you that much," I said carefully.

"I'm just tired of everyone giving me that look."

"What look?"

"The one where they're wondering if I'm gonna drop over. The one you're giving me right now!" His voice rose with a sudden edge. "I'm not some fragile little flower! I wish everyone would just relax and back the hell off."

His resentment reignited my frustration. "Jon, we're all just really worried about you!"

"Well, you don't need to be!" His brows furrowed, his face tense with defiance. "I don't need people worrying about me. I've got this."

The words stung.

How can he say that after everything?

My voice cracked as I struggled to stay calm. "Oh my God... are you kidding me? You scared the shit out of everybody! How many times in the last week have you almost died? You *literally* did fucking die!" I stressed each word with deliberate pauses. "Of *course* people are worried about you!"

"Well, I don't want the attention." His tone was cold, his expression hard.

Hurt swirled in my chest. This was new—resentment from Jon, aimed at me.

From the hall came the frantic scratching of Maize's nails. Her toy had undoubtedly rolled under the dresser again, out of reach. Normally, we'd laugh about whose turn it was to go fetch it.

Not today.

Jon stood, clearly eager for the distraction.

"So you want me to back the hell off?" I asked bitterly, quoting his words.

He didn't reply, avoiding my eyes as he left the room.

***

My thoughts swirled—a dark, tangled mess of anxiety, frustration, and dejection. I wasn't even sure how we'd ended up here. I only knew one thing: I needed to go home.

I grabbed my backpack, shoving books, my sketchpad, and a notepad inside.

I just need to go. I'll sleep in my own bed. Maybe when I wake up, this whole thing will feel like a bad dream.

I was stuffing a few more things into the bag when he walked back into the room. He stopped short, his eyes locking on my half-packed bag.

"What are you—don't go. Please?" His voice had a desperate edge. "I… can we talk?"

I froze, keeping my back to him. I didn't want to look at him.

I didn't want to leave, either. That was the last thing I wanted. My lower lip trembled.

"Jon, I don't know how to do this with you," I said, my voice quivering. "If you won't let me do all of it."

He came around to my side of the bed and gently pulled me into a hug.

"I know," he whispered. "God, Vee, don't cry. I'm so sorry. Please let me fix this? Please don't leave."

Three *pleases* in a row. Was that officially begging? Not that he had much to apologize for. He was entitled to his feelings. But so was I. We were both hurting, both overwhelmed.

I nodded and pulled back, wiping my eyes before sitting on the bed with one leg tucked under me. He sat beside me, turning to face me fully.

"I'm sorry I've been so bad at this," he said, his voice raw. His golden eyes, usually so vibrant, looked despondent.

"I don't want you to be sorry," I replied softly, meaning it. "You have nothing to be sorry for. None of this is your fault. But…" I hesitated, searching for the right words. "It feels like you're shutting me out. When you say you're fine, and I know you're not… Jon, it's okay to not be fine. Nobody expects you to be fine."

He nodded, his expression somber. He looked down, gathering his thoughts. Then he sighed.

"The stairs make me tired," he admitted. "Everything makes me tired. And... I haven't figured out how to be this person yet. As much as I hate it for myself, I hate it more for you. I hate that you're worried, and it's because of me."

His voice broke slightly, and he swallowed hard.

"I know it must have been scary for you. And now, too. I know it's hard being with me. It's way more than you signed up for."

His sudden candor was both refreshing and heartbreaking. He was talking about me being scared, but for the first time, I saw something I'd never seen in him before: fear.

The last traces of my frustration melted into empathy.

"I signed up to be with you," I said firmly. "No matter what. And I have been. I know you're dealing with the physical trauma, but Jon, we've all shared the emotional trauma. I really thought I was going to lose you. Do you understand that?"

He nodded slowly, anguish etched into his features.

Tears welled up again, hot and insistent, but I blinked them away. I wasn't done.

"That first night in ICU? I was afraid to go to sleep. I watched your heart monitor all night because I was terrified it would stop. And then, a few days ago..." My voice cracked, but I pushed through. "I thought you were going to die in Tamara's car."

I exhaled shakily, my hands gripping the edges of my shirt sleeves. "I'm not trying to be a control freak. I'm not trying to obsess over your numbers, or nag you, or—"

"Stop," he whispered, wiping a tear from my cheek. He pulled me into another hug, and I buried my face in his shoulder. His scent was familiar, grounding, his arms a steady reassurance.

"I'm so, so sorry, Vee," he murmured into my ear. "You're not a nag. Never. I love you, and I need you. I'm lucky to have you looking after me... even if you are a bit of a control freak."

I pulled back, meeting his eyes. He was grinning, his amber gaze warm again, and he winked.

“Hey!” I protested, laughing softly despite myself.

“It’s okay,” he said, brushing a strand of hair behind my ear. “I know how your beautiful brain works.” His voice softened. “This is my fault. I need to work on my communication.”

“I just want you to be honest with me,” I said, my tone steady. “Not just about how you’re feeling physically, but emotionally too.”

“I know,” he replied. “I need to do better. I will. I promise.”

He kissed my forehead, and I leaned into him, feeling the tension of the day finally start to release.

I love it when he does that.

***

The rest of the afternoon had been uneventful—a welcome reprieve. Mike had stopped by for a while, offering a refreshing break from the earlier tension. Things between Jon and me felt... better. The heated argument, though difficult, had been a catalyst for a deeply healing conversation. I felt hopeful that our relationship was stronger for it. It had to be.

By 5 PM, we were back upstairs in his room. I could tell Jon was tired and ready to relax. I was mentally drained, still processing everything we’d said to each other. The emotional weight lingered in the air between us, though now it felt less oppressive, more like a companionable silence as we settled in.

I adjusted the pillows and sank back into the bed beside him. “What should we watch?” I asked absently. “Something boring, ’cause I might fall asleep.”

Jon didn’t answer. I glanced over, expecting him to grab the remote, but instead, I found him looking at me with an unreadable expression. His gaze was soft, yet intense.

“I want us to be okay,” he said quietly.

I nodded, unsure where this was going. “Me too.”

For a long moment, we sat in silence. Then, he shifted, angling himself toward me. His movements were deliberate, cautious—as if whatever he was about to say carried weight.

"Can we try something?" he asked, his tone tentative. "A better way to communicate?"

Oh God. Where is this going?

I held my breath, bracing for another hard conversation. But something about his demeanor was different. There was a calmness to him that I couldn't quite place.

He took my hand, catching me completely off guard. Without saying anything, he pressed my palm to his chest.

"Do you feel?" he asked softly.

I blinked, unsure how to respond. I could feel his heartbeat, yes—but this wasn't just literal, I didn't think. At least, not entirely.

This is so out of character for him.

I stared at him, my mind swirling with questions and emotions. And then, he met my eyes and said, "I'm here."

The air shifted. I don't know how else to describe it. There was a stillness in the room, a strange kind of energy that I swear I could feel. It wasn't just his heartbeat beneath my hand—it was something more. Something electric. It made the hairs on the back of my neck stand up.

The moment stretched, expanding outward. Time seemed to slow. I became hyperaware of everything: the occasional bird chirps outside the window, the glint of sunlight catching a dust particle midair, the warmth radiating from his body. And his eyes—his beautiful amber eyes—they seemed brighter, more vivid than usual, like they held some kind of light within them.

What the hell is happening right now?

I tried to ground myself, but the sensations were too strong. Everything about this felt inexplicably profound. Overwhelming, yet calm. Surreal, yet undeniably real.

"Hey," Jon said gently, his voice breaking through my spiraling thoughts. His tone was soft, kind, grounding.

He didn't let go of my hand. Our eyes stayed locked as he said, "You can check my blood pressure fifty times a day if it makes you feel better. We can do that. But... if you just need to feel that I'm okay, then I'm *here.*"

He pressed my hand a little tighter to his chest for a moment, then released it. His gaze was steady, and he tilted his head slightly, a small grin tugging at his lips. "Okay?"

I nodded, but words failed me. My thoughts were a jumble. Did I want to laugh? Cry? Kiss him? All of the above?

I kept my hand on his chest for a few more seconds, reluctant to break the connection. Finally, I found my voice, though it sounded strange to my own ears. "Can I have a hug?"

He smiled, pulling me close. His arms wrapped around me, and I nestled against him, breathing him in. For the first time all day, I felt truly at peace.

***

I wasn't sure how long we stayed like that. Time itself felt irrelevant, an artificial construct that didn't belong in this moment. All I knew was that I was blissfully content, wrapped in an incredible sense of peace and euphoria. It was so overwhelming, so surreal, that part of me wondered if he'd drugged me.

Somewhere, in the back of my mind—the analytical part of my mind—questions swirled. But I didn't want to break this spell, this beautiful calm that had enveloped us. Not yet.

I felt confused, yet comforted. Overwhelmed, yet completely at ease.

Eventually, I couldn't help myself. I had to ask.

"So... what was that?" I whispered, still holding on to him, not ready to let go.

He didn't answer right away. I pulled back slightly to see if he was still awake. He was. His eyes held a glimmer, like he was amused that I even needed to ask.

"That," he said simply, "was us sharing a moment."

I let his words settle, turning them over in my mind. It was such a pure, uncomplicated answer to a question that felt so layered, so full of meaning.

Let it go, Via. Don't ruin it. You just can't help yourself, can you?

"But... how? I mean, what did you *do?*"

He chuckled softly, and sighed. "What I was *trying* to do," he said, "was show you that not everything needs to be analyzed."

I couldn't help but smile at the irony. He caught it too.

After a pause, he continued, his voice quieter now. "I wanted to show you what I meant earlier—about there being more to me than just numbers. I wanted you to connect with me, on a deeper level."

My mind raced. What did I feel? Energy?

It was energy.

Is that really what he meant? Could that be it?

Don't ask him, Via. Just accept it.

"I did," I whispered.

"Good." He kissed the top of my head. "We can check in with each other in lots of ways. Sometimes, we don't even need words, if we're paying attention enough. We can just... feel it."

His words lingered in the air, so profound and unexpected that I found myself wondering if this was tied to... I could barely bring myself to think it.

Is this from his near-death experience? Is that what this is? Could he share that with me, somehow?

You're losing your damn mind, Via.

I looked into his eyes, searching for something—clarity, maybe, or confirmation. But all I saw was warmth. Calm. That quiet, glowing confidence he had about him. It didn't matter where this came from. It didn't need an explanation.

For God's sake, Via. Just shut up and kiss him.

So I did. Tentatively at first, unsure if it was the right moment. But he leaned in too, his lips soft, his breath warm against mine. The kiss deepened, his tongue brushing gently against mine, and suddenly I didn't care about questions or plans or logic. I didn't care about anything but this.

***

The hollow chime of the doorbell echoed upstairs, freezing us in place. A second later, the click of the lock and the creak of the front door opening brought our moment to an abrupt halt.

"Hello!" called a familiar voice from downstairs.

Recognizing Ben, Maize bolted from the foot of the bed and thundered down the stairs, sounding more like a herd of elephants than a single dog. I could hear Ben laughing and greeting her as she practically tackled him.

"You've got to be fucking kidding me," Jon whispered, his tone dripping with exasperation.

I laughed, rolling off him and hopping out of bed. "I'll go down first," I offered with a wink, as he adjusted himself under the covers.

When I reached the kitchen, Ben was unloading containers from a brown carryout bag. The smell of Italian food filled the room, making my stomach rumble. I realized I hadn't eaten since my granola bar at breakfast. Jon's lack of appetite was starting to mess with my eating schedule too.

"I didn't wake you guys up, did I?" Ben asked, glancing up from the bag.

I stifled a smirk. "Nope. We were just upstairs, relaxing."

A minute later, Jon appeared in the doorway.

"Hey, man! I brought you some pasta and bread."

Jon wrinkled his nose, eyeing the bag suspiciously.

"Come on," Ben coaxed. "I know you love the food from this place. Besides, you could use the carbs! Gotta have more than a protein shake."

"Umm-hmm," Jon grumbled, grabbing a breadstick and taking a small bite, more out of politeness than interest.

"Jill insisted I bring your dinner, and make sure you eat it," Ben added with a laugh.

Jon raised an eyebrow. "First week as a new dad, and you're already blaming stuff on my sister?"

I laughed as Ben flushed slightly. "She really did ask me to come," he insisted.

"How's the little peanut, anyway?" Jon asked, his tone softening.

"She's amazing. I could bring her over tomorrow if you're feeling up to it."

"Yeah, I'd like that," Jon said genuinely.

Ben stayed for about ten minutes, chatting and making sure Jon ate at least a little. Jon was polite but clearly not thrilled about the extended interaction. He gave Maize a meatball before taking his medication.

Ben watched as he absently emptied a pill from each bottle into his palm. "How're you feeling today?"

Jon's eyes flicked to mine, and in that moment, it felt like we silently replayed our earlier conversation. His response was carefully measured. "I'm okay."

"Doing okay with those?" Ben asked, gesturing to the pills.

"Yup," Jon replied flatly, not bothering to look up. Then he stood and stretched. "I'm wiped. I think I'm ready to crash. Vee?"

I nodded. It was barely 7 PM, but the day had felt endless. While Jon took Maize outside for her evening romp, I started cleaning up.

"How's he doing today?" Ben asked, glancing out the patio doors.

"He's good. We had some company earlier. He's just a little tired, I think."

Ben nodded. "He looks tired."

I hesitated, unsure whether to mention the incident on the stairs, and then decided against it. For the first time, I started to see how all the constant checking in—while well-meaning—might feel smothering from Jon's perspective.

Chapter 33

The next morning, I sat alone on the couch in the front room. The house was empty, and quiet as usual for this time of day. I was really getting used to this. The lack of roommates.

I loved my roommates, don't get me wrong. They were calm and reasonable, especially when compared to the typical chaos of college dorms or the drama that seemed to orbit our age group in general. That's why we had become friends in the first place. Why we'd agreed to live together in an off-campus apartment, trading the "normal" college experience for something quieter, something more us.

Still, the solitude was nice.

The early sun on this April morning was especially bright, blaring through the large bay windows and throwing light oblongs across the room and floor. I could hear the birds, and see the green grass taking over the melancholic brown-scape of winter. I knew the air was still brisk in the mornings, but while enjoying the warmth of the indoors I could easily tell that spring had arrived.

Any other year, this kind of morning would have filled me with excitement—a cabin fever sort of restlessness, eager for what was to come. The bleakness of winter would be a memory, replaced by the promise of warmth, growth, and new beginnings.

But this year was different. Everything was different.

I still felt a flicker of excitement, still appreciated the beauty around me, but it was tempered by an undercurrent of anxiety. A gnawing unease reminded me that nothing was quite the same anymore. And deep down, I knew it never would be again.

Maybe it was in part because Jon and I had had our first official fight the day before. I'm not sure I could even call it a fight. *Was it a fight?* Yesterday, I had reconciled it as our metaphorical come-to-Jesus moment. That label felt better. More productive.

My friend Dawn and her boyfriend Troy had been together for two years—not even as long as Jon and I. But Dawn and Troy fought like an old married couple, complete with bickering and petty spats that occasionally made things awkward at parties.

That wasn't us.

Jon and I didn't fight like that. Never, ever. Not once.

We have some new stuff to figure out. But I think we're dealing with it. Yesterday was weird.

Are we okay?

The little notebook I was using to log his vitals lay waiting on the coffee table. An unwelcome part of our new routine, and the source of a reserved, dismissive side of Jon that prior to yesterday, I'd found both baffling and off-putting. But now it was different. As important as I still believed it was, I felt like I had a new understanding of why he hated it. And I'd decided to let it go. For the morning, at least. Things between us still felt too fragile.

It's too soon to rock the boat, Via.

***

I could hear Jon in the kitchen, preparing breakfast for Maize. Her little barks and throaty grumbles filled the air—her way of talking. And, of course, he talked back to her.

I loved how much he loved her. It said so much about who he was—his kindness, his patience.

I turned from the window as Jon walked into the living room. His gaze dropped to the notebook on the coffee table, and when he looked up, our eyes met.

He knew that I knew he'd seen it. His expression carried the weight of unspoken acknowledgment. He knew what came next—what was supposed to happen—but I stayed silent.

Be quiet, Via. Not today.

I braced myself for a sarcastic remark, a wisecrack to break the tension. That's what I expected. But what he did instead caught me completely off guard.

Jon motioned for me to come over.

Confused, I hesitated, then crossed the room to meet him.

Without saying a word, he reached for the stethoscope Tamara had left on the shelf a few days earlier. He turned toward me, holding it out. His gaze was steady as he handed me the earpieces to put on.

What the fuck?

I gingerly complied, stunned not only by his acceptance of the ritual he'd so adamantly claimed to hate, but by the fact that he was now inviting me to do it this way.

Out of character didn't even begin to describe what was happening. Holding the end of the stethoscope, I felt an unexpected pang of inhibition.

He noticed my hesitation and grinned at my awkwardness. With a slight nod of encouragement, he gently guided my hand to his chest.

Then, as if it were the most natural thing in the world, he pulled me closer, wrapping his arms around me in a loose, comforting hug. He pressed a soft kiss to my temple and then stood quietly, holding me, allowing me to listen.

The crystal clarity of his heartbeat through the stethoscope captivated me, steady and rhythmic even through his T-shirt. For a moment, I forgot the purpose entirely, lost in the quiet reassurance of that sound.

Focus, Via.

I pulled myself back to reality and, watching the second hand on the wall clock behind him, started counting his heartbeats. When 10 seconds had passed, I multiplied by 6. 84 bpm. Acceptable. And also...

It sounded *beautiful*. I could have melted in his arms at that moment.

I lingered a few seconds longer than I needed to, before dropping my hand and slightly pulling away. I didn't want to make it weird.

It's already weird, Via.

"Good," I remember saying, trying to sound matter-of-fact. "You're good!"

He didn't even acknowledge my observation. He didn't seem to care at all.

Instead, he placed his hand lightly on the back of my neck, tilting my head so that our eyes met.

"Are *we* good?" he asked softly.

Still immersed in the moment, I answered with a deep, sincere smile.

I knew this was his way of ensuring that we'd moved past what had happened the day before. I nodded, and he kissed me. *Holy fuck*. I suddenly became acutely aware of how turned-on I had become. I truly don't think he had any clue how sexy that entire gesture was; it was simply his way of extending the olive branch.

But I had never been more attracted to him than I was at that moment.

There was something undeniably sensual about his willingness to let me be close to him in that way. It wasn't lost on me that this was the second time in 24 hours he had initiated such an intimate exchange. He was really trying, just like he'd promised, and I fully appreciated his efforts.

"Let me fix this," he'd said. I hadn't even realized it could be fixed. And yet, somehow, he intuitively knew how to make me feel not just less anxious—but fully secure. That was a feat in and of itself.

***

The emotional weight of the morning lingered well into the afternoon. While Jon seemed to move on effortlessly, I found myself turning over the moment in my mind. There was something unspoken between us, something profound I couldn't quite name. The person I'd known and loved for years had, in the span of a week, evolved into someone both familiar and new. Physically, the changes were straightforward—explainable. But beneath the surface, there was something else. Something I couldn't pinpoint. It felt strange. Alluring.

I watched him now—not with worry, but with curiosity.

What was it?

When Ben arrived with Abby in tow, I welcomed the distraction. Something about feeding a baby felt refreshingly normal.

"How's Jill?" I asked, grabbing the diaper bag as Ben wrestled with the carrier.

"She's still sore," he said, sighing. "But she's getting around better. My parents left for the airport this morning, so I think she's looking forward to some peace and quiet."

I nodded, understanding. Abby started fussing almost immediately. "She sleeps in the car, at least," Ben added with a half-smile.

The reprieve was short-lived. Within minutes, Abby was outright bawling, her tiny face scrunched in protest. The cycle of fussing, quieting, then wailing again had me convinced: babies were a pain in the ass.

"Is that normal?" Jon asked, watching from the couch. "Do you even get any sleep?"

"It's colic," Ben explained, bouncing Abby slightly. "The pediatrician says she's fine and that she'll grow out of it."

Hopefully sooner rather than later.

I offered to hold Abby so Ben could eat the sandwich I'd made him, though I doubted it was a fair trade. Dutifully, I took her, trying to channel my inner "Aunt Via." The title had a nice ring to it, even if the role came with endless crying.

Abby squirmed, her little cries growing louder. After a few minutes, Jon intervened, scooping her from my arms with ease. To my surprise—and everyone else's—she stopped fussing instantly.

"What is it with you?" Ben asked, his voice tinged with awe as he chewed his food.

Jon shrugged, flashing a smile. "I guess I'm her favorite."

"I know who to call when she won't sleep at night," Ben quipped.

Jon held her for the rest of the visit. She didn't so much as whimper. Ben and I were equal parts impressed and bemused. I couldn't deny there was something endearing about watching him with her—soft smiles, gentle movements, and an almost magnetic calmness.

Ben returned again the next day, jokingly asking if Jon was free to babysit. "She must like your energy," he teased.

I laughed along, but the comment stuck with me.

Energy.

A thought tugged at the edge of my memory—an echo of Jon taking my hand that night, his heartbeat steady beneath my palm, the air charged with something unexplainable. I wasn't sure what Ben meant, but I couldn't help wondering if he was right.

Chapter 34

Out of the blue the following week, Jon said, "Oh yeah, I have a doctor's appointment on the 5th. If you want to come."

I had to consciously mask my surprise, my thoughts scrambling for a casual reply. "Your follow-up? With Dr. Brookens?" I asked, keeping my tone even.

"Yeah," he said, shrugging like it was no big deal. "I mean, only if you want to. And if you're free. Don't skip any classes or anything."

This wasn't just "a doctor's appointment." This was *the* first major follow-up since It happened. A huge deal. The doctor would be checking to see if the medications were working, if his ejection fraction had improved, if his heart was showing any signs of recovery. These results would determine the timing and complexity of his ICD surgery.

I struggled to keep my voice calm. "Of *course,* I want to come," I said, my sincerity shining through. "There's absolutely nothing more important to me. Thank you for asking."

Jon shrugged again, like it didn't matter either way, but I could tell it did. And it meant the world to me.

***

I was helping Mike update his website, the shop empty for the hours he'd blocked off for me to work. The timing was perfect. Sharron was back from her trip, and Jill felt well enough to get out of the house. She, Ben, and Abby were spending the afternoon with Jon. He could catch up with family while I focused on the site.

Mike and I started with casual talk. Like everyone else, he was concerned, but trying to toe the line between a well-meaning check-in and what Jon would surely call harassment.

"When's his next appointment?" Mike asked.

"On the 5th," I said, the weight of it settling between us.

Mike hesitated, as if deciding how much to say. "Man... I hope—" He stopped mid-thought, looking pensive. "I hope he gets good news. I just want him to be okay."

I nodded. "Me too. I'm going with him."

Mike raised an eyebrow, his surprise obvious. I laughed, already knowing what he was thinking. "He invited me. On his own—I didn't even ask."

"Wow," Mike said with a chuckle. "That dude really loves you."

I blinked, caught off guard. "Well, yeah... what does that have to do with anything?"

Mike just grinned and shrugged, not answering. Then he shifted topic. "You've been around him more than anyone this week. How's he doing? You know... with everything. Not being able to play..." He paused. "I worry about how he's handling it. Mentally."

I exhaled, understanding Mike's concern. "It bothers him. He hasn't picked up a guitar yet." Then I added, "But he's writing music. So, that's something."

"Good. I know he needs an outlet. This can't be easy for him. But honestly, he's been so quiet about everything—I just can't tell how he's really doing."

I let out a dry laugh, his observation cutting close to home. "Tell me about it." I debated how much to say but decided to confide just a little. "Actually, we had some words over that exact thing last week."

Mike tilted his head, encouraging me to go on.

"We're good," I clarified quickly. "But... man, he can be stubborn. I told him he needs to stop shutting us out and let us know how he's feeling—mentally and physically. Otherwise, how are we supposed to help?"

Mike gave a thoughtful nod. "How'd he take it?"

"Surprisingly well." I smiled. "I think that's why he invited me to the appointment. He's trying." I paused, searching for the right words. "But I don't understand why he was so resistant. Like, why wouldn't he just be real about how he's doing?"

Mike sighed, looking conflicted. "Yeah, I get that. I really do. But..." He hesitated, as if carefully weighing his next words. "You've got to see it from a guy's perspective."

I frowned, taken aback. "A 'guy's' perspective? What does that even mean?" My frustration crept into my voice despite my best effort to hide it.

"Well... I'm just saying..." Mike trailed off, looking uncertain, like he wasn't entirely sure how to articulate his point. After a pause, he pressed on. "Let's be real—these last two weeks have been brutal, but even before that... it's been a rough year. For him, for everyone."

I nodded, silently agreeing.

"And he's not even done yet," Mike continued, his tone heavy. "This surgery coming up... it's a big deal. Like, life-altering. And he knows it."

We all know it.

What does this have to do with a "guy's perspective?"

Mike hesitated, watching my reaction. I motioned for him to go on. With a reluctant sigh, he added, "I think... maybe he's afraid he's going to lose you. Over all of this."

I blinked, startled. "What?" I tried not to sound offended, but the words stung. "I've been here through everything!"

Mike nodded quickly. "Yeah, yeah—I know. Everybody knows that. It's just... it's a lot. And I think Jon might feel a little insecure."

"Insecure?" I repeated, incredulously. "Jon? What the hell does he have to feel insecure about? He's the whole damn package. Smart, gorgeous, talented—the nicest guy I've ever met. He could literally have anyone he wanted!"

Mike chuckled. "Yeah, maybe. But he doesn't want anyone else. He wants you. Long-term. And... I think he's scared that all of this—" he gestured vaguely,"—is going to be too much for you. That you'll eventually want something simpler. Someone healthier. Someone without all this baggage."

I sat silently, processing his words. It was finally starting to sink in. "Oh my God," I said slowly. "Did he actually tell you that?"

Mike laughed lightly, raising his hands in mock surrender. "I'm not saying he used those exact words. Maybe he did, maybe he didn't. But it's true. And I can't really blame him. If I were in his position, I'd worry about it too."

I shook my head, still trying to wrap my mind around it. "He knows I love him, right? I'd never leave him over this. That's insane."

Mike's expression softened, almost sympathetic. "Of course he knows. Look, you've seen Jon at his absolute worst, and you were amazing through all of it. But it's not about you. It's about him."

"That's crazy!" I said, frustrated. "He's the toughest guy I know. He survived death. Literally! How many people can say that? Male ego is so stupid."

Mike laughed. "Yeah, you're not wrong. And I agree—Jon is seriously badass."

I rolled my eyes but couldn't help smiling as he let me vent about the absurdities of the male psyche. The shared laugh seemed to lighten the mood.

"Seriously," Mike said, leaning forward, his tone sincere. "Don't worry too much about this. He's dealing with it in his own way, and honestly? I think he's handling his shit pretty damn well."

I thought back to our argument. To the conversation that followed. To how Jon had been trying, really trying, since then. "Yeah," I said quietly. "He is."

Mike met my gaze, his expression uncharacteristically earnest. "Look... Jon's struggling. And yeah, it's scary as hell. But if you ever need to talk, I'm here. I know you love him. So do I. He's like a brother to me. And I want to be his best man at your wedding. So, we're going to get through this. Right?"

I felt a lump rise in my throat at his openness but managed to nod. "Right."

***

I turned back to the computer, blinking back tears, and refocused on the work at hand. Mercifully, Mike changed the subject, letting me know that Shawn was flying in for a visit the following day. He'd only be staying one night, and going home the next afternoon, but he wanted to visit Jon in person. I appreciated his effort. It would do Jon some good. Visitors always seemed to lift his spirits, even if only for a little while.

"I was thinking," Mike said, "we could all hang out at Nikki's? Shoot some pool. Nothing big, just us. We'll keep it low-key. I thought you could bring Jon over, and Shawn could surprise him."

The idea was sweet, and no doubt Jon wouldn't be expecting to see Shawn. It would be the first time all the members of *FR* had been together since before It happened. The thought stirred a mix of emotions, since there was technically no more "FR." I knew Jon carried a heavy weight of guilt over being the reason. But maybe seeing Shawn and the others rally around him would remind him he wasn't alone in this.

"That sounds like a great idea," I said, my voice warm with agreement.

***

On the ride home, Mike's words played over in my mind, reframing the past few days with startling clarity. Ever since our argument, I'd been so focused on Jon seeing things from my perspective that I hadn't stopped to consider his. It wasn't until Mike broke it down for me that I realized the depth of Jon's insecurities—and how much they colored his actions.

And now, it all clicked.

In the days since, Jon had been nothing short of incredible, going out of his way to meet me where I needed him. Whether it was sharing how he felt physically or simply being present in a way that made me feel secure, he was doing everything I'd asked for—and more.

That made his invitation to his cardiologist appointment even more meaningful. Knowing what I now did, it was clear how much trust it took for him to offer me a front-row seat to something so personal and uncertain. Vulnerability wasn't easy for Jon, especially when the outcome of that visit could go either way.

No wonder Mike looked surprised.

***

When I arrived back at Jon's, Jill and Sharron were in the living room, folding a basket of tiny clothes. Jon was reclined in the chair beside Jill, his arm wrapped protectively around Abby, who was nestled against his chest. Both of them were fast asleep.

"Isn't that adorable?" Sharron beamed, nodding toward them.

I smiled.

"I tried to take her when I realized they were sleeping," Jill said, her voice hushed. "But she scooted away like she didn't want to leave. So, I figured I'd let them be."

We chatted quietly until Maize padded over from her spot on the floor. She rested a paw on my foot, her eyes expectant.

"Gotta pee, girlie?" I asked, and Maize snorted in response.

"Wow," Jill remarked, amused. "Looks like she has a favorite, too."

"Second favorite," I corrected, heading toward the back door, Maize trotting at my heels.

Outside, I spotted Ben sitting in the far corner of the patio, a chair dragged into the shade. He had a cigarette between his fingers and seemed startled to see me.

"I thought you quit," I said, unable to hide my grin.

"I did," he replied, holding my gaze as he took a long drag. He exhaled slowly, admitting, "Bought a pack the other week when everything went to hell. When these are gone, I'm done. Want one?"

I hesitated, then accepted.

"Still asleep?" he asked, offering me a light.

"Yep."

Ben chuckled softly, almost to himself. "That's crazy."

It clicked then—maybe it wasn't just amazement. Maybe it was frustrating for him. The fact that Jon could soothe Abby so effortlessly when no one else could. Jon had sensed it, too. A few days ago, he mentioned how Ben seemed "weird" around him, but I'd brushed it off.

"I bet it's hard, seeing her settle so easily with him," I ventured.

Ben looked genuinely taken aback. "God, no. I appreciate it so much."

He paused, his gaze distant, as if wrestling with his thoughts. "It's just..." He trailed off, then sighed. "Humbling. I keep replaying what happened in the hospital. Every time I see him, it's like I'm back there. I don't even know what to say to him."

I took a drag, unsure how to respond. Ben's raw honesty left little room for comfort.

Then, almost as if to escape the weight of the moment, Ben shifted gears. "You know what he said to me the other day?" His tone was lighter now, tinged with disbelief.

It's hard to tell.

"What?"

"He told me I should start my own accounting business."

I considered that. "That's... a big change."

Ben nodded, the baffled expression on his face betraying the magnitude of Jon's words. "That's just it. I've been toying with the idea for years—never told anyone, though. And then, when Jill got pregnant, I buried it. Too risky, you know?"

He looked at me then, his eyes searching for an answer I didn't have. "How could he have known that?"

I stayed silent, leaving the question hanging in the air.

Chapter 35

I asked Jon if he felt up to heading over to Nikki's the following evening. He perked up immediately at the suggestion. I don't even know why I offered to drive us. When the time came, Jon gave me an incredulous look. "It's right there!" he said, gesturing dramatically. "We can walk."

Of course we'd walk.

Jon's face lit up when Shawn answered the door. The two embraced, Shawn clapping him on the back while diving into a story about the annoying woman who'd sat next to him on the plane. If Shawn noticed the weight loss, he didn't let on. No sideways glances. No questions about how Jon was feeling. No mention of It. I silently thanked him for the effort—Jon needed this. A little normalcy.

"Congratulations on the new job!" Jon said as we settled in.

Shawn stopped mid-step, slightly puzzled. "Aw, man, I'm still working FOH at Majestic."

Jon frowned briefly, looking confused, but smiled and brushed it off as a misunderstanding.

***

The night was relaxing and low-key, as promised. We lounged in Nikki's back room, chatting while Mike and Shawn played a well-matched game of pool. The sound of laughter and clinking glasses filled the air, adding to the easy atmosphere.

At one point, Shawn's phone rang. He glanced at the screen, groaning. "Shit, it's work. I gotta take this." He rolled his eyes apologetically as he stepped out of the room.

Five minutes passed before Nikki spoke up. "Geesh, what's taking him so long?"

"Ahhh, they probably have some dipshit new tech who can't figure out the board," Mike said with a dismissive wave.

Shawn worked as the A1 sound engineer at a major Cleveland music venue. When he wasn't touring, it was his job to make sure everything sounded perfect and to manage the tech crew. Sometimes, even when he wasn't on the clock, they'd call him for help.

Ten minutes later, Shawn reappeared, his expression somewhere between restrained excitement and disbelief. Finally, a grin broke free. "Another round of drinks, guys! I just got a promotion!"

Cheers erupted around the room. Nikki squealed in delight, and Cary raised his glass in an impromptu toast.

Shawn held up his hands to quiet the noise, his grin widening. "I'm Venue Manager now! I'll be running the whole back-of-house."

He turned toward Jon, who leaned casually in the doorway.

"Congratulations," Jon said, his smile easy and genuine. His eyes seemed to hold an even deeper warmth, one of unspoken understanding.

Shawn shook his head, laughing. "You must have a sixth sense or something!"

Jon chuckled, but before he could respond, my attention was pulled across the room. Cary was staring at me, wide-eyed and brimming with questions yet to be voiced. His expression practically screamed, *What the hell is going on?*

Not now. Don't start, Cary. Jon needs a normal night.

I locked eyes with Cary and, making sure no one else was watching, pointed at him sharply—the same way my mom used to point at me as a kid when she wanted me to be quiet. Then, I mimed zipping my lips.

Cary frowned but seemed to get the message. Whatever he'd been about to say, he swallowed it. Instead, he busied himself collecting glasses and headed to the kitchen to mix more drinks.

After a moment, I followed him in.

"What the fuck was that?" he hissed as soon as I stepped through the doorway. His eyes blazed with frustration as he motioned toward the other room.

"I don't know," I said evenly, keeping my tone calm. "But now is not the time."

Cary looked like he wanted to argue, but instead, turned to refill the empty glasses.

I felt Jon's arms wrap around me from behind, his familiar warmth easing some of the tension. He kissed the crown of my head. "Everything okay in here?"

"Perfect!" I said cheerfully, turning to kiss him on the cheek.

Cary didn't say another word, but as Jon and I left the kitchen, I could feel his questions lingering, heavy and unanswered.

***

Returning home exhausted, Jon and I went straight to bed. I drifted off easily and stayed under for hours, but around 3:30 am, I jerked awake, my chest heaving from a nightmare I couldn't shake. It had dragged me back to the hospital—reliving that first agonizing night in the ICU. Even awake, the vividness lingered.

My stomach churned as I sat up, glancing over at Jon. He was sleeping soundly on his back, as usual, completely still. Too still. The gears in my mind started spinning. I thought about It. About heart block. About his medication. I told myself everything was fine. They'd adjusted the dose. They said it wouldn't happen again.

He's fine. He's just sleeping.

But the thought wouldn't let go.

The dim light from the streetlamp slipped through the blinds, outlining his silhouette. I stared at his chest, straining to see it rise and fall. Was he breathing? Of course, he's breathing.

Leave him alone. He needs sleep.

I lay back down, trying to rationalize my panic, but it gnawed at me. My hand hesitated before reaching over to rest gently on his chest. I thought I could feel the faint movement of his breath. Maybe?

Oh, for God's sake, Via. He's fine. You're overreacting.

Still, doubt crept in, tightening its grip. I pressed a little harder, desperate for reassurance. He stirred, shifting slightly under my touch. Relief flooded through me, followed quickly by guilt for waking him. But then he reached up, his hand finding mine, lacing his fingers through mine like it was the most natural thing in the world.

A moment later, he turned toward me, propping himself up on his elbow. "Are you okay?" he asked softly, his voice low with concern.

I blinked back tears, overwhelmed by both my fear and his gentleness. "Yeah," I said, my voice unsteady. "I just wanted to make sure you were okay." A lump formed in my throat as I added, "I had a bad dream. It's nothing. I'm sorry for waking you."

"Don't be sorry." He brushed a strand of hair away from my face, his touch soothing. "Do you want to talk about it?"

I shook my head.

Definitely not.

"Alright," he said after a pause. "Well, then come here." He lay back down, pulling me close and adjusting the blankets over us both. "Give me your hand."

I slipped my arm under the blanket, and he gently guided my hand to his chest. This time, he slid it beneath his shirt, pressing it against his bare skin. His heartbeat thudded steadily beneath my palm, grounding me in the moment. He wrapped his hand over mine, applying just enough pressure to make sure I could feel it clearly.

"I'm okay," he whispered. "I'm right here, with you."

I closed my eyes, his words echoing from the first time he'd done that. "*I'm here.*"

I don't know who fell asleep first, but for the first time in weeks, I slept deeply, my fears quieted. And I found myself falling asleep that way every night after.

Chapter 36

The evening before Jon's follow-up with Dr. Brookens had arrived faster than expected. We were outside, sitting by the fire pit. The warm, early-May air wrapped around us, and Maize roamed freely in the expansive backyard, her silhouette barely visible against the pine row in the distance.

I'd been thinking about the upcoming appointment all weekend. Though Jon hadn't spoken much about it, I couldn't help but think it weighed on him too. He'd already gone for bloodwork, an EKG, and an echocardiogram earlier in the day, but in true Jon fashion, he hadn't mentioned a word about any of it. I was trying hard not to badger him—it felt like he had enough of that from everyone else—but the silence gnawed at me.

Finally, my own nerves got the better of me. "So... how are you feeling about your appointment tomorrow?"

Jon had been leaning forward, elbows resting on his knees, staring into the fire. He turned his head slightly, his expression impassive. After a long pause, he shrugged. "I don't know... I'm not sure it matters much how I feel about it." He glanced at me then, smirking faintly, before turning back to the flames.

"Well, it matters to me," I said softly, nudging him to open up.

That made him sit up and face me fully, his eyes catching the flicker of the firelight. "Okay then," he said with a wry grin. "How are you feeling about my appointment tomorrow?"

The sudden shift caught me off guard. "I—uh..." I stumbled, annoyed that he'd flipped the script so effortlessly. Still, I wanted to be honest. "I'm a little nervous. But whatever happens, we'll deal with it." I leaned closer, hoping to convey my sincerity. "I'm in this with you."

He gave a half-smile and nodded, turning his gaze back to the fire. For a moment, the crackle of the flames filled the silence. Then, after a beat, he spoke again, his tone quieter. "You know this might not be good news... don't you?"

My chest tightened. "I know," I said carefully. "To be honest, I don't even know what I should be hoping for at this point. But 'good news' is subjective. And Jon, you're here. You're alive. That's already the best news I could ever ask for."

His lips quirked into a smile, though I couldn't tell if it was more sarcastic than sincere. I pressed on. "Seriously. We're here, sitting in your backyard. Sixteen days ago, I wasn't sure I'd ever get to tell you I love you again. So no, I'm not scared of what the doctor says tomorrow. I'm just grateful we made it this far."

His smirk softened into a gentle, almost wistful smile. "I might not ever be the same again," he said quietly, his tone warm but laced with a seriousness that reminded me he wasn't just preparing himself—he was preparing me, too.

"I'd expect not," I replied.

"I mean... I might never fully recover."

"Yeah. Dr. Brookens already warned us about that."

"This surgery is going to set me back even further."

I met his gaze, unwavering. "I know. It's gonna suck."

Jon stared at me for a long moment, searching my face. Then, finally, he laughed—a real, full laugh—and leaned back in his chair, shaking his head in mock defeat.

I moved over, straddling him in the chair and leaning down to kiss him. "I'm with you, babe," I murmured. "And I love you."

Just then, Maize came barreling up the yard, barking happily. She leaped onto Jon's lap, wiggling her way between us. We both laughed, and that was the perfect end to the conversation. Maize had a way of knowing when to lighten the mood.

***

The following morning, I woke at the crack of dawn, my thoughts already racing. Next to me, Jon was still fast asleep, seemingly unbothered by the weight of the day ahead. How did he stay so calm? Had he made peace with the worst-case scenario? His comments last night certainly made it seem that way.

I lay there for an hour, circling through my own anxious thoughts, until the alarm finally broke the quiet. Jon lazily silenced it with a groan, rolling over. When he opened his eyes, he looked surprised to find me already wide awake.

"Wow," he said, smiling softly. "You're up early."

The morning sun slipped through the blinds, painting golden stripes across the bed. In the soft light, his eyes gleamed warm, like honey. I couldn't decide whether to be more amused or irritated by how relaxed he was—and how damn adorable at the same time.

"I couldn't sleep," I admitted. "You, on the other hand, seem well-rested."

"Umhmm. Slept like the dead. Or, in my case, half-dead. Sometimes dead..." He grinned mischievously. "Maybe—"

"Oh my God, what is *wrong* with you?" I groaned, trying not to laugh as I cut him off.

"I think we're about to go find out," he teased, his eyes sparkling with that irreverent humor I couldn't help but love.

I couldn't hold back my laughter anymore and tossed a pillow at him. He caught it easily, laughing as he reached out to grab my arm, pulling me onto him. I ended up straddling him, and Maize lifted her head from the foot of the bed, watching us with sleepy curiosity.

"I'm sorry you didn't sleep," he said, his expression softening. "Will you do something for me?"

I raised an eyebrow.

"Try not to worry so much."

I rolled my eyes.

As if it's that easy.

He took my hands in his, threading our fingers together. Then, with gentle care, he brought my right hand to his lips, pressing a tender kiss to my fingers.

"We can't change the past, Vee. And we can't control the future. Worrying doesn't help anything. But what we can appreciate is this—what we have right now, in this moment."

He kissed my left hand next, his warm eyes meeting mine.

"It's the little things," he said, smiling. "There's nowhere I'd rather be than here, in this bed, with you. The sun is shining, my dog is at my feet, and I'm grateful for all of it."

His words melted me. Hot tears slipped down my cheeks before I could stop them, and I wiped at them with a shaky smile. "I love you," I whispered, bending down to kiss him.

I didn't want to move. I didn't want the moment to end. But we had somewhere to be.

***

Dr. Brookens' office was adjacent to the hospital. He didn't keep us waiting. I was surprised when he entered in under five minutes. He always carried a brisk but friendly demeanor, and while he didn't mince words, he had a way of making me feel at ease. He greeted us warmly before settling into his chair.

"So!" he began, leaning back casually. "How have you been since I last saw you?"

The open-endedness of the question threw Jon off. I didn't blame him—it felt strange, given the circumstances.

"I'm doing okay. I'm good," Jon replied hesitantly.

Brookens raised an eyebrow, a trace of amusement on his face. "Good? That's it?"

Neither of us quite knew how to respond. Brookens straightened and flipped through a folder. "You ended up back in the hospital with third-degree AV block," he said, more a statement than a question.

"Yes, sir," Jon confirmed.

"That must have been scary," Brookens remarked, his tone neutral. He waited for a response that didn't come. Then, with a quick glance at Jon, he added, "Maybe not for you?" He turned to me. "But I bet it was for you."

His bluntness caught me off guard, but I nodded. "Yes, it was."

An awkward silence lingered before Brookens smiled and gestured toward me. "I'm glad you're here. It's natural for you to see things from different perspectives. That's okay—it's good you're here together."

Brookens set his notes aside. "May I take a look at your bruising?"

Jon stood, unbuttoning the lightweight black shirt he'd worn—a shirt I'd always thought looked great on him. It slid off his shoulders as he moved to the exam table, revealing the fading evidence of trauma.

His chest was still a mosaic of bruises, the deep blues and greens replacing the harsher purples of the first week. The hues extended to his ribs, sides, and even a faint stripe across his back, blending where the defibrillator pads had left their marks. Those had faded to nothing more than faint outlines now.

Brookens pressed lightly around Jon's back. "Your burns have healed nicely," he noted before placing his hands on either side of Jon's ribs. He applied careful pressure as he palpated his way forward.

When his fingers reached a spot towards the front, Jon flinched. Brookens immediately froze. "Sorry," he said, his tone genuinely apologetic. "I'll go lighter."

Switching to one hand, he continued with a gentler touch, ending at Jon's sternum.

Brookens stepped back and nodded. "You still have some noticeable swelling. It's going to take some time to heal, so be cautious with your movements. Don't overdo it."

He moved on with the rest of the exam, which took long enough to make me worry he'd found something wrong. But at last, he stepped back, draping the stethoscope around his neck.

"Okay," he said cheerfully.

Thank God.

"How do you feel right now?" Brookens asked.

"I feel fine," Jon said, buttoning his shirt. When our eyes met, he gave me a quick wink, and I felt my face flush slightly. It was wild how even now, in a clinical setting, he could still do that to me.

What the hell is wrong with you, Via? Get it together. This isn't the time or the place.

I was embarrassingly aware of how my emotions—and apparently my hormones—seemed to override logic lately. Everything felt different now, like something had shifted, as though my internal wires had gotten crossed.

"Your EKG looks great," Brookens said enthusiastically, flipping through his notes. "Have you felt any irregular heartbeats this week? Skipping or PVCs?"

Jon shook his head. "None."

"Well, I didn't hear any either." He sat the clipboard aside.

"Let's talk about your echo," he said, his tone shifting slightly. "As you know, this test shows us how well your heart is pumping blood. When you left the hospital, your ejection fraction was at 37%—which, frankly, isn't good. But yesterday, your EF measured at 46%."

He paused, glancing between us, waiting for our reactions.

"That's significant," Brookens emphasized, leaning forward. "To see that much progress in such a short time is remarkable. It means your heart is responding well to treatment."

The words settled over me like a warm blanket. I couldn't help but smile now.

"This is encouraging," Brookens continued. "Obviously, we're not out of the woods yet—there's still a long way to go. But this tells me what I was hoping to see: you're on the path to recovery. You're young, healthy, and fit. That gives you a huge advantage."

Jon nodded, processing the words. I could feel the tension in the room beginning to ease.

And then, after a pause that felt like it could swallow the room, he added, "Which brings us to the timeline for your procedure."

Here we go.

"You absolutely need an ICD," Brookens said, looking directly at Jon. "With CPVT, your risk for dangerous arrhythmias remains. But I think your heart will continue to recover. If your ejection fraction keeps improving, we'll have a much better scenario. But we need more time to be sure."

Jon nodded, his expression thoughtful. "So... what's next?" he asked cautiously.

Brookens smiled. "What's next, for now, is more of the same. But let's talk about the medication you're on."

Jon's reaction was instant. His jaw tightened, and I could see the frustration in his eyes.

"I know," Brookens said gently. "I know it's hard on you. But it's working. It's keeping your heart rhythm stable, and that's critical right now. I want to be clear, this is not necessarily the long-term solution. As we refine your treatment plan, we'll be able to have deeper conversations about whether to discontinue amiodarone. You'll need a brief hospital stay during the transition, but the goal is to shift you back to a milder antiarrhythmic if we can. The medication will serve as your primary defense. The ICD will be your safety net."

Jon glanced at me, clearly gauging my reaction. I couldn't hide my relief, and when he saw it, he offered a genuine smile. "I guess that sounds like a plan," he said, his dimples deepening.

Brookens nodded, pleased, but then his demeanor shifted to a more focused, serious tone.

"How's your appetite been?" Brookens asked Jon, flipping through his notes.

Jon shrugged but shook his head slightly. "Not great, to be honest."

"Well," Brookens said, "I'd like to see you regain the weight you've lost. Try to eat more with your meds. That should help curb the nausea."

When he asked about Jon's blood pressure throughout the day, I was ready. I pulled the little notebook from my bag and handed it over, feeling a small surge of pride that my persistence was about to pay off.

Brookens looked genuinely impressed. "Well, now, why doesn't this surprise me?" he said with a laugh, flipping through the pages. "You've been doing your homework, haven't you?"

Brookens spent a moment examining the data. "So, it seems like your blood pressure is higher, and your pulse is lower in the mornings. Then, as the day goes on, they reverse?"

Jon and I exchanged a glance. In hindsight, that sounded about right.

"That makes sense," Brookens said, closing the notebook and handing it back to me. "This isn't from the medication—it's your body compensating."

He leaned forward, his tone serious. "Right now, we're still seeing more benefits than drawbacks with this drug. So, I need you to stick with it a little longer."

He assured us the worst of the side effects would resolve soon, and reminded Jon of the regular blood tests and screenings he would need. Then he leaned back in his chair. "Other than that, it's straightforward. We'll have more follow-ups like this. As part of the pre-surgery prep, there'll also be another series of diagnostic tests, and a counseling session."

Jon looked skeptical. "Counseling?"

Brookens smiled, clearly anticipating the reaction. "Yes, really. It's just an hour, and every ICD patient completes it. It's a chance to sit down with a clinician and talk through the secondary effects of having the device. An ICD impacts daily life, and we want to make sure you're familiar with all the resources available to you—and your family—during the adjustment."

Jon sighed unenthusiastically. "Alright," he said, resigning himself.

"For now," Brookens continued, "just focus on rest and recovery. I know it's tough to slow down when you're used to being active." He glanced at me, and I exaggeratedly nodded. Brookens chuckled.

"Well," he said, "you can start easing back into things. Don't go running any marathons yet," he teased, earning a small grin from Jon. "But you can drive. Maybe return to work—just partial days, to start. See how you feel."

He leaned forward, meeting Jon's gaze. "Listen to your body. When you're tired, rest. You'll need a lot of it, but finding the balance between your physical and mental health is just as important. Does that make sense?"

Jon and I exchanged a glance, then nodded in agreement.

Brookens leaned back, scanning both of us. "Any questions for me?" he asked.

I shook my head. Unsurprisingly, Jon didn't have any either—the big talker that he was. It seemed like the appointment had reached its natural conclusion. I grabbed my bag, preparing to leave.

As we stood, Brookens added, looking directly at Jon, "This is a tough diagnosis. But you're doing well. And I know you've got a lot of people who care about you. I don't think our unit has ever had to manage the number of visitors we saw while you were there." He chuckled.

Jon offered a small smile, while I replied, "Yes, and thank you all for being so accommodating. Your nurses were incredible."

Brookens nodded, visibly pleased. "Well, I can tell you that Jon wasn't just popular with the visitors. The staff loved him too."

"Oh, I know," I teased, glancing at Jon. "Carolynn, especially. She adored him."

Jon's smile widened, though he looked slightly embarrassed.

Brookens laughed. "Oh, absolutely! She's still talking about you. They all are."

The thought struck me before I could filter it. "Maybe we could stop in and see her? I'd love to thank her again for everything she did."

Jon shot me a glance, clearly less enthusiastic about the idea, but Brookens seemed delighted. "I believe she's working today," he said. "And I'm sure she'd love to see you. Just be prepared for a lot of hugs."

We all laughed, and I couldn't help but notice Jon's subtle shift, as though he were already inching toward the door.

Brookens returned to his earlier point. "The thing is, Jon, you're fortunate—not just with your progress, but because you have an amazing support system. And," he paused, looking between us, "you two have each other. I'm no relationship counselor, but I can tell you, the bond I've seen between you two is stronger than what I see in most couples twice your age."

Jon and I exchanged a glance, both of us beaming. He reached for my hand, intertwining our fingers. The compliment felt unexpected but deeply appreciated.

"Thank you," I said earnestly.

Brookens waved it off. "I mean it. You two are young and just getting started, but if I could offer one piece of advice? Every relationship faces challenges. You might think of all this as getting the hard part out of the way early. If you can handle this, you can handle anything."

We both nodded, taking his words to heart.

"Here's the key," he added. "Be there for each other, yes. But also allow yourselves to be vulnerable. If you're scared, or worried, or feeling off—say so. Talk to each other. That's just as important as being strong."

The sincerity in his tone was touching. "We will," I assured him, while Jon nodded in agreement.

Brookens grinned. "Good. You two are going to be just fine." He punctuated his words with a wink.

With that, we said our goodbyes and made our way out.

***

Neither of us spoke right away. I intentionally waited, curious if Jon would say anything about the visit. We stepped into the elevator, the doors closing with a soft whoosh. He leaned casually against the wall, hands in his pockets. Finally, he glanced at me, a half-smile tugging at his lips.

"So... that was a little weird, wasn't it?"

I couldn't stop the grin that spread across my face.

Oh, you have NO idea how weird that got for me.

The thought almost made me laugh out loud. I was still a little flustered over my reaction—my completely out-of-place reaction—to him earlier.

But I knew the "weird" Jon was referring to was Brookens' unorthodox approach.

"I think he's brilliant. I love him!" I said.

We agreed that the doctor had made some great points. By the time we crossed the parking lot, my mood was still buoyant. I pulled Jon's keys from my bag, anticipating what he'd want before he even had to ask. I held them up, and as he stretched out his hand, I dangled them playfully for just a second before dropping them into his palm.

We shared a deep, knowing smile. The exchange needed no words; it was a silent acknowledgment of the excellent news we'd just heard.

Jon opened the passenger-side door for me, and I slid into the seat. Once he closed his door and settled behind the wheel, I leaned over impulsively and kissed him, deeply and passionately. I pulled back just as I felt his breath hitch and caught the unmistakable gleam in his eyes.

"So... are we good?" he asked, his smile turning sly.

"SO good!" I replied, my own grin so wide it hurt.

For a moment, we both stared straight ahead, letting the intensity of the moment dissolve into a warm, comfortable calm.

Finally, Jon turned to me. "Do you seriously want to go see Carolynn?"

The cloud-nine feeling hadn't left me. "Hell yes!" I said with a laugh.

***

By the time we arrived home, it was nearing noon. The morning had felt much longer—though Jon had received the best possible news, the emotional weight of it all left us both drained.

"You should call your family and tell them the good news," I gently prompted as we stepped inside.

"I will," he said, waving it off. "But not right now. Come sit with me." He patted the couch cushion beside him, a small smile playing on his lips.

I joined him, noticing the way his posture softened as he leaned back. He must be exhausted, I realized. Despite how composed he'd seemed at the doctor's office, I imagined the relief had come with its own kind of weight.

"Hey there," he murmured, dimples deepening as his arm stretched out in invitation.

Without hesitation, I nestled into him, the familiar warmth of his presence immediately grounding me. His scent—simple and clean, just aftershave and deodorant—wrapped around me, comforting in its familiarity. His fingers drifted through my hair, sending small tingles down my spine.

I closed my eyes, letting the moment envelop me. The last few weeks had changed the way I saw everything. Every little thing I might once have taken for granted now felt like a treasure. The rhythm of his breathing, the weight of his arm around me—all of it felt profoundly significant.

As my body relaxed, so did my mind, until I felt the pull of sleep creeping in. I adjusted slightly, resting my head on his chest. Then I heard it—his heartbeat. Strong. Steady. The sound that had become both a comfort and an anchor.

The moment felt electric, as if being this close completed some invisible circuit between us. The air itself seemed charged, humming with an almost imperceptible energy. I stayed like that, listening, my drowsiness replaced by a quiet awe.

That's when I noticed the familiar ache—butterfly feelings in my lower body.

I was confused by my sudden arousal. And so, my instinct was to pretend it wasn't happening. Still... I let my hand run across his abs. *God he's sexy.* The sexual energy was intoxicating.

I felt him caress the back of my neck. He lightly touched my chin, tilting my face up towards his. I hesitated. I wanted him in a way that was hard to describe. It felt primal.

But is he ready?

As if to answer my question, he kissed me, his soft tongue brushing mine.

After a moment, he pulled back. "Are you going to finish what you started in the parking lot?" he whispered, a devious smile on his lips.

Absolutely.

I remained hyper attuned to his body.

Being with him felt so natural and familiar.

Yet so exhilarating and new.

Afterwards, we enjoyed the quietude, still embracing.

His eyes were so beautiful it was unreal. I found myself wondering how I got so lucky as to have this magnificent man beside me.

Jon kissed my forehead, breaking the silence. "I don't know how I got so lucky," he said softly.

I smiled, appreciating how much those words meant—more than he probably realized.

Lately, it seemed like he always knew what I was thinking.

That used to baffle me, but now it just felt... right. Natural.

My gaze lingered on him, my thoughts wandering to places I couldn't quite explain. Was it the fact that we'd almost lost everything that made me feel so intensely about him now? Or had something shifted in him, something I didn't yet understand?

Probably both.

Whatever it was, it drew me in—his strength, his vulnerability, his quiet resilience. And though the thought of almost losing him still haunted me, I was profoundly grateful. Grateful for this moment. Grateful for the chance to hold on to him.

Chapter 37

Friday evening, we sat around the firepit in Jon's backyard. Just our usual friend group. Jon had spontaneously decided we should have a cookout—the first of the season. It was last minute, but I was thrilled he felt up to it.

Now, as the sunset painted the sky in deep orange and fuchsia, we took our seats around the fire. Kyle had been hanging out with us earlier, pestering everyone, until his mom called him home for a bath and bed. Jon convinced him to go by promising he could come back in the morning to play video games.

Great.

With the little ears gone, our conversation turned to more adult topics—namely, Cary's latest girlfriend drama. He'd been dating Emily for about four months. Not long, but considering Cary's dating history, it was long enough to suggest he might have caught feelings.

Turns out, Emily had been two-timing him. Cary only found out when the other guy, Craig, called to introduce himself. Neither had known about the other until one of Emily's coworkers mistook Craig for Cary. In an unfortunate but hilarious turn of events, Cary and Craig devised a plan: Cary invited Emily on a date, and when it was time to pick her up, both he and Craig were waiting at her front door.

The reaction had been epic, and ironically, Craig and Cary became friends out of the ordeal. Craig was even sitting with us now, laughing as we grilled Cary about his next move with Emily.

Cary, however, was desperate to change the subject. "Okay, okay, guys," he said, throwing up his hands. "Enough. She called me this evening, I didn't answer. What more do you want?"

Then, trying to redirect the attention, he turned to Jon with a more serious expression. "Anyway, now that the dust has settled... I just... I have to ask you, man. I've been thinking about it."

Oh, shit, Cary. Don't.

Not here, in front of everybody.

Cary stammered, clearly unsure how to phrase his question, though it was obvious where he was headed. "What was it like?" he finally asked.

Jon's face remained neutral, almost curious. "What was what like?" he replied slowly, his sincerity masking the sparkle in his eyes. He was toying with Cary.

Cary shifted uncomfortably. "You know... everything that happened. I just wondered what it felt like."

He still wouldn't say the word.

Jon let the silence hang for a beat before responding. "You want to know what it's like to die?"

Whoa.

A pause followed, tense and heavy. "I mean... yeah," Cary admitted at last.

"It felt great," Jon deadpanned. "I can't wait to do it again."

The group froze, stunned into silence.

Then Jon's sly grin slowly spread, and his laugh broke the tension. Chuckles rippled around the fire, the humor cutting through the awkwardness.

"You're an asshole," Cary mumbled.

Jon grinned wider. "If you're going to bring up tough topics, I'm at least going to make you squirm."

His smile lingered, but I caught the sincerity beneath his words. He was right—it was a difficult topic. Even I had struggled to bring it up with him.

Jon softened his expression as he glanced at Cary. "It's cool," he said. "You're not the first to ask. I guess I should get used to it. Everyone wants to hear a bright tunnel of light story."

Jon's smile faded, and he seemed to drift into thought. He'd mentioned earlier in the week that a few people—one of his guitar students, and another coach on Kyle's soccer team—had danced around the same question. As private as Jon was, the curiosity had both amused and annoyed him.

"Is that not how it was, then?" Nikki asked quietly, her knees drawn up to her chest like she was waiting for a campfire ghost story.

I felt protective of him. "We don't have to talk about this," I whispered.

Jon squeezed my hand gently, reassuring me. He turned back to the group and sighed. "I can't say it wasn't like that... or that it was," he said carefully, staring into the fire. "Because the truth is, it feels like a dream. All of it. And honestly... I have trouble knowing what was real and what was just... me... shifting." He paused, adding, "Or maybe that was the realest part of all."

The word *"shifting"* hung in the air, specific yet vague.

"Well... was it scary?" Nikki asked hesitantly.

"No," Jon said quickly, his smile returning. This time, there was no sarcasm, no distance—only sincerity. "In fact, it felt more like... just... a transition, into a different state of consciousness. No, it wasn't scary. Not at all."

***

Later, as we relaxed in bed, Maize snored loudly at our feet. Jon casually wrapped an arm around me. "Thanks for sticking up for me earlier," he said softly.

I froze, already assuming he was referring to the conversation around the fire. "I just didn't want you to feel like you owe anybody anything," I said carefully. "You're not obligated to talk about It if you don't want to."

He was quiet for a moment before replying, "I guess I just don't want to say the wrong thing."

The wrong thing? What does that even mean?

I waited, letting him continue.

"It's easy enough to sense the answers people expect," he said finally. "I mean, everyone has their beliefs, their own personal views. But I think, deep down, they're all looking for the same thing: reassurance that they don't have to be afraid."

My thoughts swirled. Jon always carried such a calm demeanor, with an almost effortless grace in the way he spoke. I doubted anyone would ever associate fear with his experience. Still, the idea that he felt a responsibility to offer comfort struck a chord. It was both heart-wrenching and admirable.

"I hope you don't feel like you have to be that way with me," I said, my voice steady. "You can talk to me. Openly. You don't have to steer me in any particular direction."

He chuckled lightly. "Oh, I wouldn't even try with you. I know you've already analyzed it all up here," he said, tapping my temple playfully.

I smiled. He knew me too well. Yet despite all my overthinking, there was still so much I didn't understand—about It, about what had happened to him, about how he had changed. My thoughts drifted back to Carolynn's words during our visit.

After greeting Jon with a bear hug and fussing over him in her warm Southern drawl, she had turned to me.

"Come here, honey bunch! Bring it in!" she'd said, enveloping me in a tight hug. Her enthusiasm nearly rocked us back and forth, and I'd felt a sudden wave of emotion. By the time she pulled back, tears were welling in my eyes.

"Thank you so much for everything," I'd said, my voice trembling. "I really don't think he'd be here right now if it weren't for you."

"Oh, sweetheart," she'd replied warmly, holding both my hands and looking into my eyes. "He did all the hard work. I was just a friendly voice guiding him home."

Guiding him home.

Her words lingered in my mind now. Where had he been, then?

Where had he gone during those moments when his heart had stopped?

The question burned within me, and I finally summoned the courage to ask. "How did you know about Mary?" I asked quietly, my head resting against his arm. "How did you know where her room was—or even *who* she was?"

He didn't answer right away, and I started to regret asking. But then he spoke. "I don't know," he said, his voice soft. "She just... felt familiar. I felt like I remembered her talking to me."

"What did she say?"

"I don't remember everything exactly. It really does seem more like a dream... a really vivid one. It was like... she called to me. So... I went to her, and we were talking. And then, at one point, she asked me if I was lost. And I said no. I told her I only came because she asked me to. And then she laughed. She said, *'well, I could feel you all the way down here. And I thought you might be lost. But if you're not, then you should go back.'"*

I listened, fascinated by his recounting of a completely implausible conversation. And yet... Mary was *real.* We *met* her. And before we ever met her, she had described Jon with striking accuracy.

The entire concept gave me chills, but in an inexplicably comforting way. "She told you to go back?" I heard the perplexity in my voice.

Jon shrugged. He gave a small, half-laugh, like he was trying to dismiss his own story.

"So, was it like when you said you remembered Carolyn talking to you? When you saw blue light?" I asked with a small smile, recalling his story about seeing Abigail.

He was quiet for a moment. "The first time... everything was so vibrant, so bright blue. And I saw the baby. And I remember Carolynn talking to me. But the second time... when you were there... I saw white light. And I talked to Mary."

His words hit me like a bolt of lightning. I remembered that moment. The look in his eyes as they seemed to drift past me. I shivered. "You saw white light then?" I whispered.

"Yeah," he murmured. "It was all around you. You looked so beautiful. And then it just got brighter and brighter until it was all I could see."

I lay against him, speechless, awestruck by his words.

"It was nice," he continued. "Before that... the medicine felt awful."

I nodded silently. I'd known it had. I could see it on his face that night.

"But then, that feeling went away, and I knew... I knew I was dying. I think? But it felt... relaxing. *Better.*"

I listened, unable to speak.

"And then, after Mary, I heard other voices—familiar ones. Carolynn... you... my dad..."

My mind raced, replaying that night from my perspective, trying to reconcile his words with my memories.

"And then I woke up, and everything hurt."

His admission crushed me. "It hurt?"

"I saw you. And I wanted to be there. I picked you. But my chest hurt so bad. It hurt to breathe."

His words shattered me, sending hot tears streaming down my face. I tried to hold back a sob, but it broke through anyway.

Jon squeezed my shoulder. "I've upset you," he said, his voice apologetic.

Get a hold of yourself, Via, or this will be the last time he opens up to you.

"No," I said quickly, wiping my eyes and forcing a deep breath. "No, you haven't. I'm just... taking it all in."

I sat with a deep appreciation for what he had shared, knowing it had still barely scratched the surface of what he'd experienced. And also recognizing that it would probably take him a while... if ever... to fully process it all himself... much less share it with me.

And that was okay.

That night, I resolved to explore what I couldn't yet comprehend. For the first time, I decided to attend the voluntary discussion on campus that Saturday, led by my new psychology professor. It was time to start asking my own questions.

Chapter 38

When I answered the front door, Kyle pushed past me, slapping me on the leg as he ran by. "You're it!"

"That's cheating," I said, smiling despite the morning energy. I hadn't had enough coffee for this yet.

Kyle wrestled with Maize on the floor for a few minutes, before throwing himself down on the couch beside Jon. "When are you gonna coach our games again?" he said in a long pitchy whine.

"Geez, buddy, it's only been 2 weeks... cut me some slack," Jon said, laughing.

"Uh-uh," Kyle persisted, sticking out his bottom lip. "Today will make 3!"

That made Jon laugh harder. "I'll tell you what," he said. "How 'bout if I come out to your game this afternoon?"

Sucker.

Kyle's face lit up. "To coach?!?"

"To watch," Jon stated firmly, still smiling.

Kyle sighed dramatically, but seemed willing to accept the deal. "Fine." He conceded.

I thought that would be the end of it, but he mumbled, more to himself than to anyone, "When are you gonna be better anyway?" Then, as if the thought had just occurred to him, he perked up. "Hey! Let me see your scar!" Without waiting for a reply, he reached out and grabbed the bottom of Jon's shirt, attempting to push it up.

"Woah, there!" Jon quickly but gently intercepted Kyle's hand. "What exactly do you think you're doing?" He kept his tone playful, but I knew the undertone. Jon's bruises were healing nicely, but they were still obvious. If Kyle saw them, there would be questions.

So many questions.

My mind jumped back to when Kyle had come to visit Jon in the hospital. He'd known then about the planned surgery, although we'd been careful to spare the details. But apparently, he wasn't aware it hadn't taken place yet.

"There's no scar, Kyle." I jumped in quickly. "He didn't have the operation yet. There's nothing to see."

"Oh." Kyle sat back. I could see he was turning this over.

Jon shot me a quick look, as if to thank me for the bail out.

"But then...," Kyle said, looking at Jon, serious now. "What if you get sick again? I thought the operation was going to fix your heart?"

Shit.

"Does that mean you could die? If it's not fixed?"

I felt a pang of sympathy then. Kyle was smart for his age—and the kid was right. He wasn't saying anything the rest of us hadn't thought, at least at first.

I also felt sorry for Jon, who looked completely caught off guard by Kyle's questioning. But as usual, he quickly composed himself, and replied to Kyle, taking on a soft, parental voice.

"Well," Jon said thoughtfully. "The doctor wants me to rest up before I have my operation. But that's not something for you to worry about, okay? I'm taking medicine for my heart. I feel good. And I'm doing well... wouldn't you agree?"

I marveled at how Jon instinctively knew to reframe the subject as a question Kyle could answer.

Kyle nodded, his big eyes relaxing as a large grin took over.

"Good," Jon said cheerfully. "'Cause I'm about to kick your butt at Mario Kart!"

"Noooo," cried Kyle in a fake bawl, jumping up and down excitedly. "I'm gonna kick YOUR butt!"

I smiled. Jon was so good with kids...

"And with that, I'm going to leave you two at it," I said, heading to gather my things for the psychology group meet-up.

"Where are you going?" Kyle asked.

"To school."

"It's Saturday!"

"I know. I'm going to a study group."

"That's weird," Kyle stated. "And boring!"

Jon and I both laughed. I bent to kiss him on the cheek.

"Remember—you're watching. *Not* coaching," I reminded him, winking.

"Yes ma'am," he said with a grin.

"Don't call me ma'am!" I called over my shoulder.

"By Via." Jon called back.

"By Via!" Kyle mocked in a sing-songy voice.

***

I was only a week into the semester, but I already felt good about my course load. Jon had been right, as much as I hated to admit it, when he'd pushed me to keep going.

Straight out of high school, I'd thrown myself into an accelerated program to earn my associate degree, getting the technical coursework out of the way early. That gave me the skills to start working real jobs for paying clients. Now, as I worked to finish my bachelor's, I had a balanced schedule—one part advanced coding, which promised countless headaches, and one part Psychology, which was shaping up to be surprisingly fascinating.

Dr. Katherine Krykowsky, or "Dr. K," as she insisted we call her, taught the course. She was a captivating woman with quick wit and a dry sense of humor—my kind of person.

I guessed she was in her late fifties, though her appearance made it hard to be certain. Silver hair and a polished demeanor gave her an air of sophistication, but her bright blue eyes and sharp energy hinted at someone younger. A faint scar trailed from the corner of her right eye, down her cheek, and under her chin. It was so subtle I might not have noticed, except she'd pointed it out on the first day.

"The scar," she'd explained, "came from a horrific car accident when I was a teenager. It's barely noticeable now, but for a long time, it made me feel disfigured. The crash also claimed my best friend's life." She paused, her tone softening. "That trauma is what led me to study psychology and human behavior."

Her openness had disarmed us all. By the end of that first class, we were hooked. She'd cracked jokes, explained the syllabus, and laid out the requirements for our final research paper—a project that would span the term.

The paper was both exciting and intimidating. We could choose any topic, as long as it met the course objectives and received her approval. She'd stressed the importance of picking a topic early to stay on track with research milestones.

Topic selection was also the focus of the voluntary group discussion that Saturday afternoon. Dr. K seemed pleased when about ten of us showed up, joking that it was "practically a crowd" for an optional session.

I'd gone because I was curious to hear what my classmates were considering. The discussions ranged widely, touching on topics like childhood abuse and cognitive development, rehabilitation programs for incarcerated parents, and the psychology of substance abuse.

When it was my turn, Dr. K asked if I had any ideas.

"Not yet," I said with a shrug, though that wasn't entirely true.

From the beginning, I'd had an inkling of what I might do. But I wasn't sure how to approach it—or even if it was appropriate. The thought of sharing it with the group made my stomach twist. I needed more time to sort it out.

***

I left the campus coffee shop a little after 2 p.m., a decaf coffee in hand for Jon. Kyle's soccer game was still going, so I decided to stop by.

There were multiple games taking place, but I easily spotted the younger kids on the far field, their bright blue Grandpoint Greyhounds T-shirts bobbing about in the afternoon sun.

I made my way in their direction, and finally spotted Jon standing at the far end of the field, hands shoved in his pockets, chatting with one of the parents.

Good. He's behaving himself. He's not overdoing it.

As I approached, a woman pushing a toddler on the swings caught my eye and waved. I vaguely recognized her as a mom to one of the kids on Kyle's team. I waved back.

"They were so excited to see him!" She said, motioning toward Jon.

I offered a polite smile. "He was just as excited as they were." Was that true? Probably close enough.

"I was surprised to see him here!" She said. Her smile faded, and she lowered her voice, as if repeating gossip. "I didn't realize he was so sick." She was almost whispering, as if she was afraid the birds might hear. "How's it going? Is he receiving chemo?"

What? Fucking hell—she thinks he has cancer.

It clicked. If she hadn't heard the details, I could see how she might have jumped to that conclusion.

"Oh, no, it's not... he doesn't need chemo," I said quickly.

Thank God, no.

Her brow furrowed in confusion, and I felt compelled to elaborate, despite my instinct to keep things private.

"He has a heart condition," I admitted, the words feeling hollow and heavy as they left my mouth. It was the first time I'd spoken them out loud.

Her eyes widened. "Oh," she said, drawing the word out like it was worse than cancer. "I had no idea..."

"He's doing well, though! He's going to be fine!" I tried to sound upbeat. Convincing.

Her polite smile mirrored mine. "Oh, yeah! Of course. He looks great... I'm sure he's doing great."

Sure, you're sure.

I waved to the little girl on the swing and continued toward the field, eager to shake off the conversation.

Seeing Jon smiling and talking with a group of kids lifted my mood. Kyle was among them, his dark hair sticking up like a rooster's comb. Things looked normal. Normal enough to pretend.

"Hey, babe." I handed Jon the coffee. "Decaf," I added with a wink.

His face lit up when he saw me. "Vee! Wow... you came! Thank you," he said, kissing my cheek.

"Ew, gross!" Kyle teased, pulling a face.

"Mind your own gross," Jon shot back, laughing. "And pay attention to the game."

"We're losing, who cares?" grumbled a spiky-haired boy.

Jon crouched slightly, bringing himself to the kids' level. "Maybe you're losing because you're over here goofing around instead of helping your team."

"It's not our turn to play!" Kyle protested.

"That doesn't matter. You should be cheering them on," Jon said firmly. Then, raising his voice slightly, he clapped his hands once. "Alright, everybody—sit here, on the sideline."

To my surprise, the kids obeyed, settling into a row.

"You can't expect to win if you're not focused." Jon's tone was calm, but commanding. "When you're not on the field, support your teammates. They need your good vibes. Keep your hearts and minds in the game." He pointed to his chest, his temple, and the field in turn.

The kids nodded, their chatter quieting as they watched the game. Even Coach Dan, further down the field, noticed the change. He gave Jon a thumbs up, his exaggerated expression making us both laugh.

"It won't last," Jon murmured to me, grinning.

But it did. The kids stayed focused, for the most part, and their team scored four goals, winning with a penalty kick.

"I can't believe that worked!" Kyle shouted, his eyes wide with excitement.

"I told you—energy matters," Jon said to the cluster of kids around him. "Put it in the right place, and it makes all the difference."

His words hung in the air, perfectly logical for a soccer game, but I couldn't help wondering about the bigger context.

***

I followed Jon back to his place, the warmth of the afternoon still lingering. I was grateful I'd gone to the game. Normally, I'd find excuses—work, errands, anything—but I was glad I'd made the time.

Watching him with the kids, I couldn't help but feel proud. I always knew they loved him, but that afternoon I saw how much they respected him, too. They calmed down because he was calm. They followed his lead without hesitation, reflecting the steady energy he put into everything.

Even the parents noticed. One of them had stopped to say so. "I teach second grade," the woman had said, sounding both lighthearted and sincere. "How much would you charge to come visit my class on Monday?" Her husband had laughed, nodding in agreement, and we'd all shared a chuckle.

But I understood what she meant.

Back in Jon's kitchen, I wrapped my arms around him, pressing a kiss to his lips. "Well done, Coach," I teased.

"I didn't coach," he said, shaking his head, though he pulled me closer.

"That's not true," I replied, smiling up at him. "There's more to coaching than yelling from the sidelines. When you talk, they listen. And what you told them today? That's the kind of advice they'll remember."

He smiled, a quiet, unguarded expression that I never got tired of seeing.

I love getting that smile from him.

"You're really good with kids."

He kissed me again. "Am I?"

"Umhm"

"Should we practice making some?" He grinned mischievously.

I giggled quietly as he squeezed my ass. "Just practice."

Chapter 39

We'd made separate plans for Friday. I'd been spending most of my time at Jon's lately, so I'd set aside the day for Krissy. It had been a while since we'd had a girls' night, and I was looking forward to it—just like old times.

Jon had company as well. Jason, one of the guys from FaultCode, was in town. Jason was a phenomenal guitarist who wrote most of his band's music, much like Jon did for FR. They'd been co-writing before It happened. Lately, Jon hadn't touched his guitar much, so when Jason called to check in, I encouraged him to hang out.

I texted Jon before Krissy and I headed to the mall to shop for her sister's birthday present.

The day flew by as we ran errands, laughing and catching up. When we stopped to grab dinner, I realized I hadn't checked my phone all day. I pulled it out, expecting a reply from Jon. Nothing.

I guess he's busy too.

After dinner, Krissy and I settled in to watch one of the scary movies we'd rented. We talked through most of it, only pausing to watch the gory parts. Slasher films weren't exactly brain teasers. By the time it ended, though, a small knot of unease had formed in my stomach. Jon still hadn't replied.

I called him. The phone rang until his voicemail picked up. I hung up without leaving a message.

Another hour passed. It was after 8 p.m. when I called again. Still no answer.

"All good?" Krissy asked.

"Yeah." My voice was steady, but my nerves were starting to fray.

Finally, I called Mike. I knew Fridays were busy at the shop, but he picked up on the third ring. He hadn't heard from the guys, and offered to call Jason. I declined, not wanting to seem like a possessive girlfriend—even though that wasn't what this was.

But the knot in my stomach tightened.

Krissy watched me carefully. "You should just go over there," she said. "I can tell it's bugging you, and I don't blame you."

"I don't even know if he's there," I mumbled, trying to play it off. But the thought made my anxiety worse.

After a bit of encouragement from Krissy, I grabbed my bag and keys. It didn't take much convincing—my nerves were already winning.

***

An unfamiliar car was parked along the curb when I pulled into the driveway. New York plates. Jason's, probably. But there was no sign of Jon's truck.

Where the hell did they go?

The front door was unlocked, so I let myself in. Maize trotted from the back of the house, nudging her cold nose into my hand. The living room was dark—unusual if someone was home.

A light was on in the kitchen, but the house was quiet. Too quiet.

The unease I'd been trying to suppress threatened to take over.

"Where's your butthead owner?" I muttered to Maize, attempting a smile at my own joke. But I was worried now. It wasn't like Jon to just go dark like this.

I wandered to the basement door. Could they be down there? Jon hadn't been in the studio much since... everything. But if he was here, why hadn't he answered his phone?

My heart thumped as I strode to the door and yanked it open. Soft light spilled into the stairwell, and I could hear laughter and a low murmur of voices.

Relief hit me first. Then confusion. Then a flash of anger.

I'd cut my plans short, raced back here, and worked myself into a frenzy, only to find him hanging out in the studio like everything was perfectly fine?

I stomped down the carpeted stairs, determined to let him know just how inconsiderate he'd been. The basement-turned-studio came into view as I rounded the corner.

Jon and Jason were there, each lounging in a black rolling chair. Jason had his feet propped up on an amp, grinning. Jon sat with a guitar across his lap, jotting something down on a notepad. The room was alive with the quiet hum of amps, guitars leaning against walls, and the faint glow of equipment lights.

Jason waved. "Hey, Via!"

Jon's smile faded as he caught my expression. "Hey, babe. What's wrong?"

I stared at him, biting back the words tumbling through my head. I'd been worried sick, imagining God knows what, while he was here—laughing, playing music, acting like things were normal.

And that's what stopped me. This *was* normal. For the first time in weeks, it actually felt like it.

"I..." I hesitated, suddenly unsure. "Why haven't you answered your phone?"

Jon looked confused, patting his pockets and glancing at the desk. "Oh, man. I guess I left it in the truck. I'm sorry."

"Where *is* your truck?"

"In the garage," he said slowly, like it was obvious.

Fuck.

Of course. I hadn't even thought to look.

"Oh," I said, forcing a casual tone. "Okay. Cool. Just checking in. Hey, Jason." I waved at him, matching his friendly smile.

Jason grinned. "Pull up a chair!"

"No, that's okay," I said, retreating. "You guys have fun."

I turned and headed back upstairs, Maize trotting at my heels.

***

I was still brooding, leaning against the counter as the coffee pot finished brewing, when I heard heavy footsteps on the stairs. Jason and Jon emerged into the kitchen.

"See ya, Via!" Jason said, giving me a quick hug. "Gotta hit the road—traffic's gonna suck."

I nodded, pouring myself a cup of coffee while they talked in the foyer. After a few minutes, I heard the front door open and close.

Jon walked back into the kitchen, grabbing a glass and filling it with water. His eyes flicked toward me. "Are you okay? It felt like you were mad when you came downstairs."

It felt?

That was an odd way to phrase it.

Why does he seem so off lately?

And why am I still so upset?

"I was just worried," I said, my voice clipped. "I didn't know where you were."

"I'm sorry." He sounded sincere. "I thought you'd be busy with Krissy all day. And I guess I left my phone in the truck when Jason and I got back from the store. I didn't even realize until you mentioned it. You know I would've answered if I'd had it."

His explanation softened me. "I'm sorry," he said again, his voice warm now, with a hint of a smile. "I can tell you're pissed—your eyes always get that bright, shiny look when you're mad."

I smirked. "Uh-huh."

Jon turned to his pill bottles, casually dropping one pill from each into his palm before tossing them back and chasing them with water.

My eyes darted to the clock. It was almost 11 p.m. The sight reignited my frustration.

"You're *just* now taking your meds?" I demanded. Forgetting his phone was one thing, but his heart medication? That was serious.

He glanced at the clock and shrugged. "I'm only a couple of hours off, Vee. It's fine."

"It's *not* fine," I snapped. "I'm glad you're getting your mojo back, and I'm happy to see you in the studio again, but you *can't* lose sight of reality. You need to take your meds. *On time.*"

His expression softened. "Vee," he said gently. "I'm sorry I worried you. Please don't be mad at me."

He closed the distance between us, standing so close I could feel the warmth of him. His hands rested on my hips, his eyes searching mine. Their softness melted the edges of my anger.

"Besides," he said with a sly grin, "I've had my mojo back for a while. And those gorgeous green eyes are making me crazy right now."

I let him kiss me, pulling me in. It always amused me when he complimented my eyes. His were the most beautiful I'd ever seen.

But when he pressed closer, I gently pushed him back. As irresistible as he was, I wasn't letting him off the hook that easily.

"It's late," I said with a sigh, grabbing my bag from the counter and heading for the door.

"What?" he asked, surprise coloring his voice. "You're not seriously driving back there tonight, are you?"

"Hey," I called over my shoulder. "I had plans too, you know."

"Yeah, but you're already here now," he said, quickly catching up and stepping in front of me to block the door. "I'll be all alone. I'm not ready for that. I might forget to take my pills in the morning."

I turned to face him, meeting his intense gaze. We locked eyes, a silent battle to see who could keep a straight face longer.

His dimples appeared first, and my frown cracked. I couldn't hold back a laugh.

"You're such an ass," I grumbled.

His grin widened. "But you love me."

***

I was sitting cross-legged on the bed, reading from my Psych text and taking notes for an assignment. It was getting late, but I'd seized the opportunity to get some work done while Jon was in the shower. When he came out, he had to move my backpack before there was room on his side of the bed. Technically, *both* sides were his, but I stayed there so often at this point, we'd already naturally worked out who's side was whose. While moving my things to the stand beside the bed, I saw him do a double take. "Isn't that Tamara's?"

Shit.

I knew immediately what he was referring to. Earlier that morning I had talked to Tamera and reminded her she could stop by for the stethoscope she'd forgotten. She told me she had several, and suggested we keep it. I didn't object. Later when I'd been picking up around the house, I had brought it upstairs and thrown it down with a few of my other things—and then forgotten all about it. Had I remembered, I would have put it somewhere more discrete. Now, I needed to explain it.

Dammit.

"Yes, it's hers, but she said we could just hang on to it."

"Do we *need* it?"

He'd asked the question cautiously, with what came across as a balance of concern and sarcasm.

"No, I suppose not." I tried to play it off by joking in my own sarcastic tone. "Of course... I *do* have a boyfriend with a heart condition, so it's probably not a terrible idea to keep one around."

"Hm. Okay," he said simply. "I guess that's fair." He flopped down on the bed.

I was bemused that he didn't reciprocate with a wisecrack of his own, and then felt a little guilty, thinking I'd possibly hurt his feelings. I thought back to my conversation with Mike... about Jon's insecurities. I didn't want him to think I was being critical, or that I was excessively worried about him.

While the reason I'd given him for keeping it *was* valid—and completely logical... it wasn't the only reason, and now I felt like I owed him a better explanation. I wasn't quite sure how I was going to smooth this over, but I knew I needed to. I thought for a minute, but continued to look at my book. I remembered Dr. Brookens' advice about communicating.

I took a deep breath. "Do you remember the morning when you let me use that stethoscope?"

God, I SO don't want to have this conversation.

"Yeah, sure." He was kicked back with his arms behind his head.

"What made you decide to do that?" This was an honest question that I'd thought about multiple times since then.

"I don't know... I mean, I knew you were going to worry yourself about getting that journal entry." Now he kind of laughed. "It was just spur of the moment. I thought it would make it easier on you. With your numbers obsession and all."

Ha. Good.

He was joking, which meant he wasn't upset.

"Oh, it *was* easier!" I agreed. Knowing I would probably regret it, I made myself keep talking before I lost my nerve. "In fact, I liked it."

A few seconds ticked by before he replied.

"You *liked* it."

This came out sounding less like a question, and more like a statement, as if he were confirming he'd heard me right.

I had never been more grateful to have a textbook in front of me. Something to look at, other than him.

I stared down at it. "Yeah. Like... I *really* liked it." I was starting to get hot, from embarrassment. "It sounded nice... and it made me feel closer to you."

Wait to go, Via. There's no walking this back, now.

I'd hoped I'd made myself seem nonchalant enough. I kept writing in my notebook, painfully aware of the silence.

Finally, after what felt like an eternity, he had apparently thought through my revelation.

"I see...," he said thoughtfully.

A few more brutal seconds of silence passed. Then he added, "Well... you sold me on that *last* part, for sure."

I didn't respond. I couldn't. I was trying desperately to concentrate on my work, but my brain was glitching.

Why the fuck did you just tell him that?

My inner voice was astounded.

After a solid minute or 2 of silence, I couldn't stand it anymore. I could sense him looking at me, so I quickly glanced over.

He was lying on his side with his head propped on his hand, studying me curiously.

"What??" I snapped, struggling not to laugh at my own embarrassment.

He shrugged innocently and shook his head. "Nothing."

But I could see the intrigue in his expression, and a hint of amusement in his eyes.

"Jeezus!" I turned back to my text. "Can we please just... *not?*"

I needed the awkwardness to be over. He said nothing else about it, and thankfully after a few more minutes of agonizing quiet, the conversation moved on—mostly thanks to the dog joining us in the bed.

Thank God for Maize.

After a while, somehow, I managed to finish my assignment. I gratefully slapped the textbook closed and dropped it to the floor beside the bed. Jon had patiently waited for me to finish, so I clicked the lamp on the nightstand down to the dimmest setting. As if on cue, Maize got up and flumped down at the foot of the bed, giving me room to curl up beside him. He draped his arm around me in a hug, and for a long time, we simply embraced. I thought maybe we'd both just drift off. But after enjoying the quiet for a while, he said softly "*Soo...* you're saying that there's a way for you to feel even *closer* to me, than we are now?"

Oh God.

I felt a burst of nervous energy, unsure where this was headed but feeling so self-conscious that I didn't know how to respond. I hoped that if I stayed quiet, he'd let it drop.

But instead, he reached over, picked up the stethoscope from the stand and brought it between us.

Fucking hell.

I felt my stomach clench.

"Are you *serious?*" I whispered, incredulously, feeling myself blush. "You really want to do this, *now?*"

"I'm glad that you told me," He replied quietly. "I don't mind. I *want* you to feel close to me."

He placed it into my hands, but I wasn't sure how to respond, suddenly feeling weirdly shy around him.

"Go ahead." He encouraged me with a faint, curious smile.

It was the ultimate gesture. I realized it was the deepest act of intimacy he could have offered me. By handing me the stethoscope, he was submitting. It felt as if he were inviting me to experience the very essence of his life.

I felt both excited and terrified at the same time, unsure which emotion would override the other. But he seemed willing, and somewhere in the back of my head I recognized that we were already way too far past the line to go back.

I timidly pushed up his shirt. Not the whole way—just partially, enough to show his abs and lower ribs. I was burning with anticipation as I put the earpieces in, and holding the end of the stethoscope, slid my hand under his shirt.

I placed the cold metal to his skin, and was instantly greeted by his heartbeat, loud and strong in my ears. I wondered if he was feeling apprehensive as well. This *had* to be weird for him. He was completely vulnerable, and certainly not in any type of context that he was familiar with.

I paused. Listening to him drove me wild with excitement. It made my entire being tingle. The way it felt was inexplicable.

But then, the intoxication of the moment took over, and I felt my inhibition slip away. Letting the diaphragm rest freely on his chest, I reached up and gently placed my hand on his neck, my fingers easily finding his pulse. He made no move to resist, but remained permissive. In fact, he reached up to caress the back of my neck.

Our eyes met. His were trusting, yet exotic—a warm, beautifully golden hue that seemed to sparkle in the dim light. I admired his exquisiteness, as his pulse throbbed under my touch. Whatever was happening felt electric.

I leaned over, lightly kissing his lips. I was pleased to hear the rhythmic contractions in his chest speed up. I kissed him more intensely, and then suddenly the teasing view I had of his chest wasn't enough, and I asked him to take off his shirt.

He complied. But then, in a single smooth motion, he turned, gracefully pulled me down onto my back, and was on top of me in an instant. This time, it was he who bent down to kiss me.

"Hey!" I whispered, trying to sound indignant. "Who said I was done with you?"

"You don't have to be done," he said playfully, with a grin. "I thought we were just getting started."

He had skillfully turned the tables, and slipped his hand under my shirt. I had only been wearing a tank top and boy-short style underwear, and it took him no time to have those pulled off. I haphazardly threw the stethoscope aside, purely preoccupied with this new agenda. As he glided his hand down to my thigh, I knew it was only a short matter of time before he discovered how excited I'd become.

One of the many things I loved about Jon was how intentional he was. His movements, his eye contact, his touch... everything seemed slow and deliberate—and very different from the sexual experiences I'd had with other guys. Sex with Jon was erotic. He had an uncanny way of gauging exactly where I was in the journey, and would always proceed accordingly.

As usual, he did not disappoint.

He delayed penetration until I was physically aching for him.

Silently begging.

That night he brought me to the hardest, most intense orgasm I had ever experienced in my life. It seemed to go on and on, starting as a deep, violent explosion that sent shock waves rippling through my core. One wave after another surged, consuming all my senses in a transcendental experience.

If God were a feeling... I finally understood it.

I didn't know it was possible to feel that good.

***

We both laid motionless for a while, letting the intoxication wane.

Finally, I stretched, and turned onto my side, facing him, ready to get comfortable for the night. I slid my arm under the pillow, but felt something cold—and remembered that I had shoved the stethoscope aside during the heat of the moment. I grabbed it and pulled it out, with the full intention of dropping it onto the floor with my textbook. But when he saw it, he raised an eyebrow and grinned mischievously. "Are we going to go again?"

I couldn't help but giggle. "Stop it. It's not like that." I insisted sheepishly.

"Really?" he quipped, eyes sparkling. "Because it sure seemed like—"

"Stop!" I shoved him playfully, cutting him off.

He laughed and shrugged, but his grin was devilish. "I mean... I can't say I saw this one coming, but hey. It's an ironic twist."

"Oh God, *please* shut up!" Laughing, I rolled over, still trying to wipe the impish smile from my face.

He leaned over me, giving me a quick kiss. "Fine."

His eyes still glittered with that same look of mild amusement he'd had a while ago. "Just sayin'... I can work with that."

"Seriously," I insisted, still smiling, but also genuine. "It's not just about *that.* I can't explain it, I just like it. It relaxes me. Especially after—"

you almost died.

This time, I cut myself short. I didn't want to finish the thought—it didn't need to be said out loud. The humor in my voice had faded, and the familiar heaviness of the situation crept back in.

"It's okay," he said, matching my shift in tone. "I get it."

He held out his arm, inviting me to scoot closer. "Come here," he added softly.

I curled in beside him, and he wrapped his arm around me.

Why *had* I enjoyed that so much? It's not like I had a full-fledged kink—despite what the adorable perv lying next to me had tried to insinuate. It was deeper than that. Harder to explain. Something inherently sexy about the sense of connectedness it brought.

And I was pretty sure he damn well understood that, too.

It was emotional. Spiritual, maybe. I cherished these moments—the spaces that seemed to stretch the distance between *It* and us. They softened the otherwise constant reminders of how little time had passed since he'd been in the hospital, teetering on the edge of life and death.

Since then, he'd become the embodiment of resilience. He'd made it easy—at least sometimes—for the rest of us to forget how close we'd come to losing him. But it couldn't have been easy for him. It was humbling to even consider.

How do we balance the magnitude of what happened with the mundaneness of every day?

In that moment, he seemed content, quietly running his fingers through my hair. So, I stayed there with him, trying not to dwell on how bad things had been, and just let myself feel the weight of the moment.

It felt... profound. And unexpectedly, I felt tears welling.

I wiped my eyes, thinking I was being discreet.

He must have noticed, though, because as I settled in and he pulled me closer with both arms, his voice turned gentle. "Talk to me. What are we thinking about?"

"Nothing. I'm fine... I swear. I'm just thinking about how grateful I am."

"I'm the one who's grateful. It doesn't quite seem fair. I have the smartest, sexiest, most beautiful woman in the world at my side. And you have a boyfriend with a heart condition."

Ouch.

Oh God.

I guessed my comment from earlier had stung more than I realized—or ever intended.

Fuck.

I turned so I could see his face. He gave me a half-smile.

I chose my words carefully.

"Honestly... I do want something better," I said, my voice steady. "I want a husband with a heart condition."

He let out a soft laugh, his smile blooming into a full grin—the real kind.

"Are you sure? You haven't changed your mind yet?"

"I've never been more certain about anything in my life."

His dimples made my heart flip.

"I need you to understand something," I continued, my throat tightening. "I have never been more in love with you than I am right now."

I didn't care if it sounded cheesy. It was the honest-to-God truth.

Chapter 40

"Hey, are you busy?" Nikki asked, when I answered my phone.

I glanced at Jon and Maize, the 3 of us relaxed and cuddling on the couch. I thought about saying yes.

"No, what's up?"

"Can you come pick me up at the shop?"

"Where's your car?"

"It's here in the parking lot. It won't start, and Mike still has another client coming in. I really don't wanna have to hang around here until he's done."

"Oh, shit. That sucks." I said, straightening up. "Yeah, I'll be over."

When I hung up, Jon raised an eyebrow like he was afraid to ask.

"Nikki wants me to pick her up from the shop. Her car won't start."

Jon smirked. "That's because she's still driving around in that piece of shit Volkeswagen."

"She loves that car!" I scolded, trying not to laugh. "Anyway, I'm going to get her. You can come along—if you can be nice."

Jon grumbled something else I couldn't catch, but stood up. "Fine." He said. "But I'm driving."

I shrugged. "Suit yourself." I picked my keys up off the coffee table and handed them over.

"My vehicle," he stated.

I shrugged again and rolled my eyes.

***

Mike's tattoo shop sat on the corner, occupying one half of an old duplex that had been converted into a commercial space, with a small parking lot out back. We pulled in next to Nikki's Jetta and headed in through the back door.

Mike was wiping down his workstation while Nikki perched in the client chair.

"Thanks for coming!" she said, hopping up when she saw us.

"What's wrong with it?" Jon asked, directing the question more at Mike than Nikki.

Mike shrugged, visibly annoyed. "Ignition switch? Something electrical. Damn thing needs a trip to the junkyard."

Jon nodded. "Wanna take a look?"

Mike glanced at the clock. "I already dicked around with it for half an hour. I've got a guy coming in soon for an arm piece, but yeah, we can go take another quick look."

Nikki and I sat on the back steps, watching the guys huddle over the car. Mike popped the hood, demonstrated that the engine wouldn't start, and joined Jon at the front. Their heads bent together, poking and prodding like they knew what they were doing.

"Do you think either of them has a clue?" Nikki asked dryly.

We exchanged a look, stifled smirks, and then laughed anyway.

"Well," I said, grinning, "we've got an artist and a musician. Unless it's a flat tire, I'd say we're doomed."

Nikki chuckled. "Yeah, I think I'm screwed. Looks like a trip to the garage."

"Or the junkyard," I added.

She rolled her eyes.

After a few minutes, we wandered over to the car. Mike turned to Nikki, wiping his hands on a rag.

"Sorry, babe. My guy's gonna be here any minute. I need to get ready."

"It's fine," she said, giving him a quick peck. She glanced at me and Jon. "Mind if I hitch a ride back?"

"Yeah," Jon said, glancing at the engine. "But give me a sec. I want to check a few more things."

Nikki raised an eyebrow at me, her eyes practically saying, *This'll be good.* "Sure!" She said it brightly, but I could hear the sarcasm in her voice.

Jon motioned for Nikki to take the driver's seat. I leaned against the door, chatting with her while Jon occasionally called out instructions. "Try it now," he'd say, wiggling wires under the hood. Each attempt yielded nothing but silence.

After a few more tries, he came around to her side. "Let me in there," he said, gesturing for her to get out.

Nikki and I stepped back, watching as Jon slid into the driver's seat and turned the key. Still nothing. But instead of getting out, he stayed there, staring at the dashboard.

We walked back over and resumed places on the steps. A few minutes later, Nikki squinted her eyes in the direction of the car. "What's he *doing?*"

I followed her gaze. Jon was sitting there, one hand flat against the dash, the other reaching underneath it. He looked... focused.

Then, without a word, he climbed out, went to the back of his truck, and returned with a small tool kit.

We wandered closer as he knelt under the dash, unscrewing the panel. The screws clinked as he dropped them into the cupholder, one by one.

"Whatcha doing, babe?" I asked, trying to sound casual.

"There's an electrical problem," he said, his voice muffled from beneath the steering column. "I think it's in here."

Nikki's eyes went wide, and she mouthed, *What the fuck?*

I shrugged. Tried not to laugh out loud.

Nikki cleared her throat. "Hey... uh, how do you know that?"

Jon didn't respond right away. He carefully removed a chunk of the interior, exposing a mess of wires.

The sight made my doubts flare. "Maybe we should just let the garage handle it," I suggested, hoping to defuse the situation.

Jon slid out from under the dash and stood, brushing a bead of sweat from his temple. His gaze shifted between the two of us, a faint hint of irritation crossing his face.

"Do you want help or not?" he asked Nikki, his tone calm but direct.

She hesitated, glancing at me before answering. "I mean... yeah. If you're sure..."

Jon tilted his head, a smirk forming. "If I'm sure I know what I'm doing?"

"Yeah..." Nikki trailed off, looking awkward.

"Well," Jon said, his smirk widening slightly, "if I'm wrong, your car won't start. Which is exactly where we are now, isn't it?"

We stood there in silence for a beat. Finally, Nikki nodded.

"Cool," he said simply, turning back to the exposed wiring. "Can you go inside and ask Mike for a rag and some alcohol? Cleaning solution? Whatever he's got." He didn't even look back at us as he spoke.

We headed toward the shop, and as soon as we were out of earshot, Nikki shook her head. "So what—he's a fucking mechanic now?"

We both burst out laughing.

"Dude, I have no idea," I mumbled.

I'd stopped trying to make sense of Jon's erratic behavior lately. He had zero experience with cars, and yet here we were, just going along for the ride—possibly straight into disaster.

***

When we returned with the supplies, Jon was on his back, wedged awkwardly under the dash, working on something overhead. I watched, mystified. His bicep flexed as he twisted a wire, and my eyes drifted to where his shirt had ridden up, exposing a sliver of toned abs. Lately, every little thing about him seemed to turn me on.

"Here you go," I said, forcing myself to focus. I set the bottle of cleaner and rag on the seat within his reach.

"Thanks, Vee," he said without looking up.

I joined Nikki back on the steps, where we sat in silence for a moment, watching him work.

"Soo... he's been kinda weird lately, huh?" Nikki asked, breaking the quiet.

I sighed. "Weird is an understatement. It's been... a lot."

She nodded thoughtfully. "He's good, though, right?"

"Yeah," I said, smiling. "He's good."

"And you two?" She raised an eyebrow at me.

I felt my smile deepen, almost devilishly, thinking back to the incredible night before.

Sweet Jeezus.

"Oh yeah," I said, locking eyes with her.

Her sly grin mirrored mine. "Good for you," she teased, nudging my leg playfully.

About five minutes later, Jon pulled himself up, sitting back on the seat. A second after that, the Jetta's engine roared to life.

Nikki's eyes went wide. "No fucking way!" she gasped, and we both rushed over.

Jon stood, sweat glistening on his brow, slightly out of breath. I felt a pang of worry, but he grinned at us.

"How did you do that?" Nikki demanded, practically bouncing with excitement. "You don't know how to fix cars!"

"And yet..." Jon said evenly, gesturing to the idling Jetta.

I hugged him, and Nikki threw her arms around both of us. "You're a lifesaver!" She stepped back. "What was wrong with it?"

"Electrical," Jon said simply, shrugging like it was no big deal. "You had a loose connection. Some corroded wires. Shouldn't be a problem now."

Nikki squealed in delight, but Jon, ever the realist, added, "You should still get a better car. This thing is going to take a shit for real one day."

Nikki groaned but couldn't stop smiling.

Jon grabbed one of the dash panels and sat back down. "Give me a few minutes to put this back together, and you'll be good to go."

"Thanks, babe," I said, squeezing his shoulder before heading back into the shop to return Mike's cleaner.

***

Back in the shop, Mike was busy with his next client, the buzz of the tattoo machine filling the air. We stayed by the privacy wall, chatting from a respectful distance.

"Jon fixed it!" Nikki said, practically bouncing.

"No shit?" Mike glanced up, sounding pleasantly surprised.

"Yep! He's putting the dash back together now, and then I'll be out of your hair," she teased.

The buzzing of the tattoo machine stopped abruptly—silence enveloping the studio.

"Did you say he's putting the dashboard back together?" Mike asked, his tone skeptical.

"Yep!" Nikki chirped, missing the undercurrent in his voice.

"What was wrong with it?" he pressed, after a long pause.

"Loose connection and corroded wires," she said, mimicking Jon's matter-of-fact delivery. "He fixed it easy enough! Didn't even take long."

Okay, so she's definitely not picking up on this.

"Fixing a bad connection isn't the hard part," Mike said finally. "It's figuring out where to look."

That landed heavily, at least for me. He was right, wasn't he? It wasn't the *fix* that was impressive—it was how Jon found the problem at all. I filed that thought away, right next to the other ***Unexplainable Things Jon Said or Did Today.***

"What kind of car?" asked the guy in the chair, chiming in like an eager participant.

"Jetta," Mike muttered as he restarted the machine.

"Oh, those are a bitch to work on," the guy lamented.

Their conversation veered into Volkswagen complaints, but my mind had already wandered. Jon fixing a car? Where did that even come from? It wasn't like he'd been sneaking out to take classes at the local trade school.

"Do you ever talk to your neighbor?" I asked suddenly, my thoughts hopping tracks.

Mike glanced up. "Who?"

"The lady next door," I clarified. "The one who runs that New Age shop."

"We've said hello," Mike said with a shrug.

Nikki rolled her eyes. "You mean *Mizz Vanessa*? The tarot lady?" She threw in air quotes for emphasis.

"Is she nice?" I pressed, ignoring Nikki's sarcasm.

Mike shrugged again. "She's quiet and minds her own business. So yeah, I guess she's a good neighbor."

Jon walked in from the lot just then, heading straight for the sink to wash his hands. I made a mental note to stop by the shop sometime. Not that I was into tarot or crystals, but... well, maybe I was curious.

"I hear you got the beast roaring again," Mike said with a smirk as Jon emerged, wiping his hands on his pants.

"Think so. For now," Jon said, his faint grin tugging at the corners of his mouth.

"You got a multimeter?" Mike asked casually once the laughter died down.

My stomach dropped.

Of course he's suspicious. He's not buying Jon's casual shrug and "just a bad connection" explanation.

Jon shook his head. "Nah." Then, without missing a beat, he turned to the guy in the chair. "What's the story behind the sleeve?"

The diversion worked, but only because the client launched into an enthusiastic breakdown of his inspiration and plans for his next piece.

I glanced at Mike, who had returned to his work. His expression was calm, but I could tell he wasn't letting this go. Neither was I. This was one more log on the fire of questions that seemed to be stacking up around Jon lately.

***

The ride home from the shop felt strange. Not because of anything Jon said or did—at least not directly. The problem was that our conversation was maddeningly mundane.

He talked about tattoos, Mike's impressive portfolio, and even asked about how the website project was going.

Not once did he mention Nikki's car or how he'd managed to fix it.

I kept waiting for him to bring it up. *Shouldn't he?* It felt weird that he didn't.

Finally, my impatience got the better of me. "So—where did you learn how to fix cars?" I asked, staring straight ahead at the road.

He laughed, that casual, effortless laugh of his. "I don't know how to fix cars, Vee. It was just a basic electrical issue."

"Well, how did you know where to look?"

He shrugged. "It's just signal flow."

Signal flow.

I understood the concept when it came to audio. But a car? One he'd never worked on before? That wasn't the same... was it?

I stayed quiet, my thoughts a tangled mess. Was he oversimplifying it? Or worse—gaslighting me?

Back at Jon's, I was still struggling to manage my mood. My confusion about him—about what had just happened—kept churning with my frustration at my own spiraling thoughts.

I needed to reset. To regain a sense of control. And for once, I thought maybe I needed to do it alone.

"Hey," I said finally. "I think I'm going to head back to my place. I need to write a research proposal for class, and all my stuff's there."

Jon's expression flickered with disappointment, but he nodded, smiling anyway. "Okay... if you must. Call me later?"

"Of course."

I gathered a few of my things and headed outside. Jon followed me into the driveway, but I didn't linger on our goodbye.

I climbed into my car and shifted into reverse.

As I started backing out, he stepped toward the window.

"Are you okay?"

The doubt in his eyes made my chest tighten.

"Yes," I said, offering him a smile that I hoped was sincere. "Love you."

He seemed to relax.

"I love you," he mouthed as I pulled out of the driveway.

Chapter 41

For some reason, I had to blink back tears the whole drive home. I couldn't explain why. Nothing had happened. Not really. Maybe *I* was the one who needed my head examined.

How was it that one minute I felt so deeply connected to Jon—like our souls were intertwined—and the next, it was like talking to a stranger? Not a *bad* stranger... just someone I didn't fully recognize.

Maybe it was all in my head.

Except it wasn't.

Now, sprawled across my bed with my psychology notebooks, I seriously considered making an actual list of all the *what the fuck* moments over the past few weeks. The things that didn't add up. The things other people had noticed, too.

But then again, what good would that do? What would I do with the list once I made it? March up to Jon and shove it in his face demanding answers? It wasn't like he'd have them.

That realization struck me with a pang of guilt. Maybe I was being unfair. He was probably just as confused by all of this as the rest of us.

Right?

If that was true, then my choice of research topic felt even more justified: *The Psychological Effects of the Near-Death Experience.* Now I just had to convince Dr. K it was a good idea.

***

I was feeling pretty good about my proposal. Not confident about the research, but confident that I'd made my case for how it fit the course objectives. I drained my glass of wine and flopped across the bed to give it one last proofread before sending it off to Dr. K.

I had barely made it through the second paragraph when the doorbell rang, followed by Kenny's warm, boisterous greeting.

Great.

He must be having company over. Not that I minded his friends—they were a blast. But they were also *loud*.

I sighed and slipped on my headphones.

I had managed a few more paragraphs when a light touch on my shoulder made me jump. I yanked off my headphones, spinning around—

Jon stood there, grinning.

"What are you doing here?" I gasped.

"Sorry," he said, his grin widening. "Didn't mean to scare you. Kenny let me in."

I struggled to compose myself. It wasn't that I was disappointed to see him—I just *wasn't expecting it.*

Then, I remembered my laptop still open to my research proposal.

Shit.

I wasn't ready for this conversation. I had already decided I wasn't going to tell him what I was writing about—at least not yet. Maybe not at all.

Part of me felt guilty. But I couldn't predict how he'd react. He had been *very* clear about not wanting to be treated like a statistics project.

But this wasn't statistics.

This was psychology.

And it was *for me*, not him.

I wanted to understand what we were dealing with—so I could support him. That was fair.

Right?

I quickly closed my laptop.

"How's the proposal coming?" he asked.

"Good!" I said, a little too fast.

He handed me a small box. "Brought you something."

I glanced down. Through the clear window, I could see the delicate chocolate drizzle on my favorite cheesecake.

Wait. What the hell?

I stared at the box, then at him. It was from *Spencer's Bakery.*

"You drove to Spencer's?" My voice was laced with disbelief.

He shrugged. "I could tell you were upset when you left, so I thought your favorite dessert might cheer you up."

God he was adorable.

And crazy.

I blinked. "But that's—" I quickly did the math. "That's, like, ninety minutes from your place. Then almost an hour back *here.*"

Should he even be driving that far? By himself?

What if something had happened?

His spontaneous decision making is questionable.

Another shrug. "I needed to keep myself busy."

Bullshit.

He must have seen the doubt on my face because he added, "Plus—I missed you. You've been staying over so much lately; it doesn't feel right without you."

That part, I believed.

I had been feeling the same way. In fact, I had been sulking about it earlier. I loved my apartment. I loved my roommates. But lately, I couldn't quite relax here. The forty-five-minute distance between me and Jon felt too far now. The underlying nervousness over everything that had happened was always simmering just beneath the surface.

I had come *so close* to never seeing him standing here again.

Now, I just wanted to touch him. Make sure he was real.

He'd left my door open when he walked in. I stepped past him, peering out into the empty hallway before quietly closing it, grateful my room was tucked away at the end.

I turned to embrace him, craving that warm, low-level rush that seemed to come just from contact. He wrapped his arms around me, and I couldn't help but notice the contours of his bicep—a reminder of how good he'd looked working on that car earlier.

And there go my hormones again.

I kissed him eagerly, his warm mouth stirring sensations elsewhere in my body. I just couldn't seem to get enough of him lately.

***

When I slipped out to the kitchen to grab plates and forks, Kenny was topping off his glass of wine.

"Want some cheesecake?" I asked.

He smirked. "Maybe later. Won't mix with my wine." Then, with a knowing look, he added, "And remind me to get some tips from you on how to snag a man who's hot as hell *and* sweet. You obviously know something I don't."

I giggled. "I got lucky."

I got really lucky.

"In all seriousness, babe," Kenny said, his tone softening. "He looks great." He winked. "And I'm glad he's feeling good enough for a *booty call*."

I laughed, my face instantly heating.

Oh god. Were we loud?

"That's *not* what this was," I protested, probably a little too defensively.

Kenny rolled his eyes. "Yeah, okay. You look like the cat that ate the canary. You're practically *glowing*, girlfriend." He smirked and slinked away with his glass.

I smiled, inside even more than out.

I *was* glowing.

Jon might not be exactly the same person he was a month ago. But physical implications aside, *Jonathan 2.0* was a pretty amazing guy.

Chapter 42

I parked in the back lot. Mike's studio was closed on Sundays, but the shop next door was open until 2 PM.

Perfect timing. No one around to notice.

Jon had wanted to stay over, and I would have loved for him to. But he hadn't brought anything with him—not even his medication. Hadn't thought about it, he'd said, when he took his spontaneous road trip to Spencer's Bakery.

Oh well. Just another byproduct of his off-the-cuff behavior lately. I'd be back at his place soon enough.

But first—this pit stop.

I rounded the building, climbing the short set of steps to the storefront I had barely noticed before.

Why hadn't I?

"Mizz Vanessa's Veil & Vessel."

The painted sign in the window was framed by twinkling white lights. A faceless mannequin stood in the display, draped in a floral-printed cloak, its neck layered with beaded necklaces and charms. A fancy lamp sat on a small table beside it, casting a warm glow.

The heavy wooden door creaked as I pulled it open. A faint musky aroma of incense curled around me as I stepped inside. The dim lighting took a second to adjust to, and for a moment, the shop felt empty.

I took a slow step forward.

The walls were lined with tapestries and shelves stacked with trinkets, each surface thoughtfully arranged. Mosaic lamps cast colorful fractals onto faded damask wallpaper. Tables were scattered throughout the space, each displaying something different—books, statues, figurines. Clothing racks lined the far wall, a mix of flowing bohemian dresses and structured Victorian-style garments.

The floorboards creaked under my steps as I wandered toward a display of candles and soaps. The air shifted, scented now with eucalyptus and sage.

I picked up a candle, inhaling deeply, appreciating the fresh, calming scent.

A quiet rustling from the back of the store caught my attention. A woman emerged, moving so fluidly she almost seemed to float.

Her long, dark hair was streaked with silver, framing sharp, yet kind, features. She wore a deep purple velvet blouse with flowing sleeves—striking, though maybe a little over-the-top for a Sunday afternoon.

She smiled warmly. "Can I help you find anything?"

I returned the smile. "I'm just looking." The words came out softer than I intended. I suddenly felt a little shy. Out of place.

She nodded. "Well, if you need anything, just ask. I'm Mizz Vanessa. But everyone calls me Ms. V."

I stopped short. "My boyfriend calls me Vee," I blurted, then quickly added, "But my friends call me Via. My name is Livia."

Good God, Via. Give her your full bio, why don't you?

Ms. V smiled, unbothered by my rambling. "It's nice to meet you, Via. What brings you in today?"

I hesitated. That was a good question.

"I'm not sure," I admitted. "I guess I was just curious."

My eyes landed on the far wall, where a large display of books was neatly categorized: **Mysticism & Occult Knowledge, Energy & Metaphysics, Spirituality & Intuition.**

My gaze drifted across the titles until one caught my attention: *"Intuitive Intelligence: Make Life-Changing Decisions with Perfect Timing."*

I picked it up, flipping it over to read the back. The description promised a practical guide to recognizing and working with intuitive energy.

Huh. Interesting.

I thought of a certain someone.

Another book caught my eye. *"The Electric Body: How the Biofield Shapes Health."*

My fingers tingled as I turned it over, reading about electromagnetic fields and how they interact with the human body.

A memory surfaced, unbidden—Jon, that night in his bedroom, taking my hand and pressing it to his chest.

Goosebumps pricked along my arms.

Ms. V's voice cut through my thoughts. "Are you interested in learning about biofields and energy?"

I hesitated. Thought carefully. Then answered honestly. "I've been thinking about it, lately. Yes."

I didn't elaborate. I wasn't sure how to articulate the feelings swirling inside me.

Ms. V nodded knowingly. "Curiosity is always the first step."

The first step into what?

I wasn't sure I wanted to go anywhere. But in a split-second decision, I closed the book against my chest. I'd buy it. If nothing else, it might help with my research.

I moved toward the counter, passing another display—a vast collection of multicolored crystals and stones. I paused, running my fingers over the polished surfaces.

"Do you know anything about crystals?" Ms. V asked, watching me with quiet curiosity.

I shook my head.

Not a damn thing.

"Crystals can be used to balance energy," she said, her voice gentle. "Each has unique properties—some offer healing, others grounding, or protection."

I barely resisted a smirk.

I could use all of that. Maybe I should buy one of each.

"Sometimes, when you're just starting out, it's best to focus on what your goals are and choose one that speaks to you." She paused. "Are you looking to balance emotions? Improve focus? Maybe you're searching for clarity?"

Something about the way she said it made me feel like she already knew the answer. Her pale eyes held mine—kind, but sharp. I studied her with equal parts curiosity and skepticism.

Was she reading me?

I exhaled a quiet laugh. "Yeah. All of those, I guess."

Then, before I could stop myself, I muttered, "And warding off bad luck."

Ms. V nodded, unfazed. She slipped from behind the counter and moved toward the display, scanning the selection before reaching toward the back.

She picked up a small, beaded bracelet and placed it in my outstretched hand.

"I think this one might suit you well," she said.

The moment it touched my palm, my breath hitched.

It shimmered under the soft lighting—not the deep purple I might have picked out for myself, but a striking mix of rich golds and browns.

No way.

"This is called tiger's eye," Ms. V said, her voice smooth.

I swallowed hard, staring at the swirling amber hues.

Seriously?

Tiger's eye?

"Tiger's eye is a powerful crystal," she continued. "It's grounding, stabilizing. And it's believed to shield against negative energies."

My fingers tightened around the bracelet.

"How does it feel to you?" she asked.

It felt *like a joke*. It felt *unreal*.

But mostly, it felt like another *what the fuck* moment in an ever-growing list of them.

"It feels amazing," I said softly.

"I'll take it."

Chapter 43

My nerves fluttered as I made my way to Dr. K's office. She'd emailed me at the beginning of the week, asking if I could meet to go over my research proposal.

Is that a bad sign?

Did she meet with everyone?

I made a mental note to ask Jaycee from class if she'd received a similar summons.

The psychology wing was on the opposite side of campus from my other classes—in one of the older buildings. Dr. K's office was what I'd call *fancy*—oak floors, tall windows framed by dark trim, and a thick rug that softened footsteps. A massive wooden desk dominated the space, with a royal-looking chair stationed behind it.

Dr. K peered at me over reading glasses and motioned for me to sit in a cushioned chair beside her desk. As if sensing my anxiety, she smiled.

"Relax, Via. I like to check in with all my students periodically. This research paper makes up the bulk of your grade, so I want to make sure everyone is staying on track."

On track?

I hadn't even *started* yet.

I forced a nervous smile.

"You're one of the first to turn in your proposal," she said approvingly.

Is that why I got called in? Or is my topic too far out in left field? Should I pick something else?

"I must say," she continued, flipping through the printed pages, "your topic choice is quite original. I don't think I've seen this one come through in all my years."

Poker face. I had no idea if that was a *good* thing or a *bad* thing.

"Is it a bad idea?" I asked hesitantly, wanting to rip the band-aid off.

"Oh, no!" She replied quickly, her gaze softening. "Ambitious? Yes. A bad idea? Not at all. I think it's fascinating, actually."

Whew. Jesus, lady, why not just start there?

"Oh. Good," I said cautiously.

Dr. K studied me over her glasses for a moment, then set them aside, folding her hands.

"This is an advanced psychology course, Via. How do you find it alongside your coding courses?"

That's it. She doesn't think I belong here.

"It's a nice contrast," I said carefully.

She nodded. "I can see that. Those of us with analytical minds often excel across disciplines."

Us?

She watched me a beat longer than was comfortable before continuing. "This paper will require an investment—solid references, case studies. I like your topic. Do you think you're prepared to dig in?"

I sat up straighter. "Yeah. Yes."

She smiled and nodded. "Good. I'm looking forward to seeing how you progress."

Some of the tension left my shoulders, but before I could fully relax, she leaned forward again.

"What inspired your choice?"

Shit.

I wasn't prepared for that.

I shrugged, keeping my expression neutral. "I just find it interesting."

She nodded, but I could feel her watching me. Assessing.

Then—too casually—she said, "How's your... fiancée, is it?"

I blinked, thrown.

Seeing my surprise, she quickly explained. "I'm not trying to pry, Via. It's just that you missed a week and a half last semester. Mr. Lewis had to submit a formal note to justify your absence. I just wanted to check in."

Fuck. She's right.

When It happened, I'd dropped everything without hesitation. To avoid academic penalties, I'd had to submit documentation. So I *guess* it was fair for her to ask. She was probably just making sure I wouldn't miss *her* class, too. And depending on the timing of Jon's surgery...

I swallowed.

"Jonathan?" I said, buying myself a second. "He's... okay. He's doing well."

"He underwent heart surgery?" she asked gently.

He will.

"He needs to be fitted with a defibrillator," I corrected. "Eventually. He's still recovering." I clamped my mouth shut, suddenly worried I'd said too much. "It might not be until after the semester's over. We're not sure yet."

She didn't press, just nodded thoughtfully. "I'm not worried about your attendance, Via. I just want to make sure *you're* okay. That you're not feeling overwhelmed."

Overwhelmed was an understatement. I'd lived in a state of overwhelm for weeks now. But sitting across from her, hearing it acknowledged out loud, made the weight of it settle over me all over again.

Still, I wasn't about to be psychoanalyzed by my own psych professor.

"I'm fine," I said firmly, pasting on a smile.

"I'm glad to hear that," she said, though her pause lingered long enough to make me squirm. Then—

"Is Jonathan the reason you chose this subject?"

Fuck.

I forced myself to meet her gaze but said nothing.

She tilted her head. "Did your fiancée have a near-death experience?"

I teetered on the edge of bolting. Or crying. Maybe both. But I was determined to *not* fall apart under her scrutiny.

"I'm not sure... well... yes. I think so."

Dr. K didn't react right away, which somehow made me stammer more.

"I mean, he hasn't said much, but I think... I think he definitely could have. He survived cardiac arrest. Twice. The first time... it was a really long time."

Jesus, Via, pull yourself together. You sound like an idiot.

I swallowed hard. I wasn't about to bring up the *other* weird shit. Not now. Not like this.

"Well," Dr. K said gently, "that *is* a near-death experience. And regardless of how much he remembers, facing our own mortality is a profound event. Not just for the person who nearly dies, but for those around them. It has a ripple effect." She paused, then added, "That's why it will make such a fantastic research paper. I understand why it resonates with you. Just be careful it doesn't become too emotionally charged."

I nodded slowly. That made sense. But I had a vested interest either way—so it may as well serve an academic purpose.

"I understand," I said. "And I intend to remain objective."

She seemed placated, sitting back in her chair. "I assume you'll be using him as a case study?"

I hesitated. "I think so."

"How does Jonathan feel about that?"

Jonathan feels fine about it, because Jonathan doesn't know.

"I haven't talked to him about it yet," I admitted. "I wanted to make sure my topic was approved first."

She studied me, then nodded. "Just keep in mind—this could be tough. For both of you."

"I know."

"I'm always available if you need guidance. Or just an ear."

There was no way in *hell* I was about to have a heart-to-heart with my psych professor, but I appreciated the offer.

"I mean it," she said, smiling. "This is heavy stuff. I would know."

She motioned vaguely to the scar on her face.

"If you need another case study, I may be able to help. Down the road."

Holy fuck.

I stood to leave, slinging my backpack over my shoulder.

"Via?" she said.

I turned.

"Have patience with him."

I waited, but she didn't elaborate. Instead, she simply nodded.

"Have a good afternoon."

My mind reeled as I walked out of the classroom, down the hall, and burst into the blinding sun.

Chapter 44

When I showed up at Jon's house Wednesday evening, he was watching the baby. Again.

Jill and Sharron were upstairs, their voices carrying down the hall.

"Baby duty again?" I teased.

He shrugged, nuzzling Abby's tiny nose. "She just missed her favorite uncle."

I smirked.

Her only uncle.

But he *was* her favorite person, and we all knew it.

We hung out in the kitchen while I brewed a much-needed cup of coffee. I had been running on fumes all day.

Maize trotted over to the patio door and sat expectantly.

"Do you mind letting her out?" Jon asked. "Or take the baby, and I'll do it."

I set my cup down and grabbed the door handle. "I've got Maize," I joked. "She'll go with me without crying."

Stepping outside, I inhaled the cool evening air, enjoying the quiet as Maize wandered into the yard. The rhythmic chirping of crickets filled the silence.

Then the door creaked open behind me. Jill stepped out, carrying a bag of trash toward the recycle bin.

"We're cleaning out the closet in the spare room," she said cheerfully.

I laughed.

Yeah, I know. I've seen it.

She paused, glancing in the window at Jon and Abby. "Okay, *seriously.* Look at those two... he is so good with that baby." She nudged me playfully. "So cute, right?"

I blinked, thrown off by her comment, and consciously tried to disguise it from showing on my face. It wasn't the first time Jill had projected her maternal desires onto our relationship, but it seemed to hit a nerve for me just then.

Not at the thought of having kids with Jon—I mean, if that ever happened, I couldn't imagine anyone better.

But still. I wasn't imagining *any* of that. How could I? There were a million other priorities and problems to think about.

I forced a smile.

That seemed to satisfy her, and she turned back inside.

I sighed, watching Maize meander up the yard. Why did her comment bother me so much?

Am I just being too cynical?

I chalked it up to exhaustion. I'd been up since 5 AM working on a client project, then sat through my 9 AM coding class, spent hours collecting research for my Psych paper, and *then* sat through another lecture.

At least tomorrow was light—just one class at 4 PM.

By the time Maize and I came back inside, Abby had finished her bottle and was sucking on a pacifier while Jon patted her back. She was pretty cute—when she was quiet. With *him*, at least. She stared up at him with wide blue eyes, utterly fascinated.

Then Jon's phone rang.

It was on the counter, face up. My stomach clenched when I saw the name.

Matt.

Jon raised an eyebrow from across the room.

"It's Matt," I said.

He rolled his eyes. "Let it ring."

After six rings, it stopped.

Then, *seconds* later—

The screen lit up again.

I exhaled sharply. "It's him again."

Jon sighed. "Just answer it. Put it on speaker."

I hesitated, then tapped the button and set the phone back down.

"You're on speaker," Jon said flatly.

No greeting. Just those three words.

"Heyyy man," Matt's voice oozed through the speaker. He didn't wait for a response before launching in. "I've got a job for you."

I bet you do.

"Yeah? What's that?" Jon asked, already sounding disinterested.

"The ATIM Expo. Two Saturdays from now."

What?

Jon was in no condition to be traveling to an expo.

"ATIM?" Jon questioned.

"Audio Technology Innovation and Manufacturing. Two of your sponsors will be there."

I shook my head. *No. Absolutely not.*

Abby shifted in his arms, making a small, restless noise. Jon adjusted her without missing a beat.

"Really, man? I'm not sure the timing is good."

Diplomatic.

Abby fussed again. Jon closed his eyes briefly, took a deep breath, and exhaled slowly.

Then, in a controlled voice, "Hey Matt. I need to call you back. I'm a little busy right now."

Silence. Then, an impatient sigh from the other end.

"Fine," Matt said. Then, sharper, "But Jon? This isn't an ask. I need to know you're going to be there."

Jon's expression didn't change. "Yeah. I hear you."

"Good." Matt hung up without another word.

Jon stared at the phone, his face unreadable—but I knew *exactly* what he was thinking.

"What the hell?" I whispered.

He brushed it off. "I'll call him later."

"But you *can't* go to that," I hissed, barely keeping my voice down as Jill and Sharron came down the stairs.

Jon gave me a look that said *later.*

Abby had drifted off while the four of us made small talk in the living room. Once he was sure she was out cold, Jon carefully placed her in the carrier.

"Good to go!" he said, grinning.

"I owe you one," Jill said brightly.

You owe him more than one.

I scolded myself for thinking it.

***

It was nearly 8 PM when Jon finally stepped outside to return Matt's call.

I stayed upstairs, flicking on the TV in his room, but I couldn't focus. I felt... uneasy.

It had been, what—not even four weeks since It happened? And already, Jon's old routines were creeping back in. Despite Dr. Brookens' strict warnings about taking it easy, he'd taken back almost three-quarters of his clients.

"It's just sitting next to someone and teaching them," he'd reasoned when I'd voiced my concern.

As if energy *wasn't* a finite resource.

But on Monday, he'd basically worked a full day—and by evening, I could see the exhaustion in his face. He *wasn't* ready. And that was doing something he *loved.*

Matt? That was another story. *Matt stressed him.*

I knew that. And yet, here we were.

Twenty minutes later, Jon came upstairs. I studied his face for signs of irritation, but he just looked... subdued.

"Well?" I asked.

He hesitated. Then, in a carefully neutral tone, "I don't have to attend the expo. Just the ceremony on the last night."

What?

I sat up straighter. "Jon—you *can't.*"

"I signed a contract, Via." His voice was quiet.

"Fuck the contract," I snapped. "FR ended their contract, so why the hell are you still on the hook for this?"

"We ended FR's contract with the *label.* For now."

For now?

I didn't like the sound of that.

"We still have contracts with the sponsors," he continued.

"So end those, too! Your health is priority one—no one is going to argue with that."

He sighed. "I *can't,* Via. It's not a good look. Who knows if those opportunities will come around again? And besides..." he hesitated. "It's good money."

I stared at him.

Who cares about money if you're not alive to spend it?

For the first time, I caught something in his eyes—doubt, uncertainty, something.

And then, softly, like he was breaking bad news—

"Via, I... I don't know how long I might be unable to work after the surgery. But right now, I'm still on track to hit my goal. We'll have a really good down payment saved for the house by next spring."

I froze.

A house.

He was still thinking about *that?*

A hot ache surged in my throat, and before I could stop them, tears blurred my vision.

"Oh my God, Jon." My voice was barely a whisper. "I don't give a fuck about a down payment. I don't need a house. I need *you.*"

Jon stilled.

I swiped at my tears. "I can't believe you would even think anything matters beyond that."

He sat down beside me on the bed, voice gentle. "I know you don't care about those things, Via. But honestly? This conference is no big deal. The ceremony is Saturday night. I just have to show up, shake some hands, and be polite to the guys who cut the checks."

"That's it?" I challenged.

He nodded. "Matt said they probably won't even know about the status of FR, or me, or any of it. It's just for show."

I exhaled, trying to let the tension drain from my body. "Where is it, anyway?"

"New York. In the city."

I sighed. I still hated the idea, but at least it wasn't some far-off place.

Jon glanced at me, a soft smile playing at his lips. "It's a plus-one event."

I narrowed my eyes.

"Would you come with me?" he asked, tone deliberately sweet.

"Really?"

He nodded. "And I think Mike and Nikki will go, too. We could stay at Tony's."

I hesitated. Then, wiping at my eyes, I nodded.

"Okay?" he pressed gently.

I sighed again, but nodded once more. Maybe it wouldn't be *that* bad.

Jon wrapped an arm around me, but then hesitated.

"Via, you're so tense." He smoothed a hand over my shoulder. "Relax, babe."

I *couldn't* relax. Today had been *draining*, and I had *so* been looking forward to a quiet night with him.

But Matt had shit all over that plan.

Jon shifted, leaning back against the headboard. "Come here."

He spread his legs and patted the spot between them, inviting me in.

I sighed but moved over, settling with my back against his chest. His arms circled me, his hands kneading at the tension in my shoulders.

Then, softly—

"Relax."

His lips brushed the back of my neck, sending goosebumps down my arms. His hands moved slowly, working at the knots. I let my eyes drift shut.

I felt… safe.

Comfortable.

Calm.

He always had that effect on me.

After a few more minutes, I gave in to exhaustion, sinking back against him. His arms tightened around me, warm and secure.

"Sorry I don't have any energy tonight," I mumbled sleepily, turning to curl up against him. "It's been a long day."

"That's okay." He took my hand, guiding it to his chest—my favorite spot.

"You can share mine."

I hadn't thought twice about my choice of words, but somewhere in the back of my mind, I had the strangest feeling—

He *had.*

Chapter 45

The event floor hummed with activity. Servers weaved through the crowd with trays of champagne, and clusters of well-dressed guests lingered near polished tables, engaged in lively conversations. The main ballroom, where the awards ceremony had taken place, was nothing short of extravagant—a massive chandelier cascaded from the ceiling, scattering golden light over the room.

I had to admit, getting dressed up and stepping into a night like this was kind of fun. It had been a while since the four of us had attended anything even remotely this glamorous.

Now that the formal part of the evening was over, the music had started, and the booze was flowing. People were loosening up—laughing, dancing, schmoozing.

Nikki and I sat at the south-end bar, people-watching while nursing our drinks. The crowd was interesting, to say the least.

A couple brushed past us, the guy in a navy suit clearly too impatient to wait for the bartender like everyone else. Instead, he leaned in between Nikki and me, aggressively flagging one down.

Nikki and I exchanged looks around him, rolling our eyes.

The woman with him—she looked about our age—stood a few steps back, her posture stiff, her expression uncomfortable.

Then she caught us making faces.

Her cheeks flushed before she let out a small, knowing laugh, rolling her eyes *with* us this time.

Finally, the guy turned, a drink in each hand. Whiskey.

He offered one to the woman.

She shook her head. "I don't like that stuff."

"Suit yourself. But loosen up. Don't ruin my night for me."

Then, without waiting for a response, he turned back into the crowd.

Nikki and I stared after them.

"What the fuck," I muttered.

Nikki scoffed, shaking her head. "Honest to God, what a *jerk*."

We laughed it off.

***

A little while later, Jon and Mike were summoned over to a table of suits—the kind of guys who *owned* the room.

We watched them schmooze for a minute before Nikki spun toward me.

"Let's go explore. There's an outdoor bar at the end, I think."

She didn't have to ask twice.

Navigating through the crowd of mingling guests, we followed the warm glow of string lights leading to the rooftop bar.

It was huge—easily the size of a small club, stretching across the top of the hotel. The night air was crisp, but the mix of outdoor heaters and lingering body heat from inside made it comfortable.

We found an empty table near the bar and the doors—perfect for spotting the guys when they came looking for us.

For a while, we chatted idly about the hotel décor, until Nikki's eyes narrowed over my shoulder.

"Well, look who's coming," she muttered.

I turned just in time to see the same obnoxious guy from earlier, ordering another round of drinks.

His date—*if you could call her that*—stood a few steps behind, looking even more miserable than before.

"She looks like she'd rather be anywhere else," I murmured.

"Wouldn't you?" Nikki smirked. "I mean, if *that* jackass was your date?"

The guy was too engrossed in chatting up someone at the bar to notice us watching.

Something about the girl made me feel bad for her.

On impulse, I caught her eye and motioned her over.

She hesitated before offering a small, nervous smile and sitting down.

"We meet again," Nikki quipped, her tone dripping with sarcasm.

I shot her a look, and she quickly adjusted her expression.

"I'm Nikki," she said, offering a hand. "And this is Via."

The girl hesitated for just a second before shaking our hands.

"Kaitlynn."

Her grip was weak. That was something she should work on.

***

We kept up our conversation—casual chatter about the hotel, the conference, the ceremony. Nothing important.

But after a while, Jon and Mike spotted us and took their seats. I introduced them to Kaitlynn, who at this point had officially joined our group.

Her date? He was still working the room, laughing too loudly, gesturing too wildly, his presence a mix of booze and bravado.

I tried to ignore him, steering our conversation toward safer topics.

But I wasn't the only one keeping tabs on him.

Every so often, I caught Jon watching him.

He never said a word.

Never reacted.

But his eyes followed the guy just long enough for me to notice.

Then, at one point, the guy—seemingly remembering Kaitlynn existed—strolled past our table and, with zero warning, planted a sloppy kiss on her cheek before disappearing toward the bar again.

Jon's eyes widened, his expression registering disbelief.

"Is that your boyfriend?" he asked, voice lined with incredulity.

It must have just clicked for him. And that somehow made his irritation even *more* amusing.

Kaitlynn hesitated, shifting uncomfortably.

"Blake?" she said shyly. "Yeah. We've only been dating a few weeks. He was the first person who was nice to me when I moved here from Pittsburgh."

Blake? Nice?

I didn't see it.

Jon seemed to be thinking, his expression flickering between confusion and disgust before he said, flatly—

"Don't go home with him."

Oh my God.

I kicked him under the table, eyes flashing a warning.

Jon met my gaze, then shut up.

***

We sat for another half-hour before Jon checked his phone, then looked to Mike.

"Are there any other douchebags we need to talk to before we can leave?"

Seriously Jon?

But the entire table—myself included—laughed.

"I think we're probably good," Mike said with a smirk.

Just then, Blake—a certified douchebag—came sauntering over, looking sloshed.

"Baby," he barely stopped as he passed Kaitlynn. "I'm gonna grab one more drink, and then we can hit the road. I have more planned for us tonight, eh?"

He pointed at her and winked.

Gross.

Jon's words echoed in my head.

"Don't go home with him."

I glanced at Kaitlynn. "We can give you a ride home, if you want."

There'd be enough room in Mike's SUV for the three of us girls to squeeze into the backseat.

She hesitated, forcing a polite smile.

"Yeah," Nikki chimed in, picking up on my cue.

Before Kaitlynn could answer, Blake was back.

Way too fast.

Had he been cut off at the bar?

His face was twisted in irritation, his movements more erratic than before.

"Come on, Kait," he barked. "Let's get outta here."

Kaitlynn looked torn, glancing at us before pushing to her feet.

Jon sat forward, voice even. "Hey, man. How about if I call you a cab?"

Blake stopped mid-step, turning slowly. His eyes scanned Jon up and down, sizing him up.

"We're good," he said flatly.

He grabbed Kaitlynn's arm and started to lead her away.

Jon didn't move. Didn't raise his voice. Just shook his head.

"Actually—I'm not sure you are."

Kaitlynn froze, eyes darting between them.

Jon looked at her, his expression steady, serious. "Don't get in a car with him."

"We'll take you home," I said quickly, trying to de-escalate the rapidly escalating situation.

Blake, already white-knuckling his keys, snapped.

"Who the fuck do you think you're talking to?" he spat.

The air tightened.

I barely had time to react before—

Blake lunged.

But he was too drunk, too sloppy—his foot clipped the leg of a chair, sending him stumbling forward.

He barely caught himself, his keys clattering to the floor.

Jon bent down before Blake could react and picked them up.

Oh, fuck.

What are you doing, Jon?

Jon stood, keys in hand. Calm. Unshaken.

"How about if I grab you a cab?" he repeated, his voice steady as ever.

Blake's face contorted with rage.

"Gimme the goddamn keys!" he snarled, lunging again.

This time, his hands actually grabbed for Jon, but—

Jon's arm shot out, reaching just past Blake's head, and—

Oh my God. He's not—

He let go.

The keys sailed over the rooftop balcony—

And vanished.

A second later, a tiny metallic splash echoed up from the fountain six stories below.

Blake lost it.

Everything happened fast.

He swung.

Mike caught his arm.

A brief struggle—

Then a security guard grabbed Blake by the jacket and dragged him off the rooftop.

And just like that, it was over.

The crowd murmured, guests staring, whispering as the tension slowly deflated.

I exhaled, still stunned, my heart pounding.

Jon. Had started a fight. With a much bigger guy.

What the fuck was he thinking?

But then again...

Had he really started it?

Blake had been drunk as hell, aggressive, and dangerous—anyone at our table, or even the bartender, could vouch for that.

Still.

The keys.

That was ballsy as hell.

I had been watching.

I had seen Jon's hand open.

The way he had let go of the keys a full second before Blake ever touched him.

There was no accident.

He had meant to do that.

The murmurs faded, the rooftop settling back into its prior hum of music and chatter.

Jon met my gaze.

I leaned closer, keeping my voice low.

"Did you drop those on purpose?"

He shrugged.

"If he can get through security, down six stories, and fish them out of the fountain—then I guess he's okay to drive."

Mike smirked.

I blinked.

Still processing.

Beside me, Kaitlynn stood frozen, looking stunned.

"We'll drive you home," Mike said to her. "But let's just hang out for a bit. Let things calm down."

That sounded reasonable.

But right now?

I was ready to go.

***

We lingered for another thirty minutes or so before finally making our way out—Jon and Mike leading the way, while Nikki and I trailed behind with Kaitlynn.

I was *so* ready to be done with this night.

We stepped into the hotel lobby, pushing through the heavy glass doors into the cool, open air. Mike's SUV was parked in a garage across the street.

Jon and Mike walked ahead, while Nikki and I hung back, still giggling about the unfortunate, phallic-shaped statues lining the entrance.

Our attempt to lighten the mood for Kaitlynn.

The three of us had *just* stepped outside when—

"There you are, you cocksucker!"

The voice came from the shadows.

Everything happened too fast for my brain to process.

A blur of movement—

A collision of bodies—

Jon was yanked off balance, shoved hard into the brick wall of the porte-cochère.

Oh, Christ!

The next few seconds exploded into chaos—a violent scuffle in the dim lighting, a tangled mass of shadows and limbs.

Then—

Something hit the pavement.

A sharp, metallic clatter.

A small object bounced, catching the light.

Skidded to a stop.

My stomach turned to ice.

A knife.

A fucking knife.

Blake—that piece of shit—had brought a goddamn knife.

But before I could even think to yell, Jon moved—his grip tightened, his body shifted, and in a single fluid motion, he twisted Blake's arm behind his back.

The move was fast, efficient.

A defensive maneuver.

One I'd never seen him use outside of playful wrestling.

One I knew his dad had taught him.

Blake cursed, struggled, but Jon didn't budge.

Then, with an angry jerk, Blake wrenched free and disappeared—vanishing around the corner.

The only sound left was our breathing.

Mike immediately rushed to Jon's side.

I think Nikki screamed.

I *know* Kaitlynn did.

I—

I was frozen, my body refusing to react.

Then—

"Go get security!" I snapped, my voice sounding foreign to my own ears.

Kaitlynn's eyes were huge, her hand clamped over her mouth.

But she nodded.

And she ran.

The moment she disappeared back inside, my legs finally unlocked and I sprinted toward Jon.

He was standing now, but hunched slightly, his breath coming too fast.

"Oh my God," I breathed. "What the *actual fuck?!* Are you okay?"

Jon nodded, but didn't speak.

He took an unsteady step, paused, steadied himself, then took a few more.

His hands raked through his hair, his chest still rising and falling too quickly.

He needs space.

He's trying to pull himself together.

Mike, Nikki, and I stood there watching, still too shell-shocked to say much else.

Then Kaitlynn returned—this time with security.

The guard approached immediately.

"Sir, are you hurt?" he asked. "Do you need medical—"

Jon waved him off. "I'm fine," he muttered between breaths. "He just... caught me off guard."

The guard nodded, then turned toward the darkened alley beyond the entranceway.

"Which way?"

Mike motioned.

Kaitlynn hadn't moved.

She stood rooted to the spot, arms wrapped around herself, her face drained of color.

Mike shot her a look—almost a glare.

Then he turned away without a word.

***

Jon had paced away from us—

Now, he was a good fifty feet down the sidewalk, his hands clasped behind his head, his movements too stiff, too tense.

I could almost feel the aftershocks rolling through him.

I wasn't aware of anything else.

Not the security guard still speaking to Mike.

Not Nikki shifting beside me.

All I saw was Jon.

This isn't good.

This isn't fucking good.

Stress could trigger his heart condition.

Being jumped outside of a conference was a hell of a stressor.

Jon stopped walking, bent over—hands on his knees.

Stood up.

Bent over again.

Come on, Jon. Breathe.

My stomach clenched, my own pulse pounding in my ears.

Then, finally—

He turned back toward us.

Thank Jeezus.

"You good?" Mike asked, watching him carefully.

Jon nodded.

But as he stepped into the light, I could see it—

The color drained from his face.

A trickle of sweat at his temples.

My heart dropped.

Too familiar.

Cold. Clammy.

This is too fucking familiar.

He leaned against the same wall he'd just been thrown into, his head tipping back against the bricks, eyes closed.

Chest still heaving.

Then, after another moment, he straightened, opened his eyes—

And saw us all staring.

His mouth twitched, a dimple barely appearing.

"I guess I had that coming," he said with a smirk.

Nikki laughed. Nervously.

Kaitlynn was still speechless.

Mike wasn't laughing.

"No, fuck that guy," he muttered, shooting another glare at Kaitlynn.

I swallowed, feeling awkwardly torn.

This wasn't *her* fault.

But still.

Why would she choose to be involved with someone like that?

I turned back to Jon, reaching for him—my fingers brushing his arm.

His skin was cold.

My stomach twisted again.

"You sure you're okay?" I whispered.

Jon nodded, forcing another smile.

"I'm okay."

I narrowed my eyes.

I've heard those words before.

Jon moved to sit on one of the concrete benches lining the path.

I blinked, slowly becoming aware of my surroundings again. Security officers were gathered near the side entrance now, a few speaking in low, urgent tones. One of them turned in our direction, hesitated, then walked back toward the group, phone pressed to his ear.

I turned back to Jon just in time to see him shift slightly, his hand brushing against his chest—just for a second. He played it off, crossing his arms instead.

Wait. Did he just—

I met his eyes, raising my eyebrows slightly in a silent check-in.

Before I could say anything, Nikki beat me to it.

"Are you sure you're okay? That was some serious bullshit."

Jon didn't break eye contact with me at first, but then he smirked and turned to her. "Yeah."

A beat passed. Then—

"Jon?" Mike's voice cut through the moment, low and wary. "You're bleeding, man."

I froze.

Jon blinked at him, almost dazed. "What?"

Mike nodded toward Jon's left arm, stepping in for a better look. "Your arm. I think he got you."

Oh. My. God.

The knife.

I hadn't even thought about it. I was so focused on the fight—on Jon handling himself, on Blake, on making sure Jon was okay in every way except the most obvious.

I hadn't noticed.

Jon must have been too pumped on adrenaline to feel it either, because his expression didn't change. But now, as Mike tilted his head to get a better view,

I saw it—the way the sleeve of Jon's jacket had been sliced through. The fabric was dark, but it glistened in the light.

Oh no. *No, no, no.*

Jon shifted, shrugging out of his jacket with Mike's help, and—

Blood.

I clapped a hand over my mouth.

Jon instinctively clamped his right hand over the back of his arm. "Don't look, Vee," he said, his voice still maddeningly calm. It was no secret that I didn't handle the sight of blood well.

He turned so Mike could get a better look.

"He stabbed you?" The words left my mouth before I could process them. My ears started ringing.

"It's not a stab wound," Mike assured us, then to Jon, "but he cut you pretty good. You're probably gonna need stitches."

Before I could react, the security guard from earlier approached. His eyes flicked to Jon's arm, then down to the blood beading along his fingers and dripping onto the pavement. "How bad?"

"It's fine," Jon said, but his hand was soaked now, a slow line of blood snaking down his forearm before splattering onto the concrete.

I tore my eyes away, swallowing against the lightheadedness creeping in.

"There's an ambulance parked around the corner. We keep them on standby for big events like this," the guard said. "Can you walk?"

"Yeah," Jon answered. He glanced at me. "Vee... you guys stay put, okay?"

I wanted to argue, but I wasn't sure I could even stand without my knees buckling. So I nodded, swallowing hard.

Just then, an EMT rounded the corner, eyes scanning the scene before locking on Jon's arm. "Oh yeah," he said, barely sparing the wound a second glance before turning to the guard. "He's gonna need stitches. Let's get that checked out."

Jon didn't hesitate, moving to follow.

"I'll go with him," Mike murmured to me and Nikki before trailing after them.

I was still fighting to keep my breathing steady, but I forced myself to speak. "Mike?"

He turned back.

"He needs more than his arm checked out," I said, keeping my voice low, trying to mask the worry coursing through me.

Mike held my gaze, understanding immediately.

A single nod.

"I know."

And then, a wink. Quick. Reassuring.

And he was gone.

I put my head down, fighting the black spots clouding my vision.

"Oh God, I'm so sorry," Kaitlynn's voice wavered. Somewhere in the background, she'd been saying that repeatedly, but I had tuned her out.

"Do you want some water?" Nikki asked.

I shook my head.

I'm trying not to puke.

I focused on my breathing, willing my head to clear while Nikki reassured Kaitlynn that none of this was her fault.

Which, sure. But what the hell had she seen in that asshole, anyway?

A few minutes later, I managed to lift my head just as another cop car pulled up to the entrance. No sirens, but the flashing red and blue lights threw chaotic patterns across the building, the overhang, and the pavement beneath us. My head throbbed in response.

This night had officially gone to hell. Granted, I hadn't predicted this exact scenario, but I *had* known coming here was a bad idea. *And fuck Matt for sending us.*

Feeling steady enough to stand, I pushed myself up.

"I'm going to see what's going on," I told Nikki and Kaitlynn, who followed me around the corner.

One of the ambulance doors was open, spilling light onto the blacktop. I could see movement inside. Mike was lingering off to the side, and when he spotted us, he headed in our direction.

"They got him cleaned up," he said. "He's going to need some stitches, but I don't think it's as bad as it looked."

A wave of relief washed over me. Small, but enough to keep me from spiraling.

"I told them he has CPVT," Mike added. "Wasn't sure if he planned on mentioning that or not, so I figured I'd go ahead and be the bad guy." He smirked slightly, but his tone was serious.

Thank God for Mike.

"Thank you," I said, meeting his eyes.

Mike shrugged it off. "You can probably pop your head in. Shouldn't be too bad now."

As I stepped toward the ambulance, I heard Kaitlynn asking, "What's CPVT?"

I ignored her. Let Nikki and Mike explain how her dipshit boyfriend could've killed mine.

One of the EMTs, a guy with a ponytail, smiled and shifted aside so I could step up into the back of the ambulance. Jon was sitting on the edge of the gurney, looking... annoyed. But when he saw me, he smiled. Two paramedics were with him—one behind him, working on his arm. I intentionally looked away, and Jon grinned. "It's alright, Vee," he said, echoing himself from earlier.

They'd hooked him up to a heart monitor. Good. At least they were taking this seriously. I knew those screens well by now. My eyes flicked to the PVC counter. 146.

In just these few minutes? My stomach knotted.

I forced myself to stay calm, but my nerves were fraying fast.

Another paramedic sat across from Jon, taking his blood pressure. "Have you ever been diagnosed with heart failure?" he asked casually.

Casually. Like he was asking if Jon had any allergies.

I tried to control my mounting anxiety.

Why would he ask that?

The question hung in the air too long. I was ready to answer for Jon if he didn't speak up.

"Yeah," Jon said finally, his voice even, his eyes dark. Pissed. "From a cardiac arrest."

The EMT didn't blink. "Okay," he said, like Jon had just told him his Starbucks order. "And when was that?"

"Five weeks ago."

The EMT nodded. "Alright."

Then he and the other guy exchanged a glance.

I didn't like the look they shared.

They know something. They see something. That's why he asked.

"Is he okay?" I asked sharply.

"I'm okay, Vee." Jon answered before either of them could.

There it was again—that look. They glanced at each other like they were silently agreeing on what *not* to say in front of me.

"Yep!" the one behind him said suddenly, overly upbeat. "We've got it cleaned and wrapped, but you're going to need a doc to close this up for you."

Jon sighed but nodded. "Fine. And thank you. I'll make sure I get it taken care of."

Bullshit.

The other one spoke, his tone calm but firmer now. "Given your history, I think the best thing would be to get you over to the ER so they can take a look at you."

Fuck.

My legs wobbled.

Jon didn't even blink. "I don't need to go to the hospital."

I spun on him. "Jon!"

His jaw tightened. "Livia," he said, his voice edged with patience. His eyes locked on mine. Steady. Unyielding.

Why are you being so goddamn stubborn?

The EMT in front of him stepped in. "Tell ya what," he said, tone easy. "You're going to need that arm stitched anyway. Why don't you just hang out here, let us give you a ride? We'll keep you on the monitor, make sure nothing else pops up. If you're feeling good, I'm sure once they sew you up, you'll be outta there in no time."

"Nothing else pops up."

IF he's feeling good...

My stomach plummeted.

Jon was not okay. And they knew it. And he knew they knew it.

All three of us were staring at him.

His eyes met mine—and I gave him the look. The one that meant *please.*

Finally, he exhaled. Sharp. "Sure. Fine."

I let out a shaky breath. At least he'd be monitored. For now.

***

Almost three hours after getting assaulted by a drunken lunatic, Jon strolled casually out of the ER.

Because of his heart condition, he hadn't needed to wait long to be seen. The paramedics had made sure of that. But also—because of his heart condition, his arm had been stitched and wrapped long before they were willing to let him leave.

Still, all things considered—he'd been lucky. That motherfucker Blake could've done real damage. In more ways than one.

Mike, Nikki, and Kaitlynn were lined up on a nearby bench waiting.

"Sorry," Jon said, flexing his bandaged arm like it was no big deal. "Stitches took a while."

For a second, the three of them just stared at him. Then Mike caught the grin spreading across Jon's face—and cracked up.

They exchanged one of those shoulder-clap handshakes guys do instead of hugging.

"Come on," Jon said, barely slowing his stride. "Let's get the hell out of here."

***

Mike had offered to drive us all the way home that night, but Jon insisted we stick to the plan and stay at Tony's, citing the convenience of proximity. I knew better. He was exhausted—but if Jon wasn't ready to admit that, I wasn't about to push the issue in front of everyone.

Mike had also offered to follow through on his promise to drive Kaitlynn home, but she opted for a cab instead. That surprised me, considering she'd waited with us all that time. But she'd just wanted to make sure Jon was okay. Before leaving, she expressed her gratitude—for everything—including the fact that Jon had declined to press charges on Blake when the cops had come to talk to him.

"You guys have already done so much," she'd said, looking genuinely touched. "You're tired. You should get to where you're going for the night."

I exchanged numbers with her before she climbed into the cab. I liked her—more than I expected to, given how the night started. She was still struggling to adjust to the city, and while I wasn't sure if we'd actually become friends, I promised to keep in touch next time we were in the area.

When we finally arrived at Tony and Beverly's, we were met with the kind of warm greeting that only they could deliver.

Over the years, Tony had become more than just a manager—he was a mentor, a friend, and one of Jon's biggest champions. I always got the sense that he saw something special in him. The kind of talent that didn't come around every day.

Bev, on the other hand, exuded a grandmotherly charm despite not having children of her own. She fussed over everyone who stepped through her door, and tonight was no exception.

"Oh, don't you girls look beautiful!" she gushed, pulling Nikki and me into a warm hug, pausing to admire our dresses.

Jon walked in last, and she held him just a little longer, her voice softer when she spoke.

"It's so good to see you, honey."

Jon smiled and hugged her back, though I could see the exhaustion in his face.

"Make yourselves at home!" Bev announced, ushering us inside.

"You guys can take the spare room. Mike and I will sleep on the pullout in the den," Nikki said to me.

I carried my bags back, immediately catching the faint scent of lavender. Bev had already thought of everything—freshly made bed, a plush floral comforter, and two stacks of neatly folded towels waiting at the foot of it. I smiled. She really was the best kind of host.

By the time I changed into something more comfortable and came back out, Jon had already sunk into the couch, looking more drained than I'd seen him in weeks. He barely spoke while Nikki and Mike filled Tony and Bev in on the drama of the night, content to just listen.

"Oh my goodness, you poor thing," Bev exclaimed, immediately fussing over Jon's arm. "Can I get you something?"

Jon shook his head. "I just need a good night's sleep."

And he meant it. Not long after, he excused himself, stopping to kiss me before heading down the hall.

"You go ahead and stay up," he murmured, his lips warm against my temple. "Try to enjoy yourself. What's left of the night, anyway."

I watched him disappear down the hallway.

"That poor dear," Bev tisked, shaking her head. "He's really been through the ringer."

The room fell silent for a moment before Mike, never one for lingering tension, clapped his hands together.

"Well," he said, "I don't know about anyone else, but now that we're parked for the night, I could use a stiff drink. Or two."

Tony's face lit up. "Excellent!" He hopped up, already making his way toward the liquor cabinet. "Ladies?"

Nikki and I both nodded.

I needed something to take the edge off.

***

We sat around talking, the warmth of a nice buzz settling in as I nursed my drink. The tension from earlier had dulled, just enough to let me enjoy myself. At one point, my phone chimed. I glanced at the screen.

Kaitlynn: *Thanks again for adopting me tonight! You guys are awesome!*

I smiled. At least something good had come out of tonight.

Eventually, the conversation in the room circled back around to the inevitable.

Tony glanced at me. "So, is he behaving himself?"

I thought about that for a second, smirked, and rolled my eyes.

We laughed.

"Yeah," Tony said knowingly. "Didn't think so." His tone was light, but then his expression sobered. "I'm sure tonight didn't help anything. But he does look way better than the last time I saw him."

He fell silent for a moment, like he was replaying a scene in his mind. Then he gave a small shake of his head, almost as if he were trying to shake the memory loose. "Man... that was really... something."

I didn't know how to respond to that. I wasn't sure I wanted to.

"Any timeline on the surgery yet?" he asked.

I shook my head. "His doctor wants to wait and give him more time. Says depending on how much he recovers, maybe his ICD won't need to be as complex."

That was the plan, anyway. But was Jon *still* recovering? Or was this as good as it was going to get?

Maybe it was the alcohol lowering my guard, but I let my next thought slip out before I could stop it.

"I don't know which scares me more—the thought of him having that thing in his chest, or the thought of him *not* having it, and needing it."

Silence followed. Everyone just... nodded.

Mike was the first to break it. He shifted in his seat, leaning forward. "There's going to be a lot of shit that changes once he gets that implant," he said. "Like... he won't be able to lean over a car hood like he did at the shop the other week."

The weight of that settled over me. One more thing to add to the list.

Then Mike continued. "And Shawn was already wondering about the PA systems at venues. Even if Jon gets back to playing one day, *could* he? With an ICD?"

Nikki frowned. "What's a PA got to do with anything?"

Mike shot her a look. "Because. Those speakers are giant magnets."

That shut all of us up.

I could feel my buzz fading, leaving behind exhaustion instead. The night had stretched on forever, and my body was finally catching up.

"I'm gonna call it," I said, pushing myself up from the couch.

The others agreed. It had been an *incredibly* long evening.

***

I woke up first, lingering in bed for a solid fifteen minutes, just watching him sleep. The slow, steady rise and fall of his chest was a welcome contrast to the night before. He'd struggled to catch his breath for too long. That had been too close.

Faint voices carried from down the hall, and the smell of bacon was already thick in the air. Carefully, I slipped out of bed, pulling on a sweatshirt and shoes, then eased the door open just enough to step through. It closed behind me with a soft click.

In the kitchen, Bev was at the stove, surrounded by a controlled chaos of sizzling pans—eggs, hashbrowns, sausage, bacon. She'd gone all out. Nikki sat at the table, her hands wrapped around a cup of coffee. Through the glass doors leading to the balcony, I could see Mike and Tony, deep in conversation over their morning smoke.

"Jon still asleep?" Nikki asked as I poured myself a cup.

I nodded, glancing at the kitchen clock. Almost nine. I must've crashed hard once I'd finally gone to bed. It was nice being here. I wouldn't have slept this well in a hotel room.

"Oh, let him sleep," Bev cooed. "Poor thing looked like he was running on empty."

I nodded again, but I knew he'd need to wake up soon—at least long enough to take his medication.

"Breakfast will be ready in ten minutes!" Bev announced, far too cheerful for the morning after a near-disaster.

As good as everything smelled, I knew Jon wouldn't be up for a big, greasy breakfast. His new eating habits meant keeping it light, and besides, he needed something bland with his pills. Dr. Brookens had been right—eating more had helped curb the nausea.

"Do you have anything plain?" I asked. "Maybe just some toast?"

Bev waved toward a cabinet. "Help yourself."

I scanned over a bag of bagels, cereal, muffins—then spotted a box of apple cinnamon Pop-Tarts. He'd eat those. No effort required, straight out of the package. Perfect.

Grabbing a foil pack and a bottle of water from the fridge, I made my way back to the guest room.

I set the water and Pop-Tarts on the nightstand. Jon moved slightly, then sat up, blinking as he took in his surroundings. He looked more hungover than the rest of us combined—despite not having had a drop of alcohol.

He stretched, rubbing at his bandaged arm—then winced, as if he'd momentarily forgotten it was there.

I hated that he was in pain again. He'd had more than his share lately.

"Thanks, Vee," he murmured as I popped open his travel case and emptied his morning dose into my hand—three pills total. My eyes lingered on the little pink one, appreciating it more than ever.

Jon took the pills from my palm, washing them down with a few swallows of water. He eyed the Pop-Tarts with disinterest but unwrapped them anyway, handing me one.

I wasn't hungry yet—I was holding out for Bev's hashbrowns—but I took a bite anyway. Mostly so he would.

Then my phone chimed from the dresser.

I grabbed it absently, expecting something from Krissy or maybe a client. But it was Kaitlynn.

I opened the message, my casual curiosity morphing into a cold, twisting knot in my stomach.

No. That can't be right.

I reread it once. Twice. A third time, just to be sure. But the words didn't change.

"Hey," I said, trying to keep my voice steady. "I need to make a call."

Jon barely looked up, just nodded.

I slipped out, my ears ringing as I moved past the kitchen—past Nikki, past Tony, past Bev, past their easy laughter, past the normalcy of it all—right out onto the balcony.

The morning sun was warm on my face. I sat down hard in one of the deck chairs, clutching my phone in both hands, staring at the message again.

I must be misreading this.

I must be.

Finally, I gathered my nerve, inhaled deeply, and hit **call**.

***

After another few minutes of wrangling my thoughts, I slid the balcony door open and stepped back into the kitchen.

Mike, Nikki, and Tony were eating, their conversation a low murmur over the clinking of silverware. Bev was still at the stove, moving between pans like a conductor guiding an orchestra.

Jon stood leaning against the counter, hands shoved in the pockets of his loose fitting jeans. A simple black T-shirt stretched across his shoulders, the bandage on his arm peeking out beneath the sleeve, and he'd thrown a black beanie on his head. The first hint of a 5 o'clock shadow framed his jaw.

Even without trying, he was attractive.

But that wasn't what caught my attention now.

Something awful sat heavy in my chest, pressing down.

I must've looked as shaken as I felt because the conversation stopped. Every set of eyes landed on me.

"Via?" Nikki asked, her fork hovering midair. "What's wrong?"

I swallowed. My mouth felt dry.

"Blake's dead," I said, the two words foreign and heavy on my tongue.

The room reacted in fragments—like a glass shattering in slow motion.

Nikki's fork clattered onto her plate. Bev gasped, clasping her hands over her cheeks. Tony and Mike exchanged a hard glance.

And Jon...

Jon didn't move. Didn't speak. He just stood there, still as stone.

The silence stretched thick and unnatural, and I found myself filling it, repeating what Kaitlynn had told me.

We'd lost track of Blake after he attacked Jon, but apparently, his night hadn't ended there. No one knew where he'd gone or what he'd been doing, but somehow, he'd managed to drive all the way back to Long Island without hurting anyone else.

His own luck, however, had run out.

He'd wrapped his car around a tree barely a mile from his house.

A good samaritan had stopped to help, but Blake had bled out in the ambulance. By the time he reached the hospital, he was already gone.

His brother had called Kaitlynn early that morning to break the news.

The kitchen remained deathly quiet. No one knew what to say.

Then finally, a sharp exhale.

"Holy fuck," Mike muttered, his voice breaking the tension.

A wave of sighs followed—disbelief, shock, something close to resignation.

"Oh my. My Lord," Bev murmured under her breath, shaking her head.

Nikki turned toward me. "Jesus, Via... if she'd gone with him..."

"She'd be dead, too."

And Kaitlynn knew it. She'd sobbed on the phone, her voice shaking as she admitted she probably wouldn't be alive if Jon hadn't intervened.

That knowledge sank into my stomach like lead.

The conversation around the table slowly resumed, everyone reacting in their own way, Bev finally pulling out a chair to sit down.

Everyone except Jon.

Jon hadn't moved a muscle since I'd spoken. He was still leaning against the counter, staring off at nothing, his jaw tight.

And then, in the dim morning light, I saw it.

His eyes glistened.

With *tears.*

The man had tried to seriously hurt him—at a minimum. Maybe worse. For most people, that would have been enough to dull any sense of sympathy. But Jon wasn't wired that way.

He blinked a few times, quickly, as if forcing himself back under control. Diverted his gaze.

Still, he said nothing.

Instead, he quietly walked past everyone at the table and stepped out onto the balcony, closing the glass door behind him without a word.

We exchanged glances around the table.

Jon needed space. This was how he processed.

I waited a few minutes, letting the noise of the room rise again. Then, slipping away from the table, I followed him outside.

The air was cool, the city just beginning to wake. Jon stood silently, his gaze was fixed on something in the distance.

Or maybe nothing at all.

"I tried," he said, his voice so quiet it almost got lost in the wind.

Yes, you did.

He had tried.

And that was the thing.

Jon had locked onto Blake from the moment he saw him. Even before he realized Blake was Kaitlynn's date, he'd been watching him.

Like he'd sensed something.

And given everything about Jon since It happened, I was willing to bet that he had.

A thousand thoughts rushed through my mind, but I pushed them all back.

Now wasn't the time for questions.

Right now, he didn't need analysis. He didn't need explanations.

He just needed me.

I stepped forward and wrapped my arms around him.

"I know," I whispered, hugging him as the sun climbed higher over the city.

Chapter 46

Tuesday was shaping up to be a productive day—which was good because Monday had been a wash. Aside from a few mandatory morning tasks, I'd spent most of the afternoon lounging with Jon and Maize.

Jon had rescheduled some of his Monday clients, redistributing their time slots throughout the week. "Just for Monday, and just for this week," he'd said—a silent admission that the weekend had been hard on him.

Honestly, it had been a draining weekend for all of us. I welcomed the downtime as much as he did.

But it also gave me time to think.

Jon's intuition had been razor-sharp lately, with everything and everyone—but Saturday night felt different, like we'd crossed into new territory.

Someone had died.

And I was convinced Jon had sensed something was going to happen long before Blake downed those last few drinks that sent everything into chaos.

In my research, I'd read about people who, after NDEs, reported experiencing psychic phenomena. Some claimed newfound psychic abilities; others discovered hidden talents. One woman even said she could "sense energies" after her near-death experience.

That one really got me thinking about you-know-who.

There was no shortage of information suggesting this stuff was real. But I struggled to categorize all the ways I'd seen these things play out in Jon's life. *Our life.*

I thought about Mizz Vanessa's extensive collection of books on the subject. I needed to go back there.

***

A car I didn't recognize was parked beside Mike's SUV when I pulled into the back lot. Good. That meant he was busy with a client and wouldn't notice I'd been in the area.

I walked briskly across the lot, veering right, around the back of the building instead of taking my usual left into the shop.

The moment I stepped into Veil and Vessel, the scent of warm incense and aged paper wrapped around me. The store's soft, ambient glow was just as I remembered, a world apart from the tattoo studio next door.

Unlike my first visit, this time I had a purpose. I headed straight for the books.

So many titles seemed relevant:

- **Beyond the Five Senses: The Science and Spirituality of Intuition** – A blend of scientific theories and metaphysical perspectives on extrasensory perception.

- **The Veil Between: How Clair Senses Connect Us to the Unseen World** – Exploring the idea that intuitive perception is a bridge between the physical and spiritual.

- **The Clairs Unveiled: Unlocking Your Hidden Senses** – A beginner's guide to Clairvoyance, Clairaudience, Clairsentience, and more.

I was still scanning the shelves when Mizz Vanessa appeared from the back of the store.

"Hello, Via!" she greeted, her voice as smooth as ever. She wore an emerald green dress today—simple, yet elegant. "It's nice to see you again."

I smiled, half-focused on the book in my hands.

"Feel free to have a seat and read through anything you like," she offered, gesturing toward a small velvet couch in the corner.

That was generous of her, considering this was a shop, not a library.

For some reason, I felt comfortable here—comfortable around her. So I took the offer, settling onto the couch with a book: **The Empath's Guide to Clairsentience: How to Feel and Interpret Energy.**

I flipped through the table of contents. This one could be interesting.

After a few minutes, I felt eyes on me. Glancing up, I found Mizz Vanessa watching me with quiet curiosity.

"Is there something specific you're hoping to learn about?" she asked.

I exhaled, more frustrated than I intended. "Clairsentience... claircognizance... clairvoyance... how do you tell them apart?"

The words tumbled out awkwardly, but if she noticed, she didn't show it.

"Well," she said, settling onto the couch beside me, "they're all ways of tapping into intuitive channels. These gifts are highly individualized, and more often than not, people experience more than one."

She paused, watching me for a reaction. I kept my expression neutral.

"Are you starting to open up to these senses?" she asked.

"No," I answered too quickly. Then, realizing how flat that sounded, I fumbled. "I mean—not me. It's not—I'm not asking for myself."

Honestly, I wasn't even sure who I was asking for anymore.

"I see," she said, thoughtful. "Someone important to you, then?"

Could she see straight through me, or what?

"It's for my boyfriend. My fiancé." The words spilled before I could filter them. Why did I always seem to lose my verbal filter around this woman?

Mizz Vanessa tilted her head. "Does he think he might be sensitive?"

I rolled my eyes. "I don't know what he thinks. He's never said. But *I* think he might be. Now."

Via, without context, you're making no sense.

The word *now* lingered awkwardly between us, but she let it slide.

"What makes you think so?" she asked.

Where do I even begin?

I glanced around, confirming we were still alone. The glow from a dozen stained-glass lamps cast soft colors across the walls, wrapping the space in a quiet warmth. Something about the atmosphere felt safe.

Something about *her* felt safe.

And so I told her.

I started with the moment everything changed—when It happened. Then, without meaning to, I poured out the rest. The subtle changes in Jon's behavior. His eerie, almost instinctive awareness of things he couldn't possibly know. The way Saturday night unfolded, his warning about Blake, the wreck. I spoke in a rush, unloading everything I'd been analyzing for weeks.

Mizz Vanessa listened, fully present. Not once did she interrupt. Not once did she look at me like I was crazy.

When I finally finished, she gave me a small, knowing smile. Not sympathetic—*empathetic*. Encouraging, even.

"It sounds like you've been blessed with some miraculous experiences," she said softly.

I blinked. *Miraculous?* Interesting choice of words.

"When someone passes through the veil," she continued, "it can unlock certain shifts—enhancing our ability to perceive and interpret the physical world."

The phrase *pass through the veil* struck me. Veil and Vessel. Her store's name made sense now.

"Jonathan's story is beautiful," she said. "I know it feels overwhelming."

That word again. *Overwhelming.* Dr. K had used the same one.

"The physical aftermath of his experience is scary, yes. But the spiritual byproduct of a near-death experience is transformative. It's very insightful of you to seek understanding of it. He's lucky to have such a supportive partner."

I *wanted* to be supportive. I really did.

She studied me for a moment before speaking again.

"I would say it sounds like Jonathan is experiencing multiple clair senses," she said slowly. "It may take time for him to understand them. But having your encouragement will surely help."

I wasn't so sure about that. But it was a nice thought.

"Why don't you take that book with you?" she offered, nodding at the one in my lap. "No charge—read it, and return it when you're done."

My eyes widened. "Oh, no—I couldn't."

I *wanted* the book, but I wasn't about to take advantage of her kindness.

"I insist," she said, already moving toward the counter. "It's a good one. And it might help clarify some of your questions."

I hesitated. She waved a hand like it was nothing.

"Really."

Then her gaze drifted to my wrist. "How are you finding the Tiger's Eye?"

I followed her eyes to my bracelet. I'd barely taken it off—except to swap it out for a silver bracelet that matched my dress on Saturday night.

Maybe I should have left it on.

I had to stifle a smirk at the thought. I wasn't superstitious... not exactly. Despite what Mizz Vanessa had told me about the stone's properties, that wasn't why I'd been drawn to it. The deep, shifting golds reminded me of Jon's eyes. And Mary...

Tiger Eyes.

She had used those exact words. Sworn to her nurse that she'd seen him, the night he coded in the ICU.

A shiver crawled up my spine, but my lips curled into a genuine smile.

"I love it."

***

I had just rounded the back corner of the building, book in hand, when a loud thunk startled me.

My head snapped to the right. Mike had just stepped outside, tossing a trash bag into the dumpster.

Shit.

He saw me and stopped short. "Hey," he said.

I casually switched the book to my other hand, shifting my body just enough to block the cover from his view.

"Hey!" I replied, watching as his gaze flicked from the Veil and Vessel side of the building to me—tracing my footsteps like he was piecing together where I'd just been.

Then, his eyes dropped to the book. He probably couldn't make out the title from where he stood, but still… he knew.

Our eyes met, and for a brief moment, something passed between us. Recognition. Understanding.

He didn't say a word about it.

Instead, he threw up a hand. "See ya tonight?"

Right. We'd made plans to get the usual group together at Jon's later.

"Yep! See you there!" I said, keeping my tone light as I crossed the lot to my car.

I wondered if this would come up later. But something in Mike's expression told me my secret was safe with him.

Chapter 47

The evening had been a good one. We hung out by the fire pit after grilling dinner on Jon's back patio—the six of us: me, Jon, Mike, Nikki, Cary... and Emily.

Yes, Cary was back with Em, the girl he had so epically busted for dual-dating him and another guy. It had taken some nudging from me and Nikki, but Em was a good person, and we all knew Cary had really liked her. *A lot.*

To be fair, as we pointed out, Cary had been a bit of a player himself before meeting her. Unlike Mike and Jon—or even Shawn, who was a perpetual loner and liked it that way—Cary played the part of the rock star, often leaving shows with a different girl each night. He hadn't explicitly told Em he wanted to be exclusive, and she hadn't assumed.

But she *had* told us she had feelings for him, too.

It was nice seeing them together in an official—and seemingly happy—relationship.

As I'd suspected, Mike hadn't said a word about seeing me leave Veil and Vessel earlier.

Thank you, Mike.

We sat around the fire until an evening rain shower forced us inside, down to the basement studio.

"Dude, the new material you're working on is badass," Cary said as we settled in.

He wasn't wrong. Live shows might be off the table for now, but Jon had been back to writing and recording. He claimed his playing wasn't back to where it had been—an unfortunate side effect of his medication—but I was convinced that was more his own insecurity than anything else.

Jon was a phenomenal musician. Even on his worst day, he was better than most other professionals. And that wasn't just my bias—it was fact. It was how he got his scholarship.

Music was his language. Deep and gritty, wrapped in metaphor and mood. That's why FR had taken off the way it did. And while he had been tight-lipped about his new material, the few pieces I'd heard were... different. Dark, layered chords. Moody as hell. Intense and beautiful.

God knows he's had enough inspiration lately.

Mike had recorded drums on one track right before our shit weekend.

"So, when are we going to go over my parts?" Cary asked.

He was a great bassist. He should be—Jon had taught him everything he knew. But he also leaned on Jon's composing skills, typically receiving his bass parts fully written for him.

Jon barely looked up. "I didn't write parts for you."

Cary paused, surprised. Then laughed.

"What—don't tell me you're replacing me with Murray?"

Murray—John Murray—was the bassist in Jason's band, FaultCode. Jon had been co-writing with Jason lately, but I was pretty sure the other John wasn't involved.

At least, I didn't think so.

Jon smirked. "Murray? Fuck no. I'd use a synth bass first."

We all laughed.

Murray was good. Really good. But his ego was a mile high, and Jon—being Jon—didn't vibe with that.

"Whew. Glad to hear that," Cary said once the laughter died down. "Just let me know when you're ready, then."

Jon shook his head. "No. I sent you the stems. *You* let *me* know when you're ready, and we'll record."

I watched as Cary's grin faded, confusion settling in.

What is happening right now?

"Seriously?" Cary asked, his voice edged with something like disbelief.

Jon met his gaze, unfazed. "Seriously."

Cary hesitated. So did everyone else.

Jon exhaled sharply, running a hand through his hair. Then, frustrated, he threw up his hands.

"Cary, you're a talented player. But I might not always be around to write your music for you. You guys shouldn't be relying on me so much."

The room fell silent.

Cary and Mike exchanged the same look that Nikki, Emily, and I did.

Ohhh fffuuuck.

A knot twisted in my stomach.

Did Jon realize how hard that landed?

The unspoken message was clear. And judging by the look in his eyes, he knew it.

He'd been thinking this over for a while.

I thought back to Saturday night—his time in the ambulance. I hadn't been there for the whole ordeal, but the three of them—Jon and the two paramedics—had been locked in a silent battle over what to do.

Blake's fight had shaken him. That much was obvious.

But now I wondered...

Had it shaken him enough to question whether he'd even be around to write music for FR anymore?

Nobody spoke.

Cary just stared at Jon, disbelieving.

Then, Jon's lips quirked, a barely-there grin creeping in. Trying to lighten the mood.

"It's time to leave the nest."

Still, silence.

His grin widened, dimples flashing. "Fly away, little bird." His eyes twinkled with amusement.

Cary shook his head, but I caught the hint of a smirk at his lips. "Dude... I know they said you didn't have brain damage, but sometimes you make me fuckin' wonder."

Jon cracked up. Hard.

The tension dissolved.

The easy banter returned, pushing aside the weight of what he had just said.

But I couldn't shake it.

And looking at Mike, I could tell... neither could he.

***

I could have stayed at Jon's that night. Logistically, it made sense. He'd expected me to.

But after what he'd said to Cary earlier, I couldn't.

No—that wasn't even right. It broke my heart. It stoked a fear in me I wasn't ready to face.

For a month, I'd been wrestling my own demons—grappling with Jon's mortality, trying to keep my anxiety in check. And I'd done a damn good job, all things considered. But now?

Now, I realized it had been easier to battle my fears when Jon had been so adamantly stubborn about being fine.

As much as his unwavering insistence had driven me crazy, it had also been a comfort.

Hell, we'd even had our big blowout fight over that very thing—his relentless stubbornness.

He was fine.

Everything with Jon had always been fine.

I told him I wanted honesty. And I believed that was true.

But now—

Even though the rest of the night had settled back into something casual, normal, chill—I could not shake the look on his face when he'd said it.

When he'd basically told all of us—not just Cary—that we shouldn't rely on him being around.

Like it was just a fact.

And maybe it was.

Who the hell knows what's been running through his head all this time?

How could any of us really know?

What he felt?

What he thought?

What he believed—about any of it?

Did he think he was going to die?

I was used to Jon's cynical, self-deprecating humor. That was just... him.

But what he'd said to Cary?

That wasn't sarcasm. That wasn't his usual dry wit.

That was genuine.

He looked serious.

Worse—he looked accepting.

And that is what rattled me the most.

His acceptance.

I wasn't ready for that.

I wasn't ready to acknowledge it with him.

Or with myself.

I needed a distraction.

Even before the night ended, I felt myself grasping for one—for something to focus on instead.

I could go home.

I had books to read.

I had a research outline to write.

I had things to do—things to keep my mind busy.

That's what I needed.

A focal point.

A point to any of this.

Anything.

So when everyone else left, I went home too.

***

I had found so many good resources for my paper.

The hardest part was going to be figuring out how to fit all the pieces together—how to make sense of everything in a way that was both structured and convincing.

I'd already organized the main points into categories and formulated my thesis.

Title: ***The Psychological Effects of Near-Death Experiences: Cognitive, Emotional, and Physiological Perspectives***

I. Introduction

- Overview of Near-Death Experiences (NDEs) as a psychological phenomenon.

- Why this topic is relevant to cognitive and psychological sciences.

• The gap between scientific explanations and subjective experiences.

Thesis Statement: Although near-death experiences (NDEs) are often interpreted through a spiritual or metaphysical lens, emerging evidence supports the idea that they result in measurable cognitive, emotional, and physiological changes. These changes, particularly in perception and personality—challenge the conventional separation between subjective experience and scientific observation, suggesting that NDEs may represent a legitimate area of inquiry into the interaction between consciousness, trauma, and human physiology. This paper argues that these aftereffects—including shifts in perception, emotion, and cognition—merit deeper investigation within the field of psychology.

II. Psychological & Cognitive Shifts Following NDEs

• Commonly reported aftereffects: heightened intuition, emotional detachment from material concerns, and shifts in personality.

• Altered cognitive function—many experiencers report enhanced creativity, memory, or abstract thinking.

- Psychological theories on how trauma rewires the brain (fight-or-flight responses, PTSD, post-traumatic growth).

Possible Citations: Case studies of NDE survivors who describe psychological shifts.

I was satisfied with this part.

But the psychic and Clair sensitive themes? That was harder.

I knew they belonged in my research—if nothing else, just to acknowledge their influence on mental health.

But there was more to it than that.

The first book I'd bought from Mizz Vanessa—**"The Electric Body: How the Biofield Shapes Health"**—had been a fascinating read.

It suggested that the electromagnetic fields of the body could influence not just physical health, but also emotional states—even the moods of those around us.

I was convinced Jon was doing *something* with energy.

I could literally feel it.

And I had convinced myself that this was why Abby preferred him, too. She could sense it.

So if animals and babies picked up on it, and I picked up on it... then maybe there was an argument to be made that this energetic ability was physiological—tangible. Measurable. Not just woo-woo.

I just needed to figure out how to make the case.

At least enough to convince Dr. K that it deserved to be in my paper.

If I could just tie everything together...

I took a breath and started adding those thoughts into my outline.

III. The Role of Perception: Exploring Clair Senses

• Reports of increased intuition, clairvoyance, clairsentience, and claircognizance in NDE survivors.

• Unclear whether these are new abilities or a result of heightened subconscious awareness.

• Theories from **"The Electric Body: How the Biofield Shapes Health"** on how the biofield (electromagnetic energy field) might interact with human perception and health.

• Potential connection between energy sensitivity and autonomic function—but more research is needed to understand this relationship.

Note to Self: *There seems to be a physiological component to these perceptual shifts, but the mechanisms remain unclear. Some sources suggest an interaction between the nervous system and the biofield, but empirical evidence is limited. Further exploration is needed to determine if there's a measurable link between autonomic function and heightened perception post-NDE.*

There.

I think this might work.

It wasn't perfect. Yet.

But hopefully, it would show Dr. K that I was doing my diligence.

***

I was reading over my outline, trying to decide if it was finished, when my phone rang.

I glanced at it, tempted to ignore it.

But I didn't have the willpower.

"Hey there," Jon's voice came through the other end.

"Hi."

"Whatcha doing?"

"Coursework."

We talked for a few minutes. Or rather, he talked.

I didn't feel very chatty.

I was aware of my one-word answers, but I wasn't motivated to say more.

"You didn't hang around tonight... you barely even said goodbye." He prodded.

"I said goodbye." I countered. "And I stayed as long as everyone else."

A pause. Then—

"Are you mad?"

"No."

Another pause.

"Did I do something to upset you?"

I closed my eyes.

Yes, Jon. You were honest. Just like I asked you to be. And now I hate it.

I didn't answer.

The silence stretched.

"Is this about what I said to Cary?"

You bet your ass it is.

I sighed. "Not directly."

"I was just trying to push him—"

"Jon, this isn't about who writes Cary's music," I interrupted. "It's about the fact that you basically told everyone they needed to stop relying on you."

Now it was his turn to fall quiet.

"Does that include me?" My chest tightened, a swirl of anxiety and frustration rising in my throat. "I mean, how am I supposed to feel about that? About what you said? Do you want me to start thinking about us as... tentative?"

"What? Via, no! That's not—"

He sighed.

"I'm just trying to be real. I want the people I care about to be prepared... in case—"

"In case what?" I snapped.

"In case anything happens, Vee. It's only natural to consider the possibility."

I hated where this conversation was going, but Jon kept talking.

I was struggling not to tune out completely, my brain glitching on his words.

"I'm just doing what any responsible person would do in my situation."

Wait—what are we talking about right now?

"That's why I've updated all my personal documents, gone over my estate planning, and... you know... made you the beneficiary."

His words hit like cold steel in my chest.

I wanted to hang up—shut this down—but my body was frozen.

Please stop talking, Jon.

"I paid off my truck."

His voice was fading in and out—not literally. Just in my head.

"And I want you to come to the DMV with me so I can add your name to the title."

"Why?" My voice felt hollow.

"Because it's still new. It should be worth a good bit. You know, if you ever need to sell it."

For Christ's sake, Jon, stop talking.

"I'd like to increase my life insurance policy, but, uh..." he laughed.

He's laughing?

"I'm not very insurable right now."

I was speechless.

Tears burned down my face.

I wasn't ready to have this conversation. Not now. Not ever.

And how could he sound so casual about it?

Like he was reading off a grocery list—not talking about life insurance policies and contingency plans.

The silence stretched between us.

Finally, his voice softened. "Via?"

I realized I'd been sitting there with my hand over my mouth, trying not to sob out loud.

Slowly, I dropped my hand, holding my breath before I spoke.

"I don't want to talk about this."

A pause. Then—

"Okay. I just... sure. Okay."

Silence.

More silence.

Then—"Via—"

"I have to go."

I hung up.

I didn't even say goodbye.

I stared at my phone, half-expecting him to call back.

But he didn't.

I threw a pen at the wall.

Very mature, Via.

"Fuck!" I yelled.

Then I grabbed a pillow and screamed into it.

I welcomed the anger.

It was better than crying.

But a second later, I heard Krissy's door open, and she appeared in my doorway.

"You okay?"

I nodded.

"Cool."

I silently loved her for not asking what was wrong.

She could clearly see I'd been crying.

"I just ordered pizza. Will you eat some when it gets here?"

"No." My voice came out sharp, but I softened. "Thanks, though."

She leaned against the doorframe. "Wanna split a joint?"

I looked at her.

We shared a grin.

"Yes."

***

"Krissy!" I yelled over my shoulder as I shuffled to the door. "Your food's here!"

Where the hell was she? Shower? Music blasting?

Damn her for making me answer the door with red-rimmed eyes.

And damn me for being so emotional. Again.

I flung open the door, ready to swap a cash tip for a pizza box from—

Not the pizza guy.

Jon.

Standing there with that same stupid yet adorable beanie yanked down over his head.

What the fuck?

We'd only been off the phone for twenty minutes. He didn't fly here.

I narrowed my swollen eyes, blinking against fresh tears.

In one month, I had cried more over this guy standing in front of me than I had cried in all my childhood, pre-teen and teenage years put together.

"What are you... HOW are you even here right now?"

"I started driving as soon as I realized you were mad."

He'd been on his way the whole time we talked?

Tears welled again.

Fuck.

"I'm not mad," I corrected, though my throat felt tight. "I'm just..."

Scared? Heartbroken?

I didn't finish the thought.

I turned and walked back to my room, leaving the door hanging open. He could either follow me in, or not.

I was too emotionally drained to care.

Krissy could get the door next time the bell rang.

Right now?

I was about to have a meltdown.

Jon was right behind me, closing the door quietly as I flopped onto my bed, curling up, knees to my chest, back turned.

The tears came hot and silent.

I felt the mattress shift as he climbed in beside me.

He didn't speak.

But then—his arm around me.

And that almost made it worse.

Because it was the one thing I craved most.

And it was the one thing I was terrified of losing.

I had asked him to be honest.

But conversations about what my life would look like without him in it?

That was not what I'd had in mind.

He pulled me closer. Held me tighter.

So close I could feel his warmth.

So tight I could feel his heartbeat against my back.

And that's how we stayed.

He was right—that night in his room—when he'd told me that sometimes, we didn't need words.

He was doing that now.

And I needed him to keep doing that.

I wanted him to hold me like this forever.

***

I woke up with his arm still around me.

By the light creeping in, it was early morning.

Had I stayed like this all night? Or had I moved, and somehow we'd ended up back in this position? Either way, the heart-wrenching sadness from the night before felt... distant.

Like a bad dream that wasn't quite real.

I might not have shown it, but I had been relieved when it was him at the door.

Yet again, he'd known exactly what I needed.

I was glad I'd had the idea to throw a day's worth of his meds into the travel case in his glove box last week.

"For times when you make spontaneous plans," I'd told him.

Which, lately, was a lot.

Still, it was nice having him here.

In my bed.

Even if the reason he'd come had started out not-so-good.

He hadn't been wrong about anything—about planning.

Now that I was less tired—and had time to process—it was...

Nope.

I still wasn't ready to think about those things.

I'd rather think about the beautiful and miraculous things.

Like Mizz Vanessa had said.

I liked her.

A lot.

***

Justin was asleep on the couch—probably after staying up all night playing video games like the grown-ass geek that he was.

Krissy was still in bed, but Kenny was already in the kitchen when Jon and I walked in.

"Good morning, beautiful," Kenny greeted me. Then, without missing a beat, he turned toward Jon. "Good morning, handsome."

We all grinned.

Kenny set a cup of coffee in front of me. "You'll have to add your own sweetener," he said absently before turning to Jon. "Coffee?"

Jon shook his head. "No, thanks. I'm avoiding caffeine these days."

"I have decaf!"

I blinked, surprised.

Since when does Kenny drink decaf?

As if reading my mind, Kenny beamed. "I picked some up last time I went to the store. Just for you, hun!"

I stared at him, deeply appreciative. That was seriously such a thoughtful thing to do.

"Wow," Jon said sincerely. "That was really thoughtful. Thank you, and I'd love some!"

And suddenly—my snarky side decided to rear its sarcastic head.

I blamed morning Via—she was significantly more unfiltered before coffee.

"Aww, Kenny, that was so nice of you!" I cooed, exaggerating my sweetness. "But you shouldn't have bothered. Jon's busy planning his funeral. He probably won't be around to drink it."

Kenny shot me a quick look from behind Jon, but I winked.

The moment he saw the mischievous glint in my eyes, he smirked and turned back around.

Jon's gaze snapped to mine.

I held it for just a beat—long enough for him to know exactly what I was doing—then I intentionally looked away.

Yeah. He got the point.

Score for Via.

Jon exhaled, shifting the subject. "What's your schedule for the day?"

"Class. Some website work. Then another class. You?"

"I work 'til three, then I've got a session with Jason."

"Really?" I said, voice dripping with sarcasm. "You're not going to tell him to just forget it? No sense starting something you might not finish, right?"

You're being bitchy, Via.

I wasn't actually mad. I was just giving him a demonstration on how **words matter.**

Kenny spun around, sensing the passive-aggressive energy in the air. "I get the feeling there's a story here?"

Jon sighed. "Yeah. I got in trouble."

Kenny and I both giggled. It was cute the way he said it.

"For being Mr. Doom and Gloom," I clarified.

Kenny playfully squeezed Jon's shoulder. "What, this little ray of sunshine? I don't believe it!"

We laughed.

The three of us drank our coffee together at the table—like a cozy little friend family.

At one point, Jon glanced around and said, "So this is what it's like to have roommates?"

"This is what it's like to have *my* roommates," I corrected. "And yes—it *is* pretty nice."

Justin grumbled in his sleep and flopped over on the couch.

"Usually," Kenny added.

We cracked up.

A few minutes later, Jon pushed back in his chair. "Well, I have to hit the road."

He stood slowly, pulling on his hat.

I frowned. "What's with that thing?"

Jon paused. "What? My hat? You don't like it?"

I shrugged. "No, it's fine, I guess. But it's not winter."

"Yeah, but you never know if it's going to be hot or cold this time of year. If I wear a hat, it keeps my head warm... then I don't have to think about whether I need a coat."

He said it so casually, as if his logic was completely sound.

I laughed.

Jon logic.

Perfectly scrambled.

But justifiable.

He leaned in, pressing a kiss to my lips. "See you later, babe."

Then, he turned to Kenny. "Good luck with your sales pitch."

I paused. Had Kenny mentioned his plans for the day?

Judging by the amused expression on Kenny's face as his eyes followed Jon to the door, he probably hadn't.

"Thanks, Jon!" he called cheerfully.

Chapter 48

Jaycee and I packed up our bags as the lecture hall emptied. She was mid-story—something spicy about her latest date with Sarah, the cute purple-haired barista from the on-campus café.

As we made our way toward the door, Dr. K caught my eye and motioned me over.

Shit.

I said a quick goodbye to Jaycee and walked over to the podium, where Dr. K was still packing up.

"I enjoyed your outline, Via."

"Enjoyed" it? Was it entertaining? Amusing?

"Do you have a few minutes to talk about it?"

I nodded, feeling instantly deflated.

Jaycee had told me her topic proposal meeting with Dr. K had lasted all of three minutes—wham, bam, thank you, ma'am.

Now here I was, being pulled aside again.

I turned toward a seat, but Dr. K stopped me.

"Actually, do you have time to grab a coffee?"

Shit. She must have a lot to say.

I nodded, trying to disguise my reluctance.

It's not that I didn't like Dr. K—I did. A lot.

But I couldn't shake the feeling of being singled out.

And I wasn't sure if it was because she thought I was doing a shitty job... or if she thought I was mentally unstable.

Probably both.

***

We made small talk on the short walk to the café.

I tried to be polite, but the nerves were setting in.

Part of me just wanted to get this conversation over with.

Inside, I waved to Sarah as we ordered drinks and took our seats.

And then—remembering Jaycee's story—I almost choked on a laugh.

Sarah would probably die if she knew I knew her bedroom business.

But I welcomed the momentary humor.

It took the edge off as Dr. K pulled a folder from her leather bag and laid it on the table.

My outline.

I crossed my legs nervously as she pulled reading glasses from her head and put them on, reinspecting my paper before peering at me over the rims.

"It looks like you've done a lot of research so far. Are you finding good sources?"

"Yes," I said. "I've found a lot of references. The hardest part is deciding what to keep."

Dr. K nodded, scanning my outline. "Mm-hm."

Oh God. Here it comes.

"You have some great threads here. This is a lot of information. You could easily complete an entire thesis on just one of these topics."

Shit.

She thinks my outline is too broad.

But then—

"But I like your approach."

Wait.

"NDE experiences are multifaceted, and attempting to tie all these aspects together for a broader understanding of their psychological impact is very compelling."

So... she *does* like it?

I wished she were easier to read.

"Thank you," I said hesitantly, bracing for the other shoe to drop.

Dr. K continued scanning my outline in thoughtful silence. Then, she paused.

"Clair Senses..." she murmured. "I was a bit surprised to see this included."

Oh my God. Here it comes.

Heat flared up my neck as my stomach twisted.

I knew it. I knew I was about to get called out for including something so fringe in a scientific paper.

"Well..." I started, but cut myself off as Sarah plopped our coffees down.

Why did I feel so embarrassed to even say this out loud?

I forced myself to continue once Sarah was out of earshot.

"I feel like I've found enough research to support that it exists... although it seems to be called different things, depending on whether you're a doctor or a spiritualist."

Dr. K smiled deeply, a small chuckle escaping.

"Well, yes, you're correct. There are ways to validate these experiences regardless of which side of the fence you fall on."

She paused, then leaned forward slightly.

"However, for a research paper, I think we can dig a little deeper—to create a stronger scientific framework."

I must've visibly deflated, because she immediately followed up.

"This is a bold and interesting angle... Clair Senses. And I think you're onto something, Via."

Holy shit.

Really?

She thought some more, her eyes still fixed on my outline.

"You make mention of biofields here. As in, energy fields?"

She glanced up, eyes sharp with curiosity.

I swallowed. "Yes. It seems like there could be a connection there, maybe? I don't know..."

I was already half-retracting—but Dr. K nodded in agreement.

"Yes. I think your instincts are good. There's actually an emerging area of research that could complement this idea—coherence. Have you heard of it?"

"No." I shook my head.

Dr. K lifted her glasses and sat back in her chair, studying me.

"I've kept up with some of the latest research in mind-body regulation. It's an evolving field, but fascinating."

She took a measured sip of her coffee, never breaking eye contact.

Then, as if she were about to share the world's secrets, she settled in.

"Coherence—especially heart coherence—is being studied in psychophysiology. It's a way to measure autonomic regulation and emotional resilience. Some researchers think heart rate variability plays a role in intuition."

I sat up straighter.

"Heart rate variability?"

She nodded.

"The beat-to-beat variations in heart rate—HRV—directly reflect autonomic nervous system regulation. And autonomic regulation, in turn, influences cognitive perception, emotional stability, and..."

She shrugged slightly. "As I've said, possibly even intuition."

Her words sank in, layering over everything I had already been researching.

"We still don't fully understand how the nervous system interacts with higher cognitive function. Some people who've had near-death experiences—"

She hesitated slightly, then continued.

"—report physiological changes. But that's what the scientific world is calling coherence."

She gave me a knowing look.

"If that interests you, I can point you toward some literature?"

I blinked.

How does she know so much about this? Has she researched it herself?

I nodded eagerly.

A few minutes ago, I'd been dreading that she was going to tell me I needed to do more research... but HRV? Coherence? *Heart coherence,* even?

I needed to know more.

Dr. K smiled and nodded, as if she could see the gears turning in my head.

"Good. I really think this might help you bridge the gap between metaphysical experiences and physiological mechanisms. It could be the missing link you're looking for—the physiological counterpart to what you're calling the 'biofield.' And a solid, scientific counterpoint to Clair Senses."

A chill raced through me.

A bolt of excitement.

She was watching me carefully, the satisfied smile of someone who had just ignited a campfire.

"Some psychologists and cardiologists are beginning to study how heart rate variability connects to emotional processing. You might find it relevant to what you're exploring. And relevant to your case study."

My breath hitched.

Oh shit. She's talking about Jon.

And she was right. The thought had already jumped to the forefront of my mind.

"You're right," I said earnestly. "Thank you for pointing this out to me."

She nodded approvingly.

Then, just as smoothly, just as deliberately—

"And how is Jonathan?"

She took a measured sip of her coffee, her eyes watching me carefully over the rim.

I tried not to visibly squirm.

"If you're going to study this, you should know—coherence doesn't just affect the person achieving it. It can also influence those around them."

Yeah, no shit.

I could feel it.

And now, I could put a name to it, too.

A fresh wave of elation coursed through me.

But Dr. K wasn't finished.

"So when the two of you are discussing coherence, you can understand it as more than just an intellectual curiosity."

She set her cup down carefully.

"There are tangible medical implications that could really benefit him."

Her words hit deeper than I expected.

Because the truth was, Jon and I weren't discussing *anything.*

And now, the weight of that silence had crept in.

The guilt rose fast and sharp—because I wasn't just studying this.

I was studying *him.*

Without his knowledge.

Dr. K must have seen it on my face, because her brows furrowed slightly.

"Via. You have talked to Jonathan about your research, haven't you?"

I shifted uncomfortably.

I hadn't even formed a reply before she asked, just as gently—

"Is there a reason you haven't brought this up with him yet?"

I shrugged, shifting again. "I guess I'm just not sure how to bring it up... or how he'll react."

She nodded knowingly.

"Well, you don't have to have all the answers before you talk to him."

Her voice was measured, but there was no room for avoidance in her tone.

"But you do owe him the conversation."

I swallowed hard.

Her gaze held mine, steady and sharp.

I felt like a bug under a microscope.

"This is an ethical issue, Via—if he's part of your research, he deserves to know."

She let the words settle, then added—

"And furthermore, this is someone who loves you. And whom you love."

Her voice softened slightly, but the weight of her words didn't.

"Informed consent isn't just a box to check—it's about respect."

I nodded, voice quiet.

"I understand."

And I meant it. Truly.

It wasn't that I hadn't already known I needed to tell him.

I did.

Sooner or later.

But this?

This new information felt *big.*

And now, it was impossible to deny—I wasn't doing this research just for scientific curiosity.

I was doing it to make sense of what was happening to Jon.

And he deserved to participate.

It was *his* life on the line.

A heavy wave of guilt settled over me.

Had I been dishonest with him?

Am I lying by omission?

I needed to fix it.

Dr. K leaned forward, her gaze steady.

"Are you afraid that once you talk to him, you won't be able to rationalize keeping this separate from your personal life?"

Fuck, Via. You've really worked yourself into a corner, haven't you?

I sighed.

Honesty.

That needed to be the best policy.

From now on.

I forced myself to meet her eyes.

"It *is* personal."

The words came out quiet—but firm.

I braced for her response.

But she simply smiled.

"I know it is. I'm just glad to hear you say it."

She let the words settle.

"But I still think you can do it."

Chapter 49

I was late getting to Jon's on Saturday. I'd had to drive two towns over to the public library for a textbook Dr. K had recommended for my paper—one I couldn't find online or at either of the local branches.

It was already close to two when I pulled in and spotted Jason's car parked along the street.

He's still here? He must've stayed over.

They'd been working on some tracks last night, putting the finishing touches on a few songs.

Mike's vehicle pulled in behind me, and he and Cary climbed out. The three of us went inside together.

Jason was on his way out, thanking Jon again for fixing the bad pickups on his favorite guitar—the culprit behind last night's delay. But as he reached the door, he caught sight of Mike and Cary and lingered in the foyer, turning to fill them in on the latest band news.

I took a seat on the couch, texting Nikki to let her know I was here. She needed my help with her photography website. Go figure.

Jason launched into an update about schedules, label drama, all the usual. I half-listened, more focused on my phone, until something caught my attention.

A music festival?

Something about proceeds going to childhood cancer research. A benefit show. A stacked lineup. He rattled off a list of names. But then—

FR. Playing.

What?

My head snapped up, ears fully tuning in now. Jason was suggesting FR join the lineup. Playing the new songs—they're fire.

Oh hell no.

But the worst part? Jon didn't seem opposed to the idea.

The fuck?

OH HELL NO.

Judging by the looks on Mike and Cary's faces, I wasn't the only one having a visceral reaction to this insanity.

"Man, are you sure that's a good idea?" Cary asked, hesitant, like he didn't want to say out loud what all of us were clearly thinking. At least, all of us with any common sense.

Jon shrugged. "A few songs isn't going to hurt. It's a one-off."

"Yeah, but your doctor seemed pretty adamant that you steer clear of performances," Cary pressed.

Jon's posture stiffened, that defiant look creeping in.

Oh, here we go.

"Well," he said, his voice taking on a clipped, mock-formal tone. "I'll run it by my doctor first, of course. Wouldn't want to do anything without his permission."

He locked eyes with Cary, staring hard enough to make me feel bad for the guy. But Mike, ever the peacemaker, chimed in before things escalated.

"Well yeah, cool. We'll see how things go."

Before anyone could push back further, the front door swung open, and Nikki stepped inside. She glanced between them, immediately sensing she'd walked in on something. With a goofy wave, she beelined for the couch and plopped down beside me.

"What the fuck is going on?" she mouthed, her back to them.

Luckily, her arrival derailed the conversation. They shifted focus, mostly on Jason wrapping up his departure.

***

With Jason gone, things settled back into their usual rhythm. The topic of the festival had been tabled—for now. But I had a bright red flag on it, flashing in the back of my mind. No way in hell was Jon performing at a festival.

The guys disappeared downstairs to mix tracks—Shawn had sent over his parts, and now it was time to piece everything together.

Nikki and I stayed in the living room. Maize curled up beside me, wisely avoiding the noise.

I filled Nikki in on Jason's brilliant suggestion. She listened with increasing disbelief, and when I finished, she said flatly, "That's a terrible idea."

"Yep."

Dismissing the whole thing for now, we turned our attention to her photography proofs, flipping through the stack to find the best shots for her website.

***

By 5:30, Cary and Mike emerged from the basement.

Nikki and I were still deep in her website—we hadn't even finished the landing page yet.

"You guys done already?" Nikki asked, surprised.

"No," Cary said, grabbing his jacket. "But I got called into work. They need me to fill in tonight, and I rode here with Mike."

"Need a ride?" Mike offered.

She shook her head. "No thanks. I'll walk." Then she hesitated, glancing at me. "Unless you and Jon had something planned?"

I did.

I needed to talk to him about my research paper. The conversation I'd been dreading all week. The one I'd resolved to have after my meeting with Dr. K.

But I was staying over. And a little more procrastination sounded pretty damn good.

"No," I said. "Jon's still busy. You can hang out. Let's finish this page."

Mike kissed her goodbye, and we turned back to the site.

Another forty-five minutes of tweaks, and we were finally done.

"Thanks, Via!" Nikki said, gathering her things. "It's really looking good! I'm excited to go live!"

I smiled, but as I watched her walk down the sidewalk, my stomach tightened.

No more distractions.

The conversation was waiting for me.

I'd been rehearsing it for two days, trying to find the right words. But I'd wanted to have way more research on coherence and HRV finished before bringing this up to Jon. If anything could justify what I was doing... it was that.

But the reference materials Dr. K had suggested were dense, packed with information that took time to unpack. And some of the texts were harder to track down than I'd expected.

So, I felt semi-unprepared—which was a dangerous place to be when talking to Jon about something this sensitive.

Still, I remembered Dr. K's words:

"You don't have to have all the answers before you talk to him. But you do owe him the conversation."

She was right. I knew she was right.

I just needed to rip off the Band-Aid.

I exhaled, glancing at Maize, curled up beside me on the couch, watching me with quiet patience.

I scratched behind her ears. "Well, girlie," I murmured. "Time to talk to your daddy. I hope he doesn't get too mad at me. If he does... I'm sorry. And I love you."

Maize blinked at me.

Yeah. I know, girl.

***

Jon sat with his back to the stairs when I came down.

"Hey, sexy," he said, not even bothering to look up. His worktable was a mess—his latest project laid out in pieces, the gutted guitar surrounded by scattered hardware.

"How do you know I wasn't Mike coming back down here?" I teased, laughing.

He snorted. "He outweighs you by almost a hundred pounds. You don't sound the same."

"What are you doing?"

"Swapping out these cheap-ass pickups for good ones." He shook his head. "Jason really needs to make better choices when it comes to gear."

He chuckled, then nodded toward the big studio chair beside him. "Grab a seat."

I flopped down, spinning to face him, even though he still hadn't turned around.

I let the quiet settle between us for a moment.

God help me.

I took a breath, forcing my voice to sound lighter than I felt.

"Hey, Jon? Can we talk?"

His hands stilled.

Shit. He knows.

For a second, I thought I saw his shoulders tense, but then he carefully set his tools down and turned to me, flashing a quick smile.

Was that forced?

"Sure, babe. What's up?"

I searched his face. There was something there—something guarded. He looked about as reluctant as I felt.

I swallowed. *Here we go.*

"So... I've been thinking..."

"Oh no," he teased, smirking. "That means I'm in for it."

I laughed. "No! No, it's nothing like that."

"Good." He exhaled, his posture easing slightly.

Then, before I could get another word out—

"I wasn't just blowing smoke earlier, Via. I really will talk to Dr. Brookens before I do anything. I won't play a show before I'm ready."

Oh.

Oh shit.

That's what he thought this was about.

If I weren't still battling my nerves, I probably would've been amused. He was bracing for a completely different conversation.

And to be fair, I *had* planned on talking to him about the festival—just not now.

But hearing him say that? *That* made me feel better. Because he wasn't ready to play a show. He had to know that on some level.

I smiled. "I'm glad to hear you say that."

And I truly was.

"Good then," he said with a quick nod, already spinning back around toward his work, apparently considering the conversation finished.

I cleared my throat. "That's actually not what I wanted to talk to you about."

He paused, glancing back at me with curiosity. "No?"

"I wanted to talk about my Psychology class."

"Oh yeah?" His brows lifted with genuine interest. "You're usually complaining about Mr. Miller. I never get to hear about your other class."

Oh, you're about to hear a whole lot more than you bargained for.

He wasn't wrong. I'd deliberately avoided talking about my Psych course for obvious reasons. And when I did talk about class, it was usually to complain about Mr. Miller—my coding professor, who had the personality of a dead leaf.

I let out a nervous laugh.

"Yeah, well... I have to write a research paper. It's a big part of the course. And we're able to choose our own topic."

"Right. You had to submit a proposal. I remember."

"Uh-huh. So..."

Here it goes.

"I'm researching the Psychological Effects of Near-Death Experiences."

He froze.

But he didn't respond.

Oh God.

Just keep going, Via.

"There's a lot of fascinating information on how cognitive abilities and intuition can change after—"

"Is it because of me?"

He cut me off.

Still hadn't moved.

But there it was—the million-dollar question.

My brain scrambled for the right response, but before I could say anything, he calmly set down his tools.

And turned in his chair.

Slowly.

His eyes locked onto mine—dead serious, dead steady.

"Is the reason you chose this topic because of me?" he asked again, deliberately, every word precise.

I swallowed. "Well, yeah. In part. I mean, what happened to you is obviously relevant."

His expression didn't change.

But he nodded. Once.

Then leaned back in his chair. His gaze dropped to the floor, like he was considering something.

"So you want to head-shrink me now?"

Oh shit.

I did not like the look on his face.

No, no. Abort mission. No way in hell was I bringing up clair senses after that comment.

"Jon, no. That's not what this is," I rushed to say. "I've been researching the psychophysiological impacts of NDEs. The mind-body connection. There's this concept called coherence—it affects both physical and emotional control. It can even heighten—"

I stopped.

I was rambling. I knew I was rambling.

And I had no idea if he was even listening.

But then his eyes flicked back up to mine.

Too calm.

Too collected.

Too calculated.

"And how exactly are you planning to study these things?"

I blinked.

"How are you going to study me?" he clarified, voice quieter now. "That's your goal, right? That's what you've been doing?"

I shook my head. No. That wasn't what this was.

But suddenly, it didn't matter what I said.

His jaw tightened, and he looked away.

I wasn't sure which was worse—when he drilled into me with those fiercely indignant eyes...

Or when he refused to look at me at all.

"I'm sure there's a way to do it," he murmured. His voice was sharp, detached. Dangerously measured. "Some way to quantify all of it. Whatever it is you want to measure."

Like HRV.

I didn't dare say it.

He already knew.

And he looked hurt.

And pissed.

"Isn't that the point?" His voice was steady, but his eyes—God, his eyes—were anything but. *"You want to see how I measure up? Stack me against the rest of your research? You need to know if I'm normal."*

"Jon—that's not true! That's not it at all." My voice cracked, desperate to make him realize my intentions. "I just want to understand. *I'm trying to understand you.*"

He didn't even blink. "I thought you did understand me."

Fuck.

There it was. That same quiet, distant tone that instantly threw me back to our first argument.

This was not how I wanted this to go.

"I thought we were connecting." His voice wavered, but only slightly. "I've been trying, Via."

And he had. God, I knew he had.

"Oh my God, Jon, we *are* connecting! I've never felt closer to you than I have lately!"

His expression flickered—like he wanted to believe me. But then—

"Yeah? So close that you have to write a whole fucking research paper about it?"

The words cut deep.

"I just want to know what you're dealing with," I pleaded. "How it's affecting you. How it's affecting us."

His frustration boiled over.

"I don't know how to answer that, Via!" His voice was raw, frayed at the edges. "I don't know what that even means, or how to give you the answers you're looking for!"

He exhaled sharply, raking a hand through his hair.

Then, softer—but somehow even heavier:

"For Chrissake, Livia... what more do you want?"

He stood. Fast.

His eyes were burning now, his whole body tense, and in one long stride, he was right in front of me.

Towering over me.

Then—he moved.

Leaning down. Hands braced on the arms of my chair. Nose to nose.

His expression was serene.

But his eyes? Jesus Christ.

"Hook me up to a monitor," he murmured, voice low, dangerous. *"A lie detector. Whatever kind of biofeedback device you want."*

He was so still.

"I'll do my best."

I couldn't move. Couldn't breathe.

"I don't know what kind of test results you're looking for, Vee. But I can promise you—if you want the truth from me, you'll get it."

His voice dropped lower—but somehow, it felt like a scream.

"I fucking love you, Livia. And beyond that?"

His jaw clenched.

"I don't know a hell of a lot anymore."

His intensity was suffocating. Scorching.

"I would tell you I'd die for you," he said, his voice quieter now. "Because that's what everybody thinks love means."

My chest tightened.

I couldn't look away.

He leaned closer.

So close his lips brushed my ear.

Then, in a whisper—low, venomous, devastating:

"Dying is easy."

I shuddered.

Because fuck.

I could feel it. The anger. The resentment. The absolute rawness of those words.

But then, suddenly, he dropped.

Kneeling.

Kneeling in front of me.

My hands were clenched in my lap, white-knuckled, but he took them in his, voice dropping back into something softer.

More fragile.

"I would live for you, Vee."

His fingers squeezed mine.

"I did." His voice cracked. *"And I am."*

His gaze was raw now. Wide open. Exposed.

"And I don't know what else I can offer."

And then—

I didn't see it coming.

His lips were on mine.

And I felt it.

Every ounce of frustration. Of desperation. Of love, of need, of fire.

It was a collision.

A goddamn explosion.

And just as fast, he pulled back.

"If you feel the need to research all of this," he murmured, eyes still locked on mine, "go ahead. Do whatever you need to do."

A pause.

"But come home to me at the end of the day… and just *be here. With me."*

***

He was still on top of me, his weight solid, comforting.

His warmth, his touch—it sent shivers through me.

I felt wrapped in him, in everything he was. The rush of endorphins, the dizzying mix of love, relief, and euphoria still pulsed through my veins.

Maybe that's what made me do it.

Or maybe it was the things he'd said.

Or the way he looked at me.

Or simply the fact that I was head over heels for him, overwhelmed by everything we'd just been through.

But before I could stop myself—

"Marry me."

Christ, Via.

What the fuck?

He froze, his lips still brushing mine.

Then—a grin.

His brows furrowed slightly, playful but confused.

"I already asked you to marry me." He pulled back just enough to look at me fully, smirking. "Long before any of this happened. *Remember?"*

I grinned back.

"I know," I murmured, still breathless.

But then, I sobered.

This was different.

"I'm not asking," I said softly. *"I'm saying. Let's just do it."*

His smile faltered.

Just a little.

His eyes searched mine. Like he was trying to figure out if I meant it.

I did.

"Via," he whispered, his voice barely above a breath. "I would fucking marry you *tomorrow.* I would marry you *right now* if I could."

He kissed me again—so tenderly, so deeply—and for a moment, I thought maybe he would say yes.

But then—he pulled back.

Looking thoughtful.

Almost concerned.

"But that wouldn't be fair." His fingers brushed my cheek. "You deserve the wedding we talked about. I want to give that to you. I don't want us rushing into some half-assed plan to get hitched just because of my stupid health."

Was that what I was doing?

Subconsciously?

Normally, he was the one making rash decisions.

He kissed me again—just once, soft and sure.

"I'd have no problem running off with you in the morning and tying the knot at the courthouse," he admitted, voice low. "But that would be selfish. I'd be afraid you'd resent me for it down the road."

Down the road.

That phrase alone sent a wave of relief through me.

We were back to talking about the future.

"Besides," he added, his dimples returning as he smirked. "There would be a lot of pissed-off people if we did that."

That was true.

Between both our families, our friends... people would be disappointed if we eloped in secret.

No.

He was right.

"You're right." I exhaled, letting out a small, breathy laugh. "I just love you so much. I want to make you mine."

Jon brushed his nose against mine, murmuring, "I'm yours, baby. Always."

I smiled. Deeply. Not just on my face. Inside.

"Next year this time..." he whispered, his eyes twinkling, full of hope. "We'll be having the wedding of our dreams. We'll both be done with school. We'll have our own place. Just us and Maize... hell, maybe we'll get her a playmate. My surgery will be over. And I'll be ticking like a clock when we say 'I do.'"

I listened, soaking in every word, letting the vision wrap around me like a warm blanket. It could happen.

Right?

There was no reason this couldn't become real.

Please, God.

Let this become real.

Chapter 50

When I got to Jon's after class on Thursday, he was already waiting.

He said he needed to stop by Mike's shop and figured I could just come with him.

When we pulled into the lot, Nikki's car was there.

I caught the flicker of disapproval on Jon's face and smirked. "She did go look at another car on Monday!" I offered, preemptively defending her.

He raised an eyebrow. "She did?"

"Yeah," I said. Waited a beat. Then, casually—

"But it was another Volkswagen."

I burst out laughing when he immediately rolled his eyes, sighing like he'd just lost all faith in humanity.

"I guess she's a slow learner," he said, sounding amazed. Then—his tone shifted.

"Come on. I have a surprise for you."

A surprise?

***

The shop was quiet, except for Mike and Nikki.

We lingered near the entrance for a few minutes, swapping recaps of the day, the usual back-and-forth.

Then—Jon shifted.

His whole demeanor changed—animated, restless energy buzzing under his skin.

He rubbed his hands together.

"Dude, I've been amped up for this all day." He turned to Mike. "When can I see it?"

See it?

See what?

Mike grinned, already moving toward his drawing table. "I think you're gonna like it," he called over his shoulder.

Jon followed.

So did Nikki and I—both curious now.

Mike peeled back a thin cover sheet, revealing a large, intricate drawing beneath it.

Jon lit up like a Christmas tree.

His grin was instant—pure excitement flashing across his face as he clapped Mike on the back like he already knew exactly what this was.

"Fuck, man, you nailed it!"

Wait—what?

I stepped closer, examining the artwork.

Mike was a hell of an artist. His work was always crisp, clean, dripping with realism. Every detail, every highlight, every surface reflection and light source was considered.

This was no different.

But the subject?

Nothing like I'd ever seen before.

My eyes roamed over the illustration, my brain processing the pieces in fragments.

The black and gray detail was impeccable—hyper-realistic.

Some of the elements were unmistakably mechanical—sharp, metallic edges, intricate gears, fragments of internal circuitry woven into the composition.

But other parts were different.

Smoother. Organic.

Bone.

Wait.

Jeezus Christ—

Was that a—

My breath caught.

My perspective shifted.

Instead of focusing on the intricate details, I finally took in the entire piece.

It was almost Giger-ish in style. Surreal. Dark. Unsettling.

But unmistakable.

It was one half of a ribcage—though obscured by an intricate weave of mechanical components seamlessly fusing into organic structures.

At about the sternum, the mechanization faded—transitioning back into human skin.

And beneath it—

A heart.

Anatomically correct.

But integrated with circuitry.

And at its center—

A keyhole.

Embedded in a circuit board.

Holy shit.

This is cool.

Mike was talking to Jon, pointing out details.

"Here... and here," he said, using his pinky to indicate two specific areas on the design. "This is where I left room. Like we talked about."

Room for what?

My breath hitched as the realization slammed into me.

This piece is for Jon.

Nikki knew it too.

She elbowed me, her eyes wide with excitement. A huge, gleeful smile on her face.

I turned back to the drawing. Then to Jon. Then to Mike.

Both of them were beaming, looking so damn pleased with themselves.

Oh my God.

Jon had commissioned Mike to design him a custom tattoo.

"I printed off a stencil," Mike said, pulling out a large sheet of stencil paper—the same artwork, but stripped down to its raw outlines. "Let's check it for size and placement."

Jon shot me a grin. "Well?" he asked, teasing.

I was speechless.

"It's incredible," I managed. But that word—that pathetic little word—didn't even scratch the surface of what I was feeling.

***

Mike held up the stencil next to Jon, eyeing it critically.

"Our measurements were good," he said, nodding in approval. "I think it's gonna sit perfect."

He motioned for Jon to slip off his shirt, grabbing a bottle of stencil tonic.

Oh, holy fuck.

Nikki and I watched—unblinking, entranced—as Jon pulled his T-shirt over his head and tossed it onto a chair.

Mike carefully cut and aligned each piece of the stencil, smoothing it over Jon's ribs, his side, his shoulder. Then—slowly, methodically—he peeled back the paper.

We all stared.

And it was breathtaking.

The tattoo—a 1:1-scale, true-to-life replica of Jon's entire left side—was haunting in its precision, a stunning convergence of creativity and intent.

Mike stepped back, admiring his work, then gestured to the same two areas he'd pointed out earlier.

"Your incisions will fall into these sections," he explained. "They'll blend right in. The scars will become part of the art."

Jon's expression softened—something reverent flashing in his eyes.

"This is perfect, man. You've blown me away."

Then—he turned to me.

"What do you think, Vee?" His grin returned, playful. "Life imitates art, right? May as well make the best of it."

I exhaled, shaking my head in awe.

"It's... it's fucking amazing," I breathed. Then, turning to Mike—"You're amazing."

"That's gonna be so hot."

Nikki's voice was not subtle. She was staring unabashedly, zero shame, zero hesitation.

We both giggled.

I couldn't even blame her for the comic lustfulness in her tone.

She was right.

We all cracked up.

"Thanks, baby," Jon teased, grinning at Mike, who was still scrutinizing the placement over Jon's ribs.

Then—Jon wiggled his eyebrows.

"You're gonna do me so good."

The room exploded with laughter.

But—*holy fuck.*

Jon's toned, sculpted body was already a work of art.

Now, with this ink—this ridiculously detailed, borderline genius piece of living artwork?

He would be a goddamn masterpiece.

"That's a really big tattoo," Nikki observed, still taking it all in. "How long is it going to take?"

"A few sessions, for sure," Mike said, still scrutinizing the placement.

His fingers pressed around Jon's ribs and sternum, applying tattoo-level pressure—a silent test. There was no trace of the bruising he'd sustained from CPR, but Mike was double-checking anyway.

"Will you be able to handle that for several hours at a time?" he asked.

Jon barely blinked.

"Sure." His voice was casual, certain. "I've been through worse."

Mike smiled, nodding in understanding.

"Well," he said, matter-of-factly, "rib tattoos are never comfortable. Just making sure everything else is healed enough."

That comment triggered a thought.

"Is it safe?" I asked, hesitating. "I mean... for you to sit through this right now? Before your surgery?"

I was thinking of the stress—the implications. The last thing he needed was something that could compromise his health.

Jon winked at me. "I can handle it."

I have no doubts.

"We've got to get at least this section done before the surgery," Mike commented, his tone shifting into business mode. "His ICD will be right there. And I don't want to get too close to that with the machine."

I caught Nikki's questioning look before Mike explained further.

"Electromagnetic field," he clarified. "No way I want to risk damaging leads or disrupting the device. Plus... he's going to need to heal from that without diverting energy to healing a tattoo."

That all made perfect sense.

Mike had just given us multiple solid reasons to do it now.

I was sold on the idea.

And—holy hell—it was going to be so hot.

Mike shrugged, glancing back at Jon.

"Sometime down the road, if you still wanna do the other side, that shouldn't be a problem."

The other side?

Ffuck.

Jon grinned. Excited. Amped. "So when are we starting?"

Mike lifted his hands, looking around the shop. "I've got all night. The stencil's on. We can do the outline if you're ready."

Jon's grin widened—but then, suddenly, he stopped.

His expression shifted, lighting up again.

"Wait." He turned to Mike, eyes bright with excitement. "The other part..."

The other part?

There's more?!?

The two exchanged a knowing look before Mike turned back to his drawing table.

He grabbed a large sketchpad, flipped it open, and pulled out another drawing.

Another piece.

He walked it over to us, holding it carefully—like he knew exactly what it meant.

It was rendered in the same style as Jon's tattoo—the perfect match.

But this one—

This one was a key.

A large, ornate skeleton key.

Intricate. Engraved with the same circuitry-style illustrations.

I blinked.

Nikki gasped.

Jon was watching me, eyes lit with quiet anticipation.

Mike grinned.

"Do you like it?" he asked. "It's the key to his heart."

My eyes snapped to Jon's tattoo—the circuit board keyhole etched over his heart.

Holy fuck.

A slow, dizzying wave of realization washed over me.

I nearly swooned.

Jon stepped forward, pulling me into his arms.

"I told you," he murmured, his voice warm, certain. *"I'm yours."*

My breath hitched.

This.

This was so much better than rushing off to get married.

How did he always do this?

How did he always manage to outdo himself with gestures so effortlessly perfect?

"I can get this tattooed on me?" I breathed, still staring at the drawing.

Jon's grin softened.

"I was hoping you would." He pressed a gentle kiss to my forehead.

My eyes snapped to Mike.

He was already smirking.

"This is beautiful," I whispered, turning the page in my hands like it was something sacred. "Where should I put it?"

Mike shrugged. "It's your tattoo. We can put it wherever you want."

I glanced at Nikki—

She was already eyeing me up and down, practically vibrating with excitement, like I was a canvas waiting for paint.

Then—Jon moved.

Gently, he took my right hand in his and stretched my arm out, palm up.

The key would fit perfectly on the inside of my right forearm.

"Here?" I asked.

We all exchanged approving nods.

Spatially, it was perfect.

But then—

A thought.

A memory.

The one that sealed my decision.

Every night, when I cuddled up to Jon, I would rest my arm across him.

My hand over his heart.

Ever since that first night—the one where he guided my hand there himself—I'd discovered that it grounded me.

Falling asleep like that brought me an overwhelming sense of security. Of calmness.

If I placed the tattoo on my forearm, our designs would line up perfectly.

Our eyes met.

Jon's smile deepened.

He knew.

"I think that's a good spot," he said softly.

It's perfect.

Chapter 51

Wednesdays were becoming a monumental pain in my ass. With multiple classes spaced just far enough apart to kill any chance of productivity, I'd given up on client work entirely. Wednesdays were now dedicated to plowing through coursework for the entire week, freeing me up for... everything else.

Jon had called while I was heading to his place, mentioning one last lesson with a new student—a guy in his mid-forties who had never touched a guitar, but was desperate to bond with his new stepson. Honestly, Jon was grossly overqualified for the job, but he never looked at things that way, and of course, took him on. A sucker for anything kid-related. But... teaching a total newbie? He was in for a ride.

I let myself in, greeted Maize with the customary smooches, and took her out for a quick pee-break. The extra time meant I could finally submit my revised outline to Dr. K. I'd added a whole section on the scientific research she'd suggested—pages I'd labored over, ensuring every argument was airtight.

After rewarding Maize with a treat, I grabbed my stuff and headed upstairs.

I stopped short the second I walked into Jon's room.

What the actual fuck?

Everything was different. Rearranged. Not just a subtle shift—but a complete overhaul. The bed, the desk, the shelves—nothing was where it had been. My mind scrambled for an explanation.

Weird.

Maybe he needed more room for his music equipment?

I flopped onto the bed—now awkwardly jutting into the center of the room at an angle. Odd choice... but whatever.

I pulled out my laptop, scrolling through my document one last time, pride swelling in my chest over the additional sections.

IV. Coherence, HRV, and the Autonomic Nervous System

• Explanation of heart coherence and its role in autonomic nervous system regulation.

• The link between HRV (heart rate variability) and emotional control.

• Studies on meditative states, breathwork, and their impact on perception.

• Connection to NDEs: Could heightened coherence explain post-NDE transformations?

V. Ethical Considerations & Informed Consent

• The ethics of researching altered consciousness in NDE survivors.

• Informed consent: ensuring participants understand the implications.

• The risk of reducing profound experiences to mere science.

• Discussion: Is it ethical to study what we don't fully understand?

VI. Conclusion & Future Research

• Psychological, cognitive, and physiological changes in NDE survivors.

• The tension between empirical inquiry and subjective experience.

• The need for interdisciplinary research blending psychology, neuroscience, and mind-body studies.

• Final Thought: Studying NDEs may not just reveal insights into the experiences, but into consciousness itself.

I'd barely scratched the surface, but already, the blurred lines between science and metaphysics were undeniable. Coherence, especially, made unsettling sense. Jon wasn't just surviving post-NDE weirdness. He was regulating his autonomic nervous system—intuitively mastering what my research was only beginning to articulate.

He didn't need my research. He just... knew. His body knew. His mind knew.

I wasn't illuminating anything for him. I was scrambling to keep up.

Yet, connecting the dots felt satisfying. Maybe I didn't have all the answers—but I was starting to see the map.

***

Jon's footsteps echoed from downstairs just as I hit send. Perfect timing. Maize, her entire body wiggling with excitement, met him halfway up the stairs. She was still bouncing between us when he leaned in for a kiss. I got half Jon, half wet dog tongue.

"Ugh! Gross, Maize!" I laughed, wiping my face. "What's up with the furniture in here, anyway?"

"I wanted to move the bed," he said, like it was the most obvious thing in the world.

"Why?"

He pointed up, grinning.

The skylight.

"You rearranged the entire room... just to put your bed under the skylight?"

"Yep," he said, dimples deepening. "Now we can watch the stars when we're lying here."

I blinked. *This guy...*

"You're ridiculous," I muttered, shaking my head.

Jon flopped onto the bed, pulling me down with him until we lay side by side, gazing up through the glass.

"Why?" he teased, smirking. "We've had some pretty good times under the stars before."

His wink made my cheeks burn.

Damn it. It was true.

And it was more than that...

We had shared a moment under the stars last summer... before everything unraveled... before It happened... before we even knew It could.

Jon had made a remark about how it wouldn't be awful if my birth control failed. He'd said he wouldn't mind having a little Via running around.

At the time, I was mortified at the thought.

But now, here, after everything... I wondered.

I wasn't even sure what I wanted anymore.

And I hated the fact that fate was trying to make our decisions for us.

Chapter 52

"Wow. That is really impressive." Dr. Brookens mused, pausing to examine the tattoo sprawling across Jon's chest and ribs.

And it was. The piece was coming together beautifully—meticulously detailed, just like the original illustration.

"Thanks." Jon said, nodding. "One more session to go."

"Did it hurt?"

"Compared to what?" Jon smirked.

Brookens chuckled, then noted, "Any evidence of your ICD will look like it's meant to be there. I can't say I've ever seen a more creative way to embrace this procedure."

Jon glanced down at his own chest, tracing the ink with his fingertips. "That was kind of the point. I wanted to do something on my own terms."

Brookens nodded. "Mike working on this for you?"

"Yeah. He's a phenomenal artist."

"Oh, for certain. Impressive." There was that word again. "He's doing a fine job."

After Jon's exam, Brookens returned to his seat, and we went over familiar territory—a repeat discussion from the last visit. Only this time, Jon's EF hadn't improved as much.

I felt a pang of anxiety. Had he been pushing too hard? Working too much?

But Brookens was quick to reassure us. "It's normal to see a big jump at first, followed by slower progress. As long as there's improvement, it's good news.

Eventually, your recovery will plateau, and that's when we'll talk surgery. For now, let's follow up next month."

Then came the moment I was dreading.

Brookens asked if we had any questions, and Jon shifted in his seat.

Oh, shit. He's actually going to ask.

"So... there's an opportunity for my band to play at a festival next month. It'd be enough to keep us relevant while we're on... hiatus."

I studied Brookens' face, searching for a reaction, but his expression was unreadable. "How far out are we talking?"

"Two weeks from Saturday."

Brookens seemed to consider this. Then, to our surprise, he said, "I've listened to your music."

Wait. What?

I shot a glance at Jon, who looked just as thrown.

Had that RN—Liz—played it for him? She was a fan.

Brookens smiled. "It's quite good. Maybe a bit intense for my old age, but you're extremely talented."

Jon nodded, unsure where this was going.

"You make an amazing frontman," Brookens continued. "It takes a lot of stamina to perform like that."

And that was the problem.

Even on the best of days, for someone in perfect health, it was exhausting.

Brookens leaned forward slightly, his tone shifting to something more measured. "Here's the thing... If you push too far with high-intensity activity, your body is going to push back. It'll let you know you're redlining."

The weight of those words settled over us.

"We have two concerns," he went on. "Your heart will likely struggle to meet that demand. And stress hormones—adrenaline, norepinephrine, dopamine—could trigger CPVT. The medication helps, but at that level of exertion, you could experience a breakthrough arrhythmia."

Breakthrough arrhythmia.

We were both watching Jon now.

"So… I can't push too far." He nodded, like he'd just been given permission instead of a warning. "I could handle a couple of songs then, just not a full set."

I blinked. *The fuck?*

Had he stopped listening after the first sentence?

I turned to Brookens.

He was watching Jon curiously, but I swore I caught the ghost of a smile at the corner of his mouth.

With a sigh, he said, "Jonathan, I'll tell you the same thing I've told you before—you need to listen to your body. If you do this, even just a couple of songs, and you feel anything unusual, you pull back immediately."

Jon nodded, accepting that.

I didn't.

Brookens must have noticed the doubt on my face because he added, "The last thing you want is to faint in front of all those people."

Jon smirked. "No, that wouldn't be good."

Brookens gestured toward me. "Especially not in front of this one. I don't think she'd be very impressed."

That got a laugh from both of us.

Then Jon reached over, took my hand, and said, "No. I definitely don't want to do that."

Something in his tone softened me. I squeezed his hand, and for the first time since this whole conversation started, I wanted to support him.

"Well," I said, glancing at Brookens. "Jon's gotten really good at managing his… situation. I've been reading about heart coherence, and I think he's been applying those concepts. Anyway—I'm sure he'll be able to regulate himself. Won't you?"

I turned to Jon just in time to catch the flicker of surprise in his eyes, followed by something else—something grateful.

He smiled at me, then at Brookens. "Yeah."

Brookens raised an eyebrow, intrigued. "Coherence, huh? I've seen a few studies—heart rate variability, stress modulation, things like that. That's great, Jon. Keep it up."

Jon glanced back at me, and I winked.

Because it was true. And more than that—I felt it.

With or without the fancy terminology, Jon had learned how to manage his state of being. So well, in fact, that the people around him could feel it too.

Myself included.

Brookens exhaled. "Alright. Just don't overdo it. And I strongly recommend getting yourself checked out afterward. Ideally by an EMT or a medical professional. At the very least, check your vitals. Okay?"

Jon nodded.

***

As the elevator doors shut behind us, Jon turned to me. "Not that I'm complaining, but... why did you stick up for me back there? I know you don't want me to play this show."

I sighed. "No, I don't. But I meant what I said. And..." I hesitated, then met his eyes. "I trust you."

Jon's expression shifted—like those three words were exactly what he needed to hear.

And I was glad I said them, because a second later, he swooped down, kissed me, and the brush of his tongue against mine sent warmth curling through me—right until the chime of the elevator broke the spell.

***

The plan was for all of us to meet up one last time before the show to finalize logistics. Normally, this would have happened at Jon's place, but Cary had asked to host instead—he was dog-sitting.

"The chihuahua from hell," he'd said over the phone.

I had laughed. I loved dogs and couldn't imagine it was as bad as he was making it sound.

When we pulled up at Cary's, Mike and Nikki were already there. Mike was crouched by Nikki's car, attempting to reattach a piece of her bumper.

Jon kneeled down to help.

From inside the house, an ear-splitting, high-pitched bark rang out. And kept going.

"Oh my god," Nikki muttered. "What is he *doing* to that poor thing?"

"Let's go see."

The moment Nikki and I stepped inside, a tiny, bug-eyed creature perched on the couch armrest erupted into another round of frenzied barking, snarling like we had just broken in with crowbars.

"That's Auggie," Cary sighed.

The demon dog couldn't have weighed more than five pounds.

"Auggie the doggie!" Nikki cooed. "Hi, sweetie!"

She extended her hand for him to sniff.

Auggie immediately bared his teeth and let out another sharp snarl.

"Auggie the *asshole*," Cary grumbled. "Last time I ever offer to dog-sit. The damn thing barks at everything. *Everything.*"

Auggie barked, to demonstrate.

I laughed. "Aww, he's probably just stressed out and homesick."

Cary glared at the dog, unimpressed.

A moment later, the front door opened again.

Auggie lost his mind.

First at Mike.

Then at Jon.

Cary sighed. "Sorry about the snarling demon."

Jon tilted his head, amused. "What's the matter, buddy?"

Auggie let out a peculiar little noise in the back of his throat, licked his lips, and sat down. Then, after a long, considering look at Jon, he wriggled his tiny butt and cautiously stepped into his lap, settling there like he had *chosen* him.

Mike smirked. Cary looked personally offended.

"I think you should take him home," Cary muttered.

We all laughed.

"I'm not sure how Maize would feel about that," Jon said, stroking Auggie's head. The tiny dog panted, his tongue lolling happily.

"He's quiet now! Maybe he just doesn't like you," I teased Cary.

"Bullshit," he shot back. "Dogs *love* me."

With Auggie finally pacified, the conversation shifted to the festival.

Jason's band, FaultCode, was headlining, and it had been his idea to bring FR into the lineup. Since their co-headlining tour had been cut short when It happened, this would be a reunion of sorts. But Jason had suggested keeping FR off the official lineup—a total surprise for the fans.

The plan was simple but brilliant.

The stage would go dark, signaling the start of FaultCode's set. But instead of FaultCode, FR would take the stage and launch straight into their new material—two unreleased songs, songs nobody had heard before.

Then, when the lights came up, the crowd would realize who they were seeing.

A shock. A treat. Something no one would have expected.

FR would play just those two songs. Then, Jon would stay onstage to play lead guitar for FaultCode's opener—a track he had co-written with Jason.

If he wasn't feeling up to it, he could leave the stage with the rest of FR. No pressure.

Easy enough.

Right?

***

Later, when it was time to take Auggie outside, Jon clipped on the tiny harness with zero resistance.

Cary, watching, scowled. "I don't trust the little asshole not to run off, but he *hates* that harness."

Auggie, who had apparently *not* gotten that memo, trotted obediently toward the door.

"I think that dog loves him," Nikki remarked as Jon and Auggie disappeared into the backyard.

I smiled.

Auggie. Abby. And everyone else.

As if reading my mind, Cary said, "Yeah, well... Jon vibes different these days."

We all looked at him.

Cary hesitated, like he hadn't meant to say it out loud.

"What?" he said defensively. "Don't act like you don't notice. Jon walks into a room, and the whole energy shifts."

I felt myself tense.

Because he was right.

Of course he was.

I just wasn't expecting him to *say* it.

And he had actually used the word *energy.*

I glanced at Nikki, who was already looking at me.

Mike shrugged. "Yeah, well," he said quietly. "It's kinda cool."

A small silence fell over the room.

Then Cary exhaled, rubbing the back of his neck. "Yeah, it is," he admitted after a beat. *"Crazy fucker."*

Mike smirked.

Chapter 53

"Man, I wish all my clients were as still as you," Mike chuckled over the steady buzz of the tattoo machine.

Jon lay back with his arms behind his head, eyes closed in serene detachment. A faint smile tugged at the corners of his lips. "Just trying to do my part so you don't screw this up."

Mike smirked. "Another hour, and this masterpiece is done."

This was the last of multiple long sessions, and I had wanted to be here for it. I watched them, half amused, half in awe. Jon had been under the needle for hours, and yet, there he was—calm, unfazed, almost disconnected. My mind flicked between two competing thoughts.

Science would say he was compartmentalizing the pain, using mental discipline to distract himself. But... what if it was more than that? Was this coherence? An altered state? His ability to tap into something unseen, something unmeasurable, was undeniable. And yet, the skeptic in me still clung to logic, to what I could prove.

"I'm going next door for a bit," I announced, already feeling the familiar tug-of-war within myself.

I needed to go see Mizz Vanessa. I had a book to return.

Mike paused, briefly glancing at Jon, almost curious to see if that would change his calm exterior. But Jon, true to form, stayed composed.

"'Kay, babe," he replied lazily.

Of course he didn't react. Why would he? Jon was the master of emotional regulation. I couldn't decide if that amazed me or unsettled me.

***

I had been more than careful with the book I borrowed, treating it like a precious artifact—no bent pages, no cracked spine. I'd read every word, analyzed every concept, and still found myself straddling the line between belief and doubt.

"Lavender tea," she offered softly, placing a delicate cup in front of me.

I inhaled deeply, savoring the floral scent. Being here felt effortless. Mizz Vanessa's presence was fluid, open, unjudging—so different from Dr. K, who always made me feel like I needed to justify every thought.

"I can't stop thinking about the book," I admitted. "But... I keep questioning everything. I feel caught between two worlds."

She gave a knowing smile. "That's where transformation happens."

Mizz Vanessa listened intently as I gushed about my research, her pale eyes bright with curiosity. When I mentioned balancing metaphysics with science, I braced for a raised eyebrow—but instead, she leaned forward, fascinated.

"Ah, yes," she mused. "The bridge between what we feel and what we can prove."

I felt a spark of kinship with her. She asked questions about biofeedback research, coherence, and the intersection of energy and awareness. I marveled at how seamlessly she floated between mysticism and science.

Suddenly, the front door to the shop creaked open, and I leaned up briefly to look beyond a display, just in time to see Jon cautiously step inside.

Shit. Had it really been an hour?

Almost.

He paused just inside, eyes scanning the eclectic shelves, the faint scent of incense meeting him. I watched him take it all in, the soft lighting reflecting off polished crystals and worn book spines.

Mizz Vanessa's gaze followed mine. And then... recognition.

Her smile stretched slowly, her eyes glimmering. She knew. This was him. *The one.* The person I had spoken about in hushed tones and fervent admissions.

"Ah," she breathed, rising gracefully. She offered Jon a wave, her smile laced with curiosity and something like reverence.

Jon spotted me. "Hey, Vee," he greeted, flashing that grin. "Thought you left me."

"Nope, just visiting," I said, feeling suddenly self-conscious, torn between the comfort of his presence and the questions his abilities stirred in me.

He wandered through the shop, fingers trailing over displays with genuine interest.

"This place is...cool," he murmured.

Mizz Vanessa's eyes never left him, a soft chuckle escaping her lips.

Jon's attention lingered over the display of stones and jewelry, pausing to admire a collection of deep green crystals.

"These are pretty. Reminds me of your eyes."

My gaze darted to Ms.V, who seemed to be enjoying our conversation—and the irony.

"What does this one mean?" Jon asked.

"Green sapphire," Mizz Vanessa purred, "symbolizes tranquility, loyalty, trust, and compassion."

She paused briefly before adding "It stimulates the heart chakra."

Jon grinned wider, dimples deepening. "See, Vee? Definitely reminds me of you. I'm starting to understand."

This moment—the way he fit so naturally into my world here, the way Mizz Vanessa seemed to see right through us both—felt heavier than it should. In the best possible way.

Was Jon naturally intuitive? Or was there something more? And which version of reality was I prepared to believe?

Chapter 54

Shawn had offered to drive us to the show in his brand-new Lincoln Navigator—blacked-out, spacious, and obnoxiously swanky. A splurge he could afford thanks to his recent promotion.

Since this was just a guest appearance, the band packed light. Mike didn't even need his own drum kit; he'd be using Doug's, which would already be set up for FaultCode. Their similar sound and playing styles meant no adjustments were needed, making the transition seamless. Aside from our overnight bags, all we had were Jon's and Shawn's guitars and pedals.

Cary was driving separately with Emily and two of her friends—his *girl posse.* It worked out well. Cary was the outgoing one, while Jon, Mike, and Shawn were all quieter.

Let the introverts ride together.

There hadn't even been a conversation about seating. Jon had immediately sprawled out in the backseat, leaving Mike to ride shotgun while Nikki and I took the middle captain's chairs.

The drive was nearly three hours with traffic.

Jon wasn't sleeping—I knew that. Every now and then, he'd contribute to our conversation, offering a comment or dry remark. But for the most part, he kept his eyes closed, his body still, seemingly focused on staying calm.

***

By the time we arrived at the venue, things were already in full swing.

The private back lot was packed with tour buses, rigs, and transport vehicles, a controlled storm of roadies and musicians weaving between them in a flurry of load-ins and last-minute adjustments.

Organized chaos.

We had barely stepped out of the SUV when a voice rang out from the loading dock.

"STETS!! Holy fuck, guys, Stets is here!"

Nikki and I exchanged a knowing look.

Here we go.

Jon barely had a second to process before Clay, FaultCode's frontman, came flying off the dock, closing the distance in record time.

Clay threw his arms around Jon, clapping him enthusiastically on the back. "Jesus, man, it's been way too long!"

Before Jon could even respond, another few guys rushed in, all eager greetings and excited laughter.

I smiled to myself—not just because it was endearing to watch their excitement, but because I knew, deep down, Jon *hated* the attention.

Not the sentiment. The *attention.*

By the time he wrestled himself free from the first wave of well-wishers, another group was already making their way over.

At the front was Brian, a tall, scruffy-looking musician/engineer from Manchester, who was in the States more often than he was home.

"Bloody hell, Stets!" he called, grinning. He pulled Jon into a tight embrace, shaking him slightly. "Damn good to see ya, mate! You had us all fucking worried, yeah? You look good!"

Jon returned the hug, responding with something polite. His tone was even. Relaxed. But I caught it—the slight awkwardness in his stance, the way his shoulders didn't quite drop all the way when Brian stepped back.

The fact that everyone knew about his health bothered him.

A lot.

But he also knew their concern was genuine. That part, he didn't begrudge. The rest—the invasive nature of it, the lack of separation between his private life and the version of himself that existed in these people's minds—was something he was still figuring out how to tolerate.

This—the warm welcomes, the questions, the way he was going to have to keep his energy up all day before even stepping on stage—was exactly what he'd been bracing himself for in the car.

FR wouldn't be playing until late, but Jon would be *on* from now until then. Engaging. Smiling. Answering well-meaning questions about the one subject he wished people wouldn't bring up.

It was going to be a long day.

And he knew it.

***

Not long after, Jessica—Clay's wife—came bouncing through.

The second she caught sight of us, her eyes lit up.

"Oh my God!!" she squealed, rushing over and throwing her arms around each of us. "It's *so* good to see you! I was going to sit this one out, but the second I heard about what you had planned, I *had* to come! We've missed you guys so much!"

Then she turned to me, gripping my hands. "*Via!* The guys got a bump in their marketing budget, and we *need* you! We want to hire you for some work!"

Before I could get a word in, she was already pulling me away.

I shot Jon a quick wave before letting Jess drag me toward a quieter spot.

As soon as we were clear of the crowd, her voice dropped, turning serious. "How's he doing?"

The excitement in her expression faded, replaced by genuine concern.

"We were all worried sick when we found out what happened."

Yeah. *Us too.*

I didn't realize how much I hated talking about It until moments like this. Probably almost as much as Jon did.

Still, I gave her the necessary details—just enough to satisfy her without opening up a deeper conversation.

Thankfully, once she was reassured, she pivoted back to her original excitement, diving into the marketing plans for the website.

***

The afternoon flew by faster than I expected.

Despite the constant motion—friends, conversations, distractions—my nerves started clawing their way up.

I kept thinking about Dr. Brookens' warning.

For God's sake, Via, it's three songs. He'll be fine.

But if he *wasn't* fine, I'd know what to look for. I'd be watching.

And I already knew exactly what he would do if something *was* wrong.

Because I'd seen it happen before.

Connecticut.

In fairness, Jon hadn't known about his condition back then.

But it had been *so close.*

And yet, he'd played it off like nothing was wrong—finished the song, *walked* off stage instead of dropping right there in front of a sea of people.

A fucking *boss move.*

But also… a terrifying one.

Fuck.

***

I kept telling myself it would be okay.

Jon needed to prove it to himself.

That despite everything—despite the way his life had been flipped inside out—*it wasn't over.*

FR's appearance tonight, however brief, was validation. A reminder that he was still *him*.

And those new tracks?

Brilliant. And absolutely gut-wrenching.

I knew exactly where they had come from, and why they had been written.

And so would everyone else, once they heard them.

This was a one-off. Jon knew that. A mere blip in his new existence filled with doctors, hospitals, and tests.

He'd still be able to record in the studio. He had his final scoring and compositions to complete for his graduate degree—enough to keep his mind occupied. But after the surgery, he'd be grounded from almost everything else.

Dr. Brookens had already warned us: *No driving for at least a couple of months. No unnecessary exertion. No stress.*

Until they figured out the right medication balance. Until they knew *how* his ICD would respond. Until they could be *sure* his heart wouldn't betray him.

Laying low wasn't just a suggestion.

It was non-negotiable.

So in a strange way, tonight wasn't just a reunion.

It was a goodbye.

At least for now.

So yeah. This mattered.

And *please, dear God, let it all be okay.*

I could feel myself starting to spiral—thoughts looping tighter and tighter, my chest getting heavier—when my phone buzzed.

A text from Krissy.

Come out to the front entrance.

What?

She must have forgotten I was out of town.

I'm in Philly, I texted back.

So am I. Come out front.

I blinked.

What the hell?

Curiosity overtook my nerves as I wove my way through the crowd, slipping past the general admission section toward the front entrance.

And then—

I saw them.

Krissy. Kenny. Justin.

Standing there, beaming.

I almost burst into tears.

"What are you *doing* here?" I gasped, pulling them into hugs one by one.

Krissy grinned. "What do you *think* we're doing here?"

And *fuck*. I was *not* going to cry. No.

A laugh bubbled up instead—nervous, disbelieving, relieved—as I quickly wiped my eyes.

Then, without hesitation, I grabbed my friend family and led them to the best spot in the house.

***

I was grateful for the royal treatment we'd seemingly been given.

The venue was massive—a sprawling main floor, wraparound upper levels with additional bars and seating, and a sea of bodies filling every available space.

I'd been here before.

But tonight, it felt different. Overpacked. Buzzing. The all-day event had drawn an impressive crowd, and the energy was thick in the air.

Above it all, the top balcony loomed—the highest tier.

Typically reserved for special VIP guests, its wings flanked the sides, while the center held the lighting booth, a glowing nerve center where house lighting and tech controlled the entire show.

Unlike most nights, no VIP tickets had been sold. Instead, the area had been reserved for a select few—performers' guests, managers, PR.

And somehow, I had been invited.

Clay and Jason had made sure of it, personally handing me a special badge that granted access. A gesture from FaultCode that hadn't gone unnoticed.

Not for my own sake—but because it spoke volumes about the respect they held for Jon, and for FR.

Jon had co-written several songs for FaultCode's set tonight. And this entire plan? *Jason's idea.*

That mattered.

We picked our spots near the middle, right beside the lighting booth—by far the best vantage point.

But it was more than that.

The entrance to the top balcony was already considered backstage access, its stairwell emerging near stage right.

Which meant—

If something happened—

If I needed to move—

I wouldn't have to fight my way through the crowd.

I could get to him.

Fast.

***

The next-to-last band finished with a surge of energy, their final notes still reverberating through the venue as the stage crew moved with precision, setting the scene for the headliner.

Except tonight—

The finale held a twist no one expected.

The transition was seamless, executed with the kind of professional ease expected at a festival of this scale. But behind the scenes, there were extra layers—meticulously planned logistics, timed cues, everything orchestrated so that when the lights went down...

It wouldn't be FaultCode.

Not yet.

It would be something else entirely.

I tried to lose myself in my friends' easy banter, their laughter rolling over me like waves. But my focus kept slipping.

My apprehension was mounting—not just because of the obvious, but because this moment was going to be *epic.* A complete blindside.

Unexpected.

New material.

A shock that would hit the audience in real-time.

And somewhere between my nerves and the raw excitement of it, I suddenly understood something I never had before.

No matter how seasoned a performer was—no matter how many shows they'd played—this moment before was always a force to be reckoned with.

And for Jon...

It had *always* been worse.

That limelight trait?

It had never really been in his DNA.

From the beginning, engagement had been a struggle. Tony had pushed. Prodded. Mentored. But Jon wasn't wired like a typical frontman—he didn't *command* the room with effortless charisma.

What he *did* have, though, was something just as powerful.

Presence.

From day one, he exuded a quiet, pent-up angst—not forced, not performed, but something so real it pulled people in. He wasn't an artist who pushed outward—he was one who drew people toward him.

That had become his signature.

And eventually, even Tony stopped fighting it.

Jon didn't *need* to perform in the traditional sense. His music, his *energy*, did all the work.

But what most people didn't see was the cost.

Those of us closest to him—especially during those late-night meetings in the diner near Creston, when Jon was still in the ICU—had only *just* begun to realize how much weight he had carried.

How much it had drained him to step into that version of himself night after night.

And now—standing here, in this moment—I felt it so much more.

Jon's ability to channel this alter ego, to slip into the performer with flawless precision, was more than just a skill.

It was a gift.

And maybe—

Maybe it was the same reason he was so good at *coherence* now.

Right?

***

And then—

Finally—

The house lights cut out, plunging the venue into darkness.

A sharp inhale from the crowd—an instant hush falling over the noise, as thousands of bodies shifted, bracing for what came next.

But this time—

There was a hiss.

Fog.

It billowed in fast, curling ghostlike from both sides of the stage, swallowing the space whole.

Then—

Sound.

A low, guttural crash erupted through the speakers—discordant, dark, shifting between harmonic minors and jarring dissonance. The intro I'd heard just once before, in the dim quiet of Jon's basement.

It was haunting.

It was hypnotic.

The first drum hit cracked through the fog like a gunshot—

And at the exact same second, a single deep blue spotlight cut through the haze, barely illuminating the silhouette standing center stage.

A few beats of stillness—tension so thick you could drown in it—

And then, the song *detonated.*

An eruption of sound and light, swallowing the venue whole in a violent collision. For a breathless moment, it was *just that*—a visceral explosion, raw and deafening.

Then came the crowd.

A tsunami of noise. A roar so loud, so fierce, that the individual voices collapsed into one unrelenting wall of chaos.

Holy. Fuck.

The reaction was *so* immediate, *so* unrestrained, that it almost didn't sound human.

I was *glued* to the stage.

Because even *I* hadn't expected this to feel so monumental.

I'd *heard* these songs before—known exactly what was coming—

And still, I felt as swept away as everyone else.

***

The next few minutes were a collision of senses. My focus ricocheted between the stage and the audience, caught in a loop of sound, light, movement, and raw *emotion*.

There was a brief lull—

The slightest transition from the first song into the next—

But it was swallowed whole by the crowd.

Another song.

Jon was in his own world now—expected, predictable. He moved through the performance as if the thousands of people watching him weren't there, completely locked into his own energy field.

But even from a distance—

I caught it.

A moment.

A glance exchanged between Cary and Shawn, from opposite ends of the stage.

They grinned.

Not a typical performance high.

Not a *this-show-is-going-amazing* kind of grin.

This was *deeper*.

I felt it in my core.

Because I knew exactly what they were thinking.

Yes—it was good to be back. Yes—this new material was on another level.

But that wasn't what their expressions conveyed.

They were here for the same reason I was.

Because this was bigger than the show.

Because this was bigger than FR.

Because there was a moment—not long ago—when we believed Jon was going to die.

Where we were *convinced* it was over.

And that weight—

That *unimaginable* weight—

Would always be heavier than *this* moment on stage.

And I realized, then—

The amazement of the fans...

The excitement of the other musicians...

As genuine as they were—

They didn't even *come close* to what this meant to us.

We had seen the mountain—

And the valley.

The shadows. The doubt. The despair.

But right now—

Right fucking now—

We were standing on a peak.

And *goddammit—*

No one deserved it more than *he* did.

***

As the second song ended, the stage lights faded into darkness.

A deafening roar erupted from the crowd—a mix of surprise, exhilaration, and the universal demand for *more.*

My stomach twisted.

This was the moment.

The exit plan they'd built in just for Jon.

He could leave now, quietly, while the lights were down, slipping offstage with the others. No one would have noticed. None of this had been expected, anyway—he could vanish, and the crowd would be none the wiser.

I glanced toward the booth. The techs exchanged nods, their postures relaxed.

Always a good sign when the techs are happy.

My gaze shifted again, landing on a small cluster of people just to the left of the booth. Their eyes were wide, their faces lit up with the afterglow of something incredible. I couldn't hear what they were saying over the noise, but it was obvious—they'd *loved* it.

I glanced down at the tattoo on my forearm.

My key.

I *loved* that they loved him. I really did. I was *proud* of him on a level I could never put into words.

But deeper than that, I felt something else.

Gratitude.

Because I didn't just love him as a performer. I *knew* him.

I knew the challenges no one else could see. I knew what it cost him to get up there and give the crowd what they wanted.

And right now, that intimate understanding wasn't letting me enjoy this the same way those strangers were.

Because *holy shit.*

How was he feeling?

After that?

I was oblivious to Krissy. Nikki. Emily. My friends were right here, elbow to elbow, but it felt like there was a million miles between me and Jon.

How the hell is he feeling right now??

The stage remained cloaked in darkness.

And then—

A guitar.

Just one.

A solo lead—eerie, melodic, completely different from the gritty, hard-hitting opening riff of FR's intro.

The light returned—but this time, it had shifted. Stage right.

The crowd screamed. He was still there.

Then, FaultCode entered, calm and composed, taking their places without missing a beat.

The audience erupted again, a tidal wave of shrieks and howls.

I hadn't realized I'd been holding my breath until I exhaled in a ragged rush.

My shoulders ached—I hadn't noticed that either.

Until Kenny slipped his arms around me from behind.

He gave me a quick kiss on the cheek, then leaned close, speaking directly into my ear. "He's amazing, honey."

***

The song neared its end.

Clay leaned into the mic, his voice booming with reverb, his arm outstretched toward Jon.

"Ladies and gentlemen—Mr. Jonathan Stetson!"

The crowd exploded.

Shouts. Whistles. Cheers.

Jon gave a single head nod.

A fucking head nod.

Christ, Jon. Take some credit.

Then, as the last chords rang out, he raised one hand in a casual wave—like something you'd do when acknowledging a neighbor while checking the mail. Understated. As usual.

And he turned and walked offstage.

I headed for the stairwell.

Clay's voice followed, still carrying through the walls.

"Now he's gonna make his exit, just like the aloof SOB we've all come to know and love."

Laughter, yells, applause.

It died down as Clay kept talking. His voice was fainter now but still clear.

"But I can't let this moment pass without acknowledging how *fucking lucky* we are to have him and Final Relapse here tonight."

Wow. I wondered if Jon knew Clay was going to go off on a speech. I highly doubted it.

"As many of you know, we had some of our time on the road together cut short. And that... well, the truth is, that could have been permanent. And for a scary fucking minute, we thought it might be."

Whoa.

Holy shit.

"So I want to make damn sure everyone here tonight appreciates the surprise they just got. And I'm not sure we can hold a candle to that performance—"

More cheers.

"—but we're gonna try to end the night on a strong note. So let's get to it."

The music kicked in again, but my focus had narrowed to a single point.

I had only one thing on my mind now.

***

I wove my way through the backstage passages, my eyes scanning for familiar faces.

Instinct took over.

I turned down a wider hallway, heading deeper into the building—*away* from the stage, *away* from the noise.

Toward the back.

That's when I spotted Mike.

He had Jon's guitar slung over his shoulder.

Why?

And where the hell was Jon?

Mike turned just as I caught sight of him. He didn't say a word—just flicked his eyes toward a side door across the way and motioned with his head.

The load-in area.

Warehouse-style. Open space. Mostly quiet now while the show carried on.

Okay. This wasn't entirely unlike Jon.

I'd learned that there were two types of performers.

Some thrived off the energy of the stage—*buzzing*, electric, high on adrenaline long after the last chord faded. Those were the ones who'd still be riding the wave right now, practically bouncing off the walls.

Then there were those who unwound together—processing, critiquing, making plans for the next thing.

And then—

There was Jon.

Jon, who usually needed quiet before re-engaging.

And especially now—I knew he would need that.

I pushed through the swinging door.

Cooler air hit my face, a sharp contrast to the lingering heat of the venue.

And then—

There he was.

Forty feet away, leaning against a massive rolling case, downing a bottle of water.

I started toward him, instinct already taking over—my mind snapping into assessment mode, my mental checklist unfolding.

Look for signs of redlining.

What had Brookens said?

Fatigue. Color change. Labored breathing. Disorientation.

The overhead lighting caught a glint of metal from the door, and the reflection pulled Jon's gaze upward—

And then we locked eyes.

And *fuck my checklist.*

I wasn't going to study him.

I wasn't going to ask if he was okay.

God knows he'd probably already been asked fifty times on his way back here.

I wasn't going to do *any* of that.

Because we'd talked about this.

Because he hated it.

Because right now—

His eyes were pulling me in.

And so were his arms.

I moved into them.

No words.

No questions.

Just *feeling him.*

Not the crowd.

Not the residual static of adrenaline.

Just—

Jon.

***

For a few moments, we stood there, wrapped in each other.

Despite the chaos happening beyond these walls—a packed venue, music pounding, thousands of voices filling the air—in this quiet, tucked-away space, it felt like we existed in our own little bubble.

Finally, I pulled back.

Jon offered me a grin.

"You were incredible," I said.

"Yeah?"

He tipped back his water, finishing the last few drops before lazily tossing the empty bottle toward a bin way too far for an easy shot.

It bounced—ricocheting off a pallet of trussing, wobbling through the air—

And somehow landed in the can anyway.

He laughed, turning back toward me, looping his arms around my waist and pulling me in for another hug.

"So... you wanna go hang out with your friends? Catch the rest of the show?"

I hesitated.

Thinking.

"What do you want to do?"

I searched his face as I asked it.

And then—a flicker.

Something in his eyes. A slight shift in his expression.

And softly, without breaking my gaze, he said it.

"I'm tired."

Just two words.

But God, the weight of them.

My breath caught—not because I was surprised that he was tired.

Of course, he was.

But because he had said it.

He had admitted it to me.

Softly. Honestly. Not because he had to—but because he felt he could.

And *that* meant more than anything else that had happened all day.

I smiled, warmth spreading through me as I leaned in, my lips finding his.

His mouth opened beneath mine.

We were still brushing tongues when the door flung open.

Footsteps.

I pulled back, turning to see Mike.

He stopped short, realizing what he'd walked in on, then threw Jon a quick, knowing smirk.

"Hey."

Jon exhaled, his forehead briefly tipping against mine before turning to face him.

Mike motioned toward the hallway.

"Tony's out here. Got a sec?"

***

It wasn't just Tony.

The rest of FR, Nikki, and two guys I didn't recognize were gathered in a half-circle in the hallway.

"Hey!" Cary's voice broke through the noise as we merged with the group, his energy still running high. He was one of the Type A performers—the ones who rode the adrenaline for *hours* after a show. "The radio station wants to do an interview!"

As he spoke, the two unfamiliar men exchanged handshakes, making quick introductions before excusing themselves from the conversation.

Then, the real discussion began.

Or at least, it tried to.

Before Cary could even finish his pitch, Jon cut him off mid-sentence.

"I think you should do it."

Cary hesitated. "Yeah... but I think they really want to talk to you."

Jon's lips curled into the faintest smirk. "Cary—you *literally* work in radio. I think you can handle this."

Cary faltered for half a second, then pressed, "You sure, man?"

Jon rubbed the back of his neck. "I'm not feeling up to it. You go."

Cary lingered a beat longer, but when Jon didn't budge, he gave a single nod and disappeared with the other guys.

Shawn turned to Jon. "You ready to head to the hotel?" he asked casually. "They have a lounge. That's more my speed."

A wave of relief washed over me.

Not just because Jon *needed* to leave, but because I knew Shawn was being genuine.

He wasn't just offering an out—he meant it. Shawn was as low-key as Jon. Plus, he ran a venue just like this for a living. He wasn't the type to stick around longer than necessary.

"Yeah. I'm ready to go," Jon said.

"Us too," Mike chimed in, glancing toward Nikki.

But then—

From down the hall, another voice rang out.

"Hey, Stets! Can we borrow you for a second?"

Jon glanced at us, reluctant—then turned and drifted toward the new conversation.

We needed to get him *out* of here.

Mike sighed, shifting Jon's guitar case over his shoulder, then turned to Tony.

"Hey... we're keeping that other shit under wraps, right?"

Tony nodded.

"Absolutely."

A flicker of something passed between them.

I got the distinct feeling I was missing something.

"What other shit?" I asked.

The three of them exchanged a look.

Then, a slow, satisfied smile pulled at Tony's face—like he was holding onto a *really* good secret. But then he shook his head, waving it off.

"It's nothing," he said—except, clearly, it wasn't.

Because a second later, like he *couldn't* help himself, he added, "I've already been approached by some label reps."

He glanced at his watch.

"And it's been what? Twenty minutes?"

A smirk.

"Wait till next week."

I absorbed this.

Tony *couldn't* help himself—this was his job, after all. Negotiating the best deals for his bands. But really? Already?

"Don't worry." Mike's voice was mild. "Jon doesn't know. And we're not telling him right now."

I looked back at Tony.

"He's right," he said.

The smirk was gone now. Tony's expression turned serious.

"We're not putting that pressure back on him," he said simply. "There's more good shit like this brewing in that brilliant mind of his... but it'll come when *he's ready*."

A beat of silence.

“No more contracts. Not now.”

I searched their faces.

“Really?” I asked, needing to hear it.

Shawn answered this time, his voice final.

“Really. Let’s not even mention it yet.”

I nodded.

We wouldn’t.

Chapter 55

We entered our hotel room, tossing our bags aside.

The familiar yet foreign scent of cleaner hit me. The stillness settled in—*not home, but calm*. A temporary space to call our own.

Jon stood in the center of the room, eyes closed, drawing in a slow, deliberate breath.

Like he was resetting.

Then he turned toward me—whipping me into his arms with a sudden, crushing hug.

"God, the quiet is nice," he murmured.

The irony of a frontman, fresh off semi-co-headlining a festival, talking about quiet *while the show was still going on*—Not lost on me.

I rested my head against his chest.

"Hey," he said, kissing the top of my head. "I need to shower. I feel gross. Why don't you go down to the lounge for a bit?"

I smiled. The others were probably down there—we'd all booked rooms at the same hotel—

But no.

I wanted to be here.

As if reading my mind, Jon squeezed me. "At least go thank your roomies for coming. Tell them I said hey. We'll catch them in the morning."

I hesitated.

Then nodded.

Yeah. That felt right.

***

The hotel lounge was a stark contrast to the venue—low lights, low music, plush booths that practically invited you to sink into them.

At the far end of an otherwise empty bar, I spotted my crew.

Mike and Shawn in the corner.

Krissy, Kenny, and Justin just a seat away.

Their conversation broke as they spotted me, motioning me over.

"He coming down?" Shawn asked.

"No," I said, shaking my head. "I think he's had enough."

They both nodded, no questions, no pushback.

The conversation moved on—seamless.

"Where's Nikki?" I asked.

Mike rolled his eyes and shrugged. "She's around."

Justin grinned. "Let me buy you a drink!"

Normally, I would've said yes in a heartbeat.

But now—I hesitated.

I wasn't really up for it.

Krissy caught my pause immediately and elbowed Justin. "She has places to be," she chided, throwing me a pointed look.

Justin smirked. "Okay. A *shot*, then."

That sounded good.

The night had been a huge success, but my nerves hadn't quite settled yet.

I nodded.

The vodka burned just right.

Justin offered me another, and I actually had to think about it.

But—I needed to get back.

Normally, I'd sit here all night, laughing, carrying on, getting lost in my friends.

But now—I *couldn't.*

I *didn't want to.*

As I hugged each person goodbye, I heard Nikki's laugh ring out from somewhere beyond the booths.

I turned, expecting her to round the corner—

But when she did, she wasn't alone.

Tamara was with her.

What the hell?

Nikki beamed as she approached, wrapping me in a hug.

Tamara followed suit, practically gushing as she grabbed my hands.

"Oh my God, Via. *That show.*" Her eyes were wild with excitement. "FR was fucking *insane*. I *swear* I heard people having ear-gasms in that crowd."

I burst out laughing.

Tamara and Nikki—so alike. *So uncouth.*

But before I could even process why Tamara was there, another familiar face walked through the door.

TJ.

Okay. *What the hell??*

"We were invited to the show!" Tamara exclaimed, bouncing on her heels. "And, oh my *God*, I'm so glad we came!"

I blinked, trying to keep up. "When did you get here?"

"We planned to come this afternoon, but I had to cover a shift." She rolled her eyes. "Didn't check in until six."

But something wasn't adding up.

And then Tamara's gaze flicked to TJ.

Then to Nikki.

And she said it.

"We just thought—since we're here—we could check in on Jon."

Everything inside me paused.

A dozen thoughts slammed into me at once.

Of course, I *wanted* them to check on Jon.

He *should* have been checked already.

But *why the hell* were they really here?

My eyes shifted toward Mike.

And *just for a second—*

He looked away.

Too quickly.

Too deliberately.

Mike.

I *knew* it.

He must have been the one to suggest this.

Mike had always been quietly protective of Jon—watching over him without making it obvious.

I bet he'd talked to Nikki, *asked* her to get Tamara and TJ here.

And suddenly—I loved him for it.

TJ cleared his throat. "Has anyone looked at him?"

They were all staring at me now.

"No."

TJ checked his watch. "Well, if there was an urgent concern, I think we'd have seen it by now."

Jeezus.

I'd been so wrapped up in what Jon *wanted* that I hadn't stopped to consider what he *needed*.

TJ lowered his voice.

"Do you think he'd let me?" He hesitated. "Just—to make sure he's recovered?"

His tone was genuine.

"These arrhythmias can be sneaky. They might not hit full force, but we still want to catch it if something's off."

Holy.

Fuck.

And *for the love of God, YES.*

I turned to Mike.

The sheer appreciation surging through me was instant.

I threw my arms around him.

"Thank you."

He just grinned—confirming *nothing*.

But he didn't have to.

I already knew.

And now—

Now I had to figure out how the hell to explain this to Jon.

Tamara stepped closer, sensing my hesitation.

"How 'bout we just come up with you?" she offered. "We won't stay—just want to check in."

I nodded.

And the three of us headed for the elevators.

***

I swiped my keycard.

A loud *click*.

The door unlocked, and I pushed it open—

Steam curled into the room from the open bathroom door, the scent of warm water and fresh soap still lingering in the air.

Jon appeared from around the corner—

And froze.

"Oh, *fuck*," he blurted, his eyes darting between the three of us standing there.

Tamara sucked in a sharp breath.

"Oh *fuck*," she whispered.

I wasn't even sure she realized she'd said it out loud.

Her eyes were locked on Jon's chest. Or more specifically—his tattoo.

I bit back a smirk. Maybe it was a gloat.

Because *damn*.

It did look good.

In hindsight, I probably should have warned him that we weren't alone.

Thank God he had pants on.

He blinked, still processing. Anyone standing there with me right now would have been awkward—but Tamara and TJ?

Yeah. This was next-level uncomfortable.

And knowing Jon, he'd already started connecting the dots.

Still without a word, he moved toward the bed, grabbing a shirt and slipping it over his head.

The tension thickened.

Then—

"That's some serious artwork," TJ said, breaking the silence.

Jon nodded, offering the smallest hint of a smile.

I realized then—most guys would flaunt ink like that every chance they got.

But not Jon.

He didn't get that tattoo for attention.

He got it for himself.

And for me.

And somehow, that made it even sexier.

"I'm sorry for barging in so late," Tamara said, her tone gentle. "Via didn't know we were coming. We surprised her downstairs."

Bless her.

I appreciated the subtle defense—especially since it was *true*.

Jon's eyes flicked to mine, scanning my expression like he was deciding whether or not to believe her.

A beat.

Then—

"Is it cool if we hang out for just a minute?" Tamara asked.

Jon's posture stiffened—just slightly. The hint of suspicion was there.

Then, just as quickly, he relaxed, settling onto the edge of the bed and motioning for us to take the chair and loveseat in the corner.

Oh God.

This was happening.

And there was *no* subtle way to do it.

I knew it.

Jon definitely knew it.

And I was *sure* he was already drawing his own conclusions about why they were really here.

You're gonna piss him off yet, Via.

Maybe.

But we were just doing what Dr. Brookens recommended.

Hopefully, he'd remember *that* before he ripped someone's head off.

Hopefully—

It wouldn't be mine.

TJ took control before the tension could spiral further.

His voice was calm, steady—all business now.

"Hey, man," he said smoothly. "I was hoping you'd let me check you over real quick. Just make sure you're all good before we call it a night."

A pause.

A *long* pause.

Jon's eyes narrowed.

Then—

"So you drove three hours to come here and harass me about my blood pressure?"

His dry cynicism cut through the air.

Tamara *snorted.*

Then laughed outright, her cackle echoing through the room.

Oh God.

That was either going to piss Jon off *more*—or completely defuse the situation.

I held my breath, waiting to see which.

TJ barely missed a beat.

"Sorry, man," he said, still unfazed. "This isn't an ambush. *Swear to God.* We've been here for hours—at the venue—watching the show. You guys sounded incredible."

Jon wasn't buying it.

Not fully.

But I could also see it—the shift.

He was already weighing the fastest way to get this over with.

His jaw tightened for a moment, but then he exhaled quickly.

"Fine. Whatever."

The irritation in his voice was barely hidden.

"But I'm *not* paying for this."

His tone flattened, but there was a glint of something else in his eyes now.

He crossed his arms, staring TJ down.

"You can send the bill to whoever put you up to it."

A *beat* passed.

Then—

We all cracked up.

A slow, shit-eating grin crept across Jon's face.

Thank *God.*

He was going to be agreeable.

Maybe nobody would lose a head after all.

Tamara slid her backpack toward TJ, who casually unzipped it and pulled out an analog blood pressure cuff and a stethoscope.

Jon arched a brow.

"They let you into the venue with that backpack?" he asked, his voice carefully innocent—but the sarcasm dripped.

Tamara didn't miss a beat.

"Nooo," she enunciated dramatically. "I left it here, in our *hotel room*. When we checked in *earlier. Before* we went to the venue. *To see you play.*"

She punctuated each phrase like she was explaining a basic concept to a slow learner.

Jon smirked.

TJ, unfazed, went about business.

Finally, he straightened and nodded.

"All good," he said—though I noticed he was looking more at me than Jon.

Then, tossing his things back into the bag, he turned back to Jon.

"Get some rest. We'll catch you in the morning!"

That was it.

Quick. Efficient. Over.

Thank God.

I cleared my throat abruptly, standing up before my face could betray me.

Would he be upset with me for this intrusion? It's not like I'd planned it. What was I supposed to do, tell them no?

I was *still* considering that question a few minutes later, as TJ and Tamara said their goodbyes and headed up to their own room one floor above.

***

"Well? Are you satisfied?" Jon asked as he rose and walked toward me slowly, just as I flipped the inside door lock. His voice was cool—detached—but edged with irritation.

"Jon," I began cautiously, turning around to face him. "I really didn't know—"

He was right there. His eyes locked onto mine, as he used his body to push mine against the wall. Gentle, yet assertive.

And *holy fuck* —the way he was looking at me right now...

"That wasn't very nice. Ganging up on me, like that." He'd lowered his voice, but it simmered with a restraint I wasn't used to hearing from him.

I could only stare back at him—unsure how to respond. I had been prepared for him to be pissed. But this—I hadn't seen coming.

He tilted his head down so that we were nose to nose and planted one hand firmly on the wall beside me. The other was on the small of my back, abruptly yanking me in close to him. It startled me, but then he lightly kissed my neck. My collar bone. The feel of his lips on my skin sent shivers all the way through.

What the hell, Jon?

I wasn't sure what to make of this... not at all.

And also, I hated how much this side of him seemed to instantly turn me on—how could he be so sweet, but exude this hint of aggression? Was he horny, or pissed off? Or both?

He would never overpower me. I knew that. But when he was this close, looking at me with that glint in his eyes, it reminded me that he easily could. And for some twisted reason that thought was making things happen.

It was insane how my body reacted to his.

"I saved my best performance for you." He said. "I hope you're ready."

Oh, I'm ready. You have no fucking idea how ready I am.

Even so, I hesitated.

I knew he needed rest. He was tired, he'd said so himself.

Yet, I could feel that not all of him had received the memo.

And right now—he didn't look like a man I should argue with.

***

The room felt significantly cooler after my shower.

I pulled the towel from my head, letting my damp hair fall over my shoulders. Fuck it. It could air-dry. The bathroom mirror was still steamed over, and I was tired.

The lamp beside the bed cast a soft, ambient glow over the room—but despite the relative brightness, Jon was already out cold.

I had known he would be.

It had been a *long* day. Mentally. Physically. Emotionally.

Especially after that last performance.

I felt a slow, wry grin tug at my lips.

He never failed to impress me.

Okay, Via. Stop gloating.

But it was undeniable.

Jon had completely, *irrevocably* altered my perception of sexy.

It wasn't anything he'd done *deliberately*, I didn't think.

It was just—him.

The way he handled things that would make most people completely self-destruct.

The things that drove me crazy about Jon weren't tangible.

They weren't things you could put your finger on.

It wasn't just the tattoo. Yeah—it was hot. But the *meaning* behind it was hotter.

It wasn't just his eyes. Beautiful, yes. But it was the raw, unfiltered emotion behind them that made them irresistible.

It wasn't just his dimples. Adorable, sure. But his *smile*—that *real, unguarded smile*—was something else entirely.

And his music—God, his music. It was melodic, undeniably brilliant. But the reasons he wrote it? *That* was where the fire lived.

And tonight—

My God, tonight.

We had all felt it.

The rage. The angst. The passion burning inside him.

Swallowing up everyone in his wake.

Because despite everything—

And in the face of everything—

It was him saying, *Fuck you. I'm still here.*

***

I climbed into bed, careful not to disturb him.

Snapped off the lamp, plunging the room into darkness.

Curled up beside him, siphoning his warmth.

Normally, I didn't sleep well in hotels.

Or anywhere, really—aside from my own bed.

And *his*.

Something about unfamiliar places always made it difficult for me to let go.

But tonight felt different.

Or maybe—I was different.

Originally, I had started my research project to track and quantify the ways It had changed him.

How It was *still* changing him.

But along the way, I realized—

I had changed, too.

Jon had taken me with him on this profound, perplexing journey.

And somewhere along the way, I started to understand myself like I never had before.

He had taught me, without even realizing it.

That first time, when he had instinctively taken my hand and pressed it to his chest so that I could *feel* that he was okay—

He had taught me presence.

Taught me to be with him, in the moment.

And it had *profoundly* affected me.

Somehow, that one gesture had become a part of us.

Something that transcended words.

It had become an unspoken language, satisfying something deeper than reassurance.

A connection that was intimate and innate—

A bridge between his vulnerabilities and mine.

He worried his condition would scare me off—that I might grow tired of dealing with it. That I might see him as weak.

But in reality, I was in awe of his resilience.

I was fascinated by him—physically, emotionally, *spiritually*.

As someone who had always struggled with anxiety, I needed reassurance.

And I had found it with him.

He always knew—

What to say.

What to do.

How to settle my mind when it raced toward the worst.

And I still wasn't sure if he truly understood the impact of that.

Or if he was just following his own intuition.

But I *wasn't the only one* who had noticed.

We all had.

As I nestled in, I realized something.

I wasn't in a strange, unfamiliar place at all.

This was familiar.

Our friends were here.

Our chosen family.

They had all come—not just for him, but for us.

Supporting us.

Loving us.

We were so damn lucky.

And suddenly, I knew.

It didn't matter where we were.

Not really.

As long as we were together.

Because with him beside me—

I was home.

I fell asleep listening to the quiet, steady rhythm of his breath.

My hand resting over his heart.

And for the first time in a long time—

I let myself believe we had all the time in the world.

Stories live differently in every reader.

If this one stayed with you, you're invited to share your reflection in a review.

Visit:

theweightoflight.net/review

Thank you for being part of The Weight of Light.

— Jae Silver

About the Author

Jae Silver writes fiction rooted in the in-between, where science meets spirit, and the human experience takes center stage.

Through quiet moments, emotional depth, and a hint of the unseen, Jae's work reflects the ways we grow, heal, and find meaning in uncertainty.

To connect or learn more, visit:

www.theweightoflight.net

Acknowledgments

To the ones who heard me, before I had language for it. To those who saw something steady, even when I flickered. I'm here because you stayed.

Thank you.

To the First Light Team

Your early eyes, open hearts, and thoughtful words brought more light to this story than you know.

Thank you for walking with me at the beginning.

Continue the Journey

The Weight of Light: Echoes of the After

The story continues in the aftermath of a moment that changed everything.

Stay Connected

Want behind-the-scenes insights, future releases, and reflections on the themes within *The Weight of Light*?

Join the mailing list:

www.theweightoflight.net/join-the-journey

Follow along: @authorjaesilver on Instagram

I didn't recognize it at the time—not for what it was. But sometimes, light shows up quietly. It's not there to explain anything. It's just waiting for you to notice how it feels.

www.ingramcontent.com/pod-product-compliance
Lightning Source LLC
La Vergne TN
LVHW091249110826
845146LV00002BA/470

9798993430621